In Her Own Words

A primary sourcebook of autobiographical
texts by women artists from the 19th and 20th centuries

Dr. Wendy Slatkin

ISBN: 1453648240
ISBN-13: 9781453648247
Library of Congress Control Number: 2010909214

Contents

Acknowledgements:
In Her Own Words

If producing a book is a labor of love, then *In Her Own Words* has endured a very long gestation period. I have been writing about women artists since the 1980s, and I edited primary source material in the early 1990s for *The Voices of Women Artists* (Prentice-Hall, 1993). That book has long been out of print, but my desire to bring these texts to a wider audience has never faltered. Through many years of teaching this material, most recently at California State Polytechnic University-Pomona, I developed a passion for autobiographical primary sources based on the responses of my students. Therefore, I would like to acknowledge all my students in my "Gender and Art" courses, taught at Cal Poly over the years, but especially the class from spring 2009 that actually used draft chapters of this book to create very interesting and educational PowerPoint presentations.

For anyone who may think that reading about the struggles of women artists from the past is a closed chapter in history, I would like to cite an article published on July 30, 2009 in the Los Angeles Times. Lubna Hussein, a journalist, was one of 13 women arrested in Khartoum, Sudan, for wearing pants. Ten of these women were flogged as punishment. Hussein has resigned her UN job granting immunity, so she can mount a legal challenge to the strict Islamic dress code. Of course there are many similar examples of oppression that one could cite, but this resonated with me, because it does not seem so far removed from Rosa Bonheur's need for a police permit to wear pants in the 1850s. Many women are actively struggling for equality, and I believe that listening to the voices of real, historical women can continue to inspire and to serve as role models for women today and for future generations.

Without the consent of the copy-right holders, this book could not have been published. We want to thank all those who generously gave permission to re-print these texts. The author has made every effort to trace and contact all copyright holders of texts included in this book. We will be happy to correct any errors or omissions, in future editions. Please contact the author at: wslatkin@csupomona.edu for any copyright issues.

I want to thank Stephanie Ignacio and Sivan Kovnator for their careful word processing. Diana Dawson kindly read this manuscript, in a late stage, and offered many valuable suggestions which I have gratefully incorporated. I would like to thank the anonymous reviewers who provided thoughtful and informed comments which molded this volume into a much better, more coherent book.

I do not think it is possible to write a book without a supportive network. My colleagues at Cal Poly have sustained me in many ways, professional and personal over the years. To Bruce Emerton, Joyce Hesselgrave, Crystal Lee, Babette Mayor, Desmond McVey, Sarah Meyer, Alison Pearlman, Chari Pradel, Deane Swick, and Noel Vernon, please accept my sincere appreciation for all your kindnesses.

My family has always been behind me, and given me the room, in both the physical and emotional senses, which I required to complete this book. My daughter, Sara Gail Cohen, has served faithfully as a very precise proof-reader and comma editor, and I want to thank her for her hard work. To Randy, my son, Josh, my mother, Helen Slatkin, and my cousin, Kitty Bateman, many thanks for all your love and support over the years.

Finally the greatest acknowledgement must go to this group of fifteen extraordinary women artists whose works of visual art and words of pain, passion, and energy made this book seem like it was all worth the effort, and much more.

Introduction:
"Writing/Righting the Woman Artist"[1]

In Her Own Words is an edited compilation of autobiographical narratives by fifteen outstanding artist/authors active from the late eighteenth century to the contemporary era. Each chapter is devoted to the writings of one of these amazing and inspiring women. The texts are presented in a concise format, accessible to all interested readers both in and out of the classroom. By reading the "writings" of an artist, we can begin to "right," or correct our interpretations of her achievements. These primary sources are so essential, that, I believe it is impossible to develop a valid interpretive strategy for these creators' works of visual art without incorporating written texts into their study. While the discipline of Art History has long recognized the importance of primary sources for male artists, the integration of similar texts for women artists, especially in the college classroom, has not been as consistent. This may be due, in part, to the lengthy and relatively inaccessible format of many of these texts. It is this gap in the literature that the present volume is intended to redress. One criterion I have used in my selection process is accessibility. Readers can easily consult the complete texts, translated into

English. Therefore, the reader is both capable of and encouraged to read the primary sources in their unedited versions. This book is intended as an introduction to these writings.

Since these writers are visual artists of historical interest, the specific, excerpted texts have been selected for their insights into the ways in which writing and making art intersect or "interface." The "interface" is an appropriate term which has been employed by Sidonie Smith and Julia Watson, leading scholars in this field, for what these authors call "women's self-representational acts," which occur at "proliferating sites of visual/textual" activity. [2] All primary sources, despite their diversity, are "self-representational acts."

This book is subdivided into three chronological "parts". Part 1 is composed of texts from the nineteenth century. Part 2 includes four key creators active in the first half of the twentieth century. And the last section of the text, Part 3, spans the later twentieth century, after the hugely important decade of the 1970s in which feminism emerged, as a significant discourse to inform the visual art and writings of these artists. All texts in Part 3 were published after 1975, bringing us into the modern world. Introductory essays for each part identify the key historical conditions relevant to an understanding of the context in which both works of visual art and written texts were produced.

Every chapter begins with an introduction, summarizing the historical significance of the artist/author. Basic biographical facts are presented, in a necessarily concise format. The subject matter and stylistic idiom of the author's visual art and surviving written texts are defined. In these chapter introductions, key theoretical issues raised by scholars of autobiography are also summarized. Of necessity, material presented in the introductions varies, somewhat, due to the state of the scholarship informing the reading of each text, as well as the nature of the individual texts.

Within each chapter, every separate entry is introduced and contextualized. The main ideas of the selected text and its position within the overall primary source are clarified to guide the reader from one excerpt to the next. Each letter is identified by date and by intended recipient. The main purpose of the letter and when it was written is specified. I have consciously limited my introductory remarks for individual excerpts to the basic, factual information needed for understanding their context. I have avoided providing extensive interpretations, in the expectation that the reader will interact with these texts to develop his/her own understandings of their meanings. The editorial process, in which the excerpts were selected is, itself, an active intervention into interpretation.

My selection process involved a series of choices: firstly, in the way I defined a "primary source," then in the chronological range of the texts, and finally by confining this group to artists from European/American cultures.

The term "primary source," in art history, covers a variety of types of texts. In the present volume, in order to achieve insight into the ways in which artists and their autobiographical writings demonstrate both continuity and change over time, primary sources have been limited to three main genres: the retrospective "autobiography," the journal/diary entry, and the letter. Issues specific to each type of text will be discussed, individually, in this introduction. As historical circumstances change, the evolution of these genres will be addressed in the "Part Introductions."

It is widely understood that the production of both visual art and writing are cultural practices embedded in historically specific contexts. Feminist art historians and scholars of women's self writing have persuasively argued for the importance of historically rooted interpretive strategies. The chapters are organized chronologically, beginning with Elisabeth Vigée-Lebrun, active in the late eighteenth century, and continuing through contemporary artists, still alive, such as Louise Bourgeois and Faith Ringgold. The chronological organization, employed here, is necessary to situate the artistic and literary work of these women into a coherent cultural framework. Social conditions, specific to the culture, control and limit the range of possibilities available to these creators both to make art and to write texts.

Most of these artist /writers lived and worked in Europe or America. This selection makes no claims to be geographically inclusive or to attempt a full global span. Published primary source materials are, currently, more readily available for Euro-American women artists. Also, by restricting the geographical range, the "Part Introductions" can integrate the visual art and textual writings into a more focused framework in which political, cultural, and creative activities can be defined, compared and contrasted.

I. Artists as "Authors"

a. Writing and Reading "as a woman": interpretative strategies

Although, it has been a fashionable, post-modern conceit to distance a "text" from the identity of the author, feminist scholars have resisted this intellectual position, and I am comfortable in stating that these texts were written by women aware of gendered differences. Norma Broude and Mary Garrard succinctly define the postmodern concept of the "author" in the following way:

> "The 'author' or artist ...is not a simple designation but a description, something that is produced by culture...The concept 'author' is not identical with the human individual who bore that name; rather it is a set of meanings generated around that name." [3]

This position became known as the "Death of the Author" theory. It did not take long for feminists to question the relevance of this theory for women authors: "the exaggerated adulation of heroic authorship was declared to be passé just when women began to take the stage as authors/artists."[4] Broude and Garrard wryly note that "a cynic might observe that postmodernism declared the very idea of a canon dead in order to avoid opening up the existing one to women and minorities."[5]

If we can accept the concept that these authors write as women, then, as readers, we can also read texts "as a woman", i.e. from a gendered perspective. As Miller has argued: "to reread as a woman is at least to imagine the lady's place—to imagine while reading the place of a woman's body; to read reminded that her identity is also re-membered in stories of the body."[6] I would encourage the reader to attempt to read as a woman, to identify with the authors who were writing as women.

b. "Reclaiming Female Agency"

One of the challenges confronting feminist art historians of the twenty-first century would seem to be the acceptance of the multiplicity, diversity, and fragmentation among women based on the seemingly infinite variety of women's individual lives and gendered identities. It can seem to be virtually impossible to define a "Woman," with any degree of historical certainty. The variables of race, class, and sexual orientation, in addition to the historical period and nationality, overwhelm the ability to clarify exactly what it means to be a "woman." It is even harder to define the complex collectivity, "women." However, we can still examine the ways in which specific individuals, who were biologically female, negotiated their lives in their own particular historical realities. This is the concept which Broude and Garrard identify as "female agency." They call for studies which "rebalance the larger picture, describing a cultural dynamic that consisted not of men's cultural dominance and women's occasional achievement but rather of a steady and ongoing participation of women in culture as active agents at every level."[7]

Art historian, Griselda Pollock, has called for a more specific "reading" of the individual creator.

"Every woman is the complex product of her specific historical and cultural framing: generations and geographies. There is neither Woman nor women. Everyone has a specific story, a particular experience of the configurations of class, race, gender, sexuality, family country, displacement, alliance..." [8]

The analysis of women artists' autobiographical texts is ideally positioned to address these concerns. Reading primary sources helps us locate the active participation of women in their cultures. Readers can begin to understand how women understood and negotiated their gendered identities, in different historical milieus, as agents of cultural change. Primary sources help tell the "specific story" of each artist/author.

At the same time, we need to respect the complex creative process of making art which necessarily involves using a formal language that cannot simply be an unmediated expression of "true feelings." We fully agree with Pollock's concerns about interpretive strategies for analyzing visual art which results in "reducing all work by women artists generically to confessional, personal or testimonial autobiography."[9]

c. On the "Identity" of the autobiographical subject for women

It is a postmodern assumption that a woman's identity should be understood as multiple and layered, as opposed to the male paradigm of the unified self. Many scholars of autobiographical texts have examined this issue. Susan Stanford Friedman was one influential literary theorist who began to challenge the male model of identity for women. In an essay first published in 1988, she asserted that:

> "...the self, self-creation, and self consciousness are profoundly different for women, minorities and many non-Western people....In taking the power of words, of representation, into their own hands, women project onto history an identity that is neither purely individualistic, nor purely collective. Instead, this new identity merges the shared and the unique. ... the self constructed in women's autobiographical writing is often based in, but not limited to, a group consciousness—an awareness of the

meaning of the cultural category WOMAN for the patterns of women's individual destiny. Alienation is not the result of creating a self in language, as it is for Lacanian and Barthesian critics of autobiography. Instead, alienation from the historically imposed image of the self is what motivates the writing, the creation of an alternate self in the autobiographical act. Writing the self shatters the cultural hall of mirrors and breaks the silence imposed by male speech" [10]

I have quoted Friedman at some length because her definition of identity, as both individual and collective, seems especially appropriate for the artist/writers of *In Her Own Words*. Friedman is arguing against literary theories which break down the connection between the real living person and the author of the autobiographical text. The term "Barthesian theory" refers to the influential French philosopher Roland Barthes.[11] In 1975, he wrote *Roland Barthes by Roland Barthes* which asserts that "no definite truth about the past self may be available... The subject is inescapably an unstable fiction." [12] In addition to countering the "Barthesian critics," Friedman also mentions "Lacanian" critics. Jacques Lacan, was a French psychoanalyst whose "revision of Freudian psychoanalysis challenge the notion of an autonomous self and proposed a split subject always constituted in language."[13] Like Barthes, his ideas have been widely read and incorporated into literary criticism. Both schools of criticism have proposed an intellectual distance between the written text and the "real" person experiencing the event. Friedman argues for a closer identification of writer and text, even when analyzing the private forms of letter and journal. Freidman believes that the "autobiographical act" connects the woman writer with larger communities of visual artists, writers and women. The last sentence, cited as the epigraph of II,a, reminds us of the value and power implicit in the act of "writing the self."

Smith and Watson have applied Judith Butler's influential concept of gender formation as performance to life narratives. Many of the texts in this book can be interpreted in the context of a "performative" theory of identity.

"A performative view of life narrative theorizes autobiographical occasions as dynamic sites for the performance of identities constitutive of subjectivity... in this view, identities are not fixed or essentialized attributes of autobiographical subjects; rather they are produced and reiterated through cultural norms, and thus remain provisional and unstable."[14]

Identities, as manifested in autobiographical acts, either visual or textual "do not affirm a 'true self' or a coherent and stable identity. They are performative, situated addresses that invite their readers' collaboration in producing specific meanings for the 'life'". [15]

Gilmore is also sensitive to the complexities of defining a coherent "identity" of the author:

"The identity an autobiography inscribes is something more like a process that variously synthesizes or is fragmented by these discourses. The contradictory and fragmented though resilient subject of autobiography structures narrative and its effects and is a fictive and textual construct."[16]

II. Primary Sources: Genres of "Life Narratives"

There are many ways in which a woman can write about her own life and many different terms in play to describe this writing. "Life narrative", the term, proposed by Smith and Watson, is a useful phrase, since it encompasses many more diverse types of autobiographical texts, than the more narrowly defined term, "autobiography." In its broadest definition, a life narrative is: "a historically situated practice of self-representation."[17] In *Reading Autobiography: A Guide for Interpreting Life Narratives*, Smith and Watson, have defined 52 "genres" of texts.[18] I find these categories useful working definitions for both the excerpted primary sources, and often for the volume in which the texts were originally published. By using these definitions, we will be able to locate similarities and differences among authors across time and space. Therefore, in both the part introductions, and individual chapter introductions, I will define the specific genre of life narrative, as identified in *Reading Autobiography,* in **bold type**.

As noted above, *In Her Own Words* uses three broad categories: retrospective autobiographical narratives, letters, and entries from a diary/journal. Each of these texts raises specific theoretical issues.

a. Autobiographical narrative: "Self-representation"

"Writing the self shatters the cultural hall of mirrors and breaks the silence imposed by male speech." [19]

Friedman's statement, quoted above, is a strong assertion of the importance of autobiographical practices for the study of women in all historical periods. Writing one's "life narrative" for publication is a powerful act. As Nancy K. Miller notes:

> "To justify an unorthodox life by writing about it, however, is to *reinscribe* the original violation, to reviolate masculine turf...The autobiographies of these women, ...are a defense and illustration, at once a treatise on overcoming received notions of femininity and a poetics calling for another, freer text."[20]

Chronologically, the retrospective "autobiography" appears first in our collection. The *Souvenirs* or *Memoirs* of Vigée-Lebrun (Chapter 1), published in the 1830s, is the earliest autobiography penned by a woman visual artist.

For our purposes, we can accept, Philippe Lejeune's working definition of autobiography: "We call autobiography the retrospective narrative in prose that someone makes of *his* own existence when *he* puts the principal accent upon *his* life, especially upon the story of *his* own personality."[21] The use of male pronouns is appropriate, since the gendering of this term has a long history, beginning with Georg Misch's *History of Autobiography in Antiquity* (1907). Misch's criteria defined the appropriate subject of autobiography to be the "writer's relationship to the arena of public life."[22] He believed that only people who have been actors in important historical events are appropriate subjects for autobiography.[23] According to Misch, only the autobiography of an "eminent person" was worthy of study, effectively excluding life narratives of most women and other colonized peoples from the canon of great works.

Feminist theorists have questioned the use of the term "autobiography" which has confined scholarly analysis to a limited "canon," excluding not only women's autobiographies, but also the genres of letters and journal entries. There is a substantial academic discourse focused on the complexities of analyzing women's autobiographical texts, dating back to the late 1970s. Since then: "Women's autobiography is now a privilege site for thinking about issues of writing at the intersection of feminist, postcolonial, and post modern critical theories."[24] Clearly it is impossible to

summarize these extensive studies in this brief introduction.[25] However, the reader should be aware that
there are many terms identifying "autobiographical
practices."

Perhaps all the texts in this volume that fall into
some sort of retrospective narrative, can be viewed as
autobiographics. Leigh Gilmore invented this term
in her important feminist theory of autobiographical
production:

> "the recurring mark in the women's autobi-
> ographies... can be found in the shared sense
> that a written record, a testimonial, or a confes-
> sional document can represent a person, can
> stand in her absence for her truth, can re-mem-
> ber her life...writing an autobiography can be
> a political act because it asserts a right to speak
> rather than to be spoken for."[26]

Most of these texts also share a very real sense of
gendered identity. Women artists were quite conscious of being women and what that meant in terms
of both acceptance of and resistance to dominant gender ideologies of their societies. Therefore, one can
use the term **Autogynography**, invented by Domna C.
Stanton, "to suggest the centrality of gendered subjectivity to the literary production of self-referential
acts."[27]

Sometimes, the term **memoir** is used interchangeably with "autobiography," but it can also be seen as
a specific genre of life narrative. A **memoir** is an au-

tobiography which "historically situates the subject in a social environment as either observer or participant. …such accounts "emphasize life in the public sphere, chronicling professional careers and activities of historical import." [28] Miller has looked at the root of the term "memoir" meaning both to recall and to record: "To record means literally to call to mind, to call up from the heart. At the same time, record means to set down in writing, to make official." [29]

If the memoir is a type of autobiography which emphasizes historical accuracy and professional achievement, then there are several texts in this book which are clearly **memoirs**. Most obviously, the autobiographies of Vigée-Lebrun (Chapter 1) and Faith Ringgold (Chapter 13) may be considered **memoirs**, since this term appears specifically in the titles of their life narratives. In addition, Cameron's *Annals of My Glass House* (Chapter 4), Kollwitz's essay, *The Early Years* (Chapter 8), and *Georgia O'Keeffe*, from 1976 (Chapter 9), are also memoirs. These writings appear in all three parts of *In Her Own Words*, spanning the full chronological range of this book.

Valerie Sanders, who has studied the memoirs of Victorian women, has defined the gender differences between male and female autobiographers in the following statement:

> "Whereas men concentrate on their careers and write, for the most part, in a stately prose style without rancor, women focus on the vicissitudes of their private lives and tell stories of

endurance and survival in a society where they had no prominence and few claims."[30]

As we will see, this emphasis on tenacity and overcoming obstacles will remain a characteristic of women's life narratives, into the contemporary era, as seen in the autobiographies of Judy Chicago (Chapter 12) and Faith Ringgold (Chapter 13).

Any autobiographical narrative is a highly self-conscious constructed text, which cannot be taken, simply and uncritically, as the "truth" of the writer's life. Art historian Mary Sheriff, who has written very perceptively on the *Souvenirs* of Vigée-Lebrun, defends her use of this primary source, even while acknowledging that some passages are not historically accurate and parts of the text may have been written by someone else.

"Whether or not this life genuinely belonged to her, whether or not she actually lived or wrote it, matters little here. This was the life she appropriated for herself...For my purposes it is enough that she acknowledges this text as the representation of her life both explicitly in the body of the work and implicitly by publishing it under her name during her lifetime...As to the 'truth' of her life—well, God only knows."[31]

The reader should be alert to the fact that life narratives cannot be accepted, transparently, as faithful, accurate records of the thoughts and feelings of a closed, fixed subject. Rather all our texts can productively be seen as types of "self representations." Ten of these fifteen artists have written retrospective autobiographical texts, or "self-representations," ranging from very brief statements to books. In addition to Vigée-Lebrun, Bonheur, Cameron, Kollwitz, O'Keeffe, Neel, Chicago, Ringgold, Bourgeois, and Saint Phalle produced some type of autobiography, although many of these texts were published posthumously.

b. Letters: "The Backbone of Biography"

A late nineteenth century biographer of Angelica Kauffmann used this wonderful expression to characterize the role of letters: "Without letters the story of a life cannot be told satisfactorily: they make, in fact, the backbone of biography."[32] Letters are included in Parts 1 through 3 and do form a strong armature, a backbone for *In Her Own Words.* Vigée-Lebrun's *Souvenirs* (Chapter 1), while not letters in the strictest sense, is written in an epistolary format. Saint Phalle also used the form of the letter for her life narrative (Chapter 15). Letters, which were actually sent to correspondents, are included in seven chapters in all three parts. Hosmer, Cameron, Morisot, Modersohn-Becker, Kollwitz, O'Keeffe, and Kahlo wrote letters which have been published and, if necessary, translated into English. Therefore, the format of the letter dominates the texts in this book.

Letters are extremely useful primary sources for art historians. Letter writing, as opposed to "autobiography", was a well established practice for women, at least since the eighteenth century. Many women in the nineteenth century were very active correspondents. Carroll Smith-Rosenberg was one of the first historians to seriously study nineteenth century private writings of hundreds of American women that were preserved in archives.[33] The study of letters revealed a virtually unknown female world of great emotional strength and complexity. [34]

Some letters, in this book, are addressed to patrons, critics, or curators. Their tone and content provide insights into the ways in which woman artists negotiated their professional careers. Other letters, to intimate friends and family members, such as those of Berthe Morisot or Georgia O'Keeffe, reflect the private voices of their authors, their more unguarded revelations, creating a sense of connection between reader and writer.

Many letters bridge the public/private dichotomy. These letters are quasi-public and function as "both private correspondence expressing the inner feeling of the writing subject and as public documents to be shared within a literary circle." [35] The preservation of the letters, alone, argues for an understanding of their significance to a more public audience, beyond the limited eyes of the intended recipient.

Sarah E. Webb has argued for collaboration between artist, art historian, and reader in the interpretation of letters written by living artists. She asserts:

"Only by writing in collaboration can the artist and the art historian right the woman artist so

that her marks are not erased....Visual marks
are made and letters written to be interpreted
as much through the act of reading/readings
as through the original act of artistic creation.
It is a story of mutual dependence between text
and image knitting these "singular women"
and those beyond the pages of this book."[36]

I believe that her ideas are equally appropriate for
the study of letter writers of the past. Two phrases in
this statement are important for an understanding of
In Her Own Words. To "right" the woman artist is to
find a correct interpretation, a key task which primary
sources can begin to address. This concept is so central to this book that I have used the phrase in the
epigraph to this introduction. To refer to a group of
women artists as "singular women" an apparent oxy-
moron, refers to both their unity in gender, i.e. as
women, and their individual natures, i.e. singularity.
Therefore the term "singular women" demonstrates
uniqueness and continuity. Each artist/author, in this
collection, is most definitely a "singular woman."

c. Diaries/journals: "Tender Compulsions"[37]

"A reader goes from one surprise to another...
One discovers terrible tragedies, or moments of happiness."[38]

Diaries of visual artists are fascinating and important primary sources. Artists often used diaries to define goals, react self-critically to their own work, and
identify potential subjects for art. The published di-
ary/journal entry is an important type of text for this

book, but emerges after letters or retrospective life narratives. Marie Bashkirtseff's *Journal* (Chapter 6), published in 1887 and translated into English in 1890, was the first influential diary. It was very widely read and its popularity inspired many women to keep journals. Four of the remaining nine artists, included in this book kept diaries which have been preserved. The diaries of Modersohn-Becker, Kollwitz and Kahlo were all published posthumously. A highly selective group of Louise Bourgeois' diary entries were included in a compilation of her writings published in 1998 (Chapter 14).

Philippe Lejeune, one of the leading theoreticians of this genre, does not make a distinction between the terms "diary" and "journal." He defines the journal or diary (since we are using the terms interchangeably) as "a form of periodic life writing ... [which] records dailiness in accounts and observation of emotional responses." Lejeune notes that the diary is "motivated by a search for communication, by a will to persuasion," [39] which is quite appropriate for Bashkirtseff's *Journal*, especially. Lejeune dates the practice of keeping a diary, among girls, in France, to the era of the July Monarchy, after 1830.[40]

Felicity A. Nussbaum invented an interesting term for the diary or journal: "serial autobiography."[41] Nussbaum perceptively notes that: "The subject of serial autobiography is a subject positioned within struggles to claim individual difference, autonomy, freedom, and privacy." [42] In the past, some scholars and theoreticians of autobiography were resistant to studying diaries. Nussbaum argues for the diary's value to scholars: "The diary and journal…are representations of reality rather than failed versions of something more coherent and unified.[43]

> "In writing to themselves, eighteenth-century women, in particular, could create a private place in which to speak the unthought, un-said, and undervalued. In writing private daily records, they could speak as subjects who re-flected and produced their multiple positions in texts and in culture as they read, reread, and revised their gendered textual formulations." [44]

Women who wrote diaries were challenging the in-visibility and the submissiveness of many of their cul-ture's dominant social codes. The visual artists in this book used their diaries in many ways, including the rehearsing of gendered identity.

d. Auto/biography

Some volumes do not fall neatly into the category of either biography or autobiography. This occurs when the text has been written by another individual, usual-ly a person who knew the artist intimately, and who is responsible for publishing the book. Frequently, these books are published posthumously. Such volumes are characteristic of biography, since the overall narrative structure has been authored by someone other than the subject. Inserted into the narrative are primary sources, such as letters, journal entries and/or recorded statements, and, occasionally, a brief, retrospective auto-biography. Scholars have invented the term, **Auto/biography** or **a/b,** for short, for these types of life narratives. **A/b** is defined by Smith and Watson as:

> "an acronym [which]signals the interrelated-ness of autobiographical narrative and biog-raphy...The term also designates a mode of the autobiographical that inserts biography/ies within an autobiography, or the converse, a personal narrative within a biography."[45]

The term **a/b** is most appropriate for the books dedicated to Harriet Hosmer, (Chapter 2), Rosa Bon-heur (Chapter 3), Berthe Morisot (Chapter 5), and Käthe Kollwitz (Chapter 8). In these cases, someone, other than the artist, wrote the book and edited the texts. The excerpts which are reprinted, here, are the actual primary sources embedded in the narrative. Scholars have accepted the authenticity of these pri-mary sources and have used them in scholarly work on the four artists.

A related concept is the **collaborative life narra-tive:** "A term that indicates the production of an auto-biographical text by more than one person thorough the as-told-to narrative in which an informant tells an interviewer the story of her life." [46]   Such texts are "multiply mediated by the interviewer and editor."[47] A translator adds yet another "collaborator" for the final text. The volumes on Rosa Bonheur (Chapter 3) and Alice Neel (Chapter 11) fit into this category.

III. An explanation of the selection/editing process

In editing this book, I have necessarily had to separate these texts from their original published form, and, in many cases, to excerpt them from a longer text, creating yet one more layer of distance from the actual writing.

The selection process for individual excerpts is based on the writer's art historical position. Since these writers are visual artists, the texts which seem most important for the understanding of their art have been prioritized. Some texts are included since they are frequently quoted by scholars and seem to be most illuminating for the art historians who have dedicated long years to the study of these creators.

The following themes recur with some consistency:

1. The early sense of artistic vocation. Often the artist/writers discuss how they decided to become visual artists.
2. Recollections about the creative process of a major work or series of works.
3. Identification of sources of inspiration and motivations for the creation of the visual art. (Sometimes there is evidence of self-criticism.)
4. The position of the artist concerning marriage and motherhood. Such comments

are often incorporated into discussions of gender roles, especially in relationship to the gender of the artist.

5. Attitudes toward recognition, popular success, and the public persona of the artist.

6. Political beliefs and opinions on contemporary feminist movements.

Conclusion

When a reader has access to a text and can read the words formulated by the artist, herself, there is a new layer of contact with the actual woman. However, the reader should remember that an autobiographical narrative as a form of "self-representation" or a "fictive and textual construct" rather than the "truth." When one combines the "evidence" of written texts with visual works of art, the possibilities for "self-representation" multiply exponentially. This creates exciting opportunities to explore identities in an intimate and satisfying way. If our ultimate goal, as art historians, is to respect the agency of women artists, the crucial importance of studying these written texts is self-evident. If the goal is to re-discover the nature of individual artists who lived to create identities manifested in "texts", both verbal and visual, then the primacy of primary sources is inescapable. Primary sources help us locate the specific individuals and break down stereotypical generalities which can characterize thinking about historical women. The survival of these primary sources allows each artist to speak in her own words.

Notes

1. Sarah E. Webb, in Kristin Frederickson and Sarah E. Webb (eds), *Singular Women: Writing the Artist* (Berkeley, Los Angeles, London: University of California Press, 2003), 248.

2. Sidonie Smith & Julia Watson, (eds) *Interfaces: Women/Autobiography/Image/Performance* (Ann Arbor, MI: The University of Michigan Press, 2002), 5-7.

3. Norma Broude and Mary D. Garrard, (eds), *The Expanding Discourse: Feminism and Art History* (New York, HarperCollins1992), 2.

4. Norma Broude and Mary D. Garrard, (eds) *Reclaiming Female Agency: Feminist Art History after Postmodernism* (Berkeley, Los Angeles, London, University of California Press, 2005), 11.

5. *The Expanding Discourse*, 4.

6. Nancy K. Miller, *French Dressing: Women, Men and Ancien Régime Fiction* (London and New York, Routledge, 1995). 47 quoted in Pollock, *Encounters in the Virtual Feminist Museum,* (New York and London: Routledge, 2007), 9.

7. Broude and Garrard, *Reclaiming Female Agency*, 22.

8. Griselda Pollock, (ed) *Generations and Geographies in the Visual Arts: Feminist Readings* (New York and London: Routledge, 1996), p. xv.

9. Griselda Pollock *Encounters in the Virtual Feminist Museum,* 149.

10. Susan Stanford Friedman, "Women's Autobiographical Selves: Theory and Practice" reprinted in Sidonie Smith and Julia Watson (eds.), *Women,*

Autobiography, Theory: a Reader [WAT] (Madison WI and London: The University of Wisconsin Press, 1998), 76.

[11] Roland Barthes (1915-1980).

[12] Sidonie Smith and Julia Watson, *Reading Autobiography: A Guide for Interpreting Life Narratives* (Minneapolis and London: University of Minnesota Press, 2001), 186.

[13] Jacques Lacan (1901-1981). Smith and Watson, *Reading Autobiography*, 133.

[14] Smith and Watson, *Reading Autobiography*, 143.

[15] Smith and Watson, *Interfaces*, 11.

[16] Ibid., 84.

[17] Smith and Watson, *Reading Autobiography*, 14.

[18] Ibid., Appendix A.

[19] Friedman, in WAT, 76.

[20] Nancy K. Miller, "Writing Fictions: Women's Autobiography in France" in Bella Brodzki and Celeste Schenk (eds) *Life/Lines: Theorizing Women's Autobiography* (Ithaca: Cornell University Press, 1988), 50.

[21] My emphasis.

[22] Smith and Watson, *Reading Autobiography*, 114.

[23] Ibid.

[24] Smith and Watson, WAT, 5.

[25] See Smith and Watson, "Introduction: Situating Subjectivity in Women's Autobiographical Practices," in WAT.

[26] Leigh Gilmore, *Autobiographics: A Feminist Theory of Women's Self-Representation* (Ithaca and London: Cornell University Press, 1994), 40.

[27] Smith and Watson, *Reading Autobiography*, 187.

[28] Ibid., 198.

[29] Smith and Watson, *Reading Autobiography*, 98.

[30] Valerie Sanders, *The Private Lives of Victorian Women: Autobiography in Nineteenth Century England* (New York: St. Martin's Press, 1989), 46.

[31] Mary D. Sheriff, *The Exceptional Woman: Elisabeth Vigée-Lebrun and the Cultural Politics of Art* (Chicago and London: the University of Chicago Press, 1996), 8.

[32] Frances A. Gerard, *Angelica Kauffman: a Biography* (New York, Macmillan and Co., 1893), xi.

[33] Carroll Smith-Rosenberg, *Disorderly Conduct: Visions of Gender in Victorian America* (New York and Oxford, Oxford University Press, 1985), 28.

[34] Ibid., 28.

[35] Smith and Watson, *Reading Autobiography*, 196.

[36] Webb, in Frederickson and Webb, *Singular Women: Writing the Artist*, 248.

[37] This is the term used by Louise Bourgeois for her journal activity, (Chapter 14).

[38] Philippe Lejeune, "The "Journal de Jeune Fille" in Nineteenth-Century France", translated by Martine Breillac in Suzanne L. Bunkers and Cynthia A. Huff, *Inscribing the Daily: Critical Essays on Women's Diaries,* (Amherst, University of Massachusetts Press, 1996), 110.

[39] Lejeune, quoted in Smith and Watson, *Reading Autobiography*, 193.

[40] Lejeune in Bunkers and Huff, *Inscribing the Daily*, 114.

[41] Felicity A. Nussbaum, "The Politics of Subjectivity and the Ideology of Genre" in WAT, 166.

[42]   Nussbaum in WAT, 166

[43]   Nussbaum in WAT, 165-66

[44]   Felicity A. Nussbaum, "Eighteenth-Century Women's Autobiographical Commonplaces" in Shari Benstock, (ed) *The Private Self: Theory and Practice of Women's Autobiographical Writings* (Chapel Hill and London, The University of North Carolina Press, 1988), 154.

[45]   Smith and Watson, *Reading Autobiography*, 184.

[46]   Smith and Watson, *Reading Autobiography*, 191.

[47]   Ibid.

Introduction to Part 1:
The Nineteenth Century; the Emergence of Women Artists as Writers

Over the course of the nineteenth century, spanning the time periods in which the six women artists included in Part I worked, there was a steadily increasing population of women artists in France, England, and the United States. While Elisabeth Vigée-Lebrun remained relatively isolated and "exceptional" in the 1780s, by around 1900 there were, literally, 1000's of active women artists.

In France, one can trace the increasing numbers of women artists by the numbers of women exhibiting works in the official Salon. In 1801, 28 (14.6%) of exhibiting artists were women. By 1835, 178 (22.2%) of artists showing works at the Salon were women.[1] In 1877, 648 women had works included in the official Salon and by 1880 1,081 women were listed.[2] The population of women artists in Victorian England grew in a parallel manner. In 1841, fewer than 300 women identified themselves as artists in the census. By 1871, that number had grown to over 1,000.[3] Women artists, who achieved some measure of visibility and success, prior to 1850, were isolated and perceived as exceptional. After 1870 there was a solid population, a "critical mass" of women artists.

This increase in the absolute number of women artists occurred despite the blatant inequality in educational opportunities. Women experienced discriminatory conditions in acquiring even a rudimentary training as visual artists, compared with their male peers. In France, in 1805, the first free drawing school for girls was opened. In 1848, Raymond Bonheur, Rosa's father became director, and in the 1850's, Rosa, with the assistance of her sister, Juliette, ran this institution. By 1879, there were 20 new schools in Paris, solely designed to train women for positions in arts industries. Artists such as Berthe Morisot and Marie Bashkirtseff, due to their high class status and professional aspirations, acquired their training in other ways. Morisot studied privately, with more established male artists, and Bashkirtseff took advantage of the opening of a separate class for women, in the early 1870s, at the Atelier Julian. Julian's provided training which was closest to the official education, available only to men, at the École des Beaux Arts.

In London, in 1842, the Female School of Art was established to train women for jobs in applied or commercial design. One woman, Laura Herford managed to gain admission into the Royal Academy, in 1860. However, the opening of the Slade School, in 1871, with its stated policy of gender equality, was helpful to aspiring women artists. Additionally, there were private art schools, such as St. John's Wood, where the

German artist Paula Modersohn-Becker studied for a time (Chapter 7).

Compared to England and France, the United States opened its art schools to women relatively early. In 1844, women were drawing from plaster casts at the Pennsylvania Academy of Fine Arts. That same year the Philadelphia School of Design for Women (later Moore College of Art) was founded to train women in practical skills for arts industries. By 1860, there was a separate anatomy class for women at the Pennsylvania Academy, and in 1877, the male nude was introduced, in a radical move, by Thomas Eakins.[4] After the Civil War, many American women artists traveled to Europe, especially Paris, to pursue their artistic training. To assist them, May Alcott wrote a handbook, *Studying Art Abroad and How to Do It Cheaply* (1879).

Women who wanted to become "fine artists" had to establish a professional identity which was distinct from both designers or "decorative artists" and amateurs. In this period, there was an important distinction between training as a "fine artist" which meant usually oil painting and the education women received at the Schools of Design which prepared women for work in the fields of art teaching and crafts production. F. Graeme Chalmers has compiled a detailed documentary history of the Schools of Art and Design for Women in London and Philadelphia. In this comparative study, he has expanded our understanding of the gendered attitudes towards art making and the ways in which art education impacted creative women other than fine artists.[5]

The growth in the population of professional women artists, during the nineteenth century, should be viewed against a dominant ideology in which gender roles were strictly segregated into "separate spheres." Women were to remain in the home, engaged in motherhood and other domestic pursuits, while men were active outside the home. Known as the "Cult of True Womanhood," this ideology was developed by bourgeois men, in the United States, between the 1820 and 1840s. The "Cult" "prescribed a female role bounded by kitchen and nursery, overlaid with piety and purity, and crowned with subservience." [6]

This ideology parallels the gender roles in Victorian society, which defined bourgeois femininity as "dependent and domestic." [7] As Pamela Gerrish Nunn notes, women living in Victorian England were not supposed to earn money: "financial dependence was expected of all but the lowest classes of women." [8] Furthermore, women artists operated in a cultural milieu with widespread beliefs in the innate inferiority of their creative powers, both intellectual and artistic. Patriarchal culture, in all three counties, proposed the "scientific" belief that women's limited achievement, in the arts, inevitably resulted from gender-linked, biologically determined deficiencies in artistic creativity and the high power of imagination. [9] Despite the misogynistic gender ideology of their era, growing numbers of women artists became increasingly visible. Many women exhibited their works, in public salons, leaving a record for contemporary historians.

The work of "professional" women artists should be viewed against the backdrop of a widespread "feminine visual culture," in which "middle-and upper-class women all over Europe through the nineteenth century, painted or drew a domestic existence." [10] Anne Higonnet has defined this activity as: "rudimentary drawing and watercolor techniques and occasionally even oil-painting skills," which were taught to women as one of the "feminine accomplishments attractive to suitable husbands."[11] Women also made albums. Higonnet mentions the photographer Julia Margaret Cameron (Chapter 4) who organized some of her photographs for presentation as albums, in relation to this type of amateur activity. Amateur art most often used imagery which reinforced the hegemonic values of bourgeois femininity: "Feminine imagery acted as self-representation in the sense that it was a means both to learn and to perform an identity."[12] Against this pervasive amateur activity, women artists struggled for professional recognition, critical attention and patronage.

The beginnings and subsequent development of feminist reform movements in England, France, and the United States certainly had a positive impact on the ability of women to function as professional artists. Harriet Hosmer left the United States, for Rome, shortly after the Seneca Falls conference of 1848, the beginning of organized American Feminism. British women had already become active in the Abolitionist and Temperance movements in the early Victorian era, and by 1850, were beginning to mount a serious suffrage campaign. In 1856, the Society of Female Artists was established. In England, women artists were active participants in the reformist campaigns for equal rights after the 1850s:

> "Women artists participated in the women's movements of the nineteenth century. They were particularly active in egalitarian feminism which campaigned from the 1850s for equal rights, higher education, paid work and legal reform....Women artists contributed to the campaigns for votes for women, who were not enfranchised in Britain until 1918 and 1928. As respectable professionals, women artists embodied many of the arguments for the greater public activity and responsibility of women. From the launch of the suffrage campaign in the 1860s they joined suffrage societies, gave money, spoke at meetings, turned their studios and dwellings into campaign centers and signed petitions." [13]

In France, the emergence of Feminism was delayed due to the authoritarian government of Napoleon III, the Second Empire. However following the collapse of this regime, at the time of the Franco-Prussian War of 1870, an active, organized feminist movement emerged. In 1878, the first Congress of Women's Rights was convened in Paris. Shortly thereafter, in 1881, the Union des Femmes Peintres et

Sculpteurs (UFPS) was founded. Recognizing the inequities in arts education, the UFPS began a campaign, in 1889, to have women admitted to the Ecole des Beaux-Arts. This goal was eventually achieved in 1897. Paula Modersohn-Becker tried to gain admission, there, in 1906 (Chapter 7).

Both the British Society for Female Artists and the UFPS provided exhibition opportunities, for their members, by staging an annual Salon. In France, although many women did submit their works to the official Salon, to be hung with male peers, the numbers of awards (most often in the lower categories of third-class medal or honorable mention) remained low. By the early 1890s, between 600 and 800 works were exhibited in the UFPS Salon. The largest Union show took place in 1906, when over 1,500 works were hung. As Tamar Garb had noted: "The sheer numbers of women who exhibited with the Union is testimony to the need it filled."[14]

With the exception of the *Souvenirs* of Vigée-Lebrun (Chapter 1), the texts, included in this part, should be positioned within this historical framework of growing feminist reform movements, increasing numbers of women artists aspiring for professional recognition, and the support of organized groups of women artists promoting women's work.

Beginning in the eighteenth century, there was an:

"explosion in both the kinds and the sheer number of life narratives....New reading publics emerged with the rise in literacy, the expansion of print media, and the increased circulation of texts, goods and people between Europe and the American colonies...there was a democratization of the institution of life writing..." [15]

Just as many women aspired to become professional artists, increasing numbers of women became published authors during the nineteenth century.

Given the pervasive impact of the hegemonic gender discourse of the era, the "Cult of True Womanhood," it is not surprising that men's and women's autobiographical writings took divergent forms. As opposed to male autobiographers, Victorian women exhibited an unwillingness to examine their achievement as progressive stages in a career. For women, self-writing most frequently took the form of diary, letter, and travel memoir. Hannah More's *Strictures on the Modern System of Female Education* (1799) assigned to women faculties of "fancy" and "memory" but denied them the intellectual faculty of "comparing, combining, analyzing and separating" ideas...she believed that women lack "deep and patient thinking" and the "power of arrangement...to link a thousand connected ideas."[16] The logical extension of this premise is that "true" autobiography was beyond women's intellectual abilities. This is one of the reasons why literary theoreticians, as noted in the introduction, have rejected the over-determined term "autobiography" in favor of more inclusive terms for women's "life narratives."

However, women were expected to be good letter writers. Letters were considered to be the most appropriate type of text suitable for women's capabilities. (Introduction, II,b). The letters of Hosmer, Cameron, and Morisot are valuable primary sources, which were preserved and published. As Valerie Sanders has observed: "For many nineteenth century women, the illusion of writing letters to a sympathetic friend was the only enabling entry into autobiographical discourse."[17] This is precisely the format of Vigée-Lebrun's *Souvenirs* (Chapter 1) and persists, into the late twentieth century, in the autobiographical "letters" of Niki de Saint Phalle (Chapter 15).

Predictably, few women visual artists active in the nineteenth century, with the exception of Vigée-Lebrun, found their lives of sufficient importance to warrant the publication of a retrospective life narrative, at least while they were still alive. However, another form of writing, the diary or journal, emerged for women as a common practice in this period. Diary keeping became widespread for young girls in France only in the 1830s (Introduction II,c). The publication of Bashkirtseff's journal in the 1880s launched a widespread interest in journal keeping (Chapter 6). In a hybrid form, diary entries and letters were often inserted into autobiographical volumes to increase authenticity or to recode, indirectly, praise for professional achievement. Such "boasting" was considered to be too self- aggrandizing to be "proper" for women writers, in this era.

Part 1 includes six chapters with texts written by important, professional women artists. The first chapter is focused on the *Souvenirs* of Vigée-Lebrun, who rose to celebrity status by creating portraits for the French Monarchy and aristocracy, in the last decade of the *ancien régime*, the 1780s. Her autobiography begins, in an epistolary format, structured as letters to a "sympathetic friend", published at the end of her life, in the 1830s. This volume can be defined, at least in part, as an **apology**: "a form of self-presentation as self-defense against the allegations or attacks of others, an apology justifies one's own deed, beliefs and way of life." [18] The English translation of the title as *Memoirs,* suggests it should be understood as a **memoir**, i.e. an historical record (Introduction, II,a).

The second chapter is devoted to Harriet Hosmer, the first American woman to achieve international celebrity as a sculptor. Her neo-classical style was consistent with many Anglo-British sculptors based in Rome in the 1850s, but her iconography reflected the growing strength and support of the contemporary American/British feminist movements. Her primary sources are letters, published posthumously in a book written by Cornelia Crow Carr, who was a childhood friend of Hosmer's and the daughter of her main patron, Wayman Crow. Carr carefully preserved these letters, and like many other letters in this era, they became historical documents which although addressed to an individual were expected to be more widely shared (Introduction II,b). Furthermore, the entire volume is a form of **Auto/biography** (Introduction, II,d).

Chapter 3 is focused on Rosa Bonheur, arguably the best known and most successful woman artist of the nineteenth century. Bonheur painted animals in a Realist style. Her fame was derived, largely, from her engravings which sold widely and brought her work to a middle-class audience. Due to her popularity and financial success, Bonheur was a role model for women artists from the 1850s forward. Her primary sources come from a volume, published posthumously, based on conversations with Anna Klumpke, a much younger American artist, companion, and protégé. Like Hosmer's volume, this text is an **Auto/biography**. It may also be defined as a **collaborative life narrative** (Introduction, II,d). The boundaries between Klumpke's and Bonheur's identities are blurred or "permeable," to the extent that there is no clear distinction between biographer and the autobiographical subject.

Julia Margaret Cameron, the focus of Chapter 4, worked in the relatively new medium of photography, creating an innovative and highly personal body of work. Her account of her origins, as a photographer, *Annals of My Glass House,* first published, posthumously, in 1889, is a fascinating record of personal myth making, in the context of Victorian gender ideology. In this sense of setting the record straight, *Annals of my Glass House* is a **memoir** (Introduction I, a), but it lacks the tone of **apology** present in Vigée-Lebrun's *Souvenirs.* Cameron's letters document her serious pursuit of professional recognition and approbation and, also, function much like Hosmer's letters, as both private/public texts.

Chapter 5 reprints letters by the noted French Impressionist painter, Berthe Morisot, mainly dating from the 1870s and 1880s. Although first published and translated in a highly edited format in the 1950s, these letters still resonate with the author's struggles to become an avant garde painter of great skill. This group of letters, addressed to the family, and especially to her sister, Edma, is similar in genre to those by Hosmer. Hosmer's and Morisot's letters are inserted into larger texts, therefore the volumes are characteristic of **a/b** (Introduction II,d).

Marie Bashkirtseff died of tuberculosis at the age of 26, but she became famous for her *Journal,* heavily edited by her family, which was published after her death, in 1887. The *Journal* was quickly translated into English and widely read. She achieved fame, as she had surmised, mainly from this text, and not from her relatively small *oeuvre* of paintings. This episodic, powerful, emotional record of a dedicated, hard working painter redefined the scale of ambition and level of professional possibilities for women artists of future generations. Bashkirtseff's *Journal* is the most famous published example of this genre from the nineteenth century (Introduction II,c).

No doubt each artist/author in Part 1, understood herself to be "exceptional" given her level of professional commitment which was at odds with the hegemonic gender ideology of her era. The desire to document these exceptional lives in published texts, whether initiated by the subject or an interested collaborator, reveals a sense of the autobiographical

will write.' I understood this reason, having been so often misunderstood, slandered that I decided to do it. ...I only retrace the facts with simplicity and truthfulness, as one would write a letter to a friend." [3]

From this statement, it is clear that Vigée-Lebrun's writing project takes the form of an **apology** (Introduction to Part I), i.e. a defense and justification of her life. Her autobiography may also be defined as a **memoir.** This is the term used as the English translation of *"Souvenirs."* As a **memoir**, it purports to provide a clear historical record (Introduction, II,a). While one could argue that Vigée-Lebrun had enjoyed an extremely prominent, even "celebrity" status, during the 1780s. She wrote her autobiography near the end of her life, when hardly any artist-colleagues were alive and few contemporaries could be expected to remember her triumphs from the pre-Revolutionary era. Therefore, her *Souvenirs* is consistent with other Victorian women who also wrote stories of "endurance and survival" [4]

Most of the *Souvenirs* are written as letters. Vigée-Lebrun begins with twelve letters, addressed to Princess Kourakin, sister-in-law to the Russian ambassador in France, under Napoleon and a friend of Vigée-Lebrun's from St. Petersburg. The middle portion of the text is composed of 32 chapters that tell her story as a narration of events: then there are nine additional letters addressed to Countess Potocka, a Polish princess. The manuscript concludes with three more chapters and a series of lively, *Portraits à la plume* or "Pen Portraits."[5]   One of these "Pen Portraits," describing Jacques-Louis David,[6] is reprinted below.

The epistolary mode was quite common in writings from the eighteenth century. Letter writing was believed to be especially well suited to women, in this period[7] (Introduction II,b). The publication of letters became an acceptable form of public writing for women and eventually epistolary novels would grow out of this form of text. Therefore Vigée-Lebrun's *Souvenirs* was written in a format which was considered to be appropriate for women, by a woman who had successfully functioned in the public sphere dominated by men and who was anxious to control the "representation" of her life, for posterity.

Like Artemisia Gentileschi, and other women artists, Elisabeth Vigée's father[8] was an artist. Daughters of artists, such as Rosa Bonheur (Chapter 3), had a distinct advantage in acquiring professional skills. Louis Vigée's early death, described in the first excerpt, forced Elisabeth to acquire painting skills though the support system of her father's professional artistic network. She could not pursue the "normal" course of study which was admission to the École Royale des Beaux-Arts, because she was female, and the school was open only to young men.

I felt that I was about to lose the very best of fathers: he was my support, my guide and it was his kind encouragement that had fostered my first attempts at painting.

I was so overcome with grief that it was a long while before I could resume work. Doyen[9] came to see us occasionally and his visits were a great comfort to us. It was thanks to him that I continued in my beloved profession, which proved to be the only effective distraction in softening my feelings of regret and steering my mind away from sad thoughts. It was during this period that I began to paint from nature, completing several pastel and oil portraits in quick succession. I also drew from nature, continuing the work at home by lamp light, usually with Mlle Boquet[10] with whom I was friendly at the time. I would go to her house in the evenings, on the Rue St Denis opposite Rue Truanderie, where her father owned a bric-a-brac shop. The route was a fairly lengthy one since we lived on the Rue de Clery opposite the Hotel de Lubert but my mother always made sure I was chaperoned. In those days Mlle Boquet and I often went to draw at the house of the painter Briard[11] and he lent us his drawings and classical sculptures to copy. Briard was a painter of middling ability, although he did paint some remarkable ceilings, noted for their fine composition. He was also a talented line artist. For this reason several young people sought him out as their teacher. He had a residence at the Louvre and in order to be able to spend more time drawing there, we would each bring a basket containing some light midday fare; the maid usually carried this. I can still remember the fun of buying delicious morsels of beef from the concierge at the Louvre gates; they were always cooked to perfection. I don't think I have eaten anything quite so tasty since.

Mlle Boquet was then fifteen and I was fourteen; we were rivals in beauty, for I have forgotten to mention, dear friend, that a metamorphosis had taken place and I was now really quite pretty. My aptitude for painting was remarkable and my process so rapid that I became a topic of conversation in high places; all this led to my making the agreeable acquaintance of Joseph Vernet[12]. This famous artist encouraged me and gave me some excellent advice: 'My child," he said, "do not follow any school of painting. Look only to the old Italian and Flemish masters; but above all, draw as much as you can from nature, nature is the greatest teacher of all. Study her carefully and you will avoid falling into mannerisms.' I have always followed this advice, for I have never really had a teacher as such. Vernet himself has proved his theory through his work, which has been and always will be justly admired.

In the following excerpt, Vigée-Lebrun recounts the meeting with her husband, Jean Baptiste-Pierre Lebrun[13] and her attitude towards the union. She attributes her acquiescence to this marriage, in 1776, to her desire to escape from the home of her stepfather. She recalls the advice she received from concerned friends, who were not aware that she had already married the spendthrift Lebrun and who tried to dissuade her from this union.

Dear friend, when my stepfather retired from business, we went to live at a mansion called Lubert on Rue de Clery, AM. Le Brun had just bought the house and was in fact living there himself. As soon as we had settled in, I went to his apartment to see his collection of paintings; his walls were adorned with examples from every school imaginable. I was thrilled to be living near so many great masterpieces and to have the opportunity of viewing them at my leisure. M. Le Brun was extremely kind and gave me permission to borrow the paintings so that I might copy them. This was no small favour, for they were both extremely fine and of great value. It was to him therefore that I owed the best form of instruction I could get; at the end of six months however, M. Le Brun asked for my hand in marriage. Nothing could have been further from my thoughts than my marrying Le Brun, despite the fact that he was an attractive man with a pleasing countenance. I was then twenty years old; I had few worries about my future since I was already earning a substantial amount of money. In short, I had no inclination to wed at all. My mother, on the other hand, insisted that I should be foolish indeed to refuse such an advantageous offer. Finally, I accepted, goaded on by the desire to escape the torment of living with my stepfather, whose bad temper had grown steadily worse now that he had nothing to occupy his time. So little inclined was I to sacrifice my freedom, that even as I approached the church on my wedding day, I was still asking myself, 'Shall I say yes or no?' Alas, I said yes and merely exchanged my old problems for new ones. I do not wish to paint M. Le Brun as a wicked man; his character was a mixture of sweetness and gaiety. He was of an obliging nature, a kind man in fact; but decimated both his fortune and my own, of which he made very free use. So, by the time I left France in 1789 I had less than twenty francs to my name, in spite of the fact that I had earned more than a million from my work: he had squandered the lot!

My marriage was kept secret for a while. M. Le Brun was officially engaged to the daughter of a Dutch art dealer with whom he was conducting some lucrative business; he begged me not to declare our union until the deal had been completed. I was only too happy to consent for I was most reluctant to lose my maiden name under which I was already quite well known. This secrecy, however, cast rather a gloomy shadow over my future. Several acquaintances who thought that I was simply about to marry Le Brun sought me out, urging me not to go ahead with such an idiotic plan. First to arrive was Auber, the crown jeweller, who confided in the name of friendship, 'You would do better to tie a stone around your neck and throw yourself in the river than marry Le Brun.' Next came the Duchesse d' Aremburg, together with Canillac and Mme de Souza, the Portuguese ambassadress; all three were so young and pretty then! They came with belated advice, for I had married two weeks previously. 'For Heaven's sake,' said the Duchess, 'don't marry Le Brun; he will make you so unhappy!' She proceeded to recite a great many stories which I did not really believe until later when I found it only too easy to confirm her words. My mother, who was present while all this was being said, could scarcely hold back her tears.

In order to increase their income, Lebrun apparently pressured his wife to accept pupils. Vigée-Lebrun is, thus, very different from Adelaide Labille-Guiard,[14] the other noted woman portrait painter in France who enjoyed teaching. Labille–Guiard even encouraged the revolutionary government to establish an art school for girls. However, Vigée-Lebrun, in this excerpt, recounts all the reasons why she disliked the role of art teacher and, therefore, did not have followers or pupils.

When I finally announced my marriage officially, these gloomy warnings ceased. I was not as downcast as I might have been, for I still had my beloved painting. I was overwhelmed with commissions from every quarter and although Le Brun took it upon himself to appropriate my earnings, this did not prevent him from insisting that I take pupils in order to increase our income even further. I consented to this demand without really taking time to consider the consequences and soon the house was full of young ladies learning how to pain "eyes, noses and faces." I was consistently correcting their efforts and was thus distracted from my own work, which I found very irritating indeed.

Among these pupils was a certain Mlle Emilie Roux de la Ville[15]; she has since married M. Benoist, Directeur des Droits reunis and the man for whom Denoustiers wrote *Lettres sur la Mythologie*. The talent, which has, since made her justly famous, was already apparent in the pastel heads she painted for me. Mlle Emilie was the youngest of my pupils, for the greatest number were older than I. I felt this made it far more difficult for me to attain their awe and respect which is an essential feature of teaching. I had set up a studio for these young women in an old attic, a disused hayloft, only to find that my pupils had attached a rope to one of the beams and were happily swinging back and forth, trying to balance as best they could. I adopted a "serious" manner and scolded them; I also gave a fine speech on the evils of time wasting. Then of course I wanted to try out the swing and soon

I was enjoying myself even more than my pupils. It must be obvious to you that a personality such as mine found it difficult to assert authority. This problem, combined with the irritation of having to revert to the ABC of painting whilst correcting their work soon made me renounce the idea of teaching altogether.

A key component of the gender ideology for women of this epoch was the role of mother. Vigée-Lebrun's account of the birth of her child however is complicated by the determination of her vocation as an artist. As Sheriff notes, as she is about to give birth and to become a mother, "she also confesses …her ignorance of female things…Thus even as she performs the quintessential role of woman, the artist reminds her readers that she cannot be reduced to this role."[16]

The pleasures of vanity such as I am now recounting dear friend, and you did insist hat I tell all, could not compare, however, with the joy I felt, when after two years of marriage, I discovered I was carrying a child. Now you will see how my devotion to art made me careless in the day to day details of life; for happy as I was at the idea of becoming a mother, after nine months of pregnancy, I was not in the least prepared for the birth of my baby. The day my daughter was born, I was still in the studio, trying to work on my *Venus Binding the Wings of Cupid* in the intervals between labour pains.

My oldest friend, Mme de Verdun, came to see me in the morning. She felt certain that the child would be born that same day and, since she was also acquainted with my stubborn nature, asked if I had everything I needed. I replied that I had no idea what it was I needed. 'That's typical of you,' she rejoined. 'A tomboy to the last, I'm warning you, that baby will be born tonight.' 'Oh no,' I said, 'I have a sitting tomorrow, it can't be born today.' Without saying another word, Mme de Verdun left and sent for the doctor. He came at once. I sent him back but he remained hidden in the house until the evening and at ten o'clock my daughter was delivered into the world. I shall not even attempt to describe the joy I felt on hearing her first cry. It is a feeling that all mothers will understand, increased by its coinciding with the relief following such atrocious pain.

Acceptance into the Royal Academy was an important form of public recognition. Vigée-Lebrun's admission to the academy, in 1783, analyzed extensively by Sheriff, did not proceed in the normal way. Despite her recollections, she was admitted only by order of the king and did not present a "reception piece." Also, she was elected simultaneously with Adelaide Labille-Guiard, who she does not mention in her account. However, her inclusion of the resistance to her election was quite characteristic of the Acadamy of the 1780s. "Fears over admitting women, and thus making the Academy, a heterogeneous, mixed body, surfaced not just in the official resolution, but in every acceptance of a woman. This was the case even though women were admitted infrequently and comprised a very small proportion of the membership."[17] As Sheriff notes, only 1/3 of 1% of all artists accepted into the academy over the course of its history were women.

A little while after my return from Flanders in 1783, Joseph Vernet, on the strength of this painting and several others besides, decided to propose me as a member of the Academie Royale de Peinture. M. Pierre, the King's painter, strongly opposed the idea; he did not believe, he said, in the inclusion of women; and yet Mme Vallayer-Coster[18], a talented flower painter, was already a member; indeed I believe that Mme Vien[19] was another. However talentless this M. Pierre might have been as an artist, for his vision extended only as far as brush technique, he possessed a certain wit; what is more, he was rich and this enabled him to receive artists in a rather luxurious fashion, artists being rather more impecunious than they are now. His opposition to my entry should have proved fatal to me, had it not been for the fact that in those days all genuine lovers of art were associates of the Academie de Peinture and they formed a petition in my favour against M. Pierre...

Eventually, I was admitted. M. Pierre then started the rumour that I had been admitted only on the Court's command. In all honesty I believe that the King and Queen were pleased to see me received into the Academy but that was the limit of their goodwill. As my entry painting I gave *Peace Bringing Back Abundance*. This painting hangs today in the Ministry of the Interior. In fact they ought to have returned it, for I am no longer a member of the Academy.

Royal support for Vigée-Lebrun was not surprising, since she had a long history of painting the Queen of France, Marie Antoinette, which she recalls in the following excerpt. The complicated task of depicting the Queen, in a public manner, is discussed extensively by Sheriff[20]. The portrait of Marie Antoinette, which Vigée-Lebrun is no doubt referencing in this text, was sent to her mother, the Austrian empress, Marie-Thérèse. This image was the first official portrait, which apparently pleased her mother. "Given that Vigèe-Lebrun's image succeeded where so many others had failed, is it any surprise that Marie-Antoinette became attached to the painter who finally pleased her mama?" [21] The other portrait, discussed here, was the notorious *Marie-Antoinette en chemise*, which raised issues of propriety, since this was an informal type of dress, usually reserved for private occasions.[22] When Vigée-Lebrun writes about her homage at the theater, recalling this public recognition as one of the most emotional moments of her life, the reader can glimpse her pleasure in the celebrity status she enjoyed in the 1780s. The anecdote of Marie Antoinette collecting the spilled brushes from a pregnant artist is a trope, which echoes the relationship between Alexander and his court artist, Apelles, complicated by the fact that it is two women so entwined. [23]

It was in the year 1779, my dear, that I first painted the Queen; she was then at the height of her youth and beauty. Marie Antoinette was tall, very statuesque and rather plump, though not excessively so. She had superb arms, small perfectly formed hands and dainty feet. Of all the women in France she had the most majestic gait, carrying her head so high that was possible to recognize the sovereign in the middle of a crowded court. However, this dignified demeanor did nothing to detract from her sweet and kindly aspect. In short, it is very difficult to convey to anyone who has not seen her that perfection union of grace and nobility. Her features were not at all regular; she bore the long, narrow, oval face of her family, typical too of the Austrian race. Her eyes were not particularly large and a shade approaching blue. Her expression was intelligent and sweet, her nose fine and pretty, her mouth was not wide, although her lips were rather full. Her most outstanding feature, however, was the clarity of her complexion. I have never seen another glow in the same way, and glowing is exactly the right word, for her skin was so transparent that it could not catch shadow. Indeed I was never satisfied with the way I painted it; no colour existed which; could imitate that freshness or capture the subtle tones which were unique to this charming face. I never met another woman who could compete in this regard.

At the first sitting, I was very much in awe of Her Majesty's imposing air; but she spoke to me in such a kindly fashion that her warm sympathy soon dissolved any such impression. This sitting produced that painting of her holding a large basket, dressed in a gown of satin with a rose in one hand. It was destined for her brother, the Emperor, Joseph II, and the Queen ordered two copies, one for the Empress of Russia, the other for her apartments in Versailles or Fontainebleau. I painted a succession of portraits of the Queen on various occasions.... In one portrait, I painted her only to the knee, wearing an orange-red dress and sitting before a table upon which she was arranging some flowers in a vase. You can imagine how I preferred to paint her without any ostentatious dress and especially without the 'obligatory' straw basket. These portraits were given to friends or ambassadors. One in particular showed her wearing a straw hat and a dress of white muslin with the sleeves pulled neatly back. When this painting was exhibited in the Salon, the evil tongues could not resist the temptation of saying that I had painted the Queen in her underwear; for it was then 1786 and the slander had already begun.

Nevertheless, the portrait was a success. Towards the end of the exhibition there was a small vaudeville play being performed entitled, I believe, *La Reunion Des Arts*.

Brogniart the architect and his wife were in the author's confidence and they booked some first class seats before coming to fetch me on the opening night and driving me to the show. As I had absolutely no idea of the surprise they had prepared for me, you can imagine my feelings when *The Art of Painting* came onto the stage and the actress playing the role proceeded to copy me in the act of painting the Queen. At that very moment the entire audience, those in the stalls and those in the boxes, turned towards me and applauded heartily. I don't believe I was ever so moved or so grateful as I was that evening.

The shyness that I had felt on my first encounter with the Queen was soon dissipated by the gracious benevolence which she always showed toward me. As soon as Her Majesty heard that I had a pretty voice she often asked me to sing with her during the sittings, usually Grétry's duets, although her voice was not always perfectly pitched. As for her manner, it would be difficult to describe it in all its amiable grace. I don't think that Queen Marie Antoinette ever missed the opportunity of saying a kind remark to whoever had the honour of meeting her and the kindness that she bestowed upon me is one of my dearest memories.

One day I happened to miss an appointment which she had been gracious enough to grant me for a sitting. I was absent because, late into my second pregnancy, I had been seized by a terrible pain. I rushed to Versailles the next day in order to make my apologies. The queen was no expecting me and had ordered a carriage to go for a ride, however without talking to the Queen's personal staff. One of them, M. Campan, received me in a cold, dry manner and addressed me in his stentorian tone: 'The Queen was expecting you yesterday Madame. She is almost certainly about to go for her walk now and will not be able to sit for you today.'

Upon my reply, that I had simply come to ask Her Majesty if she could sit for me another day, he went off to find the Queen. I was straightway invited to enter her chambers where Her Majesty was finishing her toilette. Holding a book in one hand, she was going over a lesson with her daughter. My heart was pounding, for my fear was more than equal to my error. The Queen turned towards me and said softly, 'I waited all morning for you yesterday. What happened to you?' 'Alas, Madame,' I replied, 'I was in such pain that I could not carry out your Majesty's wishes. I have come today to receive fresh orders, and then I shall leave immediately.' 'No, no, don't go,' continued the Queen. 'I would hate to think that your journey had been a wasted one.' She dismissed the barouche and sat for me. I remember being so eager to show my gratitude for her good will, that I seized my paintbox with great enthusiasm, causing it to overturn; my brushes and pencils were scattered all over the floor. I bent down in order to redress the consequences of my clumsiness. 'Leave them, leave them,' said the Queen, 'your condition is too far advanced for you to bend safely.' However much I tried to dissuade her, she went on to pick them all up herself.

The most famous image which survives from this long association between artist and queen was the large scale painting, known as *Marie-Antoinette and Her Children*, exhibited in the Salon of 1787. Sheriff has written a detailed, insightful analysis of this work.[24] The following excerpt is devoted exclusively to the creation of this major image of political propaganda and its subsequent fate.

The Queen was most assiduous in teaching her children those sweet ways which made her so dear to all who knew her. I have seen her showing her daughter, then aged about six, how to dine properly; her companion was a local country girl whom she was taking care of; the Queen insisted that the latter be served first, saying to her daughter, 'It is you who ought to serve her.'

The last sitting I obtained from Her Majesty was at Trianon, where I painted her head for the large canvas; I included her children in this painting. I remember that the Baron Breteuil, then a minister was present and for the duration of the sitting he did nothing but criticise the other ladies of the court. He must have thought me either deaf or exceedingly good natured in order to trust me not to repeat his spiteful remarks to those concerned. The fact is I never spoke a word of what he said to anyone, although I have not forgotten it either.

Having finished the Queen's head as well as separate studies for the Premier Dauphin, the Madame Royale and the Duc de Normandie, I returned to this painting which had become so important to me and completed it in time for the Salon of 1788. The sight of the frame alone being carried in gave rise to scores of unpleasant remarks! 'So that's where our money goes!' Several other comments of this nature were relayed to me, causing me to expect the most strident criticism. Finally I sent on the painting, but I no longer had the courage to follow it and discover its fate, so frightened was I of being abused by the public. My terror grew to such a size that I developed a temperature; I went and locked myself in my room. I was still there, praying to the good Lord for the success of 'my' Royal Family, when my brother burst in with a crowd of friends to say that I had received universal acclaim.

After the Salon the King brought this painting to Versailles. However, it was M. D'Angevilliers, then Minister of Arts and Keeper of the Royal Palaces, who presented me to His Majesty. Louis XVI was kind enough to talk with me for some time and said that he was very pleased with my work; then he added, still looking at the picture, 'I know nothing about painting; but I have grown to love it through you.' My painting was hung in one of the rooms in Versailles, and the Queen always passed it on her way to mass. When the Dauphin died in the early part of 1789, the sight of the picture moved her greatly, refreshing the memory of the cruel loss she had recently sustained. Indeed, she was not able to pass through this room without bursting into tears. Finally she asked M. D'Angevilliers to take it down. The queen, of course, with her usual grace, told me of her intention straight away and also the reason for her decision. In fact, the preservation of this painting is due almost entirely to the sensitivity of the Queen; for the ruffians and bandits, who came there shortly after to hunt out their Majesties, would have almost certainly destroyed it with their knives, just as they attacked the Queen's bed, tearing it to shreds!

Throughout her life, as is evident in the following text, Vigée–Lebrun remained emotionally committed to the political/cultural milieu of the *ancien régime*, the cultural epoch which flourished before the

35

French Revolution. In this statement, she formulates her attachment to this era. She employs an analogy based on gender to describe the ways in which women had more autonomy and cultural capital in the pre-Revolutionary era as compared with the situation under the Revolutionary government and subsequent dictatorship of Napoleon.

I dined several times at Saint-Ouen, home of the Duc de Nivernais: his house was so beautiful and the friends who met there were the most amiable set imaginable. The Duc de Nivernais, who is always quoted as the model of a cultured, refined sensibility, was also dignified and gentle in his manner without being in the least bit affected. He was especially noted for the respect he showed to women, of whatever age. I would have considered him supreme in all these regards, if I had not known the Comte de Vaudreuil, exquisite courtesy with a politeness that was even more touching since it came straight from the heart. Besides, it is so difficult today to explain the urbane charm, the easy grace, in short all those pleasing manners which, forty years ago, were the delight of Parisian society. The sort of gallantry I am describing has totally disappeared. Women reigned supreme then; the Revolution dethroned them....

Following her forced departure from France, Vigée–Lebrun traveled to Italy, like all serious male artists. This was the excuse, which her husband used to defend her departure. [25] Gita May, author of a recent biography of the artist, notes that:

> "Le Brun turned out to be remarkably and even courageously loyal to his wife...he steadfastly defended her in the face of the mounting Terror in the form of numerous petitions defending her moral character against the calumnies spread by her enemies...In 1794, at the height of the terror, Le Brun finally found himself forced to sue his wife for divorce on the grounds of desertion... Yet when, in 1802, Vigée-Lebrun finally returned to France after pursuing a phenomenally successful career as a portraitist all over Europe... she would resume living with her ex-husband in their house on the rue de Cléry." [26]

One of her most interesting encounters in Italy was with the famous artist Angelica Kaufmann.[27] Despite Vigée-Lebrun's positive impression of Kauffmann, she is also careful to distance herself from her influence. She deliberately notes that "she did little to inspire me." She is also critical of the style of her paintings. Here Vigée-Lebrun seems to be careful to align herself with the "Rubeniste" tradition of the late Rococo, as opposed to Kauffmann's more linear, neo-classical "Poussiniste" style.

I have seen Angelica Kaufmann; I was extremely keen to meet her. I found her most interesting; apart from her fine talent, she was intelligent and witty. A very delicate seeming woman, she might easily pass for fifty; her health became impaired after her first marriage for she had the misfortune to marry an adventurer who ruined her. She subsequently remarried, and her present husband, an architect, is also her financial advisor. We had some long and interesting conversations during the two evenings I spent with her. Her speech was genteel and well informed but due to her lack of enthusiasm and my own dearth of knowledge she did little to inspire me.

Angelica possesses a few paintings by the great artists, and I also saw several of her own works while in her home. I preferred her sketches to her paintings, for the colour of the former resembled that of Titian[28].

Another intriguing anecdote from her sojourn in Italy, is the artist's visit with Felice Fontana, [29] Director of the Museum of Physical and Natural History, in Florence. The Florence museum contained over 1,500 anatomically correct parts made of wax. Like her account of the birth of her daughter, this encounter highlights the complexity of Vigée-Lebrun's own understanding of herself as both a woman and an artist.[30]

One particular meeting during my stay in Florence has stayed fresh in my memory after many years, namely that with Fontana. You may have heard how this great anatomist had constructed a model of the interior of the human body, every part, every detail of which was ingenious, sublime. He showed me his study, filled with pieces of the human anatomy made from flesh coloured wax. The first object I observed was a model of the eye and I marveled at the mass of almost imperceptible ligaments surrounding it, along with scores of other tiny details, a work useful to both physicians and philosophers. It is not possible to contemplate the structure of the human body without feeling convinced of some divine power. Despite what a few miserable philosophers have dared to say, in M. Fontana's laboratory one kneels and believes. Until that moment I had espied nothing to make me feel uncomfortable; but noticing a life size female figure that seemed perfectly real, Fontana urged me to take a look; he lifted the sheet covering the model's stomach; underneath lay a perfect replica of human intestines arranged as they would be inside our body. This sight made such an impression upon me that I was nearly sick. I could not rid my mind of this sight for several days; indeed I could not look at anyone without mentally stripping them of their clothes and then their skin and soon my nerves degenerated into a deplorable condition. When I next saw M. Fontana, I asked his advice as to how I might best relieve myself from the extreme susceptibility of my imagination:

'I know too much, I see too much and all this has shaken me to the core.' 'That which you describe as a weakness and a misfortune,' he replied, 'is in fact the source of your strength and talent, moreover, if you wish to diminish the inconvenience caused by this sensitivity, then stop painting.' As you can imagine, I was not tempted to follow his advice; to paint and to live have but one and the same meaning for me. I had given thanks to Providence on many occasions for my excellent powers of sight, and yet I had complained about my gift like a fool to the celebrated anatomist.

In the third volume of the *Souvenirs,* Vigée-Lebrun introduced an interesting format. She wrote essays describing individuals, which she termed "pen portraits." From an art historical point of view, the most interesting one "sketches" the famous painter, Jacques-Louis David.[31] The life-long political antagonism between Vigée-Lebrun and David is also played out, in this text, in specifically gendered terms. When confronted with one of her portraits, David was forced to admire her work. Apparently the highest praise for a painting is to say it was the work of a man. He is forced to admit that his own portrait was inferior and, therefore, seemed to be painted by a woman.

Pen Portrait of David

I was keen to seek out the company of all famous artists, especially those distinguished in my own particular field. David was a frequent visitor to my house, and then suddenly he stopped appearing. I met him elsewhere in society and thought I would cajole him in a friendly way on the subject. "I do not like," he said, "to be part of a hierarchy," "What?" I replied. "Do you think I treat the people from the court better than the rest? Don't you think I receive everyone with the same welcome? He continued to insist on his point, although jokingly. "Ah," I said laughing. "I believe you suffer from pride; it hurts you not to be a Duke or a Marquis. I am quite indifferent to title and am equally happy to receive all, provided they are amiable people."

From then on David never came back. He even directed the hate that he bore some of my friends towards me. This came to light later, when he procured some heavy tome written against M. De Calonne, in which the author had not forgotten to drag up all the infamous slanders of which I was the object. This book sat permanently on a stool in David's studio, and was always open at the very page upon which I was mentioned. Such wickedness was both so insidious and so childish that I would have found it difficult to believe, had I not been informed of the fact by Duke Edward Fitz-James and by the Comte Louis de Narbonne, as well as others of my acquaintance, who all remarked upon it, and on several occasions.

However it must be said that David loved art so much that no petty hatred could prevent him from appreciating talent wherever saw it. After I left France, I sent the portrait of Paisiello, which I had just finished painting in Naples, to Paris. It was hung in the Salon beneath a portrait by David, who was evidently not satisfied with his work. Approaching my painting, he looked at it for along time and then, turning towards some of his pupils and other companions said: 'One would think that my painting was done by a woman and the portrait Paisello [sic] by a man.' M. Le Brun overheard him say this and reported it back to me; moreover, I know that David always took the time to praise my work whenever the opportunity presented itself.

It might seem that such flattering praise for my work made me forget the personal attacks leveled at me by David, but one thing I could never forgive was his atrocious conduct during the Terror: he exercised a cowardly persecution against a large number of artists, including Robert,[32] the landscape painter, whom he had arrested and thrown into prison with a cruelty that touched on barbarity. It would have been impossible for me to renew my acquaintance with such a man. When I returned to France, one of our most famous painters[33] came to call upon me, and during the conversation said that David was eager to see me again. I did not reply, and as the painter was a very astute man, he understood that my silence was not of that type referred to in the saying 'we who say nothing mean yes.'

Vigée-Lebrun's bold writing project, the first retrospective autobiography by a woman artist, is an outstanding example of one woman's effort to reclaim a measure of control over her posthumous reputation. As such this autobiography is an excellent example of "female agency" discussed in the Introduction (I, b). This text provides insights into the ways in which an exceptionally successful woman artist negotiated her professional life and her personal life as wife and mother. The author seems to be constantly aware of her position as a woman and writes from a gendered perspective. However the inherent complications of being both a woman and a public celebrity are present in almost every page of the volume. Vigée-Lebrun treads the fine line between ambition and modesty, between pride in her achievements and humility. This humility was not doubt reinforced by nearly thirty years of public neglect. Because Vigée-Lebrun wanted to be remembered as both an artist, a supporter of the monarchy, and as a woman her identity is complex and layered. At times, especially in her memory of giving birth to her daughter, the contradictory roles seem to collide in a painful way, but at other points in her story her resilience, and perseverance permit her to speak with clarity, in her own words, about her artistic legacy.

Notes

1   All the texts, in this chapter are excerpted from: *The Memoirs of Elisabeth Vigée-Lebrun*, trans., Siân Evans (London: Camden Press, 1989). Information on historical persons, is also taken from this edition, unless otherwise indicated. Published by permission of Camden Press, London, England.

2   Joseph Baillio, *Elisabeth Louise Vigée-Lebrun: 1755-1842* (Fort Worth: Kimbell Art Museum, 1982), 6.

3   Quoted in Gita May, "A Woman Artist's Legacy: the Autobiography of Elisabeth Vigée Le Brun" in Frederick M. Keener and Susan E. Lorsch (eds), *Eighteenth -Century Women and the Arts* (New York, Westport CN and London: Greenwood Press, 1988), 228.

4   Valerie Sanders, *The Private Lives of Victorian Women: Autobiography in Nineteenth Century England* (New York: St. Martin's Press, 1989), 46.

5   May in Keener and Lorsch, *Eighteenth -Century Women and the Arts*, 227.

6   Jacques Louis David (1748-1825) was the most important artist of his generation.

7   Ruth Perry, *Women, Letters and the Novel* (New York: AMS Press, 1980), 68ff.

8   Louis Vigée was a professor at the Académie de Saint Luc and died in 1768.

9   Gabriel-François Doyen (1726-1806) was a painter.

10   Mlle Bouquet was a member of the Académie de Saint Luc and exhibited two portraits in 1751.

11   Gabriel Briard (1725-1777) was a history painter, who was elected to the Académie royale in 1768.

12   Joseph Vernet (1714-1789) was a French painter noted for imaginary landscapes and marine paintings.

13   Jean-Baptiste Pierre Lebrun (1748-1813) was an art dealer and collector.

14   Adelaide Labille-Guiard (1747-1803) was a noted portrait painter and skilled artist in pastel and oil.

15   Vigée-Lebrun may have used a shortened name for this particular student, Marie-Guilhemine de Laville Leroulx (1768-1826) best known for her *Portrait of a Negress* in the Louvre (1800), now known as Marie-Guilhemine Benoist. See Gita May, *Elisabeth Vigée Le Brun: the Odyssey of an Artist in an Age of Revolution* (New Haven and London: Yale University Press, 2005), 29.

16   Mary D. Sheriff, *The Exceptional Woman: Elisabeth Vigée-Lebrun and the Cultural Politics of Art* (Chicago and London: University of Chicago Press, 1996), 42.

17   Sheriff, *The Exceptional Woman*, 79.

18   Anne Vallayer-Coster (1744-1818) was a talented and successful still life painter.

19   Marie-Therese Vien Rebould (1738-1805) was the wife of Joseph Marie Vien. Vien is best known as the professor of Jacques Louis David and the Director of the French Academy in Rome from 1775 to 1881. She exhibited at the salon from 1757 to 1767.

20   Sheriff, chapter 5, in *The Exceptional Woman* and also "The Portrait of the Queen: Elisabeth Vigée-Lebrun's *Marie-Antoinette en chemise* in Norma Broude and Mary D. Garrard, (eds) *Reclaiming*

Female Agency: Feminist Art History after Postmodernism (Berkeley, Los Angeles, London: University of California Press, 2005), 121ff.

21   Sheriff, *The Exceptional Woman*, 164.

22   Sheriff, *The Exceptional Woman*,143-5, and Sherriff, "The Portrait of the Queen" in Broude and Garrard, *Reclaiming Female Agency.*

23   Sheriff, *The Exceptional Woman*, chapter 4.

24   Sheriff, "The cradle is empty: Elisabeth Vigée-Lebrun, Marie-Antoinette and the Problem of Intention" in Melissa Hyde and Jennifer Milam, (eds) *Women Art and the Politics of Identity in Eighteenth Century Europe* (Burlington VT: Ashgate, 2003).

25   Sheriff, *The Exceptional Woman*, chapter 7.

26   May, *Elisabeth Vigée Le Brun*, 35-36.

27   Angelica Kauffmann (1741-1807) was a Swiss born history and portrait painter, who had worked in England, but then moved to Rome.

28   Titian (1485-90-1576) was a leading artist of the Venetian school, noted for his oil paint technique.

29   Abbé Félix Fontana (1730-1803). See note, in Evans, *The Memoirs of Elisabeth Vigée-Lebrun*, 125.

30   Sheriff, *The Exceptional Woman*, chapter 1.

31   David (1748-1825).

32   Hubert Robert (1733-1808) was an important landscape painter of his generation.

33   This artist is identified as Baron Gros by Evans, *The Memoirs of Elisabeth Vigée-Lebrun*, (see note 11, 351). Antoine-Jean Gros (1771-1835) was a pupil of David and official painter of large scale works for Napoleon.

Chapter 2. Harriet Hosmer (1830-1908): Letters

Among the limited number of exceptional, successful professional artists of the nineteenth century, Harriet Hosmer occupies an even more isolated position. She is the first women to forge a prominent international career in the medium of sculpture. By the time she was 30, she had established herself as a neoclassical sculptor, working as an expatriate in Rome. She financially supported herself with commissions and replicas of her better known works, such as *Zenobia* (1859). In her move to Rome, she was following other American male sculptors such as Randolph Rogers,[1] William Wetmore Story,[2] and William Henry Rinehart.[3] Although she is the most famous woman sculptor of the mid-nineteenth century, she was not the only woman to become a professional sculptor in this era. Other artists such as Edmonia Lewis (1843?-1909?), Anne Whitney (1821-1915), Vinnie Ream Hoxie (1847-1914), and Emma Stebbins (1915-82) created sculpture and received public commissions.

Novelist Henry James[4] coined the condescending label "The White Marmorean Flock" to describe this group of sculptors, which has unfortunately remained attached to them. As Charmaine Nelson notes:

"James's labels indexed the (im)possibility of the female sculptor in the nineteenth century, his use of quotation marks around the term 'lady sculptors' indicating their sex/gender difference as the source of his discomfort and his objection to their presence in the colony and public visibility as professional women artists." [5]

Hosmer and other women sculptors were employing a highly respected stylistic idiom and were competing with their male colleagues on a technical level. Their expertise allowed them to move from a previously impossible role, i.e "woman sculptor," to one of true professional recognition.

Hosmer was the only surviving child of her father, a physician, who raised her in a relaxed and free-spirited fashion, following the death of her mother and other siblings from tuberculosis. After being expelled from three different schools in the area around her native Boston, she attended the boarding school of Mrs. Charles Sedgwick, in western Massachusetts, at the age of 16. There she met her life-long friend, biographer and patron Cornelia Crow (later Carr). Cornelia's father, Wayman Crow, would become Hosmer's supporter, providing the funds for her trip to Rome and the true beginning of her professional career. By 1849, Hosmer was back in Boston studying with sculptor Peter Stephenson.[6] However, as her decision to become a sculptor solidified, the limitations for training in the United States were obvious. When the medical school of Boston would not permit her into anatomy classes, she went to Saint Louis, the Crow's hometown, to study anatomy there. By 1851, as the first letter describes, she had clarified her determination to become a sculptor. To say this was an unusual choice for an American woman, would be an understatement.

In 1852, with the support of Wayman Crow and the companionship of the famous actress Charlotte Cushman,[7] Hosmer traveled to Rome and entered the studio of John Gibson.[8] Living in Rome was very important for Hosmer's career. There, she could study with established sculptors and hire practitioners to help enlarge or reduce her designs. The letters from Rome document the freedom and variety of her social life and the professional opportunities which were not available to her in America. In a study focused on Edmonia Lewis, Nelson has succinctly summarized the advantages of Rome for these woman sculptors:

"The energetic pursuit of professional recognition, unchaperoned social mobility, rigorous physical activity, the independent maintenance of living environment, financial self-sufficiency and independence, and an overwhelming rejection of heterosexual marriage: the life these women led was simply not possible to the same degree in mid-nineteenth-century America."[9]

The largest collection of neoclassical sculpture ever assembled was exhibited in 1876 at the Philadelphia Centennial Exposition. However, by this date, Neoclassicism, focused on idealized imagery from the ancient world, was losing favor in post-Civil War America, an era of rapid industrialization and cultural changes. Although Hosmer, like Mary Cassatt[10] received commissions for the 1893 World's Columbian Exposition, her submission statue *Queen Isabella* was mainly ignored. After 1900, she lived out her remaining years, in seclusion, in Watertown, Massachusetts, her birth place.

Stylistically, Hosmer's sculpture fits firmly within the expectations of the neoclassical movement of her era. Her forms, which are executed in marble, are characterized by smoothly flowing contours and the reliance on neoclassical modes of anatomy and drapery. However, the themes which she selected for these works differ markedly from her male contemporaries. For example, in her sculpture, *Beatrice Cenci* (1853-55), Hosmer depicts a heroine who was executed for her participation in the murder of her cruel father. Based on an historical event, which occurred in 1599, this story had inspired a number of works of art in the Baroque era. Closer to Hosmer's own time, the Romantic poet Shelley had written a verse drama about Beatrice Cenci's courage, glorifying the tyrannicide. Numerous authors were moved by the story. Julia

Margaret Cameron (Chapter 4) created photographs of Cenci in the 1860s.[11]

For the subject of Hosmer's most famous statue, *Zenobia*, she chose the Queen of Palmyra, whose army was defeated by the Romans in 272 CE. Zenobia was marched, in chains, through Rome. The record of her heroism has survived in texts, such as Christine de Pisan's *The Book of the City of Ladies* as a "woman worthy", i.e. an example of virtue in courage, learning, and dignity. Scholars have determined that Hosmer's conception of Zenobia was informed by the text of Anna Jameson, a noted English authority on art and women's rights.[12] Therefore we can state that in the *Zenobia*, Hosmer was creating a feminist role model for Victorian women. This is appropriate since, in the 1860s, most of Hosmer's regular clients were English noblewomen.

A few years after her death, in 1912, her lifelong friend Cornelia Crow Carr published a book, *Harriet Hosmer Letters and Memories*[13] which included all the letters excerpted in this chapter. This biography, which preserved Hosmer's correspondence, is an extremely valuable record of the "voice" of this pioneering creator. The letters of greatest interest to art historians were addressed to the Crow family (with one exception) and span a fairly confined period between 1848 and 1861. These primary sources describe the social networks of the American expatriate community in Rome. Although written to members of the Crow family, the letters were meant to be read by more than the correspondent. Letters were often semi-public documents intended "to be shared within a literary circle"[14] (Introduction II,b). Clearly their careful preservation also argues for an understanding of the significance of the letters as historical documentation of the life and career of an exceptional artist. The entire volume, as written by Carr, is an example of the genre of **Auto/biography** (Introduction II, d). In this instance, letters are the primary sources and autobiographical portion of the text, while the biographical parts were written by Cornelia Crow Carr.

Artists of both genders, active in the seventeenth or eighteenth centuries, often adopted a subservient and deferential tone when writing to their patrons. However, the style of Hosmer's letters is intimate, similar to what one would expect to read in letters between family members. In earlier periods, artists were clearly of a lower, artisan class compared to their wealthy, aristocratic patrons. Hosmer, perhaps, did not see the class differences between herself and the Crow family as so extreme. Her own father was a physician and she had attended the same school as Cornelia Crow, putting them on a more equal footing as friends, rather than as artist to patron. However, she is very appreciative and respectful of the financial support she is receiving from Wayman Crow, enabling her to live and work in Rome, as is evidenced in one of the letters from 1854, excerpted below. All letters close with the salutation, "Yours, H.".

In the first letter, addressed to Cornelia, Hosmer writing from Boston, asserts her love of music, and then, states her unusual preference for creating sculpture. Her self-conscious choice of sculpture, over painting, is rationalized by the concept of sculpture being a "far higher art". This argument is a long standing issue in art theory going back, at least, to the Renaissance and the "paragone" arguments of the era of Michelangelo and Leonardo.

Dear C:

You can't imagine how delightful are the musical rehearsals in Boston every Friday afternoon-once a week, at least, I am raised to a higher humanity. There is something in fine music that makes one feel nobler and certainly happier. Fridays are my Sabbaths, really my days of rest, for I go first to the Athenaeum and fill my eyes and mind with beauty, then to Tremont Temple and fill my ears and soul with beauty of another kind, so am I not then literally "drunk with beauty"?

And now I am moved to say a word in favor of sculpture being a far higher art than painting. There is something in the purity of the marble, in the perfect calmness, if one may say so, of a beautiful statue, which cannot be found in painting. I mean if you have the same figure copied in marble and also on the canvas. People talk of the want of expression in marble, when it is capable of a thousand times more than canvas. If color is wanting, you have form, and there is dignity with its rigidity. One thing is certain, that it requires a longer practice and truer study, to be able to appreciate sculpture as well as one may painting. I grant that the painter must be as scientific as the sculptor, and in general must possess a greater variety of knowledge, and what he produces is more easily understood by the mass, because what they see on canvas is most frequently to be observed in nature. In high sculpture it is not so. A great thought must be embodied in a great manner, and such greatness is not to find its counterpart in everyday things. That is the reason why Michael Angelo is so little understood, and will account for a remark which I heard a lady make, a short time since, that "she wondered they had those two awful looking things in the Athenaeum, of 'Day' and 'Night'; why don't they take them away and put up something decent?" Oh, shades of the departed!

The next letter, addressed to her patron, Cornelia's father, Wayman Crow, was written from Rome, and is dated December 1, 1852. Here she clarifies her choice of Gibson as her mentor. This letter also identifies the social circles in which she is moving and, also, notes the presence of her father, who is living with her.

Dear Mr. Crow:
Can you believe that this is indeed Rome, and more than all that I am in it? I wrote you from Liverpool, and after that delayed sending you any word till I could say I was in this delightful place which I now consider my home. I will

say nothing of Italy or of what you already know, but tell you at once of the arrangements I have made for the present in the way of art. Of course you know that Mr. Gibson, the English sculptor, is the acknowledged head of artists here. He is my master, and I love him more every day. I work under his very eye, and nothing could be better for me in every way. He gives me engravings, books, casts, everything he thinks necessary for studies, and in so kindly, so fatherly a manner that I am convinced Heaven smiled most benignantly upon me when it sent me to him.

I saw Mr. Terry[15] last night, there was quite an assembly of artists, Mr. Gibson, Crawford...,[16] Spence,[17] and others... I was a little disappointed in Rome when I first came, but now I feel how beautiful and grand the city is, and already look upon it with loving eyes. We are a jolly party in ourselves, Miss Cushman, Miss Hayes, Miss Smith (an English lady), Grace Greenwood, Dr. Hosmer, and myself. I am away all day, but try to make up for that at other hours, and doubly enjoy myself. We see Mrs. Sartoris frequently, and already I love her dearly. She is very like Mrs. Kemble,[18] who, by the way, is to be here in January. She (Mrs. Kemble) went with us in London to the British Museum and various other places.

Remember me to the beloved old professor, whose instructions I value more highly every day, as I see how invaluable they are.

About five month's later, in an exuberant letter to Cornelia Carr, Hosmer has settled into her life in Rome and confidently declares: "I wouldn't live anywhere else..."

Dear C:

I have not the least idea that I shall see America for five years at the inside. I have determined that, unless recalled by accident, I will stay until I shall have accomplished certain things, be that time, three, five, or ten years. My father will make a visit in about three, I suspect, or when he wants very much to see me, and then it will be my turn to visit him. As by that time you might forget how I look, I have caused to be taken a Daguerre of myself in daily costume, also one for the Pater. They are, like Gilpin's hat and wig, "upon the way."

You ask me what I am doing, and in reply I can say I am as busy as a hornet. First, I am working on your Daphne, and then making some designs for bassi-relievi. I reign like a queen in my little room in Mr. Gibson's studio, and I love my master dearly. He is as kind to me as it is possible for you to imagine, and he is, after Rauch,[19] the first sculptor of the age.

Don't ask me if I was ever happy before, don't ask me if I am happy now, but ask me if my constant state of mind is felicitous, beatific, and I will reply 'Yes.' It never entered into my head that anybody could be so content on this earth, as I am here. I wouldn't live anywhere else but in Rome, if you would give me the Gates of Paradise and all the Apostles thrown in. I can learn more and do more here, in one year, than I could in America in ten. America is a grand and glorious country in some respects, but this is a better place for an artist.

I am looking forward to our summer in Sorrento, for they say it is the loveliest spot on earth....

Many of the artists/authors in this book address the conflicts between their professionalism and the roles of wife and mother. In the following letter to Wayman Crow, dated August, 1854, Hosmer clearly states her position that "an artist has no business to marry." Hosmer believed that the dedication required of an artist and the role of a married woman, as defined in the Victorian era, were incompatible. This position is closely related to her contemporary Rosa Bonheur (Chapter 2), who also did not marry but different from the lives of Vigée-Lebrun (Chapter 1) or Morisot (Chapter 5), who did marry and have children.

Dear Mr. Crow:

I have your letter of June 13th. I have been fancying you all in Lenox, and see that I was not wrong.

By this time Bessie S. is Mrs. R. You see, everybody is being married but myself. I am the only faithful worshipper of Celibacy, and her service becomes more fascinating the longer I remain in it. Even if so inclined, an artist has no business to marry. For a man, it may be well enough, but for a woman, on whom matrimonial duties and cares weigh more heavily, it is a moral wrong, I think, for she must either neglect her profession or her family, becoming neither a good wife and mother nor a good artist. My ambition is to become the latter, so I wage eternal feud with the consolidating knot....

In the following letter to Crow, from October 1854, she expresses her appreciation for his support: "...it is to you that I owe all." Hosmer believed that the financial support of a sympathetic patron was essential for her professional success.

Dear Mr. Crow:
...Now, dear, Mr. Crow, I dare say you will say, 'What is the girl driving at?' Why, simply this, that you have understood my case well enough to lay me under an obligation, so great that if I were to realize your fondest hopes of me, I could never repay you. One thing is past denial, that however successful I may become in my profession, it is to you that I owe all. The great thing in every profession and most certainly so in art, is to get a good 'start', as we Yankees say, and then all is right. But without this good start, I want to know what a young artist is to do? One may model till one is blind, and if one gets no commissions for one's works, what is the use of it, for a work can never be really finished till it is in marble. I need not complain. When I look around and see

other artists who have been here for years and still are waiting for a 'start' and then think what a friend I have in you, *sensa complimenti,* I wonder why I have been so much more blessed than my neighbors. Every successful artist in Rome, who is living, or who has ever lived, owes his success to *his* Mr. Crow. The Duke of Devonshire was Mr. Gibson's. Mr. Hope was Thorwaldsen's.[20] And I never read the life of any artist who did not date the rising of his lucky star from the hand of some beneficent friend or patron. You know the world pretty well, and therefore know that people in general wait for someone to lead the way, and then they are ready to follow, but the one to lead that way is not sent to every poor soul who wants it. It is very inspiring, too, to know that there is somebody who has great faith in you. You seem to work up to that faith and you do the very best you can, not to disappoint the one who hopes so much from you. I don't want to be 'puffed up with my own conceit,' as the Bible hath it, but at the same time I am determined that you shall not be wholly disappointed in me. I don't mean that you shall say, five or ten years hence, 'Well, I expect that girl would do something, but she never has.' If I have the use of my legs and arms, I will show you that I haven't arms in vain. I am not very easily cast down, but have great faith, too, as well as yourself, and I have received a lesson, which I shall not forget, and which will do me a vast deal of good....

That same month, October 1854, Hosmer, wrote to Cornelia describing the importance of the environment of Rome for her chosen career path. No doubt responding to Carr's wish to see her friend, Hosmer is steadfast in her commitment to Rome, "…my heart's best love is for Italy."

Dear C:

…I am taken to task for being an alien to my country, but do you know when one has lived in Rome for some time there is no place afterwards. It is a moral, physical and intellectual impossibility to live elsewhere. Everything is so utterly different here that it would seem like going into another sphere, to go back to America. Everything looks homey and the dear Italian tongue sounds as natural as English and everything is beautiful, I glory in the Campagna, the art divine, and I dearly love the soft climate. I should perish in the cold winters at home, besides, I shall be positively tied here after this. I hope to have a studio and workmen of my own, and how could I be absent, for 'quando il gatto e fuori,'[21] etc? Ah, there is nothing like it! I admire America, but (and I hear your reproaches) my heart's best love is for Italy. I wonder is Daphne has yet reached you? I hope you will like her and look upon her as a near relation. I an making a statue now that is to become yours one of these days. It makes me so happy to think that you will all have the very first things I send from Rome,–my first bust and first statue.

I know they are going into kind, good hands, and I feel tenderly for them. You can't guess how busy I am from morning till night, nor how an artist must study and work to produce anything worthy of the name of art. Here have I been pegging away for more than two years, and I have learned just enough to feel that I know nothing; but *pazienza, col tempo tutto—forse.*[22]

By February 1858, when Hosmer was working on what would be her most famous sculpture, the *Zenobia*, she wrote a letter to Mrs. Crow, to inform her on the progress of this important work. This letter provides insight into the ways in which the costume and facial features were selected. It documents the precision and care with which Hosmer selected all the details and the willingness with which she consulted experts. As noted above, we know that she selected the theme of Zenobia in consultation with the noted British art historian and critic Anna Jameson, but, in this letter, she also reports on her trip to Florence, where she conducted her own research and consulted with an authority on ancient art.

Dear Mrs. Crow:

Before you get this I shall be as deep in Palmyrene soil as the old monks of the Cappucini are in the soil of Jerusalem. I have not yet begun the Zenobia, as I am waiting for a cast of the coin; not that, as a portrait, it will be of great value to me now, but the character of the head determines the character of the figure. When I was in Florence, I searched in the Pitti and the Magliabecchian Libraries for costume and hints, but found nothing at all satisfactory. I was bordering on a state of desperation, when Professor Nigliarini, who is the best of authorities in such matters, told me if I copied the dress and ornaments of the Madonna in the old mosaic of San Marco, it would be the very thing, as she is represented in Oriental regal costume. I went and found it. It is invaluable; requiring little change, except a large mantle thrown over all. The ornaments are quite the thing; very rich and very Eastern, with just such a girdle as is described in Vopiscus....

Many women artists wrote about their attitudes toward feminism. The last letter is dated March 1861, and is addressed to an unknown correspondent. In this statement, Hosmer clearly articulates her position on women's rights. Although distancing herself from the most radical wing of "bloomerism," which refers to the wearing of pants, known as "bloomers," she does recognize the importance of education and the need to allow women the freedom to "fight their own way through the world" as she has done. She also recognizes the more open society of America, by expressing her belief that equal rights will come, first, in her native country, despite her love of Italy.

Dear——:

...I had a discussion yesterday with Mr. May... he is a great woman's rights man.... he thinks every woman should have the power of educating herself for any profession and then practicing it for her own benefit and the benefit of others. I don't approve of bloomerism and that view of woman's right's, but every woman should have the opportunity of cultivating her talents to the fullest extent, for they were not given her for nothing, and the domestic circle would not suffer thereby, because in proportion to the few who would prefer fighting their own way through the world, the number would be great who would choose a partner to fight it for them; but give those few a chance, say I. And those chances will be given first in America. What fun it would be to come back to this earth after having been a wandering ghost for a hundred years or so and see what has been going on in flesh while we have been going on in spirit!

Unlike Vigée-Lebrun, Harriet Hosmer did not set out to write a coherent life narrative. Her surviving letters were preserved and eventually published because of the effort of her childhood friend, Cornelia Crow Carr. The support of Carr and her family on both financial and emotional levels was an essential component of Hosmer's brave decision to launch a career as a sculptor in Rome. When Hosmer wrote these letters, she may have known they would be preserved and read within a personal circle, but perhaps she was not aware that they would eventually be published in a longer memoir by Carr. It is even possible that she was resistant to this type of attention, since the volume was published four years after her death, and some three decades after her period of greatest fame and productivity. However, as a correspondent, she was quite aware of her distinctive position as both woman and sculptor. Her sense of identity seems to be less conflicted because she assiduously avoided the traditional gender roles of wife and mother, to devote herself fully to the pursuit of her profession. Her letters record the voice of a woman who joyously communicated to her patrons the details of her daily life in Rome with full awareness of her highly exceptional choice of career. To decide to be a sculptor for a woman was such a remarkable choice that it was surely apparent, to Carr, by the 1850s that her letters were important documents of the unusual life of an unusual woman artist. For Hosmer, her agency came mainly in the commitment and creation of a body of important marble statues many of whose themes spoke to the contemporary feminists of her era. She delegated the survival of her voice and posthumous reputation to her lifelong friend, choosing to maintain her silence and privacy towards the end of her life.

Notes

[1]   Randolph Rogers (1825-1892) was an American sculptor based in Rome and known as one of the leading American public monument makers.

[2]   William Wetmore Story (1819-1895) was a neoclassical sculptor, in Rome, after 1856.

[3]   William Henry Rinehart (1825-1874) was a second generation neo-classical sculptor.

[4]   Henry James (1843-1916).

[5]   Charmaine Nelson, "Edmonia Lewis's *Death of Cleopatra*: white marble, black skin and the regulation of race in American neoclassical sculpture", in Deborah Cherry and Janice Helland (eds) *Local/Global: Women Artists in the Nineteenth Century* (London and Burlington VT: Ashgate, 2006), 225.

[6]   Peter Stephenson (1823-1861).

[7]   Charlotte Cushman (1816-1876) was an "internationally renowned American actress...who provided ...a model of the possibility of a successful, independent professional woman." (Nelson, "Edmonia Lewis's *Death of Cleopatra*", 225). Cushman had adopted the role of mentor to many of the younger women, chaperoning them on the long voyage to Rome; encouraging them to pursue their art professionally...assisting them in obtaining studio space and instruction; securing patronage; and even boarding them in her large apartments...Cushman and the sculptor Emma Stebbins were partners. See Nelson, "Edmonia Lewis's *Death of Cleopatra*", notes 4-5, 241.

8   John Gibson (1790-1866) was an English sculptor who had studied with Antonio Canova (1757-1822) and Bertel Thorwaldsen (1768-1844). By the 1840s, he was one of the leading neoclassical sculptors, in Rome.

9   Nelson, "Edmonia Lewis's *Death of Cleopatra*", 224.

10   Mary Cassatt (1844-1926) was an American painter and printmaker associated with the Impressionists and active in France after 1875.

11   Sylvia Wolf, *Julia Margaret Cameron's Women* (Chicago, IL: The Art Institute of Chicago, distributed by Yale University Press, 1998), 59.

12   Susan Waller, "The Artist, the Writer and the Queen: Hosmer, Jameson, and Zenobia" *Woman's Art Journal*, vol. 4 (Summer, 1983).

13   New York, Moffat Yard and Co., 1912.

14   Sidonie Smith and Julia Watson, *Reading Autobiography: A Guide for Interpreting Life Narratives* (Minneapolis and London: University of Minnesota Press, 2001), 196.

15   This may refer to Benjamin Terry, a comic actor and father of Ellen Terry, a famous actress in the later Victorian period.

16   Thomas Crawford (1813-1857) was the first American sculptor to settle in Rome, in 1835. He is known for a series of public monuments for various sites in the United States.

17   William Blundell Spence (1814-1900) was a noted English art dealer, who was influential in building the collections of the South Kensington Museum (now known as the Victoria and Albert Museum) and other British institutions, with Italian art.

[18] Fanny Kemble (1809-1893) was a famous British actress, abolitionist and author.

[19] Christian Daniel Rauch (1777-1857) was a German sculptor known for his neoclassical work in bronze for aristocratic patrons.

[20] Bertel Thorwaldsen (1768-1844) was a Danish sculptor, who, following the death of Canova became the leading Neo-classical sculptor in Rome.

[21] When the cat's away,...

[22] Patience, with time everything can be done.

Chapter 3. Rosa Bonheur (1822-1899): *Rosa Bonheur, her Life, her Works*, by Anna Klumpke

Rosa Bonheur was the most famous woman painter of her generation, during the years of the French Second Empire (1855-1870). She was the most prominent woman artist to establish an international reputation, since Vigée-Lebrun (Chapter 1). Bonheur, like Vigée-Lebrun, was the daughter of an artist. She developed her expertise in animal paintings, and achieved widespread fame and wealth, not only from the sale of her paintings, but also from royalties on engravings of her works. Bonheur was the first woman painter to receive the cross of the French Legion of Honor which was presented to her, personally, in 1865, by the Empress Eugénie. Her most famous work, *The Horse Fair* (1853), was eventually purchased by Commodore Cornelius Vanderbilt, who donated it to the newly formed Metropolitan Museum of Art, in New York City, ensuring her fame not only in France and Britain but, also, in the United States. Her international success made her an inspiring role model to the next generation of women artists, including the American, Anna Klumpke (1856-1942), who would become her official biographer.[1]

As the daughter of an artist, Bonheur received her early training, with her siblings, at home. Her father, Raymond Bonheur, was active in the utopian movement of Saint-Simonianism, which preached radical religious and political ideas, such as greater equality between the sexes. The Saint Simonians prayed to "God, Father and Mother of us all." The Saint Simonians also believed that artists had special leadership roles to play in the "avant-garde" of the future social order.

Bonheur's first popular success, *Plowing in the Nivernais*, shown at the Salon of 1849, established her fame. She achieved financial independence with the international recognition of *The Horse Fair*. She eventually bought a château, in the Forest of Fontainebleau, and lived a quiet domestic life with Nathalie Micas. Following Nathalie's death, she found companionship with Klumpke, who was thirty years younger. Rosa Bonheur's life was unconventional in many ways. In addition to being an independent, wealthy and famous woman painter, all the strong emotional attachments of her life were with women. She is also known for her unconventional dress. Early on in her career, Bonheur chose to wear men's trousers. In order to do this, legally, she had to apply for a police permit, which required regular renewals. Bonheur's attitudes about gender roles were complex and generally resistant to the dominant culture's strong polarization of gender roles. She strongly identified with the animals she painted and believed in metempsychosis, the migration of human souls into animal forms. She also believed in the immortality of the soul and referred to her mother, who died when Rosa was quite young, as her "guardian angel."[2]

Bonheur devoted herself, throughout her life, to the realistic depiction of animals in naturalistic settings. She kept a small "zoo" on her property and used these animals as subjects later in life. As an *"animalier,"* an artist specializing in the depiction of animals, she could avoid human subjects. This protected her from the politically volatile subject of rural workers, as depicted in paintings by her contemporaries Courbet[3] and Millet.[4] Her focus on animals permitted her to gain a broad range of support; wealthy patrons purchased her paintings and a middle-class audience sought out her engravings. Stylistically, her paintings were rendered in a precise, finished, academic style and demonstrated her technical competence. Thus, she could appear to be both modern and timeless.

The text from which these following excerpts are taken, is characteristic of **Auto/biography** (Introduction II, d), a similar genre to Carr's *Harriet Hosmer Letters and Memories* (Chapter 2). *Rosa Bonheur: sa vie, son oeuvre* (*Rosa Bonheur, her life, her works*) by Anna Klumpke was first published, in French, in 1908. In this blending of narrative voices, we have a legitimate primary source which Gretchen van Slyke, the translator, has called *The Artist's (Auto) biography*. The first English translation of the entire text was published in 1997. The book is divided into three parts. In Part I, Klumpke tells the story of meeting Bonheur, and how she came to live with her and inherit her estate.

However, Part 2, from which most of the following excerpts are taken, "gives the impression that Rosa Bonheur is telling her life story in her own words. Yet, it was entirely written by Anna Klumpke."[5] Part 3 is a mixture of the two voices. Most of this section reads as if Bonheur is speaking directly to the reader. The conclusion, written by Klumpke, in the first person, describes the artist's death and burial and the issues concerning the will.

This format is a **collaborative life narrative** (Introduction, II, d). In this instance the translator, van Slyke, is yet a third participant. However, scholars have freely quoted from this source, even prior to its English translation, and have accepted these statements as accurate records of Bonheur's beliefs, at least at the time of her conversations with Klumpke towards the end of her life.

Although *Rosa Bonheur: sa vie, son oeuvre* was published posthumously, the conversations were clearly part of a self-conscious autobiographical project between Klumpke and Bonheur. Like Vigée-Lebrun (Chapter 1), Rosa Bonheur outlived her era of greatest fame and visibility. When Impressionism and Post Impressionism emerged, one can easily imagine her, in the 1890s, isolated in her Chateau, seeking some form of immortality through the creation of a life narrative.

The first excerpt, from the beginning of Part II, recounts Bonheur's memory of how she began to study art. Following the death of her mother, when she was 11, her father attempted to place her in a number of situations, including a private school in

Paris. However, Rosa was mischievous; after cutting down the school mistress's flowers, she was expelled. This excerpt is fascinating for its insights into the progression in her education from drawing to plaster casts, which replicates the formal training at the Ecole des Beaux-Arts, from which Bonheur was excluded, due to her gender. Also, the importance of role models is emphasized. Bonheur's father tries to inspire her with the example of Vigée-Lebrun: "Seek your way, try to surpass Mme. Vigée-Lebrun, whose name is on everyone's lips." Vigée-Lebrun's *Souvenirs* (Chapter 1) appeared in 1835, right around the time Bonheur was 13. Surely the publication of her autobiography reminded people of her professional success. This is a clear example of the importance of roles models for aspiring young women artists.

When I got home, my father put a plaster cast and some pencils and paper down in front of me and said: 'Daughter, since the only thing you can do is draw funny little men, these are your tools from now on. Try and learn how to use them so that you can earn your keep and lead a decent life.'

Despite his severe tone, I was delighted. It was just what I wanted to hear. At long last I was going to be able to draw to my heart's content, without anyone scolding me for it!

Back in our little studio in the rue des Tournelles, I worked desperately hard, lovingly drawing copies of the plaster casts my father gave me, not even pausing when friends dropped in. As soon as he came home in the evening, he'd inspect my day's work. He corrected my mistakes more severely, I think, than those of his pupils, but if I managed to draw something decent, he was glad to congratulate me.

One day my father left his paints home. I grabbed them, tore down to buy a few cherries, and then began painting my first still life on a little canvas I dug out of a corner of the studio. I can still see the surprise on his face. 'That's very good', he said, hugging me. 'Keep on like that, and you'll turn into a real artist.' He patted my hair and said in an emotional voice: 'Maybe, daughter, I'll fulfill my own ambitions through you!'

Soon he agreed to set me up in the Louvre. Now I could work in this sanctuary to my heart's content! I was so happy that the whole first day my hand shook like a leaf and I couldn't draw a single stroke. When I got home that evening, my father saw how upset I was and asked: 'What's wrong with you? Are you sick?' I threw myself sobbing into his arms and wailed: 'I'm so overwhelmed with joy that I couldn't even draw today, but this is the last time that you'll have to complain about me being so lazy'....

...During evenings at home, in order to take my mind off our many worries and the haunting thoughts of my poor dead mother, I'd sometimes draw plaster casts of animals by lamplight.

I soon realized that there was a real advantage to working like this. The shadows stood out so clearly that I could engrave in my mind the shapes of the oxen, sheep, and horses with surprising ease. A sculptor named Mene,[6] a very talented friend of my father's, had made many of these models. I found these wonderful casts so interesting that I began making my own. Having learned to handle the trowel as well as the paintbrush, I created a whole herd of miniature animals, ewes, wethers, rams, oxen, bulls, horses, and deer. I was the one who gave my brother Isidore his first lessons in modeling and sculpting.

'Seek your way, daughter,' my father said again and again. 'Seek your way try to surpass Mme Vigée-Lebrun, whose name is on everyone's lips these days. She's a painter's daughter, too, and she did so well that by the age of twenty-eight she got into the Royal Academy, and now she's a member of the Academies of Rome, Saint Petersburg, and Berlin.'

These words haunted me night and day, and I ran them over and over in my mind. Yet it seemed to me sheer madness to follow her path.

'Couldn't I become famous,' I once asked my father, 'by just painting animals?'

'Of course,' he replied, 'and I'll repeat what a French king once said: 'Si Dieu le veut, tu le peux.' [If it's god's will, you'll find a way.] Let this be your motto.'

From that day on I worked especially hard copying drawings by Salvator Rosa[7] and Carl Dujardin.[8] I liked pictures with horses, dogs, or sheep, and my favorite painters were Paul Potter,[9] Wouwermans,[10] and Van Berghem.[11] As I said in the *Ladies' Home Journal,* I found the old masters simply fascinating. That's why I cannot say often enough to beginners: fill your head chock full of studies; they're the true grammar of art, and you can only gain from spending your time this way.

The art students who had made fun of me stopped jeering when they saw my copies.

I finally sold my first painting and made one hundred francs. What joy! I thought I'd really made it! Little by little I lined my father's pockets.

In the next excerpt, Bonheur recounts the events leading up to the commission for *Ploughing in the Nivernais.* This excerpt also foregrounds the financial pressures under which she was working.

When I got my prize, the ministry chimed in, on a onetime basis, with a magnificent Sèvres vase, plus the commission for *Ploughing in the Nivernais.* That came to be the name of the painting, but the government only asked me for a ploughing motif similar to two of my paintings in the Salon. I was to be paid three thousand francs.

I'll never forget my father's joy at this double triumph. He felt that my success was truly his own. Hadn't he been my only teacher? Another thing added to his legitimate pride: he loved the government honoring his daughter, and its advent had nourished his dreams.

I was certainly delighted, too. When I picked up the first installment of fifteen hundred francs at the Finance Ministry, I was walking on air. Those three big banknotes made a triumphal entrance at home. We'd never seen so much money all at once.

I decided to paint a team of six oxen yoked up two by two. Getting down to work, I also had in mind to celebrate the ploughman's art of opening those furrows from whence comes the world's bread.

Needing to work from nature away from Paris, I accepted an invitation to spend the winter of 1848 with the family of one of my father's friends, M. Mathieu, a distinguished sculptor who was teaching at the Chateau de la Cave in the Nievre. Nathalie went with me. Her presence, along with her encouraging words, were good for my work. Intent on finishing this piece for the Salon of 1849, I painted amazingly fast.

Alas! I cannot help feeling a twinge of pain whenever I think of my *Ploughing in the Nivernais*. Although it really made my reputation, what gloomy memories it calls back. A few days before my father died, he made another proud inspection of my work. He embraced me and said: 'You're right on the heels of Vigée-Lebrun. So it's not in vain that I made her your role model.' Poor Father, despite his long and ever worse suffering, he had no idea that the money I got for this painting was meant to pay for his funeral expenses.

Bonheur discusses the genesis and the reception of her most famous composition, *The Horse Fair*, in the following excerpt. She notes the inspiration of the Parthenon frieze and the resistance of the French government to the theme. The Fine Arts Minister of the Second Empire, de Morny, preferred the subject of haymaking. When the government did not purchase, *The Horse Fair*, the painting traveled to Belgium and then to London, where Bonheur followed it. This visit helped establish her reputation in England. *The Horse Fair* has been the subject of much scholarly attention. James M. Saslow has identified the figure in the center as a self-representation of Bonheur, building a case for understanding her cross-dressing as "an attempt to claim male prerogatives and create an androgynous and proto-lesbian visual identity." [12] Whitney Chadwick has discussed the work in the context of public debates on animal rights and vivisection. Chadwick notes that, during the Victorian era, there is a close identification between animals and women.[13]

...after my father died, my only teachers were the artists in the Louvre and good nature herself, whose magnificent book lies ever open before our eyes. Memories of those artists combined for me with nature's teachings.

That's why I would happen to think about the Parthenon friezes while in a crowd of horse dealers trying out their beasts. 'And why not do something like that?' I asked myself. My idea was not to imitate, as you can surely guess, but to interpret, which inspired me to do countless compositions and studies. I wanted to paint this work on a canvas at least eight feet by sixteen, much larger, therefore, than my *Ploughing in the Nivernais.* One morning as I was getting down to work, I received a surprise invitation from M. de Morny, then the Minister of Internal Affairs, who also oversaw the Division of Fine Arts. He wanted me to go see him in his office.

This happened shortly after the December Days. Several of my father's political friends had fallen victim to this coup d'etat; some were exiled, others deported to Africa, where they died far away from their families. Now I was a staunch supporter of the Republic and felt deeply troubled by these events. When I entered the office of the man who had masterminded the overthrow, I was trembling inside. Expecting a tiger, I was dumbfounded to find just the opposite: a true gentleman of imposing stature, full of grace and distinction. With a sparkle in his eye and a smile on his lips, he spoke with perfect elegance and courtesy.

'Mademoiselle,' he said emphatically, 'I've taken the liberty of asking you here because His Majesty's government recognizes your rare merit and wishes to honor you by commissioning a work for the state museum. Do you have some sketches among which we could choose the subject that would allow you to develop your talent to your best advantage?'

His charming welcome and proposal promptly reassured me, and I replied with obvious satisfaction: 'M. le Ministre, I'll be delighted to show you my sketches for *Haymaking* and *The Horse Fair.*'

'Very good, mademoiselle, he said, 'please come back with your studies, and I'll look them over with you.'

At our next audience, after examining my drawings, M. de Morny said: "Mademoiselle, both compositions are charming, but I prefer the rustic motif because it does more honor to your overall reputation. You're famous for your oxen and sheep, but you've painted too few horses for us to ask you to paint a scene as turbulent as a *Horse Fair.* We've not seen enough of your horses."

M. de Morny chose the sketch I liked least of all, told me the dimensions of the canvas, and said I'd be paid twenty thousand francs.

Even though I was very flattered by the honor, I insisted on showing that I could paint horses just as well as oxen. So I replied, with my artist's independence: 'M. le Ministre, I'm preparing a composition that means a lot to me. I've always loved horses, and I've been studying how they move since tender childhood. I know in particular how remarkable the Percherons are, with their superb high necks and withers. I was meaning to paint a *Horse Fair*. With your permission, I won't begin *Haymaking* until this one's done.'

M. de Morny made no objection.

'Take whatever time you need, mademoiselle, "he replied. "*Haymaking*" will be welcome at any time. We would be sorry to hamper you in any way.'

So I kept going on my *Horse Fair*. It would even have seemed indecent to hurry, since my father was no longer there to share in my delight and benefit from my small fortune. Yet my canvas was ready for the Salon of 1853. It was wildly successful, and the jury unanimously declared that from then on anything that I sent to the Salon would be automatically accepted.

After the Salon, what was I going to do with *The Horse Fair?* I sent it to the Ghent exhibition (1854). The Royal Society for the Encouragement of the Fine Arts of Ghent showed me delicate homage by giving me a magnificent brooch with a cameo engraving of my paintings. Since this token of esteem came from the land of Rubens and Van Ostade I was deeply moved. Yet my canvas, no doubt because of its huge size, still didn't have a buyer. That same year there was to be an exhibition in Bordeaux. I promptly sent down my painting, only too happy to associate my birthplace with my first great triumph. I would have been overjoyed to see my painting in the Bordeaux museum, and I made them an offer for fifteen thousand francs. The city commissioners, who thought I was being presumptuous, turned me down. I didn't take that too well.

While my canvas was trotting all over the globe, I moved my studio from the rue de l'Ouest to 32, rue d'Assas. There, with an entire house, a courtyard, and garden, I could work at ease and parade all the animals in Noah's ark through the premises (end of 1853).

Meanwhile, my painting's success at Ghent had made such a sensation in the French press that M. de Morny, to whom I had sold another painting from the Salon of 1853, *Cows and Sheep*, showing them on a sunken road, finally understood how wrong he had been to appear hippophobic in the fore-mentioned interview. One day while I was working on *Haymaking*, the Marquis de Chennevieres, then the director of the Fine Arts Division, came into my studio and very nicely asked me to substitute *The Horse Fair*, which M. de Morny had turned down, for the painting I was working on. Much to my regret, I could not yield to his request. I had just sold *The Horse Fair* the day before.

As it happened, a London art dealer, namely M. Gambart, had come to inquire about the price. Nathalie, who took care of my financial affairs, promptly replied: 'It won't leave France for less than forty thousand francs.'

M. Gambart accepted on the spot, knowing full well that Bordeaux had refused to take it for fifteen thousand. Once everything was settled he told me he wanted to show *The Horse Fair* in London, at Pall Mall, then throughout the major cities of England. He also intended to call for subscriptions to get it engraved by Thomas Landseer,[14] the brother of Sir Edwin Landseer,[15] the painter.

Although Bonheur was quite radical in her lifestyle and choice of career, her political views were conservative. She was a strong supporter of the authoritarian government of the Second Empire. In the next excerpt, Bonheur describes her encounters with the imperial family and the award of the Legion of Honor. This was a moment, in her career, when she was receiving the most prestigious form of recognition of any women artist of her generation. Her relationship to the monarchy rivaled the status achieved by Vigée-Lebrun in the *ancien régime.*

In the first part of the excerpt, Bonheur discusses the visit of the Empress to her studio, in 1864. She then recalls her trip to the Tuileries Palace to meet Emperor Napoleon III. The last part of this excerpt concerns the visit of the Imperial Prince, who also traveled to Bonheur's chateau. In the final part of this text, she recounts the arrival of the Empress to present her with the medal of the Legion of Honor.

On June 14, 1864, a few days after that letter from Duke d' Aumale, I was in my studio working on *Deer at Long Rocks*— you know the painting I'm talking about: a stag with a huge rack of antlers followed by a whole family of does and fawns—when all of a sudden I hear carriages rumbling, bells jingling, whips cracking. All this commotion stops dead at my door. A second later Nathalie bursts into my studio shrieking: 'The Empress! The Empress is coming! Quick, off with your smock. You've just barely got time to put on this skirt and jacket,' which she handed me. In less time that it took to say it, I had changed clothes and thrown the doors to my studio wide open. The Empress was already on the threshold, her ladies-in-waiting, officers, and uniformed court dignitaries following close behind. With that sovereign grace that made her the queen of Parisian fashion, Her Majesty approached. Giving me her hand, which I kissed, she said that while out for a drive in the neighborhood she'd had a sudden whim to come meet me and visit the studio. I said I was deeply honored and showed her my paintings and drawings there. She praised them all but seemed to prefer the one I was working on, *Deer at Long Rocks*, which brought forth several remarks.

Obviously hoping to keep me entirely under the spell of her visit, which lasted about an hour, she commissioned a painting for her private collection and invited me to come have lunch sometime at Fontainebleau. As she was leaving, she gave me her hand, which I kissed once again. This must have pleased her, for she promptly drew me forward and kissed me.

I painted *Sheep by the Sea* for her. It was shown at the Exhibition of 1867 before going to the Tuileries. I don't know what has happened to it since September 4 and the Commune.

Shortly after that memorable day, I received a specific invitation... I put on my black velvet dress uniform with the gold buttons. My narrow sleeves and drooping skirts must have looked funny in comparison with the enormous crinoline hoop dresses that were fashionable back then. Then I had myself driven to the foot of the grand staircase of the chateau at Fontainebleau...

...The Emperor and the Empress made their entrance; followed by the general who had brought me my invitation...I was introduced. When the Emperor himself gave me his arm and sat me down to his right for lunch, I was terribly disconcerted. Throughout the entire meal he never once stopped talking to me and looked after my every need...

After lunch the Empress invited me for a little boat-ride on the Carp Pool. Rowing all by herself, she talked about art while we went round the pond. All of a sudden the young Imperial Prince appeared on the shore, and Her Majesty called out: 'Come, child, and shake the hand of Mlle Rosa Bonheur. At home she has a zoo you'd really like.'

'Oh!' he exclaimed, 'let's go see it right away.'

Two or three days later he popped in, and he often came back. You know that I've never liked to wear men's clothes in front of important visitors. That's why I once asked the Prince to wait a second or two. Since he seemed a bit impatient, Celine confessed that I needed time to get a skirt on.

'But I wanted to see her in her smock and trousers,' he replied.

That gave me a good laugh. Whenever he showed up after that, I made a point not to change my clothes...

...At the time the Emperor was on his way back from Algeria, having left the Empress as a regent sovereign until his return. A year, almost to the day, had gone by since Her Majesty's first visit to my studio. On the afternoon of June 10— and I knew only from the newspapers that she had come down to Fontainebleau to await the Emperor—she once again popped in unexpectedly, creating the same surprise and excitement. I was in the garden and barely had time to rush in and cover up my trousers.

'Mademoiselle,' she said, 'I am bringing you a jewel from the Emperor. His Majesty has given me permission to inform you that you've been made a knight in the Imperial Order of the Legion of Honor.'

As she spoke, she opened up a little jewel case and removed a gold cross. Deeply moved, I knelt at her feet. But there was no pin for the cross. Her Majesty bent over my worktable to look around for one. One of her officers found what she needed, and the Empress pinned the red ribbon with that glorious star over my heart. Then she raised me up and kissed me, saying: 'You're finally a knight. I am so pleased to be the godmother of the first woman artist to receive this high honor. I wanted to devote my last act as regent to showing that, as far as I'm concerned, genius has no sex. Moreover, to underscore the importance that I attach to this great act of justice, you won't be part of a 'batch.' Your nomination will be announced a day later than the others, but in a special decree headlined in the *Moniteur.*'

The next text is written by Anna Klumpke from her recollections of conversations with Bonheur. In this fascinating excerpt, Bonheur again returns to the issue of clothing and the role of women in her society. From these comments, one can sense her deeply conflicted attitudes towards the gender roles of her culture. Her famous and often repeated statement is in this excerpt: "Why shouldn't I be proud to be a woman?" This attitude indicates that at least some of the credos of the Saint-Simonians, as filtered through her father, stayed with Bonheur throughout her life. She also makes the surprising assertion that she has remained a virgin her entire life. Her attitude toward marriage is consistent with Hosmer's (Chapter 2), and she seems proud to have avoided a traditional heterosexual marriage.

I strongly disapprove of women who refuse to wear normal clothes because they want to pass themselves off as men. If I thought trousers suited women, I would have given up skirts altogether, but that's not the case; so I've never advised my sisters of the palette to wear men's clothes in ordinary circumstances.

If you see me dressed this way, it's not in the least to make myself standout, as too many women have done, but only for my work. Don't forget I used to spend days and days in slaughterhouses. Oh! You've got to be devoted to art to live in pools of blood, surrounded by butchers. I was also passionate about horses; and what better place to study them than at horse fairs, mingling with all those traders? Women's clothes were quite simply always in the way. That's why I decided to ask the prefect of police for permission to wear men's clothing.

But these are my work clothes and nothing more. I've never been upset by jeering idiots. Nathalie set no store by them, either. It didn't bother her at all to see me in men's clothes. Yet, if you're the least bit offended, I'm quite ready to put on skirts, all the more since I only have to open a closet to find a whole assortment of women's clothes.

Out in the woods I wear an overcoat, felt hat, big boots, and often spats. Yet at home I prefer patent leather ankle boots. As you know, that's one of my coquetries." ...

Trousers have been my great protectors...I've often felt proud to have dared break with traditions that would have made me drag skirts everywhere, making it impossible for me to do certain kinds of work. As for my women's clothes, when I began to get famous, Nathalie gave me a very clever bit of advice: 'Don't even try to be a fashion plate,' she said, 'just pull together an outfit that'll stand outside the vagaries of feminine elegance. Hang on to it your whole life long, and it'll become your trademark.' Nathalie was right. I followed her advice and took up Breton dress modified to my taste. I confess I've often looked a bit ludicrous with my narrow sleeves, vest, and full pleated skirt, but Nathalie used to console me by saying: 'Enough of that nonsense. People will know Rosa Bonheur by her petticoats, just like Napoleon by his little hat.'

Since I've been living at By with all my animals, I've hardly had time to play the great lady. Visitors have to take me as I am. Yet if I go out or do something official, I always put on a dress and feathered hat. Oh! the hat problem! Fashionable hats have been my bugbear for a long time.

Not a one would ever stay on my head since I didn't have a chignon to poke pins through. One day a friend of Nathalie's took the bull by the horns and got me wearing a dowager's bonnet. Hats like that were all the rage back then, even for elegant young ladies. It was a fatal bit of advice. I regret to say I did what she said, and I've had at least one notorious misadventure because of it.

Two years ago (October 8, 1896) when the Czar and his wife were visiting Paris, the Minister of Fine Arts wanted them to meet some celebrities of the French art-world during their tour of the Louvre. I was honored to receive an invitation.

As usual in such circumstances, I put on my beautiful black velvet dress and my little feathered bonnet. With my short hair, the only reason it stayed on was because of a chin strap going from ear to ear. You can imagine what that looked like.

As soon as I arrived at the Louvre, I would've given anything for my gray felt hat. I was the only woman in a crowd of men, all decked out with medals, since the only ones invited were artists in the Legion of Honor. Everyone was staring at me. I didn't know where to put myself. It was quite an ordeal, and that day I really longed for men's clothes. Seeing how embarrassed I was, M. Carolus-Duran[16] was brave enough to come up and give me his arm. I took it gratefully and hung on for dear life.

Reassured by his support and cheered by the welcome my colleagues gave me, I forgot a bit how ridiculous I looked. Yet my ordeal was not over. A few days later the illustrated papers came out. I as terribly put out when I recognized myself in a silhouette that became the laughing-stock of all...

Despite my metamorphoses of dress, none of Eve's daughters appreciates subtlety more than I. Though I'm gruff, even fierce by moments, my heart has always remained perfectly feminine. Had I liked jewelry, I certainly would wear such finery. Nathalie did, and I never criticized her for it.

Why shouldn't I be proud to be a woman? My father, that enthusiastic apostle of humanity, told me again and again that it was woman's mission to improve the human race, that she was the future Messiah. To his doctrines I owe my great and glorious ambition for the sex to which I proudly belong, whose independence I'll defend till my dying day. Besides, I'm convinced the future is ours. I'll give you just two reasons. Americans march at the forefront of modern civilization because of the wonderfully intelligent way they rear their daughters and respect their wives. On the other hand, the Orient wallows in hopeless barbarism since husbands there don't have enough respect for their wives, which is why the children don't love their mothers.

Our timid beauties of old Europe are too easily led to the altar, like ewes going to sacrifice in pagan temples.

A long time ago I understood that when a girl dons a crown of orange blossoms, she becomes subordinate, nothing but a pale reflection of what she was before. She's forever the leader's companion, not his equal, but his helpmate. No matter how worthy she is, she'll remain in obscurity.

My mother's wordless devotion reminds me that its men's nature to speak their minds without worrying about what that may do to their mates.

Sure, there are some fine husbands who are eager to make their wives' qualities stand out. You know a few. Yet I've never dared go stand before the mayor with a man. Still, unlike the Saint-Simonians, I consider the sacrament of marriage essential to society. What a great idea to give human law the power to establish a contract so powerful, so exalted that not even death can dissolve it.

When I read the enlightening account of Auguste Comte's doctrines in Littré's *Positive Philosophy*, I was struck to find something I've thought for a long time: the institution of widowhood for both men and women is an admirable idea. Children need it for their peace, well-being, and protection. What happened to us so long ago? My father couldn't bear being alone, as I've told you. A year before he died, the woman who took my mother's place gave him a son, and I paid for most of his schooling. Well! rumor had it that I was his mother, not his benefactress. That can be forgiven, but never ever forgotten!

Like Rachel,[17] George Sand,[18] and so many others, I certainly could have taken advantage of the indulgence generally conceded to prominent women. Then people could have said whatever they please about me. Instead, I've always led a pure, decent life. I've never had lovers or children.

Even though my father sometimes scolded me for my free, boyish ways, he can at least rejoice up in heaven. He used to call me his most precious asset, and I've remained without stain my whole life long."

In the final excerpt, Bonheur discusses the growing numbers of women artists, and her involvement in the Union des Femmes Peintres et Sculpteurs (UFPS) (Introduction to Part 1). Her attitude towards this organization is deeply ambivalent. She publically supported the group, assuming the position of honorary president, but she also wanted women to be judged by the same standards as male artists. As we will see, Kollwitz grapples with similar issues when she serves on the jury of the Berlin Secession (Chapter 8).

"I think young artists bear me more of a grudge for being a woman than for being old. They can't forgive me for having proved that the sex of the artist doesn't matter. I'm afraid this tension will never be resolved. Yet today women can compete for the Rome prize. That's great, since I'm not afraid of a fight. Otherwise, we'd have to resign ourselves to women-only shows. I can't bring myself to that. I can't even see that kind of show without thinking about Muhammad's notion of paradise, where our Muslim sisters have to have their own Garden of Eden.

Yet I agreed to be the honorary president of the Society of Women Painters and Sculptors, but only out of affection for Mme Demont Breton,[19] a very talented painter, and in memory of Mme Leon Bertaux,[20] the sculptor and first president of the Society.

My stand is altogether different. I think that as soon as women can aspire to the highest honors, there's no reason for them to form groups that shut out men. They'd do better to seize every opportunity to show that we women can be as good as men and sometimes even better."

Like Harriet Hosmer, Rosa Bonheur also chose to remain unmarried, and therefore her career as a painter was left uncomplicated by the demands of marriage and motherhood. However her gendered identity is nonetheless complex due to her lifelong emotional attachments to women and her unorthodox lifestyle as well as her celebrity status. Like Vigée-Lebrun, she was very concerned about her posthumous reputation and legacy and therefore undertook an autobiographical project, in collaboration with her companion and heir. While Bonheur had enjoyed great success in her lifetime, by the 1890s when she worked on the book with Klumpke, her era of greatest success was also past. Her desire to record her memories of her life and her own positions on issues of the day gained urgency with her advanced age. Also like Vigée-Lebrun, she lived past the political era in which she had received her greatest triumphs, the Second Empire, and into the time of the Third Republic. No doubt her desire to remind the public of the imperial largess was another strongly motivating factor in her autobiographical project.

Bonheur asserted her own sense of "female agency" by working with Klumpke to "set her record straight" even though it was no doubt understood that the book would only appear after her death. Bonheur's voice as recorded by Anna Klumpke, seems to maintain full awareness of her tenuous and complex position as a famous, much decorated woman artist. She always maintains an awareness of herself as both a woman and an artist and buoyed by the utopian ideals of Saint Simonianism, she manages to combine both roles into a powerful personality. She also displays a marked sense of embarrassment about her unorthodox life style and choices. This ambivalence is also evident in her conflicted position about the UFPS and her "sisters of the brush." While supporting the efforts of feminist artists, she is simultaneously critical of their efforts on behalf of other women artists. Rosa Bonheur's **a/b** is a complex narrative, interwoven between the life stories of both Klumpke and Bonheur, and is an appropriate type of text to reveal her multifaceted identity as both woman and artist.

Notes

1   Gretchen van Slyke (translator) *Rosa Bonheur: the Artist's (Auto) Biography* (Ann Arbor, MI: University of Michigan Press, 1997), p. xii. All quotes are taken from this translation, published by permission of the University of Michigan Press.

2   Albert Boime, "The Case of Rosa Bonheur: Why Should a Woman Want to Be More Like a Man?" *Art History,* vol. 4 (December, 1981).

3   Gustave Courbet (1819-1877) was a French painter and leader of the Realists.

4   Jean-Francois Millet (1814-1875) was a French painter, known for his peasant scenes.

5   Slyke, *Rosa Bonheur: the Artist's (Auto) Biography,* xiii.

6   Pierre Jules Mene (1810-1877).

7   Salvator Rosa (1615-1673) was an Italian painter of dramatic landscapes in the Baroque era.

8   Carl Dujardin (also known as Karel) (1626-1678?) was a Dutch landscape artist.

9   Paulus Potter (1625-1654) was a Dutch painter, noted for his animal imagery.

10   Philips Wouwermans (1619-1668) was a Dutch artist who was famous for his paintings of horses.

[11] Van Berghem alternately spelled Nicolaes Berchem (1620-1683) was a Dutch landscape painter.

[12] James M. Saslow "Disagreeably Hidden: Construction and Constriction of the Lesbian Body in Rosa Bonheur's *Horse Fair*" in Norma Broude and Mary D. Garrard, *The Expanding Discourse: Feminism and Art History* (New York: HarperCollins, 1992), 189.

[13] Whitney Chadwick, *Women, Art, and Society*, 4th edition (London and New York: Thames and Hudson, 2007), 189ff.

[14] Thomas Landseer (1795-1880) was a noted British printmaker.

[15] Edwin Landseer (1802-1873) was the most famous British animal painter of the Victorian era.

[16] Carolus-Duran (1837-1917) was a French artist who was one of the leading fashionable portrait painters of the Third Republic, after 1870.

[17] Rachel (1821-1858) was a famous French actress known for her many lovers.

[18] George Sand (1804-1876) was the pseudonym of an important French woman novelist, also famous for her affairs, especially with the composer Frederic Chopin.

[19] Virginie Demont-Breton (1859-1935) was a painter and daughter of the successful academic painter Jules Breton, who served as the second President of the UFPS.

[20] Hélène Bertaux, (1825-1909) was a sculptor and the first President of the UFPS.

Chapter 4. Julia Margaret Cameron (1815-1879): *Annals of My Glass House* and Letters

Julia Margaret Cameron is widely regarded as one of the most innovative and important photographers of the Victorian era. No other woman of her generation achieved the same level of professional recognition in the medium of photography. Cameron's photographs were original in both style and content. Her work is preserved in major museums, and her images have been studied, in great detail, by scholars. The critical literature on Cameron is quite extensive. Cameron's colleagues were male. Most frequently, scholars cite Oscar G. Rejlander[1] and Henry Peach Robinson[2] as "Cameron's most serious rivals for notoriety and sales."[3]

Julia Margaret Pattle was born in 1815, into a family based in Calcutta, India. Her father was a wealthy merchant for the East India Company. During her youth, she traveled with her family in Europe. She was educated in France and spent time with her maternal grandmother. She returned to India in 1835 and married Charles Hay Cameron, in Calcutta in 1838. Cameron was a distinguished jurist and member of the Supreme Court of India. Between 1839 and 1852, she bore five children. The family returned to England in 1846, but it was not until 1864, when her children were older, that she began her work in the relatively new medium of photography. Cameron did not have any formal training in photography as none existed in her era. The family had purchased property on the Isle of Wight and Cameron began making photographs from her home. By the following year, 1865, she had produced a substantial corpus of photographic work. She had her first exhibition, in London, and sent her photos to exhibitions around the continent. Most of her photographs were created between ca. 1865 and 1875, when she moved to Ceylon. She died in Ceylon a few years later, in 1879.

As Sylvia Wolf has discussed, Cameron's personal circumstances encouraged her to break away from the hegemonic gender roles defined for women of her class. During the period of her photographic activity, her husband was ill, and she assumed the business affairs of the household, in addition to her maternal responsibilities. Wolf also notes that the household was in "distinct financial distress" by the early 1860s, which provided some motivation for her efforts to sell her photographs.[4] The issue of Cameron's "amateur" versus "professional" status is an interesting one to explore in the context of the widespread amateur female activity in the visual arts (Introduction to Part I).

"During the mid-nineteenth century, wealthy members of the upper classes had leisure time and money with which to engage in the amateur study of the arts and sciences. This was considered a noble enterprise...When Cameron first took up photography, she worked within the context of this kind of amateur endeavor which is why art journals of the period and modern books on photography frequently refer to her as an amateur...as we begin to realize the extent of her commercial activity, it becomes all the more tempting to call her a professional—one who made money on her work... The respect professional artists received must have appealed to Cameron, for she sought similar recognition. By declaring the greatness of her photographs, Cameron placed herself alongside the professionals she knew— men like Tennyson,[5] Watts, [6] and Herschel[7]. By engaging in the commercial market and by exercising her ambition, she stepped beyond the bounds of amateurism and assumed the authority of a respected professional." [8]

Cameron's use of the medium of photography was innovative, both in terms of the types of subjects she created and the formal appearance and soft focus that she habitually employed. This style is seen, historically, as a forerunner of the movement of "Pictorialism". Although Cameron had no formal training as an "artist", she was clearly conversant with the trends of Victorian painting and sought to use photography in a way that would rival paintings. Cameron's goal was to elevate the medium of photography to compete with painting. This ambition is clearly stated in the letter to her mentor, Sir John Herschel, reprinted below. During her lifetime her portraits earned the unconditional respect of critics and scholars.

Cameron's subjects for her photographs were always people rather than views of nature or still lifes. She focused on a range of types, but basing her work, on academic hierarchies, she employed human figures. In the mid 1860s, she collected her works and presented them in the form of an album to Lord Overstone. The album format was used extensively by amateur women artists (Introduction to Part I).[9] The *Overstone Album* is divided into 3 groups. In the first group "Portraits," Cameron created a body of photographic portraits of many of the notable figures of her era. Her sitters included the painters Dante Gabriel Rossetti,[10] Watts and William Holman Hunt.[11] She photographed poets, such as Alfred, Lord Tennyson and Robert Browning.[12] She was friendly with and created portraits of scientists including her mentor Sir John Herschel and Charles Darwin.[13] She also photographed leading religious and intellectual figures of her era, for example, Thomas Carlisle.[14]

In the next section, "Madonna Groups," Cameron created allegorical images, using "conceptually ideal images, with references to the subject matter and the tenets of Italian Renaissance painting."[15] The third group "Idylls and Fancy Subjects" includes images directly inspired by history and literature.

In a frequently quoted article, "*Cupid's Pencil of Light*: Julia Margaret Cameron and the Maternalization of Photography," Carol Armstrong provides a perceptive analysis of Cameron's project, especially in the context of her many images of children. Armstrong demonstrates that Cameron's iconographic repertoire reveals a highly original sensibility attuned to Victorian gender ideology, conventions in the visual arts, and the specific properties of the photographic medium. In an analysis of one of Cameron's photographs, *Cupid's Pencil of Light*, Armstrong notes that:

"This Cupid represents drawing under the aegis of Photography—in the guise of light—rather than Photography under the aegis of the master arts of drawing and painting: Photography in the image of its own process, its own mode of production, rather than Photography ruled by the technical decrees of the established: Photography under the sway of the Mother, rather than the law of the Father...As exemplified in *Cupid's Pencil of Light*, Cameron's photography is often self-reflexive, as much about photography per se as it is about anything else. Indeed, it is fair to say that over and over again, Cameron sought to allegorize her own photographic practice and to define it alternatively by allegorical means—as something although different from technical mastery, pertaining, rather to the domestic, the incestually familiar and the feminine." [16]

Armstrong makes an important link between Cameron's internalization of her maternal role, within the Victorian family, and her choices of subjects in many of her images. Cameron raised eleven children: five biological children, five orphaned relatives, and one foster child.[17] Also, there were two grandchildren in her household.

Cameron created her first photographs using a camera, presented to her by her daughter and son-in-law. This was a bulky device composed of two wooden boxes which held glass plates, 11" x 9". She soon moved to an even larger format, capable of processing an 11" x 15" negative on a glass plate. Using the sun for light, this format involved long exposures. She used a "wet collodion" process, and Herschel advised her on technical issues. This process was very demanding, involving the coating of the plate in a light sensitive solution of silver nitrate, placing the wet plate into the camera frame, and, then, developing the plates, immediately. Prints were exposed to the sun for an extended period. [18]

In a major catalogue, published in conjunction with a traveling exhibition of Cameron's images of women, Wolf discusses Cameron's formal, esthetic choices, reversing the earlier more misogynistic interpretations of scholars like Helmut Gernsheim.[19] Gernsheim accepted Cameron's own version of the blurred focus, taken from the *Annals*, as a "fluke". He attributed her softly focused images to technical "error." Wolf, however, defends Cameron's consistent soft focus as a conscious aesthetic preference:

"Cameron's aesthetic rose from the combination of chance and design. During the first two years of her career, she made 9-by-11 inch plates and utilized a lens with a short focal length. This yielded an image in which only one shallow plane would be in sharp focus and the rest of the image would fall off into progressive blurriness....Had she been dissatisfied with the result, she could have changed cameras or photographed her subjects differently. But Cameron immediately recognized the artistic value of the error. When she graduated to a larger camera in 1866, with 15-by-12 inch plates and a lens with a long focal length, she had more options, but by then the selective focus of her early pictures had become part of her creative vision." [20]

Cameron's most important primary source is her brief, autobiographical essay *Annals of My Glass House.* It was written in 1874 and published, posthumously, in 1889, in the catalogue that accompanied an exhibition of her photographs in London. It reappeared in 1927 as an article in *The Photographic Journal.* "As the primary source document of one of the most brilliant nineteenth-century photographers, *Annals* has been a reference for all the major exhibitions and publications on Cameron's life and work and widely quoted in monographs and catalogues on Cameron's photography." [21] Like the *Souvenirs* of Vigee-Lebrun, this text is also a **memoir,** an official record of a professional life (Introduction II, a). The narrow focus on Cameron's career as a photographer makes this text read like a sort of "authorized" version of her unusual, indeed unprecedented, artistic activity.

This text is consistent with Leigh Gilmore's definition of women's self-narrative as **autobiographics** (Introduction II,a). Despite its brevity, and the fact that it remained unpublished and in the collection of the family until a decade after her death, Cameron writes a narrative of her life as a photographer "where self-invention, self-discovery, and self-representation emerge within the technologies of autobiography."[22] *Annals of My Glass House* is also very thoroughly suffused with an awareness of her role and identity as a Victorian woman and, so, can also be seen in the context of Stanton's concept of **Autogynography** (Introduction II, a).

'Mrs. Cameron's Photography", now ten years old, has passed the age of lisping and stammering and may speak for itself, having traveled over Europe, America and Australia, and met with a welcome which has give it confidence and power therefore, I think that the 'Annals of My Glass House' will be welcome to the public, and, endeavoring to clothe my little history with light, as with a garment, I feel confident that the truthful account of indefatigable work, with the anecdote of human interest attached to that work, will add in some measure to its value...

Therefore it is with effort that I restrain the overflow of my heart and simply state that my first camera and lens was given to me by my cherished departed daughter and her husband, with the words, 'It may amuse you, Mother, to try to photograph during your solitude at Freshwater.'

The gift from those I loved so tenderly added more and more impulse to my deeply seated love of the beautiful, and from the first moment I handled my lens with a tender ardor, and it has become to me as a living thing, with voice and memory and creative vigor. Many and many weeks in the year '64 I worked fruitlessly, but not hopelessly–....

I longed to arrest all beauty that came before me, and at length the longing has been satisfied. Its difficulty enhanced the value of the pursuit. I began with no knowledge of the art. I did not know where to place my dark box, how to focus my sitter, and my first picture I effaced to my consternation by rubbing my hand over the filmy side of the glass. It was a portrait of a farmer of Freshwater, who, to my fancy, resembled Bolingbroke. The peasantry of our island is very handsome. From the men, the women, the maidens and the children I have had lovely subjects, as all the patrons of my photography know.

This farmer I paid half-a-crown an hour, and, after many half-crowns and many hours spent in experiments, I got my first picture, and this was the one I effaced when holding it triumphantly to dry.

I turned my coal-house into my dark room, and a glazed fowl-house I had given to my children became my glass house! The hens were liberated, I hope and believe not eaten. The profit of my boys upon new laid eggs was stopped, and all hands and hearts sympathized in my new labour, since the society of hens and chickens was soon changed for that of poets, prophets, painters and lovely maidens, who all in turn have immortalized the humble little farm erection.

Having succeeded with one farmer, I next tried two children; my son, Hardinge, being on his Oxford vacation, helped me in the difficulty of focusing. I was half-way through a beautiful picture when a splutter of laugher from one of the children lost me that picture, and less ambitious now, I took one child alone, appealing to her feelings and telling her of the waste of poor Mrs. Cameron's chemicals and strength if she moved. The appeal had its effect, and I now produced a picture which I called 'My First Success'.

I was in a transport of delight. I ran all over the house to search for gifts for the child. I felt as if she entirely had made the picture. I printed, toned, fixed and framed it, and presented it to her father that same day: size 11 in. by 9 in...

I believe that what my youngest boy, Henry Herschel, who is now himself a very remarkable photographer, told me is quite true—that my first successes in my out-of-focus pictures were a fluke. That is to say, that when focusing and coming to something which, to my eye, was very beautiful, I stopped there instead of screwing on the lens to the more definite focus which all other photographers insist upon.

I exhibited as early as May '65. I sent some photographs to Scotland—a head of Henry Taylor, with the light illuminating the countenance in a way that cannot be described; a Raphaelesque Madonna, called ' La Madonna aspettante'. These photographs still exist, and I think they cannot be surpassed. They did not receive the prize. The picture that did receive the prize, called 'Brenda', clearly proved to me that detail of table-cover, chair and crinoline skirt were essential to the judges of the art, which was then in its infancy. Since that miserable specimen, the author of 'Brenda' has so greatly improved that I am content to compete with him and content that those who value fidelity and manipulation should find me still behind him. Artists, however, immediately crowned me with laurels, and though 'Fame' is pronounced 'The last infirmity of noble minds', I must confess that when those whose judgment I revered have valued and praised my works, 'my heart has leapt up like a rainbow in the sky', and I have renewed my zeal.

The Photographic Society of London in their *Journal* would have dispirited me very much had I not valued that criticism at its worth. It was unsparing and too manifestly unjust for me to attend to it. The more lenient and discerning judges gave me a large space upon their walls which seemed to invite the irony and spleen of the printed notice.

To Germany I next sent my photographs. Berlin, the very home of photographic art, gave me the first year a bronze medal, the succeeding year a gold medal, and one English institution - the Hartly Institution – awarded me a silver medal, taking, I hope, a home interest in the success of one whose home was so near to Southampton.

Personal sympathy has helped me on very much. My husband from first to last has watched every picture with delight and it is my daily habit to run to him with every glass upon which a fresh glory is newly stamped, and to listen to his enthusiastic applause. This habit of running into the dinning room with my wet pictures has stained such an immense quantity of table linen with nitrate of silver, indelible stains, that I should have been banished from any less indulgent household...

When I have had such men [Thomas Carlyle] before my camera my whole soul has endeavored to do its duty towards them in recording faithfully the greatness of the inner as well as the features of the outer man.

The photograph thus taken has been almost the embodiment of a prayer. Most devoutly was this feeling present to me when I photographed my illustrious and revered as well as beloved friend, Sir John Herschel. He was to me as a Teacher and High Priest. From my earliest girlhood I had loved and honoured him, and it was after a friendship of 31 years' duration that the high task of giving his portrait to the nations was allotted to me. He had corresponded with me when the art was in its first infancy in the days of Talbot-type and autotype. I was then residing in Calcutta, and scientific discoveries sent to that then benighted land were water to the parched lips of the starved to say nothing of the blessing of friendship so faithfully evinced.

When I returned to England the friendship was naturally renewed. I had already been made godmother to one of his daughters, and he consented to become godfather to my youngest son…

Women were expected to be good letter writers, since the letter was the form of text deemed most suitable to women's intellectual "limitations." Cameron was an extensive letter writer and some of her correspondence has survived.[23] The following letters were semi-public documents, carefully preserved, and, ultimately, expected to be shared within a limited circle (Introduction II, b).

In a letter addressed to her mentor, the scientist John Herschel, dated December 31, 1864, Cameron discusses the key issue of focus and provides a succinct insight into her ambitious goal for her photographic work, to bring it to an equal plane with painting.

[I] believe in other than mere conventional topographic photography– map-making and skeleton rendering of feature and form without that roundness and fullness of force and feature, that modeling of flesh and limb, which the focus I use only can give, tho' called and condemned as 'out of focus.' What is focus—and who has a right to say what focus is the legitimate focus? My aspirations are to ennoble photography and to secure for it the character and uses of High Art by combining the real and ideal and sacrificing nothing of Truth by all possible devotion to Poetry and beauty. But I need not tell you what my aims and efforts are. Your eye can best detect and your imagination conceives all that is to be done and is still left undone...

The following letter, to art critic William Michael Rossetti,[24] written in 1866, shows how aggressively Cameron promoted her works. Wolf has observed:

"that Cameron asked Rossetti to write for a paper with good distribution [which] shows her to be savvy about the marketplace and about the dissemination of news in the popular press. That she asked him to write anything at all is startling, for even though it was common for men to ask for favors, it was outside the realm of feminine restraint for a Victorian woman to do the same. No review, friendly or otherwise, is on record from Rossetti." [25]

My dear Mr. Rossetti

I have never heard *from* you and only once *of* you since the afternoon when you very devotedly did your best *for* me and I in my turn did my best with you, for I verily believe I have never had more remarkable success with any photograph, but I should like to know if you yourself are of this opinion for I have never heard even whether you approve of the picture!

I have printed two special copies for you and addressed them care of Colnaghi and they *now await your claiming them.* Do so soon I pray and tell me what you think of all my late Photography. Your careful criticism was never brought to light—but now if you would in any current Paper notice that my Photographs are all for sale at Colnaghi's you would I think help me on.

I am under a promise to *stop* Photography till I have recovered my outlay, that is to say, to take no *new* pictures and limit myself to printing from the old and depending on their sale—but this duty—and my delight therefore can only be in the past till a lucrative present sets me afloat again.

Have you no means of introducing any friendly Paragraph into any Paper that has *good* circulation?

I myself delight in both those Pictures of you—but if you judge differently I would not have you otherwise than quite candid with me. I never print out the hand holding the umbrella because I always remember proudly it is Browning's hand!!!

I have had an anxious time helping a devoted sister and two brothers to nurse Philip Worsely thro' an almost mortal illness- but he is this time *surviving* tho' far too advanced in tubercular disease ever to recover. A most interesting and most afflicted creature with a mind of great power that o'er informs its very shattered tenement of clay.

For the *first* time for 26 years I am left without a child under my roof—but they are doing well and struggling to improve and I must not grudge the sacrifice of their sweet society. I should like to hear about your Mother and dear Christina, *all* about her health. I long to know the success of your journey abroad with her.

Your brother went to my gallery and his enthusiasm as reported to me was one of my great rewards.

I was going to write and ask him to tell *me* in direct person what I was told he said of the Photography but thought the writing to me would bore him. I believe you are not bored and I feel I have a little more claim upon you from the ties of old and I hope enduring friendship.

With kind remembrances from my Husband
Yours always truly
Julia Margaret Cameron.

As you did not go to the gallery I urge you to see at Colnaghi's my late large pictures. Mr. Wynfield too never went! and that surprised me. My book there held the one great fact that to my feeling about his beautiful Photography I owed *all* my attempts and indeed consequently all my success.

The following letter, addressed to Blanche Ritchie, cousin of Cameron's close friend Anne Thackeray, is dated May 14, 1872. Here, she writes asking for candid, honest feedback on 45 prints which she had sent to Ritchie. She refers to herself, humorously, as "Priestess of the Sun".

Dearest
This above all be true-(as I said when I summoned your Mother to the magical floating tub for the first seeing of the Photos) give no praise that is meant to gratify me at the expense of one just criticism, so tell me first which of all the Photos *now* do you like the best? The St. Agatha. The Queen Clotilda. The Holbein Mary—and which one of the *three?* The Seven Stars. The Calypso. The Votive Offering.

Give me detailed criticism on each. There is only *one* set of these last studies in which you have not moved—the set of Mary Queen of Scots—all the others are just prevented from being quite perfect in the still sitting and then the pictures would be perfect—The Seven Stars might have been entirely perfect but for some movement which is quite discernible.

Notwithstanding they are beautiful pictures. People marvel at the *variety* not at the beauty. Those only who don't know you in all your expressions think them idealized just as so many think I idealize and glorify my beautiful Madonna [Mary Hillier] but I know all her expressions—and know all the beauty and I nearly fixed for ever what I saw of you in the glass house but then movement comes because you are not *yet* so practiced a sitter as my Angel of the Tomb [Mary Hillier].

The Tennysons are greatly delighted with your picture. Mrs. Tennyson says she has never known me so successful. She and Alfred both prefer the same. It is not the one I prefer and not the one that Hallam prefers and not the one that Horatio [brother of Alfred Tennyson] prefers. Horatio, Hallam, and I all prefer the same one. I won't *enlighten* you any more because you are to give us the light of your opinion and true eye—and your dear Mother is to tell me also, *all* she thinks. Blanche and Gussie have seen none of this last set nor has our cherished Annie Thackeray. Tell me whether you like the names chosen.

Hallam returned to Marlboro' [Marlborough School] today. I did not like to see him go but I have the heart of a Coward. HE wished to go. I saw dearest Mrs. Tennyson this morning and Alfred offered me a drive but I had your parcel to send off to you and letters to write and I couldn't go. You know my letters average three hundred every month and I got dreadfully in arrears by making holidays or *bits* of holiday with you and Annie Thackeray so I *can't* come on Monday as Lady Margaret has proposed which I am sorry for on all accounts; and now post hour is coming and the house has been beset this whole afternoon with visitors so that I have to be quite savage and declare I will see no one till the bag is closed and so farewell for today. You and your Mother are to have six photos as gifts—16 in all have been sent this time, 29 last time, and as *ten* were purchased so that after this time 'orders is business'!!!

With my love to your Mother and all salutations to you from the Priestess of the Sun and from Apollo himself

Yours lovingly
Julia Margaret Cameron.

Cameron's personal friendship with Tennyson, referenced in the preceding letter, eventually led to the invitation, by England's poet laureate, to create a set of illustrations for his famous poetry cycle, *The Idylls of the King,* based on the Arthurian legends. This was the last major project which occupied Cameron prior to her departure for Ceylon. According to Debra N. Mancoff, modern critics have dismissed this series, either ignoring it or viewing it as "camp."[26] Mancoff argues for a more sincere understanding of these works, in the context of Victorian readings of Tennyson's poems. "The nature of Tennyson's and Cameron's friendship, moreover, bound them together in a shared interpretive vision. Just as Cameron often signed her negatives 'From Life', Tennyson sought to instill an authentic vitality into his legend." [27] Mancoff concludes: "She was…responding as an artist through her medium; Cameron's *Illustrations* gave a tangible human dimension to the mythic world." [28] On November 29, 1874, the first edition of Tennyson's poems was published. Cameron was initially disappointed in the appearance of her images, printed as small woodcuts, and she seized on Tennyson's suggestion to publish a new volume with the photos in their original size. To achieve this, she wrote the following letter to Sir Edward Ryan,[29] who was connected to the London Times for support. The letter documents her determination and level of commitment to obtaining an appropriate format for her photos. As noted in her letter to Rossetti, Cameron used her pen as a weapon in her drive to find a public audience for her photography.

Just now I *think* you can help me and I do not think but feel sure, that you will help me if you can…

I have worked for three months putting all my zeal and energy to my high task. But my beautiful large photographs are reduced to cabinet size for his people's edition and the first illustration is transferred to wood cut and appears now today when *12,000* copies are issued. I do it for

friendship not that I would not gladly have consented to profit if profit had been offered. Doré[30]
got a fortune for his *drawn* fancy illustrations of
these Idylls. Now one of my large photographs,
the one for instance illustrating Elaine, who is May
Prinsep (now Hitchens) at her very best would
excite more sensation and interest than all the
drawings of Doré—and therefore I am producing a volume of these large photographs to illus-
trate the Idylls—12 in number all differing (with
portrait of Alfred Tennyson) in a handsome half
morocco volume priced six guineas—I could not
make it under for it to pay at all.

The photographs will also be sold singly at
16 each to those who prefer single copies, then
the set would come to L10.8. for the 13 pictures
without the binding whereas the *book* is only six
guineas. It will make a beautiful Xmas Gift Book
or Wedding Gift Book—The Elaine of May Prinsep and the Enid of another lovely girl are as all
agree *not* to be surpassed as Poems and Pictures
and the King Arthur all say is magnificent mys-
tic mythical, a real embodiment of conscience
with piercing eyes and spiritual look and air. You
will smile over Merlin. Mrs. Tennyson said my Merlin was an old darling. The oak is a hollow tree
off Alfred's own grounds, and this is the tree in
which my husband stood.

Now what I want *you* to do for me is since
Mr. Dasent is your friend to get this work noticed
in the *Times*—even if Mr. Dasent has left the *Times*

he has influence—Do persuade him. Shew him this note and plead for me—I am not asking him to compromise his judgment. I am asking him to praise what he and every high artist says is worthy of praise and well it may be for I have striven to *perfect* this work. I have taken *180* pictures to obtain 12 successes—This is the work of the last *three months* and then the experience and labour of 10 previous *years* has all been brought into play. The hiring of the armour and the models has all cost me a great deal and I *hope* to get one single grain of the momentous mountain heap of profits the poetical part of the works brings in to Alfred...

I am going to dedicate the book to the Crown Princess [of Germany] because of her most amiable friendly letter to me. She was so charming towards me.

And now lest I should be late for the afternoon service I say goodbye and God bless you.

Yours ever
Julia Margaret Cameron.

Shall I send you the publisher's letter about my photographs of these Idylls? They say they are beyond all praise yet they are *gifts* to them.

On receiving your answer I will send you a copy of the Book for presentation to the writer [i.e. the prospective reviewer] if I may.

Cameron's autobiographical text and letters reveal a woman determined to establish a new level of respect and professionalism for photography. Her identity depends on two seemingly contradictory components, the full acceptance of Victorian upper-class expectations for woman as wives and mothers and the role of serious photographer. That she could merge these roles to create an astoundingly original photographic *oeuvre* is remarkable. The texts included in this chapter are of two distinct types, the autobiographical statement that records her development as a photographer and letters to friends and colleagues to promote her work. In both types of self writing Cameron manages to fuse her identity as a woman and her aspirations for her work.

Her determination and commitment to her photographic project raises her above class and gender expectations but is fully consistent with other woman artists. Cameron was around fifty years old when she began her work in photography. As we have seen with Vigée-Lebrun and Bonheur, painters began their training no later than their teens. By seizing on photography as her artistic medium, Cameron had the opportunity to become a serious artist, at an age when Victorian women were supposed to be grandmothers, well outside of the public eye. This is clearly a highly original mode of "female agency". There is no doubt that her work provided her with a creative outlet which enriched the last decades of her life. We can only be grateful to this remarkable woman who has given us a substantial group of photographs of both stylistic and iconographical originality, which has fascinated audiences from the Victorian age into the contemporary era.

Notes

1   Oscar Rejlander (1813-1875) was a Swedish photographer, active in England from the 1850s.

2   Henry Peach Robinson (1830-1901) was an English photographer who studied with Rejlander in 1858 and wrote *The Pictorial Effect in Photography* (1869).

3   Sylvia Wolf, *Julia Margaret Cameron's Women* (Chicago, IL: The Art Institute of Chicago, 1998, distributed by Yale University Press), 52.

4   Wolf, *Julia Margaret Cameron's Women*, 47-49.

5   Alfred Tennyson (1809-1892) was the Poet Laureate of the United Kingdom from 1850 to his death, in 1892.

6   George Frederick Watts (1817-1904) was a noted British painter.

7   Sir John Herschel (1792-1871) was an astronomer and scientist who also experimented with chemistry. His most important photographic contribution was the invention of sodium thiosulphite, or "hypo" fixing agent.

8   Wolf, *Julia Margaret Cameron's Women*, 215-16.

9   The *Overstone Album*, now in the Getty Museum (Los Angeles) was exhibited, with an accompanying catalogue, in 1986.

10 Dante Gabriel Rossetti (1828-1882) was one of the leading painters of the Pre-Raphaelite Brotherhood.

11 William Holman Hunt (1827-1910) was an important British painter and a founding member of the Pre-Raphaelite Brotherhood.

12 Robert Browning (1812-1889) was a famous British poet.

13 Charles Darwin (1809-1882) was a British naturalist and famous for publishing the first texts developing the principles of natural selection.

14 Thomas Carlyle (1795-1881) was an important essayist and historian.

15 Violet Hamilton, *Annals of My Glass House: Photographs by Julia Margaret Cameron* (Claremont, CA: Scripps College, 1996), 43.

16 Carol Armstrong, "*Cupid's Pencil of Light*: Julia Margaret Cameron and the Maternalization of Photography" *October*, vol. 76 (Spring, 1996), 117-119.

17 Wolf, *Julia Margaret Cameron's Women*, 23.

18 Hamilton, *Annals of My Glass House: Photographs by Julia Margaret Cameron,* 26.

19 Helmut Gernsheim, *Julia Margaret Cameron: her life and photographic work,* (1st ed. London: Fountain Press, 1948; 2nd edition London, Gordon Frazer, Millerton NY: Aperture, 1975).

20 Wolf, *Julia Margaret Cameron's Women*, 33.

21 Hamilton, *Annals of My Glass House: Photographs by Julia Margaret Cameron,* 17.

22 Leigh Gilmore, *Autobiographics: A Feminist Theory of Women's Self-Representation* (Ithaca and London: Cornell University Press, 1994), 42.

23 The following texts are from letters, reprinted in Gernsheim, *Julia Margaret Cameron: her life and photographic work* .

24 William Michael Rossetti (1829-1919) was an art critic and brother of Dante Gabriel Rossetti.

25 Wolf, *Julia Margaret Cameron's Women,* 213.

26 Debra N. Mancoff, "Legend 'From Life': Cameron's Illustrations to Tennyson's *'Idylls of the King'* " in Wolf, *Julia Margaret Cameron's Women.*

27 Ibid., 90.

28 Ibid., 104.

29 Retired chief justice of Bengal, Ibid., 87.

30 Gustave Doré (1832-1883) was a French artist who was known for his wood and steel engraved illustrations.

Chapter 5. Berthe Morisot (1841-1895): Letters to her Family

As one of the most talented painters in the Impressionist movement, Berthe Morisot is usually included in an elite "canon" of "great" women artists. Her paintings display all the hallmarks of delicacy, energy, and originality, characteristic of her more famous male Impressionist colleagues, Monet,[1] Renoir,[2] and Degas.[3] Her art and her life have been the subjects of extensive scholarly attention, over the past 20 years.

Born into an upper-middle class French family in 1841, Berthe and her sisters Edma and Yves received drawing lessons. In this class milieu, "minor drawing room accomplishment," i.e. the ability to make art on an amateur level, was widespread (Introduction to Part I). However, from this base in gender and in class specific expectations, Morisot pursued her study of art with unusually fierce energy and drive.

Both Berthe and Edma exhibited a determination and willingness to work, which exceeded the gendered amateur level of mere "accomplishment." One insight into the special personality of Berthe Morisot is the frequently quoted statement by the sisters' first drawing teacher, Joseph-Benôit Guichard.[4]

"Considering the character of your daughters...my teaching will not endow them with minor drawing-room accomplishments; they will become painters. Do you realize what this means? In the upper-class milieu to which you belong, this will be revolutionary, I might almost say catastrophic. Are you sure that you will not come to curse the day when art, having gained admission to your home, now so respectable and peaceful, will become the sole arbiter of the fate of two of your children?"[5]

Unlike her sister Edma, whose marriage interrupted her painting career, Berthe married the brother of the prominent painter Édouard Manet[6] and continued to painting steadily throughout her life. She contributed works to every Impressionist group show, except the one held following the birth of her only child, Julie, in 1879.

Many contemporary critical appraisals of Morisot's paintings have fixed on her "femininity" and interpreted her talent as a natural delicacy and capriciousness appropriate to her sex. Modern scholars understand that Morisot's self-conscious selection of style was not determined by her gender but by a deliberate choice of artistic means. The difficulties she encountered in capturing "the spontaneous" are revealed in her letters. Her works should be understood in the context of other works by Impressionists, such as Renoir and Monet, and distinguished from the art of other contemporary women, such as Marie

Bashkirtseff (Chapter 6). Morisot read Bashkirtseff's diary in 1890, and discussed it in one of the letters, excerpted here. Being a woman did not automatically establish an instinctual affinity with Impressionism.

Most of Morisot's subjects reflect her world view as a Parisian woman of the *haute bourgeoisie.* Her paintings are focused on the domestic world of women, children, and the home. Most frequently, members of her family, including her sisters and their children, her daughter, and her servants, are the subjects of her works. Women are viewed in the home, in private gardens, or in urban parks. She rarely depicted men, only occasionally using her husband (usually paired with her daughter) as a subject.

Morisot's correspondence provides valuable insights into the intimate circle of an upper middle class, avant-garde woman artist. Her letters were edited, in an excerpted format, by her grandson, Denis Rouart in the 1950s.[7] The correspondence was translated, into an English edition, at that time. As a family venture, Berthe's letters were interspersed with other primary sources from intimate friends and other family members. It is intriguing to consider the extent to which the published letters in this volume were edited to omit anything that might prove embarrassing or inconvenient for the family. As we can tell from the complete letters by Kahlo (Chapter 10), often discussion of art matters would be interspersed with many other more personal issues. Especially within a family correspondence, one wonders how frequently the discussion of artistic issues, of concern to art historians appeared within the broader context of family relations. Because these letters are addressed to an intimate family circle, it is less relevant to see them as quasi-public documents. However, the very fact of their preservation testified to the internal family support for Morisot's work as an artist. Like Hosmer and Bonheur, one can see this book as an **Auto/biography** (Introduction, II,d). Exactly like Carr's volume on Hosmer (Chapter 2), it is the well-preserved letters, the primary sources, which provide the autobiographical as opposed to the biographical component of the text.

Within this group of primary sources, Morisot's letters to her sister Edma speak most directly to the key issues of greatest interest to art historians. All of the following texts, except the last letter, are addressed to her sister. To what extent does choice of professional identity as an artist overwhelm the author's understanding of herself as a "woman?" Why does she select the "avant-garde" style of Impressionism, while most other women artists painted in more conservative styles and submitted works to the official Salons or exhibiting with the UFPS (Introduction to Part 1). What personality traits were specific to Berthe Morisot which allowed her to pursue her career through all the stages of marriage and motherhood, while her sister Edma stopped painting after her marriage? In what ways did Morisot accept the gender ideology of her dominant class and culture and in what ways did she manage to resist them to provide space for the production of her art?

Early in 1869, Edma married a naval officer and moved away from Paris, her sister and her entire familial support group. When Edma married, Berthe lost not only her sister, but also her painting partner. Their correspondence centers on the changes and choices in their lives. Berthe's letters are one half of a dialogue. Berthe, still searching for her mature style, struggled on alone. Unlike Hosmer and Bonheur, Morisot accepts the gender ideology of her class and time and consoles Edma in her choice of marriage over painting. In response to a letter from her sister, Berthe adopts a voice in which she attempts to help her sister adjust to her changed circumstances.

March 19, 1869: If we go on in this way, my dear Edma, we shall no longer be good for anything. You cry on receiving my letters, and I did just the same thing this morning. Your letters are so affectionate, but so melancholy and your husband's kind words made me burst into tears. But, I repeat, this sort of thing is unhealthy. It is making us lose whatever remains of our youth and beauty. For me this is of no importance, but for you it is different.

Yes, I find you are childish: this painting, this work that you mourn for, is the cause of many griefs and many troubles. You know it as well as I do, and yet, child that you are, you are already lamenting that which was depressing you only a little while ago.

Come now, the lot you have chosen is not the worst one. You have a serious attachment, and a man's heart utterly devoted to you. Do not revile your fate. Remember that it is sad to be alone; despite anything that may be said or done, a women has an immense need of affection. For her to withdraw into herself is to attempt the impossible.

Oh, how I am lecturing you! I don't mean to. I am saying simply what I think, what seems to be true.

The correspondence continued, and, about one month later, Berthe is still trying to console Edma. However, she is also respectful of the need for women to have independent activities. In Edma's case, she is assuming that she will become pregnant and, therefore, occupied with the demands of motherhood.

April 23, 1869: I am not any more cheerful; than you are, my dear Edma, and probably much less so. Here I am, trapped because of my eyes. I was not expecting this, and my patience is very limited. I count the days passed in inaction, and foresee many a calamity, as for example that I shall be spending May Day here with poultices on my eyes. But let us talk about you. I am happy to think that your wish may be fulfilled. I have no knowledge of these matters, but I believe in your premonitions. In any case, I desire it with all my heart, for I understand that one does not readily accustom oneself to life in the country and to domesticity. For that, one must have something to look forward to. Adolphe would certainly be surprised to hear me talking in this way. Men incline to believe that they fill all of one's life, but as for me, I think that no matter how much affection a woman has for her husband, it is not easy for her to break with a life of work. Affection is a very fine thing, on condition that there is something besides with which to fill one's days. This something I see for you in motherhood.

Do not grieve about painting. I do not think it is worth a single regret.

Edma did become pregnant and in the following winter (1869-70), she returned home to stay with her family during her "confinement." Morisot painted *Mme. Morisot and her Daughter Mme. Pontillon (The Mother and Sister of the Artist)*[8] about a week before the birth of Edma's first daughter. It is a fascinating image on many autobiographical levels. Art historian, Marni Riva Kessler has suggested that the painting, like the correspondence, was an attempt to re-claim the intimacy of their relationship, disrupted by Edma's marriage. Pregnant Edma is a signifier of the domestic and maternal realm, from which Berthe, still unmarried, was excluded. [9]

However, this painting also occupies a place in the correspondence of Berthe and her relationship with

Édouard Manet. She intended to submit it to the jury for exhibition in the Salon of 1870. The events which ensued, in which Manet retouched portions of the canvas, provides insight into the insecurities and anxieties Morisot was experiencing in this early phase of her career. She expressed her distress to her sister in this letter.

March, 1870: Mother wrote to you at the time Puvis[10] told me that the head was not done and could not be done; whereupon great emotion; I took it out, I did it over again. Friday night I wrote him a note asking him to come to see me; he answered immediately that this was impossible for him and complimented me a great deal on all the rest of the picture, advising me only to put some accents on mother's head. So far no great misfortune. Tired, unnerved, I went to Manet's studio on Saturday. He asked me how I was getting on, and seeing that I felt dubious, he said to me enthusiastically: 'Tomorrow, after I have sent off my pictures, I shall come to see yours, and you may put yourself in my hands. I shall tell you what needs to be done.'

The next day, which was yesterday, he came at about one o'clock; he found it very good, except for the lower part of the dress. He took the brushes and put in a few accents that looked very well; mother was in ecstasies. That is where my misfortunes began. Once started, nothing could stop him; from the skirt he went to the bust, from the bust to the head, from the head to the background. He cracked a thousand jokes, laughed like a madman, handed me the palette, took it back; finally by five o' clock in the afternoon we had made the prettiest caricature that was ever seen. The carter was waiting to take it away; he made me put it on the handcart, willy-nilly. And now I am left confounded. My only hope is that I shall be rejected. My mother thinks this episode funny, but I find it agonizing.

I put in with it the painting I did of you at Lorient. I hope they take only that...

Manet has never done anything as good as his portrait of Mademoiselle Gonzales[11]; it is perhaps even more charming now than when you saw it. As for our friend Chavannes,[12] everybody agrees that his picture is very good: this proves that I was right and mother wrong.

Good-bye–I embrace you, write to me, and tell me as much about yourself as I tell you about myself.

About 4 years later, following her own marriage to Eugène Manet, Morisot seems more certain of her path and more fully dedicated to the Impressionist principle of painting "en plein aire" or totally outdoors. Like the other members of the Impressionist circle, Morisot is determined to paint while observing the motif. This letter was written while she was vacationing in the resort town Ryde, on the Isle of Wight.[13] Morisot documents, with some humor, the difficulties she encountered in attempting to capture the views which attracted her interest.

Summer 1875: It is not too expensive here, and it is the prettiest place for painting-if one had any talent. I have already made a start, but it is difficult. People come and go on the jetty and it is impossible to catch them. It is the same with the boats. There is extraordinary life and movement, but how is one to render it? I began something in the sitting room, of Eugène. The poor man has taken your place. But he is a less obliging model; at once it becomes too much for him....

Nothing is nicer than the children in the streets, bare-armed, in their English clothes. I should like to get some of them to pose for me, but all this is very difficult. My English is so horribly bad, and Eugène's is even worse...

The little river here is full of boats, a little like the river at Dartmouth in the photographs Tiburce sent us. I am sure you would like all this very much, and that it would even give you a desire to start working again. The beach is like an English park plus the sea; I shall have to make a water-colour of it, for I shall never have the courage to set up my easel to do it in oil.

At Ryde, everything takes place on the pier, which is interminably long. It is the place for promenading, for bathing, and where the boats dock.

I found a superb Reynolds there, for a little less than two francs. My black hat with the lace bow made the sailors in the port burst out laughing.

You should really write me a little. Cowes is very pretty, but not gay; besides, we constantly miss our home life. Eugene is even more uncommunicative than I.

I have worked a little, but what rain we have had for a week! Today we have been to Ryde. I set out with my sack and portfolio, determined to make a water-colour on the spot, but when we got there I found the wind was frightful, my hat blew off, my hair got in my eyes. Eugene was in a bad humour as he always is when my hair is in disorder-and three hours after leaving we were back again at Globe Cottage. I nevertheless took the time to take a little walk through the big town of Ryde, which I decidedly find even drearier than Cowes. There are more people in the streets but fewer boats on the water; and the pretty little river adds a lot of charm to the place. Anyway I am happy with our choice, which is a rare thing.

At Ryde there are many shops, and even a picture dealer. I went in. He showed me water-colours by a painter who, I am told, is well known; they sell for no less than four hundred francs apiece-and they are frightful. No feeling for nature–these people who live on the water do not even see it. That has made me give up whatever illusions I had about the possibility of success in England. In the whole shop, the only thing that was possible and even pretty was by a Frenchman; but the dealer says that sort of thing does not sell.

Like so many others, Morisot read Marie Bash-kirtseff's *Journal* (Chapter 6). Morisot's comments demonstrate her continuing belief in the separate realm of women and reinforce her commitment to the gender ideology of her era, the dominant culture's understanding of the essential nature of "Woman." They also reflect her continued dedication to the impressionist painting style.

Autumn 1890: My admiration is dampened because of her [Bashkirtseff's] mediocre painting; the "Meeting" and the rest are awkward, commonplace, almost stupid, and very difficult to reconcile with her alert style, with so much intellectual boldness and grace. I associate in my mind two books by women: *Recits d'une soeur* and hers. The truth is that our value lies in feeling, in intention, in our vision that is subtler than that of men, and we can accomplish a great deal provided that affectation, pedantry, and sentimentalism do not come to spoil everything.

The last excerpt of this correspondence is a moving "last will" to her daughter, Julie. Her final letter reinforces, poignantly, the continued bonds between Berthe, her sister, Edma, and Edma's daughter,

Jeannie. The strength of her identification with her Impressionist colleagues is documented. She also remembers some of her fellow Impressionists, who were united in their continued struggle for recognition of their artistic achievements.

March 1, 1895: My little Julie, I love you as I die; I shall still love you even when I am dead; I beg you not to cry, this parting was inevitable. I hoped to live until you were married...Work and be good as you have always been; you have not caused me one sorrow in your little life. You have beauty, money; make good use of them. I think it would be best for you to live with your cousins, Rue de Villejust, but I do not wish to force you to do anything. Please give a remembrance from me to your aunt Edma and to your cousin Gabriel give Monet's *Bateaux en reparation*. Tell M. Degas that if he founds a museum he should select a Manet. A souvenir to Monet, to Renoir, and one of my drawings to Bartholomé.[14] Give something to the two concierges. Do not cry; I love you more than I can tell you. Jeannie, take care of Julie.

Like Cameron, Morisot largely accepted her culture's expectations for women of her class. She married and became a mother, and seems to have internalized the gender ideology of her era. Also in a consistent fashion, she maintained her privacy throughout her life, broken only by the brief emergence of her

Impressionist canvasses at the Impressionist exhibitions. Similarly, her writings are also private letters carefully preserved and eventually edited and published all within her immediate family circle. Where she emerges from this conformity, is in the embrace of the radical painting technique of Impressionism. Because the movement embraced a range of themes from contemporary life which could be adapted to a woman's life, Morisot could participate fully with her male colleagues. Their respect for her technical virtuosity is well known. Morisot's unique "female agency" is in the passionate embrace of a new energy and immediacy in the handling of paint which is radical even from the standards of her colleagues Monet and Manet. Freed from the need to sell her works to make a living, Morisot broke away from her generation of women artists in the pursuit of an avant-garde style. Marrying into the Manet family, with one brother already established as a leading member of the avant garde, ensured a supportive family environment. The careful preservation of her paintings and letters documents the strength of this family environment for her success and posthumous reputation. Even in the highly edited version of her family correspondence we can hear the level of commitment to becoming not just another "woman artist", but a painter of significance, different from any other woman of her generation.

Notes

[1] Claude Monet (1840-1926).
[2] Pierre Auguste Renoir (1841-1919).

[3] Edgar Degas (1834-1917).

[4] Joseph-Benoît Guichard (1808-80) was Professor at the Ecole des Beaux- Arts in Lyons 1862 and Director from 1871. From 1868, until his death, he directed a municipal course in drawing and painting for girls. Note 3, page 213 in Denis Rouart (ed) *Berthe Morisot: the Correspondence with her Family and her Friends* (Betty W. Hubbard, translator) first ed. Percy Lund Humphries and Co. Ltd., Mt. Kisco NY: second edition, Moyer Bell Limited, 1987). All quotes are taken from this edition published by Permission of Moyer Bell Press.

[5] This was recorded by their brother Tiburce. Ibid., p. 19.

[6] Édouard Manet (1832-1883).

[7] Rouart (ed) *Berthe Morisot: the Correspondence with her Family and her Friends.*

[8] This painting is in the collection of the National Gallery of Art, Washington, D.C.

[9] Marni Reva Kessler, "Reconstructing Relationships: Berthe Morisot's Edma Series" *Woman's Art Journal,* vol. 12, no. 1 (Spring-Summer, 1991), 24ff.

[10] Pierre Puvis de Chavannes (1824-1898) was a French painter.

[11] Eva Gonzales (1849-1883) was a French painter who studied with Manet.

[12] Pierre Puvis de Chavannes (1824-1898).

[13] This is the same island where Julia Margaret Cameron lived (Chapter 4).

[14] Paul-Albert Bartholomé (1848-1928) was a French painter and sculptor.

Chapter 6. Marie Bashkirtseff (1858-1884): *Journal*

Marie Bashkirtseff's short life and painting career have been overshadowed by the enormous influence of her *Journal,* published in 1887. This diary is a key document for the history of women artists' narratives (Introduction I,c).

Born into a family of Russian aristocrats, Bashkirtseff spent most of her life in France. Her family first settled in Nice but then moved to Paris. In 1877, she decided that she wanted to become an artist and began her training at the Atelier Julian. Julian's separate women's class provided the most complete training available to women, in Paris, in the 1870s (Introduction to Part1). Bashkirtseff created a well-known painting showing this women's class working from the live model, a young boy modestly draped in a loincloth. Between the beginning of her studies and her death, from tuberculosis, in 1884, she produced several hundred works. She exhibited paintings at the Salons of 1880, 1881, and 1883. Two of her paintings were shown, posthumously, at the Salon of 1885. The Union des Femmes Peintres et Sculptures (UFPS) organized a retrospective exhibition of her works which numbered over 200 paintings, drawings, pastels, and, even, five works of sculpture (Introduction to Part 1). While Bashkirtseff accomplished a good deal artistically, her life was prematurely cut short before she could create a substantial body of mature paintings.

Her most famous painting is *The Meeting*, exhibited at the Salon of 1884. It was purchased by the French government of the Third Republic and was reproduced in both engravings and lithographs. Stylistically, Bashkirtseff aligned herself with the naturalist school, led by Jules Bastien-Lepage.[1] This group of artists used a technique which was looser than the linear, polished style still taught at the Ecole des Beaux Arts and Julian's and employed by the most conservative academic painters. However it was more finished than the much more visible brushwork of the Impressionists, such as Monet, Renoir or Morisot (Chapter 5). The painting depicts an inventive subject, six impish street urchins. As Rozsika Parker and Griselda Pollock note that what she found in this theme "was difference, a liveliness and freedom from the artifices which she as a woman of the upper class experienced as restriction to her life." [2] That longing for freedom was frequently expressed in her journal and will be highlighted in several of the excerpts reprinted below.

Her *Journal* is a very important primary source that made her famous when it was published in 1887. This is the first diary, or journal, in this book, because, keeping a diary for young girls was a historically situated practice in France emerging in the 1830s (Introduction II,c). Only a few of these diaries were published after 1860. As Philippe Lejeune, the leading scholar of this genre had observed: "In most cases, (47 diaries) the diary was published after its writer's death. The diarist died, often of tuberculosis...Two purposes operated in conjunction: the desire to cultivate the memory of the deceased, but primarily, the desire to instruct the living." [3] Both commemoration and the desire to use her example as a role model must have been active within Bashkirtseff's family to motivate the publication of her diary.

Bashkirtseff left 84 handwritten notebooks, which were carefully edited by her mother. Scholars, such as Colette Cosnier, who have compared the *Journal* to the handwritten manuscripts, have noted a range of omissions, alterations, and suppressions, including excerpts which deal with issues of sexuality and her politically active feminism.[4] Despite this censorship, the diary was a revolutionary work. It was widely read and discussed when it first appeared in print. Contemporary scholars have confirmed the importance and influence of Bashkirtseff's *Journal*. Lejeune notes that its publication created a "major shock":

> "This diary is a complete subversion of the 'moral order' diary, a proud claim to self value, a commitment to revealing the truth... it is ahead of its time, as the Eiffel Tower was in 1889. It foreshadows a line of diaries where introspection, active contestation of the condition of women and interest in writing stand out as defining features."[5]

When the diary was translated into English in 1889, it created a sensation in England. One late Victorian reviewer, Marion Hepworth Dixon wrote, in 1890, "It is this *Journal* with which the world is now ringing, and which it is hardly too much to say is likely to carry the fame of Marie Bashkirtseff over the face of the civilized globe."[6]

The *Journal*'s influence also spread to the United States. Margo Culley, in the introduction to her selection of American diaries, refers to Bashkirtseff's *Journal* as a:

> "diary of self-absorption...[which]became phenomenally popular...a kind of Marie Bashkirtseff cult developed in America. Women ... began keeping journals with the explicit expectation that their journal would make them famous, too....The wide popularity of her journal in America clearly gave American women 'permission' to pay that kind of sustained attention to the self."[7]

The impact of Bashkirtseff's *Journal* was immense. Even in this volume, there are references to the *Journal* from both Morisot (Chapter 5) and Modersohn-Becker (Chapter 7). As we will see in Part 2, Modersohn-Becker, Kollwitz, and Kahlo, following Bashkirtseff's example, were active journal writers. Well into the twentieth century, Louise Bourgeois also kept a journal and even wrote a brief essay about the importance of her diary for her creative process, "Tender Compulsions" (Chapter 14).

All scholars are struck with the ambitious statement of the preface, this first excerpt, in which Bashkirtseff makes a bid for immortality with her journal. She accepts that she is going to die before producing a substantial body of paintings. It is her journal, which she expects to be widely read, which will insure her posthumous fame.

When I am dead, people will read my life, which to me seems very remarkable. Were it not so it would be the climax of misery. But I hate prefaces and editors' notes, and have missed reading many excellent books on this account. That's why I've wished to write my own preface. It could have been dispensed with had the whole diary been published; but I think it best to begin with my thirteenth year, the preceding part being too long. The reader, however, will find sufficient data to go upon in the course of this narrative, for I frequently make references to the past, now for one reason, now for another. Suppose I were to die now quite suddenly, seized by some illness; perhaps I should not know of my danger; they would conceal it from me; and, after my death my drawers would be ransacked, and my family would discover my Journal, and, having read, would destroy it. Soon afterwards nothing would remain of me—nothing...nothing...nothing!...It is this which has always terrified me. To live, to have so much ambition, to suffer, weep, struggle—and then oblivion!...oblivion...as if I had never been. Should I not live long enough to become famous, this Journal will be of interest to naturalists; for the life of a woman must always be curious, told thus day by day, without any attempt at posing; as if no one in the world would ever read it, yet written with the intention of being read; for I feel quite sure the reader will find me sympathetic...And I tell all, yes, all....Else what were the use of it? In fact, it will be sufficiently apparent that I tell everything...

In the next except, dated May 1877, one of the main themes, self-absorption, even a certain level of narcissism, is clearly expressed. Bashkirtseff pierces the pretentious self-sacrifice, often proposed as a model for women, and delves more directly into the selfish motivations which often propel actions.

Would you like to know the truth? Well, remember what I am going to tell you—I love nobody, and shall never love, but one person, who will gracefully pamper my self-love...my vanity.

When you feel yourself beloved, you do everything for *the other* one, and then there is no feeling of shame; on the contrary, it makes you feel heroic.

I know very well that I would never ask anything for myself; but for another I would do a hundred meannesses, for it is by mean actions that one rises.

This again proves clearly that the finest actions are done for self...To ask for myself would be sublime, because it would cost me...Oh! How horrid even to think of it!...But for another it is a pleasure, and it looks like self-sacrifice, like devotion, like charity personified.

And on such occasions you believe in your own merit. You really believe yourself to be charitable, devoted, and sublime.

In the following three excerpts, all from October 1877, Bashkirtseff provides insight into the beginning of her work at the Atelier Julian and the level of expectations and ambition which she is bringing to her study of art.

October 6: Every time he [Julian] corrects my drawing he asks with some distrust if I did it alone.

I should think so indeed. I have never asked for advice of any of the pupils, except how to commence the study of the nude.

I am getting rather used to their ways—their artistic ways.

In the studio all distinctions disappear: you have neither name nor family; you are no longer the daughter of your mother; you are yourself; you are an individual with art before you—art and nothing else. One feels so happy, so free, so proud!

At last I am what I wished to be for so long. I wanted it so long that I cannot quite realize it.

October 10: Don't suppose I am doing wonders because M. Julian is surprised. He is surprised because he expected to find the whims of a rich young girl and a beginner. I need experience but my work is correct and like the model. As for the execution, it is just what may be expected after a week's work.

All of my fellow-students draw better than I do, but none of them can get it as like and true in proportion. What makes me think I shall do better than they, is that, although I see their merit, I should never be content to draw no better than they, whereas generally the beginners are continually saying, "Oh! If only I could draw as well as such or such a one!"

These women of forty have practice, work, and experience; but they will never do more than they are doing at present. As for the young ones, they draw well, and have time before them, but no future.

Perhaps I shall never do anything, but it will be from impatience. I could kill myself for not having begun four years ago, and it seems to me that it is too late.

We shall see.

October 11: It's all very well to say it's useless to regret the past, but every minute I say to myself, "How good it would be if I had begun working three years ago. By this time I should be a great artist, and I might," &c. &c.

M. Julian told the studio servant that Schaeppi and I were the most promising ones.

You don't know who Schaeppi is. She is the Swiss girl. Goodness, what a dialect! And M. Julian added that I might become a great artist.

I know it from Rosalie.

It is so cold that I caught cold; but I *forgive* that, if I can only draw.

And why draw?

...to get all that I have been crying for since the world began. To get all that I have wanted, and still want. To get on by my talent, or in any way I can, but to get on. If I had *all that*, perhaps I should do nothing.

In the following excerpt, dated April 13, 1878, Bashkirtseff writes one of the most flagrant assertions of pure ambition ever penned by a woman up to this time. This is precisely the sort of statement which seemed to be most shocking for her contemporaries, since it deviated dramatically from the gender ideology of this era, which expected modesty, self-sacrifice, and self-effacement in bourgeois women.

At twenty-two I shall either be famous or dead.

You think perhaps that one works only with eyes and fingers?

You who are *bourgeois*, you will never know the amount of sustained attention, of unceasing comparison, of calculation, of feeling, of reflection, necessary to obtain any result.

Yes, yes, I know what you would say…but you say nothing at all, and I swear to you by Pincio's head (that seems stupid to you; it is not to me)—I swear that I will become famous; I swear solemnly—by the Gospels, by the passion of Christ; by myself—that in four years I will be famous.

Bashkirtseff expresses her frustrations in this next excerpt dated January 2, 1879, about the restrictions which her class and gender imposed on her freedom of movement. Unlike Morisot, she struggled against these limitations and even worked actively with the UFPS to achieve greater equality with her male colleagues (Introduction to Part 1). In this era, artists assumed the role of a *flaneur*, a spectator who roams the streets observing his society. Bashkirtseff demonstrates a feminist awareness of her different position, due to her gender, in the cultural milieu of late nineteenth century Paris.

What I long for is the freedom of going about alone, of coming and going, of sitting on the seats in the Tuileries, and especially in the Luxembourg, of stopping and looking at the artistic shops, of entering the churches and museums, of walking about the old streets at night; that's what I long for; and that's the freedom without which one can't become a real artist. Do you imagine I can get much good from what I see, chaperoned as I am, and when, in order to go to the Louvre, I must wait for my carriage, my lady companion, or my family?

Curse it all, it is this that makes me gnash my teeth to think I am a woman!—I'll get myself a *bourgeois* dress and a wig, and make myself so ugly that I shall be as free as a man. It is this sort of liberty that I need, and without it I can never hope to do anything of note.

The mind is cramped by these stupid and depressing obstacles; even if I succeeded in making myself ugly by means of some disguise I should still only be half free, for a woman who rambles about alone commits an imprudence. And when it comes to Italy and Rome? The idea of going to see ruins in a landau!

"Marie, where are you going?"

"To the Coliseum."

"But you have already seen it! Let us go to the theatre or to the Promenade; we shall find plenty of people there."

And that is quite enough to make my wings droop.

This is one of the principal reasons why there are no female artists. O profound ignorance! O cruel routine! But what is the use of talking?

Even if we talked most reasonably we should be the subject to the old, well-worn scoffs with which the apostles of women are overwhelmed.

After all, there may be some cause of laughter. Women will always remain women! But still…supposing they were brought up in the way men are trained, the inequality which I regret would disappear, and there would remain only that which is inherent in nature itself. Ah, well, no matter what I may say, we shall have to go on shrieking and making ourselves ridiculous (I will leave that to others) in order to gain this equality a hundred years hence. As for myself, I will try to set an example by showing Society a woman who shall have made her mark, in spite of all the disadvantages with which it hampered her.

Bashkirtseff's hard work and determination began to produce results. Her account of winning a prize at the competition at Julian's, is lively and insightful. In this entry, dated January 14, 1879, she appreciates the support and attention while also recognizing the limitations of her profession. Criticism remains highly inflected with gendered expectations. As in the era of Vigée-Lebrun (Chapter 1), the highest form of complement is to say that the painting appeared to be the work of a young man.

I was unable to get up till half-past eleven after sitting up all night. The competition was judged this morning by the three masters—Lefebvre[8], Robert Fleury[9], and Boulanger[10]. I only reached the studio at one o' clock, and then only to learn the result. The elder girls had been examined this time, and the first words that greeted my ears as I entered were: "Well, Mlle. Marie, come along and receive your medal!"

And indeed there was my drawing fastened to the wall with a pin, and bearing the word: "Prize." I should have been less surprised had a mountain fallen on my head.

I must explain to you the importance and real meaning of these competitions. Like all other competitive examinations, they are useful, but the rewards are not always the proof of the tastes and natural ability of the individual. For it is unquestionable that Breslau, for instance, whose picture comes fifth in the list, is superior in every way to Bang, who comes first after the medal. Bang goes *piano e sano*[11], and her work is like good honest carpentering; but she always takes a high place, because women's work is in general rendered painful by its weakness and fancifulness, whenever it is not of a strictly elementary character.

The model was a lad of eighteen years, who, both in form and color, strikingly resembled a cat's head that one would make with a saucepan, or a saucepan in the form of a cat's head. Breslau[12] has painted some figures which would easily win the medal; but this time she has not succeeded. And further, it is not execution nor beauty which is most appreciated down below, for beauty has nothing to do with study, you may have it in you or not, execution being only the complement of other more important qualities; but it's above all *correctness*, boldness and *perception* of truth. They don't consider the difficulties, and they are right; therefore a good drawing is preferred to an indifferent painting. What, after all, do we do here? We study; and these hands are judged solely from that point of view. Mine is a perfect swaggerer. These gentlemen despise us, and it is only when they come across a powerful, and even brutal, piece of work, that they are satisfied; this vice is very rare amongst women.

It is the work of a young man, they said of mine. It is powerful; it is true to nature.

'I told you that we had a stunner up there,' said Robert Fleury to Lefebvre.

'You have won the medal, young lady,' said Julian, 'and it was awarded with honours; the gentlemen did not hesitate.'

I ordered a bowl of punch, as is the custom down-stairs, and Julian was called. I received congratulations, for many present imagined that I had reached the height of my ambition, and that they should get rid of me.

Wick, who won the medal at the last examination but one, is this time the eighth; but I console her by repeating to her the words of Alexandre Dumas,[13] who says so truly:—'A failure is not a proof that we have no talent, whereas one successful piece of work is a proof that we have.' This definition is, after all, the one most exactly applicable to these matters.

A genius may do a bad thing, but a fool can't do a good one.

In the following journal entry from June 20, 1882, Bashkirtseff indulges in a form of textual daydreaming of travels to Spain and to Italy. She returns again to the restrictions of her life as a women and her acute awareness of the limitations of her freedom.

Ah, well! Nothing new. An interchange of visits and painting...and Spain. Ah! Spain, it is one of Théophile Gautier's[14] books which has caused all that. Is it possible? What! I have been to Toledo, Burgos, Cordova, Seville, and Granada! Granada! What! I have visited these countries whose very names it is an honour to utter; eh, well! It is delirium. To return there! To see those marvels again! To return alone or with some of one's fellow-comrades; have I not suffered enough through going there with my relatives! O poetry! O painting! O Spain! Ah! How short life is! Ah! How unfortunate one is to live so little! For to live in Paris is only the starting-point of everything. But to go on those sublime travels—travels of connoisseurs, of artists! Six months in Spain, in Italy! Italy, sacred land; divine, incomparable Rome! It makes my head swim.

Ah! How women are to be pitied; men are at least free. Absolute independence in every-day life, liberty to come and go, to go out, to dine at an inn or at home, to walk to the Bois or the café;

this liberty is half the battle in acquiring talent, and three parts of every-day business.

But you will say, "Why don't you, superior woman as you are, seize this liberty?"

It is impossible, for the woman who emancipates herself thus, if young and pretty, is almost tabooed; she becomes singular, conspicuous, and cranky; she is censured, and is, consequently, less free than when respecting those absurd customs.

So there is nothing to be done but deplore my sex, and come back to dreams of Italy and Spain. Granada! Gigantic vegetation! Pure sky, brooks, oleanders, sun, shade, peace, calm, harmony, poetry!

In the excerpt from July 30, 1882, Bashkirtseff absorbed her discussion with her professor at Julian's, Tony Robert-Fleury. She summarizes his concerns over the degree of her discipline and vows to begin working on a new painting "something which will make them leap with astonishment." Again her ambition is quite clearly stated.

Robert Fleury came this evening, and we had a discussion about the picture...and work in general. I do not work in a satisfactory manner. For two years I have had no continuity of ideas, and so I am never able to pursue a study to the end. That is very true...he says that in order to prove to me that I make as much progress as possible considering the manner in which I work, and that the other young people work longer and better. Nothing is so effectual as perseverance and continuity; whereas a good week now and then, followed by idleness, goes for little, and does not allow of progress. But, it's true, I was ill, traveling, and without a studio...Now I have everything, and if I do not set to work I must be worthless.

The picture is a good one; I will do it well. This week my painting has been bold, but...to rid me of my despair he would have to say something more exciting; in fact, that I am as powerful as... one of the most powerful; that I can do whatever I choose; that...And he tells me, when I complain, that it is absurd, and that he has never seen any one do more in so short a time. Four years! Then he tells me that the most gifted or the most fortunate do not succeed in less than seven, eight or even ten years. Oh it's too bad!

There are moments in which I could dash my brains out. Rhetoric is of no use. I must produce something which will make them leap with astonishment, nothing else will restore my peace...

Bashkirtseff began to suffer from tuberculosis in 1884. In her journal entry from April 1, 1884, she notes, for one of the first times, that she is ill, even while she continues working in the Louvre.

I go to the Louvre this morning with Brisbane (Alice). Not that she is very interesting, as

Breslau, for instance, would have been. There is no exchange of ideas; but she is good, and fairly intelligent; she listens to me, and I think aloud. It is an exercise. I talk of what interests me, and of what I should desire. Of Bastien, naturally, for he has taken an enormous place in my conversations with Julian and Alice. I like his painting extraordinarily, and I shall seem to you very blinded if I tell you that those old dusky paintings in the Louvre make me think with pleasure of the living pictures bathed in air, with speaking eyes, and with mouths just about to open.

Well, that is my impression this morning, I do not give it as final.

I cough, and though I do not get thinner it seems to me that I am ill, only I do not want to think of it. But why then have I such a healthy look, not only in colour, but in size?

I look for the cause of my sadness and I find nothing, unless it be that I have hardly done anything for a fortnight.

About 18 months later, she recognizes the course of her illness and her impending death. She is suffering from the same illness as Bastien-Lepage, and, in fact, both artists died in 1884.

Such disgust and such sadness.
What is the good of writing?
My aunt has left for Russia on Monday; she will arrive at one o' clock in the morning.

Bastien grows from bad to worse.

And I can't work.

My picture will not be done.

There, there, there!

He is sinking, and suffers terribly. When I am there I feel detached from the earth, he floats above us already; there are days when I, too, feel like that. You see people, they speak to you, you answer them, but you are no longer of the earth; it is a tranquil but painless indifference, a little like an opium-eater's dream. In a word, he is dying. I only go there from habit; it is his shadow, I also am half a shadow; what's the use?

He does not particularly feel my presence, I am useless; I have not the gift to rekindle his eyes. He is glad to see me. That's all.

Yes, he is dying, and I don't care; I don't realize it; is something which is passing away. Besides, all is over.

All is over.

I shall be buried in 1885.

In the final entry, written just months before her death, she records her condition, and tells of a visit by Bastien-Lepage. Even at this advanced stage of her illness, she retains her humor and self-awareness of the impression she makes on her colleague. Her journal records a woman of great intelligence who lived her life and also observed it with a detached objectivity, which seems remarkable.

I have a terrible amount of fever, which exhausts me. I spend all my time in the *salon*, changing from the easy-chair to the sofa.

Dina reads novels to me. Potain came yesterday, he will come again tomorrow. This man no longer needs money, and if he comes, it is because he takes some little interest in me.

I can no longer go out at all, but poor Bastien-Lepage comes to me; he is carried here, put in an easy-chair, and stretched out on cushions—I am in another chair drawn up close by, and so we sit until six o' clock.

I was dressed in a cloud of white lace and plush, all different shades of white; the eyes of Bastien-Lepage dilated with delight.

"Oh, if I could only paint!" said he.

And I—

Finis. And so ends the picture of this year!

The publication of Bashkirtseff's journal had an impact beyond the relatively narrow confines of the art world of the 1890s. She inspired an entire generation of young women to write her lives and find the creative space to liberate themselves from the gendered limitations of the ideology of the era. Her impact and "agency" occurs with the publication of the journal, rather than from her visual art, whose development was curtailed by her early death. Even in the carefully edited form of the published diary a new woman emerged, who embraced a level of personal freedom, ambition, and autonomy shocking to her contemporaries. From the 84 handwritten notebooks, the nearly 700 published and translated pages were more than adequate to paint a picture of a young woman living in Paris and internalizing the new feminist ideas in circulation. While actually writing the diary it is possible that Bashkirtseff was not committed to its publication. However, from the preface it is clear that she had a measure of control over the editing process and fully intended the world to read her most intimate thoughts. Unlike the extremely private Morisot, Bashkirtseff was a young woman who was determined to become a celebrity. This makes her unique among the group of artist/writers discussed in the preceding chapters. Remaining unmarried, Bashkirtseff's identity emerges in the fragmented, discontinuous mode of the journal with clarity and consistency. This is a woman of great ambition, who is committed to working as hard as necessary to become a painter. She applied that same level of discipline in the virtually daily maintenance of the journal, using the relatively new diary format to redefine herself and eventually to present herself to the world.

Notes

[1] Jules Bastien-Lepage (1848-1884).

[2] Introduction by Rozsika Parker and Griselda Pollock in *The Journal of Marie Bashkirtseff*, Mathilde Blind, trans., (reprinted London: Virago Press, 1985), xxvii.

[3] Philippe Lejeune, "The *journal de jeune fille* in Nineteenth–Century France" in Suzanne L. Bunkers

and Cynthia A. Huff (editors) *Inscribing the Daily: Critical Essays on Women's Diaries* (Amherst, University of Massachusetts Press, 1996), 108-09.

4   These issues are summarized in Parker and Pollock introduction to *The Journal of Marie Bashkirtseff.* See Colette Cosnier, *Marie Bashkirtseff: Un Portrait Sans Retouches* (Paris: Editions Pierre Horay, 1985).

5   Lejeune, in Bunkers and Huff, *Inscribing the Daily: Critical Essays on Women's Diaries*, 119.

6   *Journal of Marie Bashkirtseff,* p. vi

7   Margo Cully, Introduction, *A Day at a Time; the Diary Literature of American Women from 1764 to the Present* (New York: The Feminist Press at the City University of New York, 1985), 7.

8   Jules Joseph Lefebvre (1836-1911).

9   Tony Robert Fleury (1837-1911) was a history and genre painter who exhibited regularly in the official Salon and was an instructor at the Académie Julian.

10   Gustave Boulanger (1824-1888) was a French painter who won the Prix de Rome in 1849 and painted in a highly polished, conservative academic style.

11   Slow and steady

12   Louise C. Breslau (1856-1927) was a Swiss painter studying with Bashkirtseff.

13   Alexandre Dumas (1802-1972) was a popular French novelist.

14   Théophile Gautier (1811-1872) was a French writer who was well known for his travel accounts.

Introduction to Part 2: The Early Twentieth Century; Private Writing Made Public (1900-1940)

Compared with the nineteenth century, the decades between 1900 and 1940, witnessed significant improvements in women's educational opportunities in the visual arts and the eventual elimination of institutional discrimination. In the United States, by the beginning of the second decade of the twentieth century, one could say that virtually all major obstacles toward equal access to training had been removed. Ironically, this became a somewhat less urgent issue, since the power and influence of art academies and their conservative technical education were waning in significance in the art world.

However, other more subtle areas of gender inequality still remained. Just as women artists began to achieve professional parity with men, the discourse of "Modernism" was becoming a significant critical tool, which continued to marginalize women. In an important study of women artists who were active during the Weimar era of the 1920s in Germany, Marsha Meskimmon has noted that:

"Women were an integral part of the social, economic and cultural exchanges characterized as 'modern' yet all too frequently their contributions to modernism as active participants... have been undervalued if not effaced. Simply, the modernist canon, as it has been constructed, leaves women (and 'woman') outside its frame as 'not modern enough.' "[1]

As we will see in Part 3, the strength of Modernism, in the post World War II era, continued to work against recognition of women artists in Euro-American culture.

Both Paula Modersohn–Becker and Käthe Kollwitz, the subjects of the first two chapters, were German. In the late nineteenth and early twentieth centuries, Germany was different in significant ways that directly impacted women artists. Important artists such as Modersohn–Becker and Kollwitz emerged later, in the early twentieth century, as opposed to the interlocking artistic environment of England, France and the United States, defined in Part 1. Germany became a "nation" following its unification after 1871 which was quite late in European history. Germany was both politically authoritarian and strongly patriarchal, in a culture still dominated by Prussian values. German middle class women began to organize into feminist groups in the 1860s, even before unification. However, the bourgeois National German Women's association, founded in 1865, largely accepted traditional gender ideology, which associated women with maternal, nurturing "instincts."[2] German feminists subordinated their political priorities to the Liberal party, dominated by men, who opposed suffrage. German women were ultimately enfranchised by the socialist revolutionary government in the immediate aftermath of World War I, not through the efforts of the bourgeois feminist movement.

Through the nineteenth century education for German girls, in sexually segregated schools, was inferior to that available for boys of similar class backgrounds. Most women employed outside the home were teachers. In 1878, there were about 1,500 women teaching in Prussian elementary schools, and by 1900, that number had exploded to 22,000. Paula Becker obtained a teaching credential before her father would permit her to study art (Chapter 7). After 1900, there were increasing numbers of women working outside the home, in jobs other than teaching, such as in sales and clerical positions, social work, and postal and railroad administration.[3]

The Verein der Kunstlerinnin, the official German women's art organization, ran independent schools for women in Berlin, Munich, and Karlsruhe. As far as we know the leaders of this organization did not promote the integration of women into the official government school for "fine arts," unlike the comparable situations in France and England. As in other countries, there were applied and decorative arts schools open to women.

Kollwitz attended the school run by the Verein, in Berlin, in 1885 (Chapter 8). This school was discriminatory to women since it cost six times the tuition of the Prussian Royal Academy, and offered a less rigorous course of study.[4] When Paula Becker studied at the same school in 1896, there were separate departments for drawing, painting, and graphics. Most of the professors were men, but a few women also taught at this school. From 1897 to 1902 Kollwitz taught figure drawing and graphics in this institution.

The impact of the schools run by the Verein became felt in the 1890s. In the early 1890s about 10% of full time artists were women. By 1907, the number of women artists grew twice as fast as male artists, with over a 100% increase in women active in the field.[5] Beth Irwin Lewis concludes that: "Women artists were quietly but steadily becoming a visible presence in the art world.[6] In her excellent study of this era, using the evidence of art publications, Lewis correlates this enlarged population of women artists with a corresponding increase in misogynist imagery in paintings by male artists:

"The growing number of accomplished women artists only served to raise the level of resistance to their presence…readers of *Die Kunst für Alle*[7] were confronted simultaneously with evidence of women as professional artists and with visual condemnation of woman as the embodiment of depraved sexuality."[8]

This is the background against which both Modersohn-Becker and Kollwitz emerged as historically important artists.

The highest mark of recognition in Germany was admission into the Prussian Academy of Art. In the early twentieth century, only "honorary", as opposed to "regular" membership, was available to women artists. This category was also used to recognize men who helped promote the arts but was never applied to practicing male artists. Following the war in 1919, Kollwitz was the only woman admitted into the Prussian Academy.

Although German women constituted between one-fourth and one-third of all published novelists in the nineteenth century, very few women wrote autobiographies.[9] Only about 500 women published autobiographies as opposed to 1000's of German men. The autobiography was a literary genre believed to be more appropriate to male identity and achievements. Georg Misch, a German, published, *History of Autobiography in Antiquity*, in 1907 in which his concept of life narrative that excluded women exercised a "profound impact" on subsequent twentieth century studies of these texts [10] (Introduction, II, a).

As one might expect, literary criticism of women's writing was strongly colored by gender stereotypes. Discussion of women's writing seemed to focus on the "unimportant and redundant detail...this contempt for the woman's world is typical of prevailing contemporary opinion. It is thus not surprising that women find it difficult to report on their own lives, especially when extraordinary events are missing."[11]

Predictably, Modersohn-Becker and Kollwitz confined their literary output to the private forms of the letter and journal entry. Both women wrote extensively and in their journal entries, especially, one can appreciate the importance of writing for their creative processes. Fortunately, their texts were preserved, and published posthumously.

The other two chapters in Part 2 find their historical framework in the post-World War I milieu of New York, for Georgia O'Keeffe (Chapter 9), and in Mexico, for Frida Kahlo (Chapter 10). In many countries, men and women experienced the traumatic effects of the war differently. While men were actively engaged in fighting, women were recruited to fill the vacant jobs abandoned due to male mass conscription. A reward for women's contribution to the war effort was the right to vote, which was granted in nineteen countries between 1915 and 1922. However, following the war, and despite these political gains, there was an anti-feminist backlash in many counties. Population losses and the need to provide employment for war veterans were two key factors which converged to promote a cultural ideology which encouraged women to stay in the home and devote themselves to childbearing and mothering. Between 1900 and 1940, the percentage of women in the work force rose only slightly.[12]

By 1935, in the United States, 41% of identified practicing artists receiving government subsidies were women.[13] This statistic is based on the census data collected by the US federal government. Although 41% still constitutes a minority, it is quite a large minority. Women were now a major component of the overall population of artists. Alice Neel received assistance from the Works Project Administration (WPA) (Chapter 11). Designs for mural projects were submitted, unsigned, and women finally had the opportunity to be judged in a "gender-blind" manner with their male colleagues.

Although O'Keeffe was 20 years older than Kahlo, both artists' periods of greatest productivity and recognition took place during the interwar decades. As we will see, both of these artists internalized the prevalent discourse of nationalism. O'Keeffe and Kahlo, with Canadian Emily Carr, are analyzed together in an interesting study by Sharyn Udall, who discusses the common ideologies and iconographical motifs among these three artists.[14]

The genres of autobiographical texts, written by the subjects of Part 2 are similar. All four artist/ authors wrote letters and Modersohn-Becker, Kollwitz and Kahlo also kept journals. Like Hosmer, Bonheur, and Morisot, Kollwitz's volume is an **auto/biography** (Introduction II,d) since her son edited her writings, posthumously. The texts of the other three artists were edited by contemporary art historians. All primary sources were published posthumously and translated into English.

Chapter 7 is devoted to Paula Modersohn-Becker, who died at the early age of 31, following complications from the birth of her only child. In this short time, she created over 1200 paintings, drawings and etchings, which is sufficient to qualify her as one of the most innovative German artists of her generation. She synthesized French Post Impressionist styles with the earth-toned palette and naturalism of the Worpswede painters, a group which includes her husband

Otto Modersohn,[15] into a body of innovative works. She was an equally prolific writer, producing over 400 pages of letters and diary entries. A selected group of her texts was first published around 1920. However, it was not until the early 1980s that a complete edition of her writings first appeared, translated into English.

Käthe Kollwitz, the subject of Chapter 8, was a much more famous woman artist than Modersohn-Becker. By the 1890s, Kollwitz had developed an innovative style of printmaking. She enjoyed widespread professional recognition in the years prior to World War I. During the Weimar era of the 1920s, Kollwitz's prints were quite famous and she was somewhat of a celebrity, at least in her native Germany. Her working life spanned much of the early twentieth century. She created prints through the 1920s and her output was curtailed only by the persecution of the Nazis, in the 1930s. Like Modersohn-Becker, Kollwitz's literary output is composed mainly of journal entries and letters to family and friends. She did write a brief retrospective autobiographical text, *The Early Years*, excerpted below. This essay is a **memoir** in its focus on her early development as an artist (Introduction II,a).

The focus of Chapter 9 is Georgia O'Keeffe, perhaps, the most famous American artist active in the 1920s. Her best known works are large scaled paintings of flowers, but she also created haunting, powerful images of New Mexico, where she eventually settled. O'Keeffe guarded her privacy and her reputation carefully, while she was alive. She did write a **memoir** in 1976 which was published in *Georgia*

O'Keeffe, excerpted below. In 1987, the year after her death, a selection of O'Keeffe's letters first appeared in a major exhibition catalogue, published by the National Gallery of Art. These letters to family, friends, and colleagues provide a much more intimate sense of O'Keeffe's voice, compared with her laconic statements published in the exhibition catalogues of her solo shows. The other texts in Chapter 9 are letters which were addressed to a range of correspondents.

Chapter 10 includes both letters and diary entries written by Frida Kahlo. Kahlo is a true "celebrity" of the twenty-first century. She is best known for her autobiographical paintings and a powerful series of self-portraits created mainly in the 1930s and 1940s. During her life, she worked in virtual total isolation. Given her immense popularity today, it is actually surprising that it was only a few years ago, in 2006, that a comprehensive collection of her letters, translated into English, was published.[16] Kahlo kept a journal during the last decade of her life, from 1944 to 1954. This fascinating diary contains images as well as texts and was published, in facsimile, with English translations and annotations, in 1995. [17]

The unifying factor among these four artist/ authors, from the perspective of life narratives, is the dominating role of private writing. All were active correspondents who used letters to discuss their works, making them important primary sources for art historians. Following the example of Bashkirtseff (Chapter 6), maintaining a diary was an important part of the creative process for Modersohn-Becker,

Kollwitz, and Kahlo. When private writing is made public, it is a powerful resource for understanding the visual art and personalities of these creative women.

Notes

[1] Marsha Meskimmon, *We Weren't Modern Enough: Women Artists and the Limits of German Modernism* (Berkeley and Los Angeles: University of California Press, 1999), 3.

[2] Amy Hackett, "Feminism and Liberalism in Wilhelmine Germany, 1890-1918" in Berenice A. Carroll (ed) *Liberating Women's History: Theoretical and Critical Essays* (London and Urbana, Chicago, IL: University of Illinois Press, 1976), 127.

[3] James Albisetti, "Women and the Professions in Imperial Germany" in Ruth-Ellen B. Joeres and Mary Jo Maynes (eds) *German Women in the Eighteenth and Nineteenth Centuries: A Social and Literary History* (Bloomington, IN: Indiana University Press, 1986), 94ff.

[4] J. Diane Radycki, "The Life of Lady Art Students: Changing Art Education at the Turn of the Century", *Art Journal* vol. 42, no. 1 (Spring,1982), 9ff.

[5] Ibid., 215.

[6] Beth Irwin Lewis, *Art for All?: The Collision of Modern Art and the Public in Late-Nineteenth-Century Germany,* (Princeton and Oxford: Princeton University Press, 2003), 207.

[7] *Die Kunst für Alle* (The art for all) was a journal that attempted to create "a new cultural politics that would transform the diverse German people into a new unified nation." Lewis, *Art for All?*, 38.

[8] Ibid., 289-290.

[9] Patricia Herminghouse, "Women and the Literary Enterprise in Nineteenth-Century Germany" in Joeres and Maynes, *German Women in the Eighteenth and Nineteenth Centuries: A Social and Literary History*, 78ff.

[10] Sidonie Smith and Julia Watson, *Reading Autobiography: A Guide for Interpreting Life Narratives* (Minneapolis and London, University of Minnesota Press. 2001) 114.

[11] Gudrun Wedel, "…Nothing More than a Woman: Remarks on the Biographical and Autobiographical Tradition of the Women of One Family, "in Joeres and Maynes (eds), *German Women in the Eighteenth and Nineteenth Centuries: A Social and Literary History*, 309.

[12] Alice Kessler Harris, "Women, Work, and the Social Order," in Carroll (ed), *Liberating Women's History: Theoretical and Critical Essays*, 330ff.

[13] Quoted in Harris and Nochlin, 63: Statistics from K. A. Marling and H. A. Harrison, *Seven American Women: the Depression Decade* (Poughkeepsie, NY, Vassar College Art Gallery, 1976).

[14] Sharyn R. Udall, *Carr, O'Keeffe, Kahlo: Places of Their Own* (New Haven, CN: Yale University Press, 2000).

[15] Otto Modersohn (1865-1943).

[16] Raquel Tibol (ed), *Frida by Frida*, translated by Gregory Dechant (Mexico: Editorial RM, 2006).

[17] *The Diary of Frida Kahlo: an Intimate Self-Portrait* (New York: Harry N. Abrams, 1995).

Chapter 7. Paula Modersohn–Becker (1876-1907): Letters and Journal

By the time of her pre-mature death at age 31, the German artist, Paula Modersohn–Becker, had created a distinctive body of works. She was the first German artist to forge an original style, developed with an understanding of the innovations of French Post-Impressionism. One of her famous images is *Self Portrait with Amber Necklace* (1906), the first nude self-portrait by a woman artist, in the history of art.

Paula Becker was born into an upper-middle-class family in Dresden, with no connections to the art world. In 1892, when she was just 16, she lived in England with relatives, and received her first regular art instruction, at St. John's Wood School of Art. This was a serious art school, which prepared students for admission into the British Royal Academy. She struggled to define herself as an artist to her family. Her father insisted that she acquire a teaching degree. Therefore, from 1893 to 1895, she was enrolled at the Bremen Seminary for women teachers. As noted in the Introduction to Part 2, there was a huge demand and an increase in the number of women teachers at this time. Only after this "practical" training was she permitted to study at the school run by the German women artists' organization, the Verein der Kün-stlerinnen. This school, segregated by gender, offered the most complete and professional instruction, then available to aspiring German women artists (Introduction to Part 2).

In 1897, she discovered the artist's colony of Worp-swede, in a small village in northern Germany. Here the artists frequently painted local peasants, set in the landscape, in a dark, earth-toned naturalistic palette. During her extended stay, from 1898 to 1899, she studied with the leading artist of the group, Fritz Mackensen.[1] She met her close friend Clara Westhoff,[2] a sculptor and future wife of the poet Rainer Maria Rilke,[3] and her future husband, Otto Modersohn,[4] who was then married.

On New Year's Eve 1900, Becker left Worspwede for Paris and entered the next phase of her life as an artist. Between 1900 and her death in 1907, she made four trips to Paris, the last one stretching from February 1906 to April 1907. In Paris, she studied at the Académie Colarossi and at the Académie Julian, where Marie Bashkirtseff had worked (Chapter 6). She even took advantage of the anatomy course recently opened to women at the official École des Beaux Arts (Introduction to Part 1).

In 1901, returning to Worspwede, Becker married the recently widowed Otto Modersohn. This created conflicts when she continued to travel, independently, to Paris. In 1906, Otto Modersohn joined Paula in Paris. She became pregnant and returned with him to Worpswede in 1907. She died just three weeks after giving birth to a daughter.

Over about a 10 year period, she created 560 paintings, over 700 drawings, and 13 etchings, none of which were commercially exhibited during her lifetime. She did submit work, in 1906, to the Kunsthalle in Bremen.[5] Her most characteristic paintings were created during the latter part of her career following her move to Worpswede, her experiences in Paris, and her marriage to Otto Modersohn. Many of her images deal with the poor peasantry around Worpswede. However, during her last prolonged trip to Paris, in 1906-7, she created a series of famous, monumentally scaled mother and child images, as well as her nude *Self Portrait*.

Stylistically, her work evolved from the tight, linear rendition, which she was taught in her academic training, to the naturalistic forms, favored by the artists of the Worspwede colony. Eventually, she developed her own unique style. This personal style clearly shows the influence of Van Gogh,[6] in her use of saturated colors, Gauguin,[7] in her smoothly flowing "synthetic" contours and flattened spaces, and Cézanne,[8] in the density of surfaces and movement away from Impressionist illusionism.

Her literary output was equally prolific. She actively corresponded with her family, friends and colleagues and many of her letters have survived. She also maintained a private journal. Like Bashkirtseff, Modersohn-Becker first became famous through her life writing rather than her visual art. The first edition of her selected letters and journal entries was published in 1917, and revised in 1920. It was widely read and reprinted many times, before World War II. In 1979, the definitive edition of her writing, containing over 400 pages, was published, in German, and subsequently translated into English. This volume includes "every known word written by the artist."[9] Therefore, unlike the letters of Hosmer (Chapter 2) and Morisot (Chapter 5), or the journal of Marie Bashkirtseff (Chapter 6), Modersohn-Becker's writings are published in a complete unedited format.

As noted above, Paula Becker's decision to become an artist met with resistance from her family. She had to convince them, especially her father, of her vocation. In this first letter, addressed to her father and dated February 27, 1897, Becker is acknowledging the receipt of a box of pastel chalks. She is writing from Berlin, where she is enrolled in the art school of the Verein der Künstlerinnen and expresses her joy at being able to look at original drawings by Michelangelo. She also recounts her experience in her life-drawing class. The letter tells us that she is fully immersed in an academic course of study in which she is grappling with the human form, in this case a male figure, indicating her seriousness and her commitment to acquiring the skills of an artist. After her years studying to be a teacher, her elation at being able to focus on her art is quite evident.

Dear Father, after a morning of hard work it is such a pleasure to sit down and thank you for that beautiful box of pastels. I keep looking at the rows of magnificent crayons and can hardly wait to begin using them.

My model right now is a little Hungarian boy, a mousetrapper, who cannot understand a single word of German, so that it is impossible to scold him when he comes every morning half an hour late. But is such fun drawing him.

Last Thursday after class I went to see the Kupferstichkabinett [Print Room] for the first time. I had stood at the glass entrance several times before, but the solemn gloom behind it always frightened me away. Yesterday I took heart and went in, feeling like an intruder in the sanctum sanctorum. An attendant came up to me and silently handed me a slip of paper on which I had to write down what I wanted to look at; "Michelangelo, drawings by"… He brought me a gigantic folio. I could hardly wait to look inside. At the same time, being the only woman in the midst of this overpowering masculinity, I would have given anything to make myself invisible. But as soon as I opened the folio and could study Michelangelo's powerful draftsmanship, I could forget the whole rest of the world. What limbs that man could draw!

We had the most amazing model that evening in life-drawing class. At first, the way he stood there, I was shocked at how ugly and thin he seemed. But as soon as he began to pose and when he tensed all his muscles so that they rippled down his back, I became very excited. How strange and wonderful, my dears, that I can react this way! That I am able to live totally in my art! It is so wonderful. Now if I can only turn this into something good. But I won't even think about that now—it just makes me uneasy.

The next two entries are from her journal and are dated October 29 and November 11, 1898. Here, she records her personal reflections on the style and iconography for her art. She uses the journal as a way to define her ideas and clarify her feelings. The journal entries show her creative thought processes, as she tries to define her own responses. These entries are significant, because she has selected the theme of a "Worpswede Madonna", already explored by Fritz Mackensen. This theme will occupy her over the next eight or so years, until her own pregnancy terminated her life. She continued to draw these women, and to be inspired by them. In the second journal entry, she is continuing to work on the nude form, using a child as a model. She also notes that she is reading Marie Bashkirtseff's diary (Chapter 6).

October 29, 1898: I sketched a young mother with her child at her breast, sitting in a smoky hut. If only I could someday paint what I felt then! A sweet woman, an image of charity. She was nursing her big, year-old bambino, when with defiant eyes her four-year-old daughter snatched for her breast until she was given it. And the woman gave her life and her youth and her power to the child in utter simplicity, unaware that she was a heroine.

November 11, 1898: I'm drawing nudes in the evening now, life-size, beginning with little Meta Fijol[10] and her pious Saint Cecilia face. When I told her that she should take all her clothes off, this spirited little person said, "Oh, no, I ain't doin' none of that." So at first she got only half undressed. But yesterday I bribed her with a mark and she complied. I blushed inside, hating the seducer in me. She is a small, crooked-legged creature. But I'm still happy to have a chance to study the human figure at my leisure again.

I am now reading the diary of Marie Bashkirtsev [sic]. It is very interesting. I am completely carried away when I read it. Such an incredible observer of her own life. And me? I have squandered my first twenty years. Or is it possible that they form the quiet foundation on which my next twenty years are to be built?

The following letter was written just a few weeks after Becker arrived in Paris for the first time. It is addressed to Otto and Helene Modersohn and documents her excitement in this large city. She also confesses to being intimidated by the scale of Paris. She writes about the physical conditions of her life and the companionship of Clara Westhoff. Her close friendship with both Otto and his wife seems to be clearly expressed in this lively, humorous, and intimate letter, dated January 17, 1900. Towards the end of this letter, she states her belief in the superiority of the German people, evidence of the pervasive nationalism of the pre-World War I era.

Whenever I have felt most helpless here in Paris, I always let my thoughts wander back to Worpswede. That is always a splendid remedy. It disperses the chaos in me and brings a kind of gentle repose. Of course, Paris is wonderful, but one needs nerves, nerves, and more nerves—strong, fresh, and receptive nerves. To keep them under control in the face of these overpowering impressions here is not easy...

The Louvre! The Louvre has me in its clutches. Every time I'm there rich blessings rain down upon me. I am coming to understand Titian more and more and learning to love him. And then there is Boticelli's sweet Madonna, with red roses behind her, standing against a blue-green sky. And Fiesole with his poignant little biblical stories, so simply told, often so glorious in their colors. I feel so well in this society of saints—and then the Corots[11], Rousseaus[12], Millets[13] that you told me about. There are wonderful pictures by Millet to be seen now at the art dealers'. The most beautiful one to me was of a man in a field who is putting on his jacket, painted against a brilliant evening sky. ...

Mornings I go to an academy (Cola Rossi). I have had some very fine critiques there, especially by Courtois[14], who has a fine feeling for *valeurs*. Collin[15], who does the more practical criticism at the start of each week, is more concerned with accuracy—

For two weeks I put up with the dirty housekeeping in a dirty atelier. But since last Sunday I have been living in a dollhouse atelier with my own furniture, i.e., one bench, one table, one chair. Everything else is made of boxes covered with cretonne. It must be grand to have money and to be able to furnish one's home here. There are so many fine secondhand shops here, and thousands of fine things. Often I get into a rage and then I go into the shops and ask what the things cost. After I've taken a good look around then I calm down and saunter away—

There are as many painters here as there are grains of sand on the beach. And among them one sees some fairly eccentric phenomena. When one is in a good mood, one can be amused by it all. But when one feels weak, one is easily overcome by the creeping malaise. "All humanity's misery lays hold of me." One sees so frightfully much misery here, much that is corrupt and degenerate. I do think that we Germans are better people...

Your Paula Becker

Clara Westhoff lives in the same house with me; she is doing over-lifesize sculpture here in Paris and sends her best regards.

If you have any plans at all to write to me sometime, then please do it on February 8. That, you see, is my birthday.

The letter written to her father the next day, January 18, 1900, is quite different in tone. She is responding to his criticism of her decision to strike out on her own, to follow her ambitions, and to go to Paris. Also, her father is not pleased about her association with Westhoff. Working without her family's support, or at least in an environment of parental disapproval, surely increased the pressure and strain on Becker, perhaps propelling her into the marriage with Otto Modersohn the following year. She ends on a resolute note, reaffirming her own decision to become an artist.

My dear father,

Many thanks for your two long letters. Don't look at the world and me so darkly. You will feel far better, and so will the two of us poor abused people, if only we could be left with that little bit of rosy hue which does, in fact, exist. In the end, though, it doesn't make that much difference to us.

So you are upset by my recent move? As far as order is concerned, it's a step forward. The old *hotel* furniture and carpets were worn and filthy beyond redemption. Where I am now everything is clean. Fairly empty, but pleasant. As to expense, both places are about the same.

It's almost like spring here now. I am sitting at an open window. Outside a friendly sun is shining. I am happy that we are being spared your cold weather, because the fireplaces here tend to tease much more than they actually warm us.

A few words about the Académie. Today I had my critique from Courtois. He hits the nail on the head, short and to the point. He has an eye for what I want and doesn't want to push me in another direction. I learned much from him today and am very happy. I have registered for a morning course in life drawing. At the beginning of each week Girardot and Collin come and criticize the accuracy of our work...

In the afternoon there is a course in *croquis*[16] also from the nude in which for two hours we draw models in four different poses. This is very instructive for understanding movement. Each of us pays a fee for this course every afternoon. That way we are not bound to it, and every so often can take a trip to the Louvre instead. The Old Masters there also do their part in helping me along.

I am taking different courses than Clara Westhoff is. In fact, my style of living is totally different from hers. Enough for today. Your two letters did depress me a little. They made you sound so thoroughly dissatisfied with me. I, too, can see no end to the whole thing. I must calmly follow my path, and when I get to where I can accomplish something, things will be better. None of you, to be sure, seems to have much faith in me. But I do.

In this journal entry dated July 26, 1900, she has returned from her first stay in Paris and has written an eerily precise premonition of the shortness of her life.[17] Becker writes poetically of her desires and her seeming acceptance that even though she will not live a long life, into old age, she still has time to accomplish something important.

As I was painting today, some thoughts came to me and I want to write them down for the people I love. I know that I shall not live very long. But I wonder, is that sad? Is a celebration more beautiful because it lasts longer? And my life is a celebration, a short, intense celebration. My powers of perception are becoming finer, as if I were supposed to absorb everything in the few years that are still to be offered me, everything. My sense of smell is unbelievably keen at present. With almost every breath I take, I get a new sense and understanding of the linden tree, of ripened wheat, of hay, and of mignonette. I suck everything up into me. And if only now love would blossom for me, before I depart, and if I can paint three good pictures, then I shall go gladly, with flowers in my hair. ..

Paula Becker married Otto Modersohn on May 25, 1901, and, as was customary in Germany, accepted his name hyphenated with hers. From this time on she is known as Modersohn-Becker. In the next journal entry from February 1903, Modersohn-Becker is using the writing process to define her goals and to clarify a direction for her painting. She is moving away from Worpswede naturalism. This is considered to be "one of her most important self-analytical statements."[18] This and the following letter are written during her second stay in Paris, a rather brief sojourn of only two months.

February 20, 1903: I must learn how to express the gentle vibration of things, their roughened textures, and their intricacies. I have to find an expression for that in my drawing, too, in the way I sketch my nudes here in Paris, only more original, more subtly observed. The strange quality of expectation that hovers over muted things (skin, Otto's forehead, fabrics, flowers); I must try to get hold of the great and simple beauty of all that. In general, I must strive for the utmost simplicity united with the most intimate power of observation. That's where greatness lies. In looking at the life-size nude of Frau M., the simplicity of the body called my attention to the simplicity of the head. It made me feel how much it's in my blood to want to overdo things.

To get back again to that "roughened intricacy of things": that's the quality that I find so pleasing in old marble or sandstone sculptures that have been out in the open, exposed to the weather. I like it, this roughened alive surface...

When I'm out in the street I sometimes feel the same mood I felt three years ago. I feel like a queen hidden behind veils, with everything rushing and roaring past me.

In the following letter to her husband, dated March 2, 1903, Paula recounts her visit to the studio of Rodin.[19] She is urging Modersohn to come to Paris, to expose himself to the range of modern art only available in the French capital. Modersohn-Becker is overwhelmed by Rodin's powerful work, which one could only see at this time in Rodin's own studio. She gains admittance to his studio with a letter from Rilke, the poet, and Clara Westhoff's husband. (Rilke will soon become Rodin's personal secretary.) Despite Rilke's friendship with Modersohn-Becker, he introduces her as "the wife of a very distinguished painter." This frequently quoted detail seems shocking today, in the way it dismisses her talent and her extensive body of work. However, it does provide some insight into the cultural obstacles facing a woman artist, especially when married to an older, more established, artist.

My dear Spouse,

Just listen, I'm getting the feeling more and more that you must come here, too. There are so many reasons why you should. But I'll tell you only one, a great reason, the greatest: Rodin.

You must get an impression of this man and of his life's work, which he has gathered together in castings all around him. I have the feeling that we shall probably never experience anything like this again in our lifetime. This great art came into full blossom with incredible determination, silently, and almost hidden from view. The impression Rodin makes is a very great one. It is hard for me to talk about any single work of his because one must keep coming back to it often, and in all one's various moods, in order to completely absorb it. He has done the work almost in spite of the rest of the world, and it exudes such a wonderful feeling—he doesn't care whether the world approves or not. Instead he has one conviction, firm as a rock: that it is beauty itself which he means to bring into the world. There are many who pay him some heed, although most of the French put him into the same pot with Boucher[20] and Injalbert[21] and whatever the names of all those other dim lights are.

But I want to tell you everything chronologically.

Armed with a little calling card from Rilke, which referred to me as *"femme d'un peintre tres distingue,"* [22] I went to Rodin's studio last Saturday afternoon, his usual day for receiving people. There were all sorts of people there already. He didn't even look at the card, just nodded and let me wander freely among his marble sculpture. So many wonderful things there. But some I cannot understand. Nevertheless, I don't dare judge those too quickly. As I was leaving, I asked him if it would be possible to visit his *pavillon* in Meudon, and he said that it would be at my disposal on Sunday. And so I was permitted to wander about the *pavillon* undisturbed. What wealth of work is there and such worship of nature; that's really beautiful. He always starts from nature. And all his drawings, all his compositions, he does from life. The remarkable dreams of form which he quickly tosses onto paper are to me the most original aspect of all his art. He uses the most simple and sparse means. He draws with pencil and then shades in with strange, almost passionate, watercolors. It is a passion and a genius which dominate in these drawings, and a total lack of concern for convention. The first thing that comes into my mind to compare them with are those old Japanese works which I saw during my first week here, and perhaps also ancient frescoes or those figures on antique vases. *You simply must see them.* Their colors are a remarkable inspiration, especially for a painter. He showed them to me himself and was so charming and friendly to me. Yes, whatever it is that makes art extraordinary is what he has. In addition there is his piercing conviction that all beauty is in nature. He used to make up these compositions in his head but found that he was still being too conventional. Now he draws only from models. When he is in fresh form he does twenty of them in an hour and a half. His *pavillon* and his two other ateliers lie in the midst of strangely intersecting hills which are covered with a growth of stubbly grass. There is a wonderful view down to the Seine and the villages along it, and even as far as the domes of Paris. The building where he lives is small and confined and gives one the feeling that the act of living itself plays hardly any role for him. "La travaille [sic], c'est mon bonheur," [23] he says.

On February 23, 1906, Modersohn-Becker left Worpswede, and her life with her husband, and returned to Paris for what would prove to be her final and longest stay in the city. About two weeks after she departed, on March 9, she wrote Modersohn the following letter, in which she acknowledges that she is ready for a permanent separation. She is spending time with her younger sister, Herma. She also indicates a desire to study at the École des Beaux Arts. Opening this prestigious school to women had been a victory for the UFPS, about ten years earlier (Introduction to Part 1).

Dear Otto,
Your many long letters lie here before me. They make me sad. Over and over again there is the same cry in them, and I simply cannot give you the answer you would like to have. Dear

Otto, please let some time pass peacefully and let us both just wait and see how I feel later. Only, dear, you must try to grasp the thought that our paths will separate.

I wish so much that my decision hadn't made you and my family suffer so. But what else can I do? The only remedy is time, which slowly and surely heals all wounds—

I am happy for you that you have sold two paintings; that ought to bring at least a little cheer to these difficult times.

I wonder if you have been good enough to mail my drawings to me? I should like to have them here for admission to the Ecole des Beaux-Arts. Even with them it is far from being a sure thing. Everyone says it is a fine place to work and that it is also cheaper. However, in case you haven't sent them off, please don't bother now. They would arrive too late, and I can still enroll in one of the private schools.

I am beginning to settle in here. This past week the weather has been wonderful, warm enough to make one walk on the shady side of the street. It is very beautiful stepping outside in the evening after the drawing lessons and see-ing the great city spread out in the blue twilight, punctuated with the lighted streetlamps—

Dear Otto, I squeeze your hand and send you heartfelt greetings.

Your Paula

During this last stay in Paris, she worked with great concentration and determination, creating many of her most mature and famous works. The next letter, dated September 3, 1906 is written prior to Modersohn's impending arrival in Paris for the winter. This letter begs him not to come, but also documents a total financial dependence on him. However in the next letter, written six days later, her ambivalence emerges, and she rescinds her earlier rejection agreeing to his upcoming visit, the resumption of marital sexual relations, and the acceptance of his desire for her to bear his child.

Dear Otto,

The time is getting closer for you to be coming. Now I must ask you for your sake and mine, please spare both of us this time of trial. Let me go, Otto. I do not want you as my husband. I do not want it. Accept this fact. Don't torture yourself any longer. Try to let go of the past—I ask you to arrange all other things according to your wishes and desires. If you still enjoy having my paintings, then pick out those you wish to keep. Please do not take any further steps to bring us back together. It would only prolong the torment.

I must still ask you to send money, one final time. I ask you for the sum of five hundred marks. I am going to the country for a while now, so please send it to B. Hoetger,[24] 108, rue Vaugirard. During this time I intend to take steps to secure my livelihood.

I thank you for all the goodness that I have had from you. There is nothing else I can do.

Dear Otto,

My harsh letter was written during a time when I was terribly upset... Also my wish not have a child by you was only for the moment, and stood on weak legs...I am sorry now for having written it. If you have not completely given up on me, then come here soon so that we can try to find one another again.

The sudden shift in the way I feel will seem strange to you.

Poor little creature that I am, I can't tell which path is the right one for me. All these things have overtaken me, and yet I still do not feel guilty. I don't want to cause pain to any of you.

Your Paula

In a letter addressed to her sister Milly, dated November 18, 1906, she acknowledges Milly's gift of money. The "review" to which she is referring was a notice of her works exhibited at the Bremen Kunsthalle, written by Gustav Pauli. She feels a public notice will help justify to her family her unorthodox decision to go to Paris and her reconciliation with Otto Modersohn.

My dear Sister,

You really seem to love me as a sister, and I thank you for it. I love you in my own way, with much reserve, but very deeply. If you feel a little cheated by me, heaven will see to it that you are compensated or that in some other way. I'm convinced that we are rewarded or punished one way or another for everything we do while we are still on this earth. The review was more a satisfaction to me than a joy. Joy, overpoweringly beautiful moments, comes to an artist without others noticing. The same is true for moments of sadness. That is why it's true that artists live mostly in solitude. But for all of that, the review will be good for my reappearance in Bremen. And it will perhaps also cast a different light on my reasons for leaving Worpswede.

Otto and I shall be coming home again in the spring. That man is touching in his love. We are going to try to buy the Brunjes place in order to make our lives together freer and more open. We will also have all kinds of animals around us. My thoughts run like this just now: if the dear Lord will allow me once again to create something beautiful, then I shall be happy and satisfied: if only I have a place where I can work in peace. I will be grateful for the portion of love I've received. If one can only remain healthy and not die too young.

I'm so happy, my dear, that things are going well for you! I think about you and your little one very often. Just learn to be patient, and the happy event will soon come. And please make up your mind now that it is not important whether it's a boy or a girl. Do you think it mattered in our case; aren't we fine girls?

Right now Otto is at Hoetger's atelier. Hoetger is doing a plaster bust of him. I am to get a cast of it. The two of them have gradually come to understand each other very well. Otto has great hopes for his own art this winter. He has many new ideas, which is a great comfort to me.

I naturally indulged myself with the money you sent. I bought myself silly trinkets, something for the head, something for the feet. A pair of beautiful old combs, a pair of old shoe buckles.

Farewell, my dear. Be happy, be good, be careful.

Modersohn-Becker lived with her husband in Paris through the winter of 1906-07. She did become pregnant during this time, and returned to Worspwede in the spring. This letter, written to Clara Westhoff, on October 21, 1907, recalls the impact of the work of Cézanne, which they first saw at Vollard's Gallery. She expresses regret that she could not see the large retrospective of his works, then on display in Paris, and her desire to meet her friend. Clearly Cézanne's paintings exerted a powerful influence on her artistic development.

Dear Clara Rilke,

My mind has been so much occupied these days by the thought of Cézanne, of how he has been one of the three or four powerful artists who have affected me like a thunderstorm, like some great event. Do you still remember what we saw at Vollard in 1900? And then, during the final days of my last stay in Paris, those truly astonishing early paintings of his at the Galerie Pellerin. Tell your husband he should try to see the things there. Pellerin has a hundred and fifty Cézannes. I saw only a small part of them, but they are magnificent—My urge to know everything about the Salon d'Automne was so great that a few days ago I asked him to send me at least the catalogue. Please come soon and bring the letters [about Cézanne]. Come right away, Monday if you can possibly make it, for I hope soon, finally, to be otherwise occupied. If it were not absolutely necessary for me to be here right now, nothing could keep me away from Paris.

I look forward to seeing you and to your news. I also send two lovely greetings to Ruth.

Your Paula Modersohn

On November 2, 1907, Modersohn-Becker gave birth to a daughter named Mathilde, after her mother, and died of an embolism 19 days later on November 20, 1907.

Like Morisot and Bashkirtseff, Paula Modersohn-Becker wrote in the two most intimate forms widely used by women, the letter to friends and family and the journal. Also, like Bashkirtseff her premature death no doubt encouraged the publication of her

private writing which predated the serious appreciation and recognition of her work as a visual artist.
Perhaps, had she lived long enough to establish a
reputation as a painter, her letters and journal may
have remained unpublished. But her abbreviated life
no doubt encouraged the publication of her writings
during World War I, only a decade after her death.

The evidence of her writing presents us with a
woman who struggled with the inherent contradictory roles of wife and mother and her ambition to be
an artist of originality and importance. These painful
conflicts and her difficulties in their resolution make
her texts compelling reading. During her lifetime this
struggle was acted out in the privacy of her writing,
while she remained virtually invisible on the public
stage. There is no evidence to suggest that Modersohn Becker wanted to become a famous writer. Her
primary outlet was in building her skills as an artist to
compete with her Worpswede colleagues and eventually to surpass them. Like Bashkirtseff, the extent of
her writing is impressive. Divided between letters and
journal entries, she applied the same tenacity and self-
discipline in her regular correspondence and journal keeping as is evident in her dedication to her art.
The surviving writings provide an intimate window
into the mind of a woman who never fully reconciled
her roles as obedient daughter and wife with her own
drive to become an artist whose works would redefine
the avant garde in Germany.

Had she survived and lived out her life I believe
that she would have achieved her goal and become

recognized as the most important German artist of her generation. Her writing would have documented her journey, in the manner of Van Gogh's letters, rather than standing in for her achievement, as it does today.

Notes

[1] Fritz Mackensen (1866-1953) was a figure painter and the founder of the painters' colony in Worpswede. He was Paula Becker's first mentor in the summer of 1897, when she first spent time in Worpswede.

[2] Clara Westhoff (1878-1954) was a sculptor and painter. She studied painting in Munich and with Mackensen in Worpswede. In 1899, she lived in Paris and studied with Rodin. In 1901 she married Rilke.

[3] Rainer Maria Rilke (1875-1926) was a poet and art critic who worked as Rodin's secretary from 1905-06.

[4] Otto Modersohn (1865-1943) was "by far the most gifted" Worpswede artist. By ca 1895 he had achieved "considerable esteem and success, as a landscapc painter By 1900 he had become something of a famous man." Günter Busch "Introduction" in *Paula Modersohn-Becker: The Letters and Journals*, edited by Gunter Busch and Liselote von Reinken, translated by Arthur S. Wensinger and Carole Clew Hoey © Tapliner Publishing Company (Evanston, Illinois: Northwestern University Press, 1990) 4-5. All quotes are from this edition

and are published by permission of Northwestern University Press.

[5] Ibid., 7.

[6] Vincent van Gogh (1853-1890).

[7] Paul Gauguin (1848-1903).

[8] Paul Cézanne (1839-1906).

[9] *Paula Modersohn-Becker: The Letters and Journals,* vii.

[10] Meta Viol was a girl who lived with her family in Worpswede.

[11] Camille Corot (1796-1875) was a noted French landscape painter who debuted at the Salon of 1827.

[12] Théodore Rousseau (1812-1867) was a French landscape painter associated with the Barbizon School.

[13] Jean-Francois Millet (1814-1875) was a French figurative painter of the Barbizon School.

[14] Gustave Courtois (1852-1923) was a French portrait painter.

[15] Raphael Collin (1850-1916) was a French painter who was known for decorative murals, e.g. the ceiling of the Opéra-comique.

[16] sketching

[17] This is similar to an entry in Marie Bashkirtseff's journal, December 9, 1883. Modersohn -Becker's involvement with Bashkirtseff was so intense that Rilke refers to her as "Marie Bashkirtsev" in a letter of January 24, 1901. (*Paula Modersohn-Becker: The Letters and Journals,* see note, p. 481).

[18] Ibid., Note, 505

[19] Auguste Rodin (1840-1917) was the most important French sculptor of the late nineteenth and early twentieth centuries.

[20] Alfred Boucher (1850-1934) was a French sculptor.

[21] Jean Antoine Injalbert (1845-1933) was a French sculptor.

[22] The wife of a very distinguished painter.

[23] Work, that is my happiness.

[24] Bernard Hoetger (1876-1949) was a German sculptor and a painter.

Chapter 8. Käthe Kollwitz (1867-1945): *The Early Years, Diary, and Letter*

While Paula Modersohn-Becker (Chapter 7) worked for much of her brief life in obscurity, without public recognition, Käthe Kollwitz was the most celebrated German graphic artist of her era and, probably, the most famous German woman artist active in any visual art medium. She produced a powerful body of works, in a range of print media and sculpture, which has ensured her continued fame and recognition as an original creator. She lived during the tumultuous years of the early twentieth century and lost one of her two sons in World War I, surviving to see her grandson killed in World War II.

Born into a family with no direct connections to the visual arts, Käthe Schmidt was educated with a strong political awareness of socialist activism. Like all other German women artists of her generation, she was educated in the schools run by the Verein der Kunstlerinnen, first in Berlin, in 1885, and then in Munich, from 1888 (Introduction to Part 2). In 1891, she married Karl Kollwitz to whom she had been engaged since 1884. Kollwitz was a doctor who practiced in a very poor, working-class neighborhood of Berlin. From this vantage point, Käthe could observe the direct effects of impoverishment on this population. During the 1890s, she bore two sons and created her first major print cycle, *The Revolt of the Weavers*, which established her reputation as one of the foremost graphic artists in Germany.

Between 1902 and 1908, she created her second important series of prints, *The Peasant War*, which was inspired by an uprising of German peasants in the sixteenth century. The leader of this revolution was a woman, "Black Anna," and the theme of this cycle coincided with two of Kollwitz's key concerns: empathy for the poor and the power of women to effect social change.

Following World War I, Kollwitz's talents were widely recognized. She became the first woman to be elected to the Prussian Academy of the Arts in 1919. In 1928, she was appointed director of graphic arts at this school. Kollwitz also participated in several activist organizations of German women artists. She served as president of the Frauenkunstverband (Women's Art Union) in 1914 and again, after the war, in 1926. She was a founding member of GEDOK (Society for Women Artists and Friends of Art). Both groups were designed to promote equality of educational and of exhibition opportunities for women artists. Her fame can be noted by her inclusion as a "floating head" in Hannah Hoch's famous Dada collage, *Cut with the Kitchen Knife*.[1]

Kollwitz survived the harsh living conditions of World War I, the loss of one of her sons, the unstable revolutionary period, and the establishment of the Weimar Republic. By the 1930s, Kollwitz witnessed the persecution of her work, along with the art of other Expressionist colleagues of her era, such as Barlach,[2] Kirchner,[3] and Modersohn-Becker, which the Nazis labeled as "degenerate" art.[4] She died in 1945, the year the War ended, leaving an impressive and lasting legacy of powerful graphic art.

Kollwitz's themes are imbued with compassionate humanitarianism. Her images often focused on the pains and on the joys of motherhood, the traumas of death and loss, and the injustices of capitalist exploitation of the working classes. After her son Peter's death, in 1914, she channeled much of her grief and anger into powerful anti-war imagery and designed a sculpted memorial for all the lost sons of Germany.

Over the course of her career, Kollwitz used every graphic medium. Her early works employed mixed media of etching, aquatint, and other intaglio processes. She was drawn to the powerful medium of woodcut in the 1920s. After World War I, she frequently used lithography, in a simplified style that imitated charcoal.

Kollwitz's writings were edited, by her son Hans, and appeared in 1948. The book was translated into English and published in an American edition, in 1955, as *The Diary and Letters of Kaethe Kollwitz*.[5] Like Carr's book dedicated to Hosmer (Chapter 2), and Denis Rouart's editing of Morisot's family documents (Chapter 5), we have a person very close to the subject, organizing the primary sources to create an **auto/biography** (Introduction II, d). *The Diary and Letters of Kaethe Kollwitz* begins, in a chronological manner, with the text, *The Early Years*, which Hans encouraged his mother to write.[6] *The Early Years* is a **memoir**, like Cameron's *Annals of My Glass House* (Chapter 4), since it focuses on Kollwitz's early professional development. Kollwitz maintained a journal for most of her active life. She also wrote letters to family, colleagues and very close personal friends, such as "Jeep."[7] With the exception of one letter to Jeep, the remaining excerpts are drawn from her diary entries, which provide insights into her creative process.

The first excerpt comes from *The Early Years*, in which Kollwitz recalls her early artistic training. She reflects on her sibling rivalry with her younger sister. Lise did not display the ambition and determination needed to become a professional artist.

I turn now from discussion of my physical development to my nonphysical development. By now my father had long since realized that I was gifted at drawing. The fact gave him great pleasure and he wanted me to have all the training I needed to become an artist. Unfortunately I was a girl, but nevertheless he was ready to risk it. He assumed that I would not be much distracted by love affairs, since I was not a pretty girl; and he was all the more disappointed and angry later on when at the age of only seventeen I became engaged to Karl Kollwitz.

My first artistic instruction came from Mauer,[8] the engraver. There were usually one or two other girls in the class. We drew heads from plaster casts or copied other drawings. It was summer, and we sat in the front room. From the street below I could hear the rhythmic tramping of men laying paving stones. Above the tall trees of the garden across the way hung the dense, motionless city air. I can feel it to this day.

I was hard-working and conscientious, and my parents took pleasure in each new drawing I turned out. That was a particularly happy time for my father, in respect to us. All of us children were developing rapidly. Konrad was writing, and we gave performances of his tragedies; I was showing unmistakable talent for drawing, and so was Lise. I still remember overhearing my father in the next room saying happily to my mother that all of us were gifted, but Konrad probably most of all. Another time he said something that bothered me for a long time afterwards. He had been astonished by one of Lise's drawings, and said to mother: "Lise will soon be catching up to Kaethe."

When I heard this I felt envy and jealousy for probably the first time in my life. I loved Lise dearly. We were very close to one another and I was happy to see her progress up to the point where I began; but everything in me protested against her going beyond that point. I always had to be ahead of her. This jealousy of Lise lasted for years. When I was studying in Munich there was talk of Lise's coming out there to study too. I experienced the most contradictory feelings: joy at the prospect of her coming and at the same time fear that her talent and personality would overshadow mine. As it turned out, nothing came of this proposal. She became engaged at this time and did not go on studying art.

Now when I ask myself why Lise, for all her talent, did not become a real artist, but only a highly gifted dilettante, the reason is clear to me. I was keenly ambitious and Lise was not. I wanted to and Lise did not. I had a clear aim and direction. In addition, of course, there was the fact that I was three years older than she. Therefore my talent came to light sooner than hers and my father, who was not yet disappointed in us, was only too happy to open opportunities for me. If Lise had been harder and more egotistic than she was, she would unquestionably have prevailed on Father to let her also have thorough training in the arts. But she was gentle and unselfish. ("Lise will always sacrifice herself," Father used to say.) And so her talent was not developed. As far as talent in itself goes—if talent could possibly be weighed and measured—Lise had at least as much as I. But she lacked total concentration upon it. I wanted my education to be in art alone. If I could, I would have saved all my intellectual powers and turned them exclusively to use in my art, so that this flame alone would burn brightly.

Kollwitz exhibited her prints with the Berlin Secession. The Secession movement and the specific history of the Berlin Secession have been studied by scholars. According to Robert Jensen, author of an important analysis of art institutions in the 1890s, the impetus for the development of these alternative exhibitions occurred at "a unique historical moment when artists attempted to shape themselves as a professional class."[9] The Berlin Secession developed later than most of the other Secession groups in other Central European cities, holding its first exhibition in 1899. Under the leadership of Max Lieberman,[10] who served as the first president, the group broke away from the older more traditional Society of Berlin Artists. The Secession promoted the "Modern" art of its members and served as an exhibition venue for French artists, such as Degas and Monet. By declaring their independence from state support, these artists were forced to rely on collectors and the art market systems.[11] In choosing to exhibit with the Secession, Kollwitz aligned herself with the more avant-garde, progressive artists of Berlin.

In the journal entry dated December 30, 1909, Kollwitz is responding to the exhibition of her etchings in the Secession show. In the privacy of her journal, Kollwitz confides her self-critical attitude towards her own work. She defines the need to simplify, stressing only the "essential". This except is quite prophetic of the stylistic direction her art would take in the next decade and also echoes some of the concerns of Paula Modersohn-Becker (Chapter 7), about a decade earlier, as she, too, broke away from naturalism to develop a more avant-garde style.

On Saturday the Secession show was opened. I went there with Hans. My things were hung well, although the etchings were separate. Nevertheless I am no longer so satisfied. There are too many good things there that seem fresher than mine. Brandenburg is excellent this time. I wish I had done his dance, his orgy. In my own work I find that I must try to keep everything to a more and more abbreviated form. The execution seems to be too complete. I should like to do the new etching so that all the essentials are strongly stressed and the inessentials almost omitted.

In the following journal entry, dated September 1913, she is writing to encourage herself to have greater confidence and exhibit "moral courage." This is precisely the quality which seems most evident in Kollwitz's art, from our perspective, so it is quite interesting to read how she uses the diary to strengthen her resolve.

I am working on the group of lovers, with the girl sitting in the man's lap. My deep depression after the summer vacation has dissipated, but I still do not have any real faith. Sometimes it seems to me that all I lack is moral courage. I do not fly because I do not dare to throw myself into the air like Pégoud.[12] Actually, with my technique—even in sculpture—I should trust myself more. Is my lack of courage a token of age? All the ifs and buts that older people are aware of. Pechstein[13] exhibits his talented sculptural sketches without any scruples. He doesn't give a hoot that they are nothing but sketches.

After August 1914, with her son on the front, the war occupied Kollwitz, incessantly. In the following excerpt, dated December 1914, after learning of Peter's death, she attempts to channel her grief into a commemorative sculptural memorial.

Conceived the plan for a memorial for Peter tonight, but abandoned it again because it seemed to me impossible of execution. In the morning I suddenly thought of having Reike ask the city to give me a place for the memorial. There would have to be a collection taken for it. It must stand on the heights of Schildhorn, looking out over the Havel. To be finished and dedicated on a glorious summer day. School children of the community singing, 'On the way to pray.' The monument would have Peter's form, lying stretched out, the father at the head, and the mother at the feet. It would be to commemorate the sacrifice of all the young volunteers.

It is a wonderful goal, and no one has more right than I to make this memorial...

My boy! On your memorial I want to have your figure on top, *above* the parents. You will lie outstretched, holding out your hands in answer to the call for sacrifice: 'Here I am.' Your eyes—perhaps—open wide, so that you see the blue sky above you, and the clouds and birds. Your mouth smiling. And at your breast the pink I gave you.

In her journal entry for January 1916, she describes her service on the jury deciding on the works to be hung in the Secession exhibition. It is interesting to note her conflicts concerning other women artists. On the one hand, she is empathetic with women artists' desires for recognition, but she is also aware that many of the works were not up to the highest aesthetic standards. Her sentiments echo those of Bonheur (Chapter 3), who also worried about women artists being judged on more lenient critical criteria.

All day devoted to hanging pictures in the Secession. Acting on the jury and hanging too is very instructive.

A show ought to have a face, and the pictures exhibited must fit into this face. From that it follows that mediocre pictures may possess the features which are fitting for the face and often must be accepted, while better pictures which have unsuitable features must sometimes, and justly, be rejected. Necessary injustice in all exhibitions...

My unpleasant position on the jury. I always find myself forced to defend the cause of a woman. But because I can never really do that with conviction, since most of the work in question is mediocre (if the works are better than that the other jury members will agree), I always become involved in equivocations.

In her journal entry on February 21, 1916, she is responding to an article on the issue of realism and the power of art to communicate with ordinary people. This excerpt underscores Kollwitz's desire to create images for a broad public audience, which she terms the "average spectator".

Read an article by E. von Keyserling[14] on the future of art. He opposes expressionism and says that after the war the German people will need eccentric studio art less than ever before. What they need is realistic art.

I quite agree—if by realistic art Keyserling means the same thing I do. Which refers back to a talk I had recently with Karl about my small sculptures.

It is true that my sculptural work is rejected by the public. Why? It is not at all popular. The average spectator does not understand it. Art for the average spectator need not be shallow. Of course he has no objection to the trite—but it is also true that he would accept true art if it were simple enough. I thoroughly agree that there must be understanding between the artist and the people. In the best ages of art that has always been the case.

Genius can probably run on ahead and seek out new ways. But the good artists who follow after genius—and I count myself among these—have to restore the lost connection once more. A pure studio art is unfruitful and frail, for anything that does not form living roots—why should it exist at all?

Now as for myself. The fact that I am getting too far away from the average spectator is a danger to me. I am losing touch with him. I am groping in my art, and who knows, I may find what I seek. When I thought about my work at New Year's 1914, I vowed to myself and to Peter that I would be more scrupulous than ever in "giving the honor to God, that is, in being wholly genuine and sincere." Not that I felt myself drifting away from sincerity. But in groping for the precious truth one falls easily into artistic oversubtleties and ingenuities—into preciosity. I suddenly see that very clearly, and I must watch out. Perhaps the work on the memorial will bring me back to simplicity.

In the next two excerpts from her journal, from May and July 1917, Kollwitz is reflecting on the feedback from her solo exhibition. She seems almost stunned by this positive attention. She then admits, to herself, that it is only by the age of 50 that she has a sense of what she has accomplished and the positive impact her work has achieved. Despite her recognition, she retains a remarkable level of humility, as evidenced in her attributing her success to "luck."

May 1917: After Easter worked concentratedly on the show. On the afternoon of Sunday, the 15th, I had the porter open the building and showed Karl the exhibition. Monday, the 16th, it was opened. It was a great success. From many sides I heard that it made a strong and integrated impression. Stahl's review, Deri's prefatory notes, Lise's review in the *Monatsheft*, Wertheimer's comments. Their praise is such that I almost think the last two at least would not be so affected by an artist who was a stranger to them. Fondness for me is also involved. For I can scarcely think that I have been so able to communicate myself or—more than that—to have been the direct mediator between people and something they are not conscious of, something transcendent, primal. Suggestion must play some part here. If my works *continue* to make such an impression—even after decades—then I will have achieved a great deal. Then men will have been enriched by me. Then I shall have helped in the ascent of man. For that matter everyone does so, but it would then have fallen to me to do so to a greater degree than others.

July 1917: My fiftieth birthday has passed. Different from the way I used to imagine it. Where are my boys?

And yet the day was good, this whole period is good. From so many sides I am being told that my work has value, that I have accomplished something, wielded influence. This echo of one's life work is *very* good; it is satisfying and produces a feeling of gratitude. And of self-assurance as well. But at the age of fifty this kind of self-assurance is not as excessive and arrogant as it is at thirty. It is based upon self-knowledge. One knows best oneself where one's own upper and lower limits are. The word fame is no longer intoxicating.

But it might have turned out differently. In spite of all the work I have done, success might have been denied me. There was an element of luck in it, too. And certainly I am grateful that it has turned out this way.

After the war, Kollwitz was in demand to make posters for various causes. In this phase of her long career, she creates some of her most famous images. The following journal entry, dated January 4, 1920, documents her sense of responsibility to "voice the sufferings of men." This is an astonishing recognition of the heavy burden that she carried for the German people.

I have again agreed to make a poster for a large-scale aid program for Vienna. I hope I can make it, but I do not know whether I can carry it out because it has to be done quickly and I feel an attack of grippe coming on.

I want to show Death. Death swings the lash of famine—people, men, women and children, bowed low, screaming and groaning, file past him.

While I drew, and wept along with the terrified children I was drawing, I really felt the burden I am bearing. I felt that I have no right to withdraw from the responsibility of being an advocate. It is my duty to voice the sufferings of men, the never-ending sufferings heaped mountain-high. This is my task, but it is not an easy one to fulfill. Work is supposed to relieve you. But is it any relief when in spite of my poster people in Vienna die of hunger every day? And when I know that? Did I feel relieved when I made the prints on war and knew that the war would go on raging? Certainly not. Tranquility and relief have come to me only when I was engaged on one thing: the big memorial for Peter. Then I had peace and was with him.

Many of her images deal with an aggressive, violent death tearing families apart.

In this journal entry, dated June 25, 1920, Kollwitz reflects on the impact of Barlach's woodcuts and discusses the differences among various print media. She is very self-critical, and, inspired by her colleague's example, she decides to attempt woodcutting again.

Yesterday I went with Professor Kern to the Secession shows and to the big exhibition in order to choose a print for the Kunstverein. Then I saw something that knocked me over: Barlach's woodcuts.

Today I've looked at my lithographs again and seen that almost all of them are no good. Barlach has found his path and I have not yet found mine.

I can no longer etch; I'm through with that for good. And in lithography there are the inadequacies of the transfer paper. Nowadays lithographic stones can only be got to the studio by begging and pleading, and cost a lot of money, and even on stones I don't manage to make it come out right. But why can't I do it any more? The prerequisites for artistic works have been there—for example in the war series. First of all the strong feeling—these things come from the heart—and secondly they rest on the basis of my previous works, that is, upon a fairly good foundation of technique.

And yet the prints lack real quality. What is the reason? Ought I do as Barlach has done and make a fresh start with woodcuts? When I considered that up to now, I always told myself that lithography was the right method for me for clear and apparent reasons.

In woodcuts I would not want to go along with the present fashion of spotty effect. Expression is all that I want, and therefore I told myself that the simple line of the lithograph was best suited to my purposes. But the results of my work, except for the print *Mothers*, never have satisfied me.

For years I have been tormenting myself. Not to speak of sculpture.

I first began the war series as etchings. Came to nothing. Dropped everything. Then I tried it with transfers. There too the results were almost never satisfying.

Will woodcutting do it? If that too fails, then I have proof that the fault lies only within myself. Then I am just no longer able to do it. In all the years of torment these small oases of joys and successes.

The next text is a letter, addressed to her lifelong friend Jeep, written in 1933.[15] She discusses, with a good deal of wry humor, the Nazi manipulation of the exhibition, which can be seen as the prelude to the notorious Degenerate Art exhibition of 1937.[16] She seems to have accepted the inevitable disruptions which will occur in her career.

Dear Jeep!

...The Academy show has opened here meanwhile. That is, it has not opened, rather it has been ready to open for two weeks. But Goering,[17] the second man in the State, has no time to open it right now. I was admitted after all and was delighted with the exhibition. You will see it in the winter. It is only sculpture—one hundred and fifty years of sculpture, down to the present. You know I wanted to have my group there, but they refused it. Instead they wanted the Mother figure that is in the Kronprinzenpalais museum, and the small bronze gravestone relief. At first I was angry that they did not want my new work; but it is just as well after all. It could not possibly have been ready in stone, and in the cement cast, as it is now, it would not have done at all. It is far from dry yet and looks horribly mottled. –

Yesterday, when I came into the old rooms and saw my own works among many others, and that they held up, I was very glad after all. Participation is good and vital, and it is sad to be excluded. For one is after all a leaf on the twig and the twig belongs to the whole tree. When the tree sways back and fort, the leaf is content to sway with it.

The day before the opening of the show my two works, the Mother from the Kronprinzen-palais museum and the gravestone relief, were taken out. So were three works by Barlach. From this and from Rust's speech I could not help concluding that both pieces were going to be put away in the warehouse of the National Gallery. That is for outdated trash. In fact, I began to fear worse things. I was afraid they would remove my figures from the cemetery in Belgium. But with a curious lack of consistency, although the works were removed from the Academy show, they are to be on exhibition in the Kronprinzenpalais again. A sequence of decisions which is hard to understand. If only the sculptures may remain in Belgium in the place for which they were made.

In the final journal entry, from November 1935, with Germany fully in the hold of Nazism, she seems resigned to the end of her active career. She notes the silence which exists concerning the Nazi policies, and she is resigned and admits, at least to her journal, that "there is really nothing more to say."

I am gradually realizing now that I have come to the end of my working life. Now that I have had the group cast in cement, I do not know how to go on. There is really nothing more to say. I thought of doing another small sculpture, *Age*, and I had some vague ideas about a relief. But whether I do them or not is no longer important. Not for the others and not for myself. Also there is this curious silence surrounding the expulsion of my work from the Academy show, and in connection with the Kronprinzenpalais. Scarcely anyone had anything to say to me about it. I thought people would come, or at least write—but no. Such a silence all around us. – That too has to be experienced. Well, Karl is still here. I see him every day and we talk and show one another our love. But how will it be when he too is gone?

One turns more and more to silence. All is still. I sit in Mother's chair by the stove, evenings, when I am alone.

Unlike the abbreviated and largely anonymous career of Modersohn-Becker, Kollwitz lived a full life in which her remarkable achievements in the full range of print media and sculpture were well known. She also seamlessly combined the roles of wife, mother and artist, using her own personal experiences, especially the loss of her son in World War I, as inspiration for her art. While she enjoyed a popular recognition of her early work, she continued to evolve as an artist and to express her personal beliefs in increasingly innovative stylistic forms. Kollwitz exercised her agency, her impact in the strong political and social messages of many of her powerful images.

Her writings were mainly in the private forms of letters to family and friends and her journal. Like Morisot, the preservation and eventually publication of these texts remained within her family and it was her surviving son Hans who edited these works, which were only published posthumously. Her brief autobiographical memoir of her early life was like Cameron's also written privately and remained unpublished until it was included in that volume. For students and admirers of her works one reads the journal with astonishment at the harsh self-criticism which she brings to the evaluation of her own work. She seems to be always striving to achieve a more powerful, more original image. The impressive evidence of this drive is the outstanding quality of her work. Unlike Bashkirtseff, Kollwitz had no pretension to achieve any sort of fame from her writings. Her public voice was clearly articulated in her remarkable images which fortunately were preserved even amidst the strife of the upheavals of two Worlds Wars and Nazi suppression.

Notes

[1] Maud Lavin, *Cut with the Kitchen Knife: the Weimar Photomontages of Hannah Höch* (New Haven and London: Yale University Press, 1993).

[2] Ernst Barlach (1870-1938) was a German sculptor and printmaker, noted for his woodcuts.

[3] Ernst Kirchner (1880-1938) was a German Expressionist painter and leader of Die Brücke.

[4] Stephanie Barron, *Degenerate Art: the Fate of the Avant-Garde in Nazi Germany* (Los Angeles: Los Angeles County Museum of Art, 1991).

[5] *The Diary and Letters of Kaethe Kollwitz,* translated by Richard and Clara Winston (Chicago: Henry Regnery Co., 1955). All quotes are from this edition and are published by permission of Northwestern University Press.

[6] Hans Kollwitz, "Introduction" in *The Diary and Letters of Kaethe Kollwitz,* 1.

[7] Beate Jeep-Bonus.

[8] Rudolph Mauer (1845-1905).

[9] Robert Jensen, *Marketing Modernism in Fin-de Siècle Europe,* (Princeton: Princeton University Press, 1994), 167. See his overview in Chapter 6, "Secessionism".

10 Max Lieberman (1847-1935).

11 Beth Irwin Lewis, *Art for All?: The Collision of Modern Art and the Public in Late-Nineteenth-Century Germany,* (Princeton and Oxford: Princeton University Press, 2003), 305-6.

12 Adolphe Pegoud (1889-1915) was a French aviator and fighter ace during World War I.

13 Max Pechstein (1881-1955) was a German painter associated with Die Brücke.

14 Eduard von Keyserling (1855-1918) was a German essayist and author of fiction.

15 This letter was published in an earlier German edition. See *The Diary and Letters of Kaethe Kollwitz,* note p. 164.

16 Barron, *Degenerate Art.*

17 Hermann Goering (1893-1946) Hitler's designated successor and commander of the German Air Force.

Chapter 9. Georgia O'Keeffe (1887-1986): *Georgia O'Keeffe and Letters*

Georgia O'Keeffe is one of the most important American artists, male or female, of the pre-World War II era. She has been the focus of widespread scholarly and popular attention. In a career that spanned most of the twentieth century, O'Keeffe created a body of works which is both personal and national, and as she states in the last letter in this collection, "I think that what I have done is something rather unique in my time and that I am one of the few who gives our country any voice of its own."

O'Keeffe was born, in Wisconsin, into a family with no special interests in visual art. With her characteristic determination, she studied at the Art Institute of Chicago and then migrated to New York City where she continued her formal instruction at the Art Students' League. After a period in which she taught art in Virginia and in Texas, she returned to New York in 1918. She had attracted the attention and gained the support of Alfred Stieglitz,[1] whose "291 Gallery" was in the forefront of taste making and reputation building. From the role of mentor, to lover, and, then, to husband, Stieglitz tirelessly promoted O'Keeffe's works in annual exhibitions held between 1916 and 1946, the year he died. O'Keeffe both accepted and resented the publicity which this relationship brought her. Her ambivalence is discussed in a study which unites O'Keeffe, Carr and Kahlo by Sharyn Rohlfsen Udall.[2] In the summer of 1929, O'Keeffe traveled to New Mexico and became strongly attached to the desert region around Taos. From this year until the time when the Stieglitz estate was settled, she summered in New Mexico. After 1949, she settled permanently in the remote town of Abiquiu, where she lived until her death in 1986. Although she continued to paint into the 1970s, her period of greatest originality and productivity is the inter-war period.

O'Keeffe is best known for a limited range of subjects. In the 1920s, she became most famous for her large-scale, close-up views of flowers. During her stays in New Mexico, she explored the motifs of the landscape, especially the hills and the trees in the area around Taos. She is well known for her imagery of cow skulls and other animal bones.

Stylistically, O'Keeffe adopted a rather precise, well blended style in her mature paintings. Her edges are sharp and her originality seems to rely more in her selected imagery, rather than in any expressive method of paint application.

For an artist who was so famous, O'Keeffe's autobiographical texts are quite brief. Prior to 1976, her only public writings were brief, impersonal statements printed in exhibition catalogues. Some of these statements are frequently quoted but they are not included in this book because of their distance from genres of "life narrative." *Georgia O'Keeffe*, an autobiographical essay, was published in 1976,[3] and the first two excerpts, printed below, are from this source. This is a **memoir** (Introduction II,a) since it traces her life as a progression towards professional success.

O'Keeffe's most interesting primary sources are letters which have survived from almost every decade of her adult life. In 1987, just after her death, her works were organized into a large scale traveling exhibition, by the National Gallery of Art in Washington, D.C. [4] This exhibition toured the country from 1987 to 1989. The volume that was published in conjunction with this major retrospective reprinted a number of her letters, providing access to a more direct and intimate voice than had been possible during her lifetime. All of the letters, excerpted below, were reprinted in this volume. Her letters addressed to many correspondents provide insights into her creative process, her inter-personal relationships, and her sense of place, especially New Mexico.

In the first excerpt, from her autobiographical essay in *Georgia O'Keeffe* (1976), she recalls her early decision to become an artist, by about age 13. She recognizes that she did not come from an environment in which being an artist, let alone a famous artist, was actually articulated.

The year I was finishing the eighth grade, I asked our washwoman's daughter what she was going to do when she grew up. She said she didn't know. I said very definitely—as if I had thought it all out and my mind was made up—'I am going to be an artist.'

I don't really know where I got my artist idea. The scraps of what I remember do not explain to me where it came from. I only know that by that time it was definitely settled in my mind. I hadn't seen many pictures and I hadn't a desire to make anything like the pictures I had seen. But in one of my mother's books I had found a drawing of a girl that I thought very beautiful. The title under it was 'Maid of Athens.' It was a very ordinary pen-and-ink drawing about two inches high. For me, it just happened to be something special—so beautiful. Maybe I could make something beautiful...I think my feeling wasn't as articulate as that, but I believe that picture started something moving in me that kept on going and has had to do with the everlasting urge that makes me keep on painting.

Later, in the same essay, O'Keeffe describes her life class at the Art Institute of Chicago and her discomfort at viewing a nearly nude male model. Although O'Keeffe's mature art did not require expertise in the nude, she was fortunate to be coming of age during a time when the study of the male nude was taken for granted, even for female art students. The restrictions and level of discrimination against Victorian women, discussed in Part 1, were disappearing, by the early twentieth century.

I have never understood why we had such dark olive green rooms for art schools. The Anatomy Class was in one of those dark-colored half-lighted dismal rooms. When I went in, the room was full. Most of the students were much older than I was. I was a little girl with a big black ribbon bow on my braid of hair. The man teaching had a soft light-brown beard and an easy way of moving and speaking. After talking a while he said, 'Come out,' to a curtain I hadn't noticed. Out walked a very handsome, lean, dark-skinned, well-made man—finely cut face, dark shining hair, and dark moustache—naked except for a small loincloth. I was surprised—I was shocked—blushed a hot and uncomfortable blush—didn't look around in my embarrassment and don't remember anything about the anatomy lesson. It was a suffering. The class only came once a week and I had to make up my mind what I was going to do about it before time for the next lesson. I still had the idea that I wanted to be an artist. I thought that meant I had to go to art school. Drawing casts in the upstairs gallery wouldn't go on forever. If I was any good at all I'd be promoted to the Life Class where there would be nude models. It was something I hadn't counted on but had to face if I was going to be an artist. I don't know why it seemed so difficult. In the summer when we went swimming down on the river a boy my age wore the least little piece of a bathing suit and I don't remember thinking anything about it except that he was blond and beautiful and laughing. The bare figure in the dismal dark classroom with everybody else dressed was different—he was definitely there to be looked at. Maybe if I had had a passionate interest in anatomy I wouldn't have been shocked. But I had no interest at all in anatomy and the long names of things—the teacher did not connect it in any way with my drawing upstairs. When the next lesson came and everyone else drifted in the direction of the Anatomy Class, I drifted in, too. I don't remember learning anything except that I finally became accustomed to the idea of the nude model.

In this first letter, dated October 11, 1915, O'Keeffe is writing to her closest friend, Anita Pollitzer (1894-1975). Pollitzer was an art student with O'Keeffe in 1914, at Columbia University Teacher's College, where they were exposed to the ideas of Arthur Wesley Dow.[5] Dow's teachings would be quite influential for the development of O'Keeffe's abstract style. Pollitzer had visited Stieglitz's gallery in June 1915, and it is in this letter that O'Keeffe confides that she would respect his opinion of her work. Writing from South Carolina, O'Keeffe reflects on her ambivalent position concerning the opinions of other and wonders: "Why should I care if anyone else likes it?"

Anita

—aren't you funny to wonder if I like your letters. I was walking up from the little bandbox post office with the mail under my arm—reading your letter this afternoon—and when I came to the part telling what Stieglitz said about 'it's worth going to Hell to get there'—I laughed aloud— and dropped all the things under my arm.

I had gone for the mail because I had worked till—what I thought didn't count—so it wasn't any use to keep on—I read your letter twice then went for a walk with about eight of the girls—it was supposed to be a run—and they were all very much astonished that none of them could keep up with me—I can run at a jog trot almost as easily as I can walk—and most girls can't, you know.

We explored much woods and country and found the quaintest little deserted house imaginable with wonderful big pink and white and yellow roses climbing on it—and funny little garden effects—all surrounded by great tall pines.

It would have been too cold to go without a coat if we hadn't run most of the way— whenever they had breath—so you know how great it felt.

I came back and read your letter again.

Anita—do you know—I believe I would rather have Stieglitz like something—anything I had done—than anyone else I know of—I have always thought that—If I ever make anything that satisfies me ever so little—I am going to show it to him to find out if its any good—Don't you often wish you could make something he might like?

Still Anita—I don't see why we ever think of what others think of what we do—no matter who they are—isn't it enough just to express yourself—If it were to a particular person as music often is—of course we would like them to understand—at least a little—but why should we care about the rest of the crowd—If I make a picture to you why should I care if anyone else likes it or is interested in it or not. I am getting a lot of fun out of slaving by myself—The disgusting part is that I so often find myself saying—what would you—or Dorothy—or M. Martin or Mr. Dow—or Mr. Bement— or somebody—most anybody—say if they saw it—It is curious—how one works for flattery—

Rather it is curious how hard it seems to be for me right now not to cater to someone when I work—rather than just to express myself.

During the summer—I didn't work for anyone—I just sort of went mad usually—I wanted to say 'Let them all be damned—I'll do as I please'—It was vacation after the winter— but—now—remember I've only been working a week—I find myself catering to opinion again— and I think I'll just stop it.

Anita—I just want to tell you lots of things— we all stood still and listened to the wind way up in the tops of the pines this afternoon—and

I wished you could hear it—I just imagined how your eyes would shine and how you would love it—I haven't found anyone yet who likes to live as we do—

Pat. Saturday night.

There is an extensive surviving correspondence between O'Keeffe and Stieglitz from the early period of their courtship. O'Keeffe met Stieglitz when she was visiting New York, in the spring of 1916. Throughout the summer and fall of 1916, they wrote each other on a more or less weekly basis. By the winter of 1916-17, they exchanged letters almost daily until O'Keeffe moved to New York, in May 1918. O'Keeffe writes the following letter, dated September 4, 1916, to Steiglitz, from Texas, where she had just arrived to assume a teaching position. Her need for Stieglitz's approval and her ambivalence about her decision to accept this job provides insight into the mind of the young O'Keeffe.

Your letter this morning is the biggest letter I ever got—Some way or other it seems as if it is the biggest thing anyone ever said to me—and that it should come this morning when I am wondering—no, I'm not exactly wondering but what I should have been thinking in words—is—*I'll be damned* and I want to damn every other person in this little spot—like a nasty petty little sore of some kind—on the wonderful plains. The plains—the wonderful great big sky—makes me want to breathe so deep that I'll break—There is so much of it—I want to get outside of it all—I would if I could—even if it killed me—

I have been here less than 12 hours—slept eight of them—have talked to possible 10 people—mostly educators—*think* quick for me—of a bad word to apply to them—the *little* things they forced on me—they are so just like folks get the depraved notion they ought to be—that I feel it's a pity to disfigure such wonderful country with people of any kind—I wonder if I am going to allow myself to be paid 1800 dollars a year to get like that—I never felt so much like kicking holes in the world of my life—still there is something great about wading into this particular kind of slime that I've never tried before—alone—wondering—if I can keep my head up above these little houses and know more of the plains and the big country than the little people.

Previous contacts make some of them not like my coming here.

So—you see it was nice to get a big letter this morning—I needed it—

I walked and heard the wind—the trees are mostly locust bushes 20 feet high or less—mostly less—and a prairie wind in the locust has a sound all its own—like your pines have a sound all their own—I opened my eyes and simply saw the wallpaper—It was so hideously ugly— I remembered where I was and shut my eyes right tight so I couldn't see it—with my eyes shut

I remembered the wind sounding just like this before—

I didn't want to see the room—it's so ugly—it's awful and I didn't want to look out the window for fear of seeing ugly little frame houses—so I felt for my watch—looked at it—decided I needn't open my eyes again for 15 minutes—The sound of the wind is great—but the pink roses on my rugs! And the little squares with three pink roses in each one—dark lined squares—I have half a notion to count them so you will know how many are hitting me—give me flies and mosquitoes and ticks—even fleas—every time in preference to three pink roses in a square with another rose on top of it.

Then you mentioned me in purple—I'd be about as apt to be naked—don't worry—! Don't you hate pink roses!

As I read the first part of your letter—saying you hadn't looked at the stuff I left for my sister to send you—I immediately thought—I'd like to run right down and telegraph you not to open them—then—that would be such a foolish thing to do.

Not foolish to me—or for me—but the other queer folks who think I'm queer.

There is dinner—and how I hate it—you know—I—...

Your letter coming this morning made me think how great it would be to be near you and talk to you—you are more the size of the plains

235

than most folks—and if I could go with my letter to you and the lake—I could tell you better—how fine they are—and more about all the
things I've been liking so much but I seem to feel
that you know without as much telling as other
folks need.

In June 1918, O'Keeffe responded to Stieglitz's
prompting, and moved back to New York City to take
up residence in his niece's studio, and, by July, they
were living together. They were married in December
1924 a few months after Stieglitz obtained a divorce
from his wife.

O'Keeffe wrote the following letter to the influential critic Henry McBride[6] in recognition of his review
of O'Keeffe's solo show of over 100 works, hung in
1923 in Stieglitz's Anderson Galleries. McBride had
written about her exhibition in the New York Her-
ald, on February 4, 1923. He also discussed two other
women artists, Clare Sheridan[7] and Henrietta Shore[8].
In this letter one can see the driving ambition which
O'Keeffe rarely showed publicly: "I like being first."
McBride endeared himself to O'Keeffe because he did
not stress her "feminine" interpretation of the flower
paintings. Her odd post script does seem to acknowledge that men and women can be judged separately, if
not on two completely different sets of criteria.

My dear Henry McBride:
    After a week of my exhibition I took myself to
bed with the grippe—it was the day before your

advice about the nunnery came out in the Sunday paper—or I might have chosen the nunnery instead.

—However—six days in bed with the grippe is a fair substitution for a nunnery—and I had plenty of time to think about my sins—.

Your notice pleased me immensely—and made me laugh—. I thought it very funny—. I was particularly pleased—that with three women to write about you put me first—My particular kind of vanity—doesn't mind not being noticed at all... and I don't even mind being called names—but I don't like to be second or third or fourth—I like being first—if I'm noticed at all—that's why I get on with Stieglitz—with him I feel first—and when he is around—and there are others—he is the center and I don't count at all.

Now these are secrets—and don't you tell all New York about it or everyone will know how to hurt my feelings—and I'll have to get a new set—

—One more thing I must tell you—Marin[9] brought his new work over last week—and the first day I was out of bed Stieglitz brought it to me to look at (first). I spent the whole day with it—

I think it by far the best he has ever done—Several wonderful sail boats—I feel like going out and robbing someone for him—So he won't have to worry about money—. I wanted to spend all that I got from my show on them—Stieglitz laughs at me—but he is quite as excited himself—.

You must see them soon—I'd like to send one of the sail boats to get you—but you will probably have to come up some other way—.

There are wonderful houses too—and a great sea—You must see them soon.

Sincerely—and thanks again for the notice
Georgia O' Keeffe

I must add that I don't mind if Marin comes first—because he is a man—it's a different class—

The next letter is addressed to Mabel Dodge Luhan[10] and written around 1925. Luhan was an author and supporter of the arts. She was known for her "salon" in Taos which included many important literary figures, such as the noted author D. H. Lawrence.[11] Luhan was instrumental in O'Keeffe's decision to visit New Mexico, in the summer of 1929. She settled O'Keeffe into the "pink house," near her home in Taos. In this letter, O'Keeffe recognizes the polarization of gender issues of her era and appeals to Luhan to write about her works in such a way that "a woman ...might say something that a man cant [sic]." However, Luhan did not publish an article about O'Keeffe at this time.

Mabel Luhan:

About the only thing I know about you—from meeting you—is that I know I don't know anything.—That I like—because everybody else knows—So when they say—'Don't you think so?' I don't think so—I don't think at all because I can't.—No clue to think from—except that I have never felt a more feminine person—and what that is I do not know—so I let it go at that till something else crystallizes.

Last summer when I read what you wrote about Katherine Cornell I told Stieglitz I wished you had seen my work—that I thought you could write something about me that the men can't—

What I want written—I do not know—I have no definite idea of what it should be—but a woman who has lived many things and who sees lines and colors as an expression of living—might say something that a man can't—I feel there is something unexplored about woman that only a woman can explore—Men have done all they can do about it.—Does that mean anything to you—or doesn't it?

Do you think maybe that is just a notion I have picked up—or made up—or just like to imagine? Greetings from us both—And kiss the sky for me—

You laugh—But I loved the sky out there

Georgia O'Keeffe—

While returning to New York, from her first summer in New Mexico, O'Keeffe wrote the following letter, addressed to Ettie Stettheimer[12] and dated August 24, 1929. It was written on stationery from a hotel in Aspen, Colorado. Ettie was one of three sisters, none of whom ever married, who lived in Manhattan and who had a close friendship with O'Keeffe and

Stieglitz, and many other influential artists and writers. O'Keeffe references both Carrie[13] and Florine,[14] also an interesting painter, in her closing salutations. In this letter, there is a wonderful, almost poetically concise summary of the experience of New Mexico and how she hopes it will inspire her art. She also justifies her return to Stieglitz and his family's summer home, in upstate New York, on Lake George.

Dear Ettie:

A week ago today I took this paper at this funny little hotel to write you because it seemed amusing. I have carried it so long that it isn't amusing me any more—However—the paper having lost its flavor isn't going to stop me.

I am on the train going back to Stieglitz—and in a hurry to get there—I have had four months west and it seems to be all that I needed—It has been like the wind and the sun—there doesn't seem to have been a crack of the waking day or night that wasn't full—I haven't gained an ounce in weight but I feel so alive that I am apt to crack at any moment—

I have frozen in the mountains in rain and hail—and slept out under the stars—and cooked and burned on the desert so that riding through Kansas on the train when everyone is wilting about me seems nothing at all for heat—my nose has peeled and all my bones have been sore from riding—I drove with friends through Arizona—Utah—Colorado—New Mexico till the thought of a wheel under me makes me want to hold my head.

—I got a new Ford and learned to drive it—I even painted—and I laughed a great deal—I went every place that I had time to go—and I'm ready to go back East as long as I have to go sometime—If it were not for the Stieglitz call I would probably never go—but that is strong—so I am on the way. He has had a bad summer but the summers at Lake George are always bad—that is why I had to spend one away—I had to have one more good one before I got too old and decrepit—Well—I have had it—and I feel like the top of the World about it—I hope a little of it stays with me till I see you—

It is my old way of life—you wouldn't like it—it would seem impossible to you as it does to Stieglitz probably—but it is mine—and I like it—I would just go dead if I couldn't have it—When I saw my exhibition last year I knew I must get back to some of my own ways or quit—it was mostly all dead for me—Maybe painting will not come out of this—I don't know—but at any rate I feel alive—and that is something I enjoy.

Tell me what the summer has been for you—I hope it has been good for all of you—

I will be in Lake George by the time you get this.

My greetings to Carrie and Florine
With Love

Georgia—

This next letter, addressed to Jean Toomer,[15] provides insight into O'Keeffe's beliefs and understandings about the gender differences between men and women. Toomer was an African-American author who had met O'Keeffe and Stieglitz in 1923, following the publication of his acclaimed book *Cane*. They maintained a friendship over the next decade. O'Keeffe clearly felt close to him, as is revealed in this letter, dated January 10, 1934,that formed part of an ongoing correspondence. She states that her center is "like a plot of warm moist well tilled earth with the sun shining hot on it." This vocabulary is so powerful that scholars have analyzed this letter carefully. Sharon Udall interprets this as a clear reference to the way she personified land forms and the way land could become in her paintings a "symbolic extension of her own body."[16] However Barbara Buhler Lynes warns us to recall that this "vocabulary was used with great frequency" by artists of both genders in the Stieglitz circle and could be seen as carrying universal rather than specifically female significance. [17]

I waked this morning with a dream about you just disappearing—As I seemed to be waking you were leaning over me as you sat on the side of my bed the way you did the night I went to sleep and slept all evening in the dining room—I was warm and just rousing myself with the feeling of you bending over me—when someone came for you—I wasn't quite awake yet—I seemed to be in my room upstairs—doors opening and closing in the hall and to the bathroom—whispers—a woman's slight laugh—a space of time—then I seemed to wake and realize that you had gone out and that the noises I had heard in my half sleep undoubtedly meant that you had been in bed with her—and in my half sleep it seemed that she had come for you as tho it was her right—I was neither surprised no[r] hurt that you were gone or that I heard you with her.

And you will laugh when I tell you who the woman was—It is so funny—it was Dorothy Kreymborg.[18]

And I waked to my room here—down stairs with a sharp consciousness of the difference between us.

The center of you seems to me to be built with your mind—clear—beautiful—relentless—with a deep warm humanness that I think I can see and understand but *have not*—so maybe I neither see nor understand even tho I think I do—I understand enough to feel I do not wish to touch it unless I can accept it completely because it is so humanly beautiful and beyond me at the moment. I dread touching it in any way but with completely acceptance. My center does not come from my mind—it feels in me like a plot of warm moist well tilled earth with the sun shining hot on it—nothing with a spark of possibility of growth seems seeded in it at the moment—

It seems I would rather feel it starkly empty than let anything be planted that can not be tended to the fullest possibility of its growth and what that means I do not know but I do know that the demands of my plot of earth are relentless if anything is to grow in it—worthy of its quality.

Maybe the quality that we have in common is relentlessness—maybe the thing that attracts me to you separates me from you—a kind of beauty that circumstance has developed in you—and that I have not felt the need of till now. I can not reach it in a minute.

If the past year or two or three has taught me anything it is that my plot of earth must be tended with absurd care—By myself first—and if second by someone else it must be with absolute trust—their thinking carefully and knowing what they do—It seems it would be very difficult for me to live if it were wrecked against just now—

The morning you left I only told you half of my difficulties of the night before. We can not really meet without a real battle with one another and each one within the self if I see at all.

You have other things to think of now—this asks nothing of you.

I[t] is simply as I see—I write it—though I think I have said most of it—...

I like you much.

I like knowing the feel of your maleness and your laugh—

James Johnson Sweeney[19] was a curator at the Museum of Modern Art in New York. He organized a retrospective of O'Keeffe's work, which opened on May 14, 1946. Although Sweeney planned to write a book about O'Keeffe, and she was co-operating with him on that project, the book was never published. In this letter, written on June 11, 1945, in preparation for the exhibition, O'Keeffe writes of her ambivalence toward the recognition and the attention which such a retrospective brings to any artist. She manages to be both proud and modest. Her pride is evident when she writes: "I am one of the few who gives our country any voice of its own." But her humility appears in: "It may not be painting, but it is something." In her conflicted statements, one can sense echoes of the deep ambivalence of successful women artists, since Vigée-Lebrun, who found fame and ambition incompatible with the gender ideology of their culture.

...I must say to you again that I am very pleased and flattered that you wish to do the show for me. It makes me feel rather inadequate and wish that I were better. Stieglitz's efforts for me have often made me feel that way too—The annoying thing about it is that I can not honestly say to myself that I could not have been better.

However—we need not go into that. But I do wish to say that if for any reason you wish to change your mind feel assured that it will be alright with me—For myself I feel no need of the showing. As I sit out here in my dry lonely country I feel even less need for all those things that go with the city. And while I am in the city I am always waiting to come back here.

Since I left New York and since seeing you I have had a girl who did some secretarial work for me last winter—collect clippings and put them together for you. I don't know how well she will have done it but she will have done something—It will be odd reading for you I am afraid—

When I say that for myself I do not need what showing at the Museum shows means—I should add that I think that what I have done is something rather unique in my time and that I am one of the few who gives our country any voice of its own—I claim on credit—it is only that I have seen with my own eye—. It may not be painting but it is something—and even if it is not something I do not feel bothered—I do not know why I am so indifferent—...

Georgia O'Keeffe was one of the most private famous artists of her generation. Her amazingly beautiful and original paintings combined with the tireless promotion by Stieglitz, one of the most influential arbiters of American Modernism, was a potent combination which kept her work in the public eye for most of her life. Knowing the level of attention which her art attracted, encouraged O'Keeffe to remain very circumspect in her published statements which were reprinted in catalogues from her New York shows during Stieglitz's lifetime. These statements are not life narratives, in the sense that we have developed that term for this book. Her memoir of 1976 is a retrospective autobiography and, especially in her recollections of her formative years prior to her emergence as an artist in New York, provides valuable insights.

However it is through the informal private medium of her letters only published posthumously, but carefully preserved and now in the collection of the Beinecke Library at Yale University that we begin to "hear" her more unguarded voice. Like much of O'Keeffe's art, her letters embody a contradiction. Had she truly wanted them to remain private, she could have destroyed them, but their preservation argues for her implicit recognition of their historical value and her approval to have them made public, although after her death when she would not have to personally experience the response.

As intimate revelations from one of the most famous, talented and original artists of her era, the letters are precious primary sources which provide a counterbalance to the exquisite, but mute legacy of her painting.

Notes

1 Alfred Stieglitz (1864-1946).
2 Sharyn R. Udall, *Carr, O'Keeffe, Kahlo: Places of their Own* (New Haven CT: Yale University Press, 2000), 288-89.
3 *Georgia O'Keeffe,* (New York: Viking Press, 1976). All excerpts from this volume are reprinted by permission of Juan Hamilton

4   Jack Cowart and Juan Hamilton, Letters selected and annotated by Sarah Greenough, *Georgia O'Keeffe: Art and Letters* (Washington DC: National Gallery of Art, 1987). All of the following notations come from this volume, unless referenced from another source.

5   Arthur Wesley Dow (1857-1922) was head of the fine art department at Columbia University's Teacher's College. O'Keeffe studied with him from 1914 to 1915 (275, note 3).

6   Henry McBride (1867-1962) was an art critic for several New York newspapers (278, note 27).

7   Clare Sheridan (1885-1970) cousin of Winston Churchill was a British sculptor known for portrait busts.

8   Henrietta Shore (1880-1963) was a Canadian-born artist, who settled in California in the mid-1920s. She painted in an abstracted organic precisionist style, using botanical and shell images which were an influence on photographer Edward Weston (1886-1958).

9   John Marin (1870-1953) was an American painter and watercolorist, in the Stieglitz circle "O'Keeffe appreciated Marin's art...she was particular drawn to his watercolors of New York skyscrapers..." (275, note 4)

10 Mabel Dodge Luhan (1879-1962) was "an author and patron of the arts...known for her sponsorship of artists and writing, first in New York and later at her home in Taos, New Mexico (280, note 34).

11 D. H. Lawrence (1885-1930).

[12] Ettie Stettheimer (1925-1955).

[13] Carrie Stettheimer (1869-1944).

[14] Florine Stettheimer (1871-1944).

[15] Jean Toomer (1894-1967).

[16] Udall, *Carr, O'Keeffe, Kahlo: Places of their Own*, 120.

[17] Personal communication, from Dr. Lynes, Curator of the Georgia O'Keeffe Museum and Director of the Georgia O'Keeffe Research Center (October 30, 2009).

[18] Dorothy Kreymborg was the wife of Alfred (1883-1966) who was a poet playwright and critic. Alfred and Dorothy spent several weeks, at Lake George, in the summer of 1925 (280, note 35).

[19] James Johnson Sweeney (1900-1986).

Chapter 10. Frida Kahlo (1907-1954): Letters and Diary

Today, Frida Kahlo is one of the most widely recognized and distinguished women artists of the twentieth century. Arguably, she is the most famous Mexican artist, male or female, of her generation. Her reputation has eclipsed that of her husband, Diego Rivera,[1] which is ironic since she remained nearly invisible as an artist during her own lifetime. Kahlo's precisely rendered, intriguing body of works, which focus most resolutely on the practice of self-portraiture, is now perceived as an empowering symbol for women of color and for women artists around the globe. Her fame has been reinforced by a well-crafted Hollywood film of her life and the facsimile publication of her diary.[2] In 2005, a major exhibition of her works was mounted at the Tate Modern, in London. This exhibition was accompanied by an important catalogue, containing a number of scholarly essays.[3] In the United States a massive exhibition was organized by the Walker Art Center in Minneapolis, in 2007, and traveled to Philadelphia and to San Francisco, maintaining the popularity of this artist.[4] In fact, the Kahlo literature, both scholarly and popular, continues to expand annually.[5]

One could argue that Kahlo's life and her art were more closely intertwined than practically any other artist of the twentieth century. Kahlo's life, from childhood, is inescapably connected with pain, disease and illness. She contracted polio when she was seven, and then, at age eighteen, she was in a horrific accident in which bones in her spine, collarbone, pelvis, right leg and foot were severely damaged. Kahlo endured a series of miscarriages and was never able to carry a pregnancy to full term. During the course of her life, she underwent about 35 separate operations.

In 1929, she married the famous Mexican, mural artist Diego Rivera. From this point on, her life was also merged with her passion for him. Kahlo traveled with Rivera to the United States, in the early 1930s, where she became acquainted with her first supporters in the art world. In 1938, Julien Levy, who owned a small gallery in New York dedicated to Surrealism, mounted her first public exhibition. André Breton,[6] who had been her houseguest in Mexico, wrote the introduction for this exhibition, in which he characterized her art with the famous phrase, "a ribbon around a bombshell." In 1939, Kahlo traveled, alone, to Paris, where Breton eventually organized a show of her work, as discussed in a letter to Nicholas Muray,[7] reprinted below. By the end of that year, her stormy relationship with Rivera led to a divorce, but they were unable to separate their lives and were remarried a year later. By the 1940s, Kahlo was increasingly plagued by debilitating physical problems, although she continued to paint. In 1953, desperately ill, Kahlo was carried on a bed into the opening reception for her first major retrospective exhibition, in the Gallery of Contemporary Art, in Mexico City. After her death, Rivera donated her house to the state as the "Frida Kahlo Museum."

Despite her physical and emotional suffering, Kahlo painted over 150 works, and about 55 or one–third of her total production was in the genre of self-portraiture. In this visual "autobiography," Kahlo invented many varied personae and presented herself to the world in any number of fascinating guises. She also painted still lives and small scale narrative paintings, often inspired by Mexican *retablos*, religious ex-voto paintings.[8]

Stylistically, her art is quite unique and sits uneasily under the umbrella of Surrealism. Kahlo was reluctant to be labeled a Surrealist, as stated in her letter to Antonio Rodriguez[9], included below. However, this was the artistic circle in which her works were recognized during her lifetime. Both the tightly linear style and the combination of veristic imagery, in incongruous juxtapositions, support her inclusion in the wide circle of Surrealism. This is an important issue which Margaret Lindauer discusses, extensively, in her chapter "The Language of the Missing Mother."[10] After summarizing the discussion of Kahlo's relationship to Surrealism, in the literature, and analyzing two key images, *My Birth* (1932) and *My Nurse and I* (1937), Lindauer concludes that: "Kahlo's production clearly is surrealist in so much as surrealism was charged with creating a 'new language' that bridges dichotomies without leveling differences....[Kahlo challenged] masculinist restrictions on subject, theory, and ideology."[11]

Kahlo's literary output consisted mainly of letters and a diary which she kept from the mid-1940s to the end of her life. Her talents as a writer, according to Raquel Tibol, her biographer and the editor of the complete collection of her letters, have never been seriously appreciated. According to Tibol, "Although Frida Kahlo never planned to have a place in twentieth century literature, she must be hailed as a writer who developed new linguistic usages to express her own existential and aesthetic tension."[12]

In her introduction to the facsimile edition of Kahlo's diary, Sarah M. Lowe defines this as a "*journal intime*, a deeply private expression of her feelings."[13] It was never intended to be viewed publicly. Lowe contrasts the immediacy of the diary to the more public and highly constructed record of the painted self-portraits, which could be seen as more of a formal "autobiography". Since nearly every drawing in the diary is spontaneous, one could see her process as closely related to "automatism." "Automatism" was the technique proposed in Breton's First Manifesto of Surrealism as an ideal technique to "bypass the rational mind and unlock the unconscious."[14] The facsimile form of the publication allows the reader to feel as if they are looking over Kahlo's shoulder in her most intimate, quiet and private moments, when she is allowing her "creative unconscious" to emerge in both text and in image.

Tibol defines "the literary element of the diary [as]

"...a series of fragments welded together by heartbreak and loneliness. It is remarkable for its verbal probing, for certain confidences conveyed with poetic intensity and supported by the magical vision through which she set free her libido, imagine a physical release despite her confinement, hold madness and looming grief at bay."[15]

This last decade of her life, from 1944 to 1954, when she worked on her diary, was marked, increasingly, by physical agonies. This is given visualization in one of the most gripping images in the journal: a small self portrait perched on a pedestal with a head, eye and hand falling downwards and the inscription: "I am disintegration" [Yo soy las desintegración...].

Most of Kahlo's other surviving texts are letters to friends and supporters. Kahlo wrote mostly in Spanish, but some of her letters, to her American friends, are written in English. These letters have been collected and translated, where necessary, in a recent volume, making them easily accessible.[16] Collectively, the letters provide a sense of the "real" Kahlo; her energy, compassion, and true warmth is communicated in these texts. Since she wrote mainly to intimate family and friends, she shared her feelings quite directly. Tibol characterizes the personality of Kahlo, as revealed in the corpus of letters, as:

"swinging back and forth between sincerity and manipulations self-complacency and self-flagellation, with her insatiable need for affection, her erotic upheavals, her touches of humor, setting no limits for herself, with a capacity for self-analysis and a deep humility." [17]

The style of Kahlo's letters is "a mixture of refinement and obscenity, artifice, aggression and vulgarity. An outlet for her passion, a desperate game..."[18]

The first letter, reprinted here was written, in English, to Dr. Leo Eloesser, a surgeon. Rivera and Kahlo were in Detroit, in 1932, where Rivera was working on the mural for the Detroit Institute of Arts. Kahlo had met Dr. Eloesser (1881-1976) in Mexico, in 1926, but they became close friends in San Francisco, in 1930.[19] Part of the popular mythology of Kahlo is that her inability to bear a child was a tragedy, that plagued her entire life. Kahlo's culture prioritized child bearing. "In post-revolutionary Mexico, one of the most significant social expectations of married women was to bear children, and women were understood to carry an intense yearning to procreate and nurture." [20] This ideology has been read into Kahlo's life by many scholars and popular biographers. However, as the following letter shows, Kahlo seems quite capable of considering this issue rationally, weighing pros and cons and seeking Dr. Eloesser's expert advice. This would seem to be at odds with an interpretation of the *Henry Ford Hospital,* as the visual documentation of her desperate desire to bear children.

Detroit, May 26th, 1932

[...] This city gives me the impression of an ancient and impoverished hamlet, it struck me as a village, I don't like it at all. But I'm glad Diego is working happily here and has found a lot of material for the frescoes he's going to do in the museum. He's delighted by the factories, the machines, et cetera, like a child with a new toy. The industrial part of Detroit is really the most interesting, the rest is like everywhere else in the United States, ugly and stupid. [...]

I have a lot to tell you about myself, though it's not very pleasant, shall we say. First, my health is not at all good. I would like to talk to you about anything other than that, for I understand you must be bored of hearing complaints from everyone and of sick people, of sicknesses, and above all of the patients, but I would like to believe that my case will be a little different because we are friends and both Diego and I love you very much. You know that well enough.

I'll start by saying I went to see Doctor Pratt, because you recommended him to the Hastings. I had to go the first time because my foot is still bad and consequently the toe, which is naturally in a worse state than when you saw me, as almost two years have passed since then. I'm not too worried about this matter, because I know perfectly well there is no remedy and not even crying helps anymore. In the Ford Hospital, which is where Doctor Pratt is, one of the doctors, I don't remember who, diagnosed it as a *trophic ulcer*. What is that? I just gaped when I found out I had such a thing in one of my paws. The important question now and what I want to consult you about before anyone is that I'm *two* months pregnant, that's why I went back to see Doctor Pratt, who had told me he knew my general condition, because he had talked with you about me in New Orleans, and I wouldn't have to explain to him again the question of the accident, hereditary factors, et cetera, et cetera. Since I thought that, given the state of my health, it was better to abort, I told him so, and he gave me a dose of *quinine* and a very strong castor oil purge. The day after taking it I had a very slight hemorrhage, *almost nothing*. For five or six days I have had a bit of bleeding, but very little. In any case I thought I had aborted and went to see Doctor Pratt again. He examined me and told me no, that he is completely sure *I didn't abort* and that his opinion was that it would be much better, instead of having an abortion, to leave the baby alone and that in spite of the poor state of my organism, taking account the small fracture in the pelvis, spine, et cetera, et cetera, I could have a child by Caesarian section without too much difficulty. He says that if we stay in Detroit for the seven months of pregnancy, he would undertake to look after me with the utmost care. I want you to tell me what you think, with complete frankness, because *I don't know what to do in this case.* Naturally, I'm willing to do what you think will be best for my health, and *Diego says the same.* Do you think it would be more dangerous to abort than to have the child? Two years ago I aborted in Mexico with an operation, in more or less the same conditions as now, three months pregnant. Now I'm only two months pregnant and I think it would be easier, but *I don't know why* Dr Pratt thinks it would be better for me to have the child. You know better than anyone the state I'm in. In the first place, with my heredity I don't believe the child could be very healthy. Secondly, I'm not very strong and the pregnancy would weaken me still more. Moreover, my situation is rather difficult at the moment, as I don't know exactly how long Diego will need to finish the fresco and if, as I calculate, it were in September, the child would be born in December and I would have to go to Mexico three months before it is born. If Diego finishes later, the best thing would be to wait for the baby to be born here, and in any case there would be terrible difficulties traveling with a child just a few days old. I have no one of my family who could care for me during and after my pregnancy, since poor Diego cannot, as much as he would like to, as he's burdened with the problem of his work and a thousand other things. So I wouldn't be able to count on him for anything. The only thing I could do in that case would be to go to Mexico

in August or September and have it there. I don't
think Diego is very interested in having a child,
since what preoccupies him most is his work and
he's perfectly right about that. Kids would come
in third or fourth place. For my part I can't tell
you if it would be good or bad to have a child,
since Diego is constantly traveling and I would
by no means wish to leave him alone and stay
in Mexico, that would only cause difficulties and
problems for both of us, don't you think? But if
you really think as Dr Pratt does, that for the sake
of my health it is better not to abort and to have
the baby, all these difficulties can be somehow
resolved. What I want to know is your opinion,
more than anyone else's, since in the first place
you know my situation and I would thank you
from the bottom of my heart for telling me clearly
what you think would be best. If the operation to
abort were most advisable, I beg you to write
to Dr Pratt, because he's probably not aware of
all the circumstances and since it's against the
law to have an abortion, perhaps he's afraid or
something and later it would be impossible to
perform the operation for me.

If, on the contrary, you think that having the
child could help me, in that case I want you to
tell me if it would be better for me to go to Mexico in August and have it there, with my mother
and my sisters, or to wait for it to be born here.
I don't want to cause you any more bothers,
you can't imagine, dear doctor, how bad I feel

about having to bother you with these things, but I write you not so much as a doctor but rather as the best of my friends and you have no idea how your opinion will help me, because I have *no one* I can count on here. Diego is very good to me as always, but I don't want to distract him with things like this, now that he has all the work on his shoulders and needs peace and quiet more than anything. I don't feel close enough to Jean Wight and Cristina Hastings to consult them about things like this, which are terribly important and if I blunder, the grim reaper could take me! That's why now that I still have time I want to know what you think and to do what is best for my health, which is the only thing I think would interest Diego, because I know he loves me and I'll do anything in my power to make him happy. I'm not eating at all well, I have no appetite and it's only with a great effort that I drink two glasses of cream a day and eat some meat and vegetables. But now I want to vomit all the time with this blessed pregnancy and I'm a mess! *Everything* tires me, for my spine bothers me and I'm also pretty done in by the problem with my foot, since I can't do any exercise and as a result my digestion is all messed up! Nevertheless, I have the will power to do a lot of things and I never feel *disappointed with life as* in Russian novels. I perfectly understand my situation and I'm more or less happy, firstly, because I have Diego, my mother and my father; I love them so much. I think that's enough and I don't ask miracles of life, far from it. Of my friends I love you most and that's why I dare to bother you with such silliness. Forgive me and when you answer this letter, tell me how you have been and accept Diego's and my affection and an embrace from Frieda. If you think I should have the operation immediately I would appreciate your sending a telegram referring to the matter in a veiled way, in order not to compromise yourself in any way. Many thanks and my best memories.[21]

The next letter, dated February 14, 1938, was also written in English. It was addressed to Lucienne Bloch,[22] a close friend of both Rivera and Kahlo's. Bloch had worked as Rivera's assistant in New York, in 1931. She lived with the couple in Detroit, when Frida suffered her miscarriage at the Henry Ford Hospital, and she married one of Rivera's assistants, Stephen Dimitroff. Kahlo was named as the godmother of their child. Because this letter is written to such an intimate friend and does not require translation, it seems to speak to us most directly with Kahlo's "true" voice. This letter is also of interest because she describes the initial contact with Levy and the upcoming plans for her first serious exhibition.

February 14th, 1938
Darling Lucy,
    When your letter arrived, I was feeling lousy as hell, I been having pains on my damn foot for

a week, and probably I will need another operation. I had one four months ago, besides the
one they made when Boit was here, so you can
imagine how I feel, but your letter came, and
believe it or not, gave me courage. Yes Kid, you
don't have any bad foot, but you are going to
have a baby and you are still *working,* and that
is really swell for a young kid like you. You don't
know how happy I am with such news, tell Dimi
that he is behaving O.K. and for your Kid, all my
congratulations. But…please do not forget that
I must be the godmother of that baby because,
in first place, it will be born the very same month
that I came to this damn world, and in second
place, I will be damn switched if somebody else
would have more right than I to be your "com-
rade", so keep that in mind.

Please darling take good care of yourself. I
know you are strong as a rock, and Dimi healthy
as an elephant, but nevertheless you should be
very careful and behave as a good girl. I think
you shouldn't monkey around too much on the
scaffolds, and besides you should eat well and
at regular hours, otherwise it is not worthwhile to
risk the whole thing. I am talking now as a grandmother, but…you know what I mean O.K.

Now I will tell you some things about myself. I
haven't changed very much since you saw me
last. Only I wear again my crazy Mexican dress,
my hair grew longer again, and I am as skinny
as always. My character hasn't changed either,

I am as lazy as always, without enthusiasm for anything, quite stupid, and damn sentimental. Some times I think that it is because I am sick, but of course that is only a very good pretext. I could paint as long as I wished, I could read or study or do many things in spite of my bad foot and other bad things, but there is the point, I live on the air, accepting things as they come, without the minor effort to change them, and all day long I feel sleepy, tired and desperate. What can I do? Since I came back from New York I have painted about twelve paintings, all small and unimportant, with the same personal subjects that only appeal to myself and nobody else... I send four of them to a gallery, which is a small and rotten place, but the only one which admits any kind of stuff, so I send them there without any enthusiasm, four or five people told me they were swell, the rest think they are too crazy.

To my surprise, Julian [sic] Levy wrote me a letter, saying that somebody talked to him about my paintings, and that he was very much interested in having an exhibition in his gallery, I answered sending few photographs of my last things, and he sent another letter very enthusiastic about the photos, and asking me for an exhibition of thirty things in October of this year and he wants to have Diego's exhibition at the same time, so I accepted, and if nothing happens in the meanwhile, I will go to New York in

September. I am not quite sure that Diego will have his things ready for then, but perhaps he will come later, and after to London. Such are the projects we have, but you know Diego as well as I do... I must tell you that Diego painted recently a series of landscapes. Two of them, if you trust my own taste, are the best things he ever painted in his whole life. They are simply gorgeous. I could describe them to you. They are different to anything else he painted before, but I tell you they are magnificent! The color, Kid, is incredible, and the drawing, gee, it's so perfect and strong, that you feel like jumping and crying for joy when you see them. One of them will be very soon at the Brooklyn Museum, so you will see it there. It is a tree on blue background. Please tell me your opinion after you have seen it.

Now that I know that I will have this exhibition in New York, I am working a little bit more to have the thirty damn paintings ready, but I am afraid I will not finish them. We will see.

Reading the *Workers Age* I noticed a great change on your group, but you still have the attitude of a good father trying to *convince* a son that he is wrong but having a great hope that the child will change with your scoldings. I think that this attitude is even worse than the bad behavior of the child. Nevertheless you are admitting little by little many things you thought were all [...] We have many things to talk about this business, but I am not going to bother you now with such stuff after all my opinion in this matter is damn unimportant.

I have many, many interesting things to tell you besides differences of opinion. In September we will talk for hours. Now I only can tell you that his coming to Mexico has been the swellest thing ever happened in my life.

About Diego I am happy to tell you that he feels very well now, his eyes don't bother him any more, he is fat but not too much, and he works as always from morning to night with the same enthusiasm; he still behaves sometimes as a baby, her permits me to scold him once in awhile without abusing too much of that privilege naturally; in one word, he is pretty swell guy as ever was, in spite of his weakness for "ladies" (most young Americans who come to Mexico for two or three weeks and to whom he is always to show his murals outside of Mexico City) he is as nice and fine boy as you know.

Well Darling, I think this letter is already a magazine for my character. I told you all I could, taking account of my bad humor in this moment having pains on my foot, etc., etc. I will send this letter today, air mail, so you will know a word about this lousy person.

Kahlo did travel to New York for her show and then on to Paris, where she had been promised an exhibition by Breton. Arrangements did not proceed smoothly and Kahlo's high level of frustration is fully vented in this letter, dated February 16, 1939, also written in English, to Nickolas Muray, a photographer with whom she was having an affair. She is distancing herself from the apolitical circles of Parisian Surrealism and expressing a sense of homesickness for Mexico.

The question of the exhibition is all a damn mess...Until I came the paintings were still in the custom house, because the s. of a b. of Breton didn't take the trouble to get them out. The photographs which you sent *ages ago*, *he never received*—so he says—the gallery was not arranged for the exhibit *at all* and Breton has no gallery of his own long ago. So I had to wait days and days just like an idiot till I met Marcel Duchamp (marvelous painter- who is the only one who has his feet on the earth, among all this bunch of coocoo lunatic sons of bitches of the surrealists. He immediately got my painting out and tried to find a gallery. Finally there was a gallery called "Pierre Colle" which accepted the damn exhibition. Now Breton wants to exhibit together with my paintings, 14 portraits of the XIX century (Mexican), about 32 photographs of Alvarez Bravo, and lots of popular objects which he bought on the markets of Mexico—*all this junk*, can you beat that? For the 15ᵗʰ of March the gallery is supposed to be ready. But... the 14 oils of the XIX century must be *restored* and the damn restoration takes a whole month. I had to lend to Breton 200 bucks (Dlls) for the restoration because he doesn't have a penny. (I sent a cable to Diego telling him the situation and telling that I lended to Breton that money—he was furious, but now is *done* and I have nothing to do about it.) I still have money to stay here till the beginning of March so I don't have to worry so much.

Well, after things were more or less settled as I told you, few days ago Breton told me that the associate of Pierre Colle, an old bastard and son of a bitch, saw my paintings and found that only *two* were possible to be shown, because the rest are too 'shocking' for the public!! I could of kill that guy and eat it afterwards, but I am so sick and tired of the whole affair that I have decided to send everything to hell, and scram from this rotten Paris before I get nuts myself... You have no idea the kind of bitches these people are. They make me vomit. They are so damn "intellectual" and rotten that I can't stand them any more. It is really too much for my character. I rather sit on the floor in the market of Toluca and sell tortillas, than to have any thing to do with those "artistic" bitches of Paris. They sit for hours on the 'cafes' warming their precious behinds, and talk without stopping about 'culture' 'art' 'revolution'" and so on and so forth, thinking themselves the gods of the world, dreaming the most fantastic nonsense, and poisoning the air with theories and theories that never come true.

Next morning—they don't have any thing to eat in their houses because *none* of *them work* and they live as parasites of the bunch of rich bitches who admire their "genius" of "artists." *Shit* and only *shit* is what they are. I have never seen Diego or you, wasting your time on stupid gossip and 'intellectual' discussions. That is why you are real *men* and not lousy 'artists' – Gee weez! It was worthwhile to come here only to see why Europe is rottening, why all this people—good for nothing—are the cause of all the Hitlers and Mussolinis. I bet you my life I will hate this place and its people as long as I live. There is something so false and unreal about them that they drive me nuts.

From these strong feelings, it is not surprising to read the following statement recorded in an undated letter to Antonio Rodriguez, from the early 1950s, concerning her relationship to Surrealism. This statement foregrounds Kahlo's strong political beliefs and her complex political attitudes toward the nationalism of her era, also discussed in Lindauer in her chapter titled "Unveiling Politics."[23]

Some critics have tried to classify me as a Surrealist; but I do not consider myself to be a Surrealist... Really I do not know whether my paintings are Surrealist or not, but I do know that they are the frankest expression of myself... I detest Surrealism. To me it seems to be a decadent manifestation of bourgeois art. A deviation from the true art that the people hope for from the artist... I wish to be worthy, with my painting, of the people to whom I belong and to the ideas that strengthen me... I want my work to be a contribution to the struggle of the people for peace and liberty.

The last two texts are from Kahlo's diary. In 1939, Kahlo left Paris, broke off her relationship with Muray, and returned to Mexico. By the end of the year, she was divorced from Rivera. In this period, she painted her most famous and complex image, *The Two Fridas.* In a text from her diary, written in 1950, she writes of a childhood memory, which she identifies as the "Origin of the Two Fridas."

ORIGIN OF THE TWO FRIDAS.
=Memory=
    I must have been six years old when I had the intense experience of an imaginary friendship with a little girl... roughly my own age. On the window of my old room, facing Allende Street, I used to breathe on one of the top panes. And with my finger I would draw a "door"........ Through that "door" I would come out, in my imagination, and hurriedly, with immense happiness, I would cross the entire field I could see until I reached a dairy store called PINZON... Through the "O" in PINZON I entered and descended impetuously *to the entrails of the earth,* where

"my imaginary friend" always waited for me. I don't remember her appearance or her color. But I do remember her joyfulness- she laughed a lot. Soundlessly. She was agile. And danced as if she were weightless. I followed her in every movement and while she danced, I told her my secret problems. Which ones? I can't remember. But from my voice she knew all about my affairs. When I came back to the window, I would enter through the same door I had drawn on the glass. When? How long had I been with "her"? I don't know. It could have been a second or thousands of years... I was happy. I would erase the "door" with my hand and it would "disappear." I ran with my secret and my joy to the farthest corner of the patio of my house, and always to the same place, under a cedron tree, I would shout and laugh Amazed to be *Alone* with my great happiness with the very vivid memory of the little girl. It has been 34 years since I lived that magical friendship and every time I remember it comes alive and grows more and more inside my world.

PINZON 1950. Frida Kahlo

Kahlo's strong, passionate relationship with Rivera led to a reconciliation and the couple remarried. One of the recurring themes of the diary is her love for Rivera. "Kahlo is endlessly inventive in her casting of their roles in their complementary and symbiotic relationship." [24] In her diary, she wrote many love poems about her feelings for Diego. In this text, she seems to summarize her complex emotional attachment to him. On the last page of this five page entry, she lists all the multiple roles of Rivera, who is all possible things to her.

Nobody will ever know how much I love Diego. I don't want anything to hurt him. nothing to bother him or to sap the energy that he needs to live-

To live the way he feels better. Painting, seeing, loving, eating, sleeping, feeling lonely, feeling pained – but I never want him to be sad and if I had my health I'd like to give it all to him if I had my youth he could have it all

I'm not just your –mother- I am the embryo, the germ, the first cell which – potentially- engendered him- I am him from the most primitive... and the most ancient cells, that with time became him...There is nothing absolute Everything changes, everything moves, everything revolves- everything flies and goes away.

Diego beginning
Diego builder
Diego my child
Diego my boyfriend
Diego painter
Diego my lover
Diego "my husband"
Diego my friend

Diego my mother
Diego my father
Diego my son
Diego =me=
Diego Universe
Diversity within unity.

Why do I call him my *Diego?*
He never was or will be mine.
He belongs to himself.

Frida Kahlo's letters, in a way similar to those of O'Keeffe, are valuable documents in which the reader can hear the unguarded voice of the artist, as she communicated to friends and family. The recently published complete edition of her letters is a valuable resource for students and admirers of Kahlo's art. Unlike O'Keeffe, Kahlo painted in the shadow of Rivera and with very, very little recognition, so her art never received the sort of critical reception to which O'Keeffe became accustomed. It is a tribute to Kahlo's strong sense of identity that she continued to paint and during the last decade of her life create the remarkable diary in the absence of any consistent or widespread support. That identity of humor energy and strength is communicated clearly in the texts of the letters. Given the popular phenomenon of "Frida-mania," it is especially important to listen to her own voice to anchor our interpretations of her paintings.

The diary is a unique and highly original synthesis of texts and images and presents Kahlo as a more self-consciously poetic writer showing us anther facet of her amazingly creative personality. Kahlo's struggle to maintain her dignity in the face of great physical pain and personal traumas has resonated with audiences around the world and anyone who admires her "painted autobiography" can gain insight into her personality though the medium of her correspondence and her diary.

Notes

[1] Diego Rivera (1886-1957).

[2] *The Diary of Frida Kahlo: an Intimate Self-Portrait* (New York: Harry N. Abrams, 1995).

[3] Emma Dexter and Tanya Barson (eds), *Frida Kahlo* (London: Tate Publishing, 2005).

[4] Elizabeth Carpenter (ed) *Frida Kahlo* (Minneapolis MN: Walker Art Center, 2007).

[5] One important study is Gannit Ankori, *Imaging her Selves: Frida Kahlo's Poetics of Identity and Fragmentation* (Westport, CO: Greenwood Press, 2002). This work, based on her dissertation at Hebrew University, contains a detailed exploration of Kahlo's iconography, leading to new interpretations of her major works.

[6] André Breton (1896-1966), a French poet, essayist and critic, was one of the founding members of Surrealism and the author of the Surrealist manifestos.

[7] Nicholas Muray (Hungary, 1892- United States, 1965) photographer, dance critic, aviator, fencing champion, was introduced to Frida in Mexico by

Rosa Rolando and Miguel Covarrubias. An initial romantic encounter became deeper when Kahlo arrived in New York to present her first individual exhibition at the Julien Levy Gallery from November 1 to 15, 1938. Raquel Tibol (ed), *Frida by Frida*, translated by Gregory Dechant (Mexico: Editorial RM, 2006), note, p. 103.

8   "When Kahlo started to paint on tin in the early 1930s it was specifically in imitation of the naïve painters of religious *ex-votos*...Kahlo was an avid collector of these *retablos* or *milagros*, as evidenced by the large number still on display in her home the Casa Azul." Dexter and Barson (eds), *Frida Kahlo*, 15-16.

9   Antonio Rodríguez (Portugal, 1908-Mexico, 1993) was an art critic, journalist, cultural promoter and photographer. He interviewed and photographed Frida, who in 1944, dedicated to him, a very surrealist self-portrait: "With love for Toño" (note, Tibol, *Frida by Frida*, 365).

10   Margaret A. Lindauer, *Devouring Frida: the Art History and Popular Celebrity of Frida Kahlo* (Hanover and London: Wesleyan University Press, 1999), 86ff.

11   Ibid., 113.

12   Raquel Tibol, "Paint—Love—Liberation: Frida Kahlo's Words" in Dexter and Barson, 191.

13   *The Diary of Frida Kahlo: an Intimate Self-Portrait* (New York: Harry N. Abrams, 1995).

14   Sarah M. Lowe, "Essay" in Ibid., 27

15   Tibol, in Dexter and Barson, *Frida Kahlo*, 190.

[16] Raquel Tibol (ed), *Frida by Frida.*

[17] Ibid., p. 8

[18] Tibol in Dexter and Barson, *Frida Kahlo,* 186.

[19] Tibol, *Frida by Frida* , note, p. 105 Dr Leo Eloesser (1881-1976) was chief of service at San Francisco General Hospital, professor of surgery at Stanford School of Medicine He was Kahlo's most trusted doctor and life long friend (Dexter and Barson , *Frida Kahlo,* 210).

[20] Lindauer, *Devouring Frida: the Art History and Popular Celebrity of Frida Kahlo* 20ff.

[21] All letters are reprinted with the permission of the Diego Rivera & Frida Kahlo Museums trust.©2009 Banco de Mexico Diego Rivera &Frida Kahlo Museums Trust. Av. Cinco de Mayo No. 2, Col. Centro, Del. Cuauhtemoc 06059, Mexico, D. F.

[22] Lucienne Bloch (1909-1999) was a photographer and close friend of Kahlo's. The daughter of Swiss composer, Ernest Bloch, she met Rivera at a banquet in Manhattan. When Rivera and Kahlo moved to Detroit, Rivera asked her to move in and care for Kahlo...Kahlo became godmother to Bloch's child. (Dexter and Barson, *Frida Kahlo* 209).

[23] Lindauer. *Devouring Frida: the Art History and Popular Celebrity of Frida Kahlo,* 114ff.

[24] Lowe, *The Diary of Frida Kahlo: an Intimate Self-Portrait,* 28

Introduction to Part 3: The Late Twentieth Century; Life Narratives in the Contemporary World (1975-2000)

The texts in Part 3 were published after 1975, while the texts in Part 2 were mainly written before 1940. This 35 year gap is not a random lapse, but reflects the destructive impact of "genocidal fascism, with its anti-feminist, misogynist, homophobic racism," as Griselda Pollock has defined the cultural disruptions of World War II.[1] The period between 1945 and 1970 was a very difficult time for women artists, who became virtually invisible in the art world.

While enjoying many of the benefits of access to equal art education, prejudice against women artists persisted in the post World War II era, reflecting the gender ideology of the culture as a whole. Between 1950 and 1970, the New York art world was dominated by the aesthetic and critical system of "Modernism" and the subsequent movement, which was a direct outgrowth of modernist principles, "Minimalism." As discussed in the Introduction to Part 2, this ideology had already become a significant issue working against women artists in the inter-war period. Many scholars have noted the masculinist gender ideology which pushed women artists to the, almost, completely

277

invisible margins of the art community in the1950s and 1960s. As Marcia Tucker stated:

"the artistic canon [modernism] …embodied the (masculine) values of the culture at large and virtually eliminated not only women but all artists of color. It upheld the value of a single standard of quality against which all works could be objectively measured and which formed a 'consensus of educated opinion'.— consisting largely of those who wished to perpetuate the values of their own kind." [2]

In their introduction to an important history of the Feminist Art movement, Norma Broude and Mary Garrard discuss the impact of Modernism: "Women artists in the 1950s and 1960s suffered professional isolation not only from one another, but also from their own history, in an era when women artists of the past had been virtually written out of the history of art."[3]

This situation began to change radically in the 1970s. The visibility of women artists was fueled by the developing feminist movement in Euro-American culture. Women artists emerged into the consciousness of the art world, and formed an influential group that rejected Modernism's monolithic approach to making works of art. They challenged the narrow aesthetic criteria which eliminated the "personal" from the sphere of "art." The slogan, "The personal is political," inspired a number of women artists to break away from the narrow aesthetic boundaries of Modernist abstraction and to begin to incorporate autobiographical references, images of the female body, spiritual icons of a "Great Goddess", and other new concepts into the visual arts. The Feminist Art movement of the 1970s broke the hold of Modernism and expanded the iconographical and stylistic options available for significant works of art.

> "It was the Feminist Art movement, with its politically forceful reinstatement of figurative imagery, portraiture and the decorative that forced an expanded definition of modernism and opened up new avenues of expression to male as well as to female artists."[4]

The historical significance of this paradigmatic shift should not be underestimated. Broude and Garrard have clearly defined its impact for the subsequent history of contemporary art:

> "We owe to the feminist breakthrough some of the most basic tenets of postmodernism: the understanding that gender is socially and not naturally constructed; the widespread validation of non-'high art' forms such as craft, video, and performance art; the questioning of the cult of 'genius'…the awareness that behind the claim of 'universality' lies an aggregate of particular standpoints and biases, leading in turn to an emphasis upon pluralist variety rather than totalizing unity." [5]

Pollock believes that there is a direct connection between women modernists who were active between 1900 and 1940 (Part 2), and the feminist artists of the later twentieth century (Part 3). She traces a strong connection across the generational divide of World War II.

"The emergence of a formally, self-consciously feminist intellectual revolution in the last third of the twentieth century was itself the product, in part, of the relatively unacknowledged and swiftly forgotten cultural and aesthetic revolution initiated by the modernist women of the first third of that century, that was not fully curated and collected and inscribed into our established narratives." [6]

As we have seen, by 1900 a large percentage of artists were women (Introduction to Part 2). Although many women, like their male colleagues were traditional painters, women participated in avant garde movements in significant numbers, as well, even if their contributions were not acknowledged. These "fore-mothers," such as Alice Neel (Chapter 11) and Louise Bourgeois (Chapter 14) became role models for the generation of women coming to artistic maturity after 1970.

In 1980, Kay Larson confidently announced, in the widely read magazine *ArtNews*, that "For the first time in western art, women are leading, not following." [7] However, in retrospect, it would appear that 1980 was a culminating moment of visibility for women artists in this decade. By 1983, coinciding with the increasing political conservatism of the Reagan administration, women were statistically under-represented in every major group exhibition in Europe and in America, as well as in commercial galleries.[8]

In the catalogue for a major traveling exhibition in 1989, *Making Their Mark: Women Artists Move into the Mainstream, 1970-85*, a number of statistics supported the decrease in visibility and recognition of women artists during the 1980s.[9] One egregious example of discrimination during these years was the large exhibition mounted in 1984 to celebrate the re-opening of New York's Museum of Modern Art titled "An International Survey of Recent Painting and Sculpture". Of 169 artists, only 13 (7.7%) were women.[10] One positive outcome of this "hang" was the formation of the Guerrilla Girls, the self-proclaimed "conscience of the art world" who remain active, today, fighting discriminatory practices.[11]

However, by the 1990s, the impact of the disintegration of modernist "uniformity" into pluralistic diversity, which had been spearheaded by the Feminist Art movement of the 1970s, could be documented, in major exhibitions. In this decade, Anglo-American curators developed a global, multicultural awareness of artistic activity. Maura Reilly, curator of the Elizabeth A. Sackler Center for Feminist Art, at the Brooklyn Museum, cites the Whitney Biennial of 1993 as "a benchmark...to include artists... [whose works] touched on many of the pressing concerns facing the

U. S. at that specific historical moment."[12] Statistically, it was also very unusual in that white males were in the minority: 36.4% were white male, 29.5% were white females, 22.7 % were males of color, and 11.4% were females of color.[13]

Cultural changes do not occur in an unbroken linear progression of successes. Therefore there are a number of statistics from the 1990s that indicate the lag in some institutions in the full recognition of women artists. However if one takes a broader view, there was clearly major improvements by the beginning of the millennium. For example, between 2000 and 2004, 37% of solo exhibitions at the Whitney Museum featured women artists, although the statistics for other major museums were considerably lower.[14]

However one can cite positive changes over time in the Venice Biennale, a major indicator of trends in contemporary art. In 1991, 25% of the artists represented in national pavilions were women.[15] However, in 2005, the Venice Biennale was curated by two Spanish women, Rosa Martinez and Maria de Corral. This was the first time that this international exhibition, which began in the 1890s, was directed by women. Their fresh perspective resulted in a better representation of women artists. In this show, 38% of the works displayed were made by women, many of whom were feminists. It was global in scope, and two of the prominent spaces showed works by Barbara Kruger[16] and the Guerrilla Girls.

One of the most important changes in the past decade has been the recognition of the global nature of artistic practices. Breaking out of the confines of a Euro/Americacentric focus curators, critics and art historians have manifested a heightened awareness of the full range of artistic practices around the world.

Indicating a sensitivity to the importance of viewing art globally, Whitney Chadwick in *Women, Art and Society* (4th edition, 2007), devoted two final chapters to an analysis of the artistic activities of women worldwide, as documented through a series of international exhibitions in cities, such as Sydney, Havana, Johannesburg, and São Paolo. According to Chadwick "Perhaps the most extensive and far-reaching representation of women artists in international biennials occurred in 1999 with exhibitions in Brisbane [The Third Asia-Pacific Triennial], Fukuoka [Asian Art Triennial, Japan], Istanbul, and Venice."[17]

The year 2007 was an exciting time for the exhibition and awareness of both historical and contemporary feminist artists. On the west coast, *WACK! Art and the Feminist Revolution*[18] brought together a massive number of works created, internationally, during the 1970s. Simultaneously, *Global Feminisms: New Directions in Contemporary Art* opened, coinciding with the inauguration of the Elizabeth A. Sackler Center for Feminist Art, at the Brooklyn Museum. *Global Feminisms* presented "a multiplicity of voices and ones that are primarily non-Euro-American, which [was designed] to call attention to the fact that feminism is a global issue.[19] This show was co-curated by Reilly and noted art historian Linda Nochlin. Judy Chicago's historically important installation, *The Dinner Party* (Chapter 12), has found its permanent home at the Sackler Center.

Most recently, in a very positive move, curator Camille Morineau used the entire exhibition space of the Pompidou Center, usually reserved for the permanent collection, to hang a show of works created exclusively by women, drawn from the museum's holdings. Opening in May, 2009, *elles@centrepompidou* marked the first time that a major museum looked to its own permanent collection and then formulated an alternative history of twentieth century art, exclusively by women.[20] One can hope that this show will inspire other museums to mine their permanent collections in a similar way.

What this does indicate collectively is a willingness to rewrite the history of contemporary art. It seems fair to state that scholars writing the history of twentieth first century art will not only include a substantial number of women but will also find theoretical perspectives in which artistic practices have been redefined by the feminist revolution of the 1970s. My positive viewpoint has been reinforced by the most recent edition of a standard text widely used in college classrooms. H. H. Arnason's *History of Modern Art* has just been revised by Elizabeth C. Mansfield, with a copyright date of 2010. The last chapter is appropriately titled "Contemporary Art and Globalization" reinforcing the importance of global perspectives as noted above. Four of the five subheadings in this chapter are directly relevant to an appreciation of the impact of feminist artists. Not only does the author include important women practitioners, but also one can argue the themes used to define contemporary practice were invented by women artists.

Under the first topic: "Lines That Define Us: Locating and Crossing Borders, Art and the Expression of Culture" Mansfield includes three women artists who were also included in either the Pompidou Show or Global Feminisms, Shirin Neshat, an Iranian filmmaker, Shahzia Sikander born in Pakistan and the Japanese artist Mariko Mori. Mansfield's second theme "Growing Into identity" and its subheading "Identity as Place" is focused on images of childhood and adolescence. Seven of the twelve artists discussed are women. However it is the women who have defined the terms of this practice and spearheaded an acceptance of issues of identity as a foreground for artistic practice. Three of these seven artists, Rineke Dijkstra, a Dutch photographer, Marlene Dumas a painter raised in South Africa under apartheid, and Tracey Emin from Britain were include in the Pompidou show. A fourth Emily Jacir, a Palestinian, was included in the "Global Feminisms" show.

The third subheading "Skin Deep: Identity and the Body" was a primary concern of Feminist art in the 1970s. Three of the six artists in this section Kiki Smith, an American, Mona Hatoum, a Lebanese artist now living in London, and Ghada Amer, born in Egypt were all included in the Pompidou show. The fourth subheading of significance, "The Art of Biography" foregrounds the importance of the individual and the personal story, which has informed the work of this entire book. Three of the five artists discussed in this section are women; the African Americans Carrie Mae Weems, and Lorna Simpson and the photographer Nan Goldin, who was also included in the Pompidou show.

What this list shows, cumulatively, is not a writing of the history of contemporary art that merely includes women in an artistic practice defined by male artists but the redefinition of art practice according to the concerns of feminist artists. I believe that Mansfield's rewriting of twenty first century art opens up very exciting possibilities for the future. Historians will continue to develop new thematic approaches to the understanding of the art practices of our world. As Pollock notes:

> "…we do not yet know what women's interventions into the art of the twentieth century signify. We have hardly begun to collect it, exhibit, it, analyze it…each event…is one experimental sentence or paragraph of the expanding cultural script. " [21]

This "expanding cultural script" is one that cannot marginalize or minimize the enormous contributions of women artists from around the world.

This introduction can only indicate a few milestones in the complex chronology of women artists of the late twentieth century. For a much more detailed record of key events for women artists and Euro-American society, the reader can consult Jenni Sorkin and Linda Teung's chronology in W*ACK! Art and the Feminist Revolution* [22] and the chronology prepared by Nathalie Ernoult in *elles@centrepompidou*.[23]

All five texts included in Part 3, partake in the explosion of life narratives in the contemporary world. As Sidonie Smith and Julia Watson note:

> "The autobiographical gesture has become endemic...We are also witnessing, in an outpouring of memoirs, the desire of autobio-graphical subjects to splinter monolithic cate-gories that have culturally identified them, such as "woman" or "gay" or "black" or "disabled," and to reassemble various pieces of memory, experience, identity embodiment and agency in new, often hybrid, modes of subjectivity."[24]

However, gender differences persisted into the twentieth century, as seen in two major compilations in which women accounted for slightly over 20% of published autobiographies. [25] This does not mean that, when compared with earlier periods, there are a small absolute number of published self narratives. Patricia K. Addis compiled a list of 2,217 published women's autobiographical writings, from the period 1946-1976, including compilations of letters and travel narratives.[26] Addis provides an index of these authors, according to their professions. Visual artists are not strongly represented: 22 names are listed under the generic term "artist," 11 as "painter," 3 as "potter," and 7 under "sculptor," for a total of 43, just under 2%.

One of the distinguishing features of the life narratives of the five artists in Part 3 is their awareness of the contemporary women's movement of the 1970s. These texts were written in a self-conscious manner, supported by a broad based cultural feminism.

Alice Neel created many innovative portraits, a type of painting which was unappreciated during the dominance of Modernism (Chapter 11). However, in the 1970s, her work was "rediscovered," and she emerged into the cultural consciousness, fueled by the Feminist Art movement and rescued from her position of critical neglect. Between 1979 and 1982, art historian Patricia Hills interviewed Neel and recorded their conversations. The texts reprinted in this chapter are excerpted from the subsequent publication.[27] This was most fortunate, since Neel, already in her 80s, passed away in 1984. This is a contemporary equivalent of Rosa Bonheur/Anna Klumpke's volume (Chapter 3), and likewise can be termed a **collaborative life narrative** (Introduction II, d).

Chapter 12's texts are excerpted from two retrospective life narratives *Through the Flower (1975)* and *Beyond the Flower (1996)* written by Judy Chicago. Today, Chicago is recognized as one of the leading "foremothers" of the Feminist Art movement of the 1970s and the creator of its most monumental and historically important installation, *The Dinner Party*. *Through the Flower* was written just before the production of *The Dinner Party*, while *Beyond the Flower* resumes the narrative with the controversial critical reception of the installation, as it toured the country in 1979.

The subject of Chapter 13, African-American artist Faith Ringgold, has written an insightful retrospective life narrative, *We Flew over the Bridge: the Memoirs of Faith Ringgold.* Art historian Lisa Farrington has summarized Ringgold's achievement in the following statement: "Ringgold has accomplished a feat only rarely achieved by an African American woman: success, acknowledgement and veneration in her lifetime as an accomplished visual artist." [28] Ringgold's autobiography uses the term **memoir** as its subtitle. This book corresponds to the sense of historical accuracy associated with that genre (Introduction II,a).

The autobiographies of both Chicago and Ringgold are characteristic of a **relational autobiography**, which presents a model of selfhood as "interdependent and identified with a community."[29] The term was first promoted by women of color who argued for a model of difference and a "call to complexity in theorizing of difference [which] multiplies these differences and raises a new issue of priority among heterogeneous differences."[30] Ringgold's retrospective life narrative has a very keenly focused awareness of herself as a feminist, African American artist. Chicago also perceives herself as a role model for future generations of women artists.

Chicago and Ringgold's autobiographies may also be understood as examples of the **Bildungsroman.** This genre originated in the form of a novel of a young man's growth and development and "has been

taken up more recently by women and other disen-
franchised persons to consolidate a sense of emerging
identity and an increased place in public life."[31] The
subtitle of Chicago's *Through the Flower* is *"My Struggle
as a Woman Artist"*. This would also be an appropriate
subtitle for Ringgold. Both Chicago's and Ringgold's
life narratives convey pride in overcoming persecution
and obstacles. Despite the changes that have taken
place since the Victorian era, this sense of struggle
and triumph is not so different from that of Vigée-
Lebrun (Chapter 1) or of Bonheur (Chapter 3), who
could have easily used this same subtitle for their retrospective life narratives. Both Ringgold and Chicago
communicate a sense of identity, which is consistent
with Valerie Sanders's definition of Victorian women
autobiographers, quoted in the Introduction to Vigée-
Lebrun's *Souvenirs* (Chapter 1):

> "Whereas men concentrate on their careers
> and write, for the most part, in a stately prose
> style without rancor, women focus on the vicis-
> situdes of their private lives and tell stories of
> endurance and survival in a society where they
> had no prominence and few claims."[32]

However, I would not characterize these books as
apologies, as the term was used for Vigée–Lebrun's
Souvenirs. The feminist movement gave both artists
support so that they felt less threatened and did not
have the same defensive need to justify their professional lives.

Louise Bourgeois (Chapter 14) is generally acknowledged as an important, innovative sculptor, whose works, especially since the 1970s, have been frequently exhibited and extensively analyzed by art historians. Her primary sources were published in a unique format, compared with other writings in this book. They appeared in an anthology, *Louise Bourgeois: Destruction of the Father, Reconstruction of the Father: Writings and Interviews 1923*-1997.[33] This volume is a compilation of a broad range of both published and unpublished primary sources spanning Bourgeois's active professional life, up to 1998.

This genre could be termed a **literary self-portrait**. Its form is influenced by Barthes's concept of identity which has been quite influential, on a theoretical level (Introduction, I,c). The editors of *Destruction of the Father, Reconstruction of the Father* self-consciously avoid the textual presentation of the artist as a unified, fixed subject narrating a coherent retrospective history. Bourgeois's primary source volume adopts the postmodern idea of fragmentation as its organizing structure. But, even within this format, one can find a connection to the actual living artist. One should recall that feminist scholars of autobiography reject the complete denial of identity between text and author. The chronological sequence of the texts does maintain a link with traditional autobiography. Furthermore, I have reprinted mainly autobiographical statements and diary entries to maintain some continuity with other texts included in this book.

Niki de Saint Phalle came to artistic prominence in the 1960s, with her playful monumental installation *Hon*, one of the earliest "goddess" images, anticipating an important theme of the Feminist Art movement of the 1970s. Her creative sculpture has been critically appreciated, and she has had opportunities to work on a large scale, uncommon for contemporary women artists. Chapter 15 reprints a brief autobiographical statement *"Niki by Niki"* which is an **Autobiography in the third person**. This genre is "a style of address [in which]…the narrating 'I' refers to the narrated 'I' in the third person."[34] The third person voice permits the author to speak in "the role of an apparent self-historian [which] may be ironic and self-deprecating, rather than heroic."[35] Saint Phalle's essay is written in a playful, lighthearted spirit, and reveals some of her key interests and perceptions about her work. This chapter also includes several letters, also published during the artist's lifetime, in an exhibition catalogue from 1992. These letters are addressed to various correspondents, including her most important artistic and personal partner, Jean Tinguely[36] and her most powerful professional supporter, museum director Pontus Hulten.[37] These texts are only "letters" in format, since they were always intended for publication and never actually mailed to the correspondent (Introduction, I,b). Saint Phalle employs the letter format as an "enabling entry" into the realm of autobiographical discourse in a manner quite similar to Vigée-Lebrun's "letters" to Princess Kourakin (Chapter 1).

Perhaps it is appropriate that the texts of Chapter 15 seem to echo, in form and in purpose, the texts of Chapter 1. It is certainly a fascinating intellectual exercise to trace the continuities and dissimilarities in cultural frameworks relevant to the artist/authors included in this book. Despite many improvements for women artists over the past 200 years, gender differences, which diminish women's equality with men, remain a powerful force. These fifteen "singular women" have used both words and visual art to overcome their inherited gender ideologies to create empowering models of professional excellence for future generations.

Notes

[1] Griselda Pollock,"Virtuality, aesthetics, sexual difference and the exhibition: Toward the Virtual Feminist Museum" in Camille Morineau, et al., *elles@centrepompidou: Women Artists in the Collection of the Musée National d'Art Moderne, Centre de Création Industrielle* (Paris: Editions du Centre Pompidou, 2009), 327.

[2] Marcia Tucker, "Women Artists Today: Revolution or Regression?" in Randy Rosen and Catherine C. Brawer, *Making Their Mark: Women Artists Move into the Mainstream, 1970-85* (New York: Abbeville Press, 1989), 198.

[3] Norma Broude and Mary D. Garrard (eds), *The Power of Feminist Art: The American Movement of the 1970s, History and Impact,* (New York: Harry N. Abrams, Inc., 1994), 16.

[4] Ibid., 12.

[5]   Broude and Garrard, *Power of Feminist Art,* 10.
[6]   Pollock, "Virtuality, aesthetics, sexual difference and the exhibition" in Morineau, et al., *elles@centrepompidou,* 327.
[7]   Kay Larson, "For the First Time Women Artists Are Leading Not Following" in *ArtNews,* 79, no. 8 (October, 1980) 64ff.
[8]   Tucker, in Rosen and Brawer, *Making Their Mark: Women Artists Move into the Mainstream,* 1970-85 (New York: Abbeville Press, 1989), 199.
[9]   Randy Rosen and Catherine C. Brawer, *Making Their Mark: Women Artists Move into the Mainstream.*
[10] Maura Reilly, "Introduction: Toward Transnational Feminisms" in Maura Reilly and Linda Nochlin (eds) *Global Feminisms: New Directions in Contemporary Art* (London and New York: Brooklyn Museum and Merrell Publishers, 2007), 22.
[11] See www.guerrillagirls.com
[12] Reilly, *Global Feminisms: New Directions in Contemporary Art,* 34.
[13] Ibid., note #114 p. 45, based on statistics compiled by the Guerrilla Girls.
[14] Reilly, *Global Feminisms: New Directions in Contemporary Art,* 20.
[15] Whitney Chadwick, *Women, Art and Society* 4th edition (London and New York: Thames & Hudson, 2007), 423.
[16] Barbara Kruger (b. 1945) is an American conceptual artist, usually linked to the "second-generation" of Feminist art.
[17] Chadwick, *Women, Art and Society* , 457.

[18] Connie Butler, *WACK! Art and the Feminist Revolution* (Los Angeles: Los Angeles Museum of Contemporary Art, 2007).

[19] Ibid , 38.

[20] *elles@centrepompidou: Women Artists in the Collection of the Musée National d'Art Moderne, Centre de Création Industrielle*

[21] Pollock, "Virtuality, aesthetics, sexual difference and the exhibition" in Morineau, et al., *elles@centrepompidou*, 327.

[22] Los Angeles, Los Angeles Museum of Contemporary Art, 2007

[23] *elles@centrepompidou:Women Artists in the Collection of the Musée National d'Art Moderne, Centre de Création Industrielle*

[24] Sidonie Smith and Julia Watson, *Reading Autobiography: A Guide for Interpreting Life Narratives* (Minneapolis and London: University of Minnesota Press, 2001), 109.

[25] Margo Cully, *A Day at a Time; the Diary Literature of American Women from 1764 to the Present* (New York: The Feminist Press at the City University of New York, 1985), 6.

[26] Patricia K. Addis, *Through a Woman' s I: American Women's Autobiography 1946-1976* (Metuchen, NJ and London: The Scarecrow Press, 1983).

[27] Patricia Hills, *Alice Neel* (New York: Abrams, 1983).

[28] Lisa E. Farrington, *Faith Ringgold* (San Francisco: Pomegranate, 2004) 101.

[29] Smith and Watson, *Reading Autobiography*, 201.

[30] Sidonie Smith and Julia Watson (eds.), *Women, Autobiography, Theory: a Reader* [WAT] (Madison WI and London: The University of Wisconsin Press, 1998), 6.

[31] Smith and Watson, *Reading Autobiography*, 189.

[32] Valerie Sanders, *The Private Lives of Victorian Women: Autobiography in Nineteenth Century England* (New York: St. Martin's Press, 1989), 46.

[33] Published by MIT Press, in 1998.

[34] Smith and Watson, *Reading Autobiography*, 185.

[35] Ibid.

[36] Jean Tinguely (1925-1991) was a Swiss sculptor and one of the founding artists of the movement, Nouveau Realisme.

[37] Pontus Hulten (1924-2006) was a distinguished Swedish museum curator, who was a powerful presence in the contemporary art world, from the 1960s to the 1990s. He was the director of the Museum of Modern Art, in Stockholm, in the 1960s-1970s and founding director of the Centre Georges Pompidou, in Paris, from 1974-1981.

Chapter 11. Alice Neel (1900-1984): *Alice Neel*, a Collaborative Life Narrative

Neel was born in the suburbs of Philadelphia, into a family with no connections to the visual arts. Between 1921 and 1925, she attended the Philadelphia School of Design for Women (now Moore College of Art)[1], which was still under the direction Mary Cassatt's friend and traveling companion, Emily Sartain[2]. Like O'Keeffe, Neel came of age, artistically, when the major institutional barriers to equal education for women had been lifted. She chose a woman's art school, not because she was unable to attend the co-educational Pennsylvania Academy of Fine Arts. However, as she recounts, more subtle gender discrimination persisted in the New York art community in which she lived and worked from the 1930s to the end of her life in 1984.

The late 1920s was a traumatic period for Neel. She married a Cuban artist, had a child who died from diphtheria, and suffered a nervous breakdown. By 1932, she had relocated to New York and was supported, during the Depression, by the New Deal assistance programs.[3] During the 1930s Neel joined the Communist Party, along with many other New York artists and intellectuals. Her commitment to painting portraits of individuals solidified in this decade. Neel painted portraits quietly, with very little recognition, through the 1940s, into the 1960s.

By the 1970s, Neel began to receive the critical attention she deserved for a lifetime of original painting. She was awarded an honorary doctorate from Moore, in 1971, and a major retrospective exhibition at the Whitney Museum, in New York, in 1974. The Feminist Art movement of the 1970s embraced Neel as a true "grandmother." She, in turn, was actively supported by the women's rights movement.

Like Vigée-Lebrun (Chapter 1), Neel's art consists mainly of portraits of specific individuals. However, unlike Vigée-Lebrun, who worked on commission for a wealthy clientele, Neel had the freedom to select her own sitters. This choice permitted her to reveal insights about her times, while retaining a specificity which never reduced her sitters to stereotypes. Neel was one of the few artists who continued to paint recognizable humans in the face of the nearly overwhelming prioritization of abstraction in the post-World War II New York art world. She painted portraits throughout her career, even when Abstract Expressionism was considered to be the only appropriate idiom of modern art. Neel refers to her art as telling "the truth." Her own nude *Self-Portrait* (National Portrait Gallery, 1980) does seem to communicate a form of "truth" with unflinching honesty.

While her style of painting did evolve, she always maintained a rather flattened space and a fluid painterly style, rejecting the traditional academic illusionism of much conservative art. Her mature art is characterized by the use of a saturated blue contour line, painted rather than drawn, and an uneven finish, often focusing on the sitter's head and hands.

The most complete primary source for Neel is *Alice Neel*, published in 1983, just a year before her death.[4] This volume is based on recorded conversations with art historian, Patricia Hills. Like Rosa Bonheur's primary source (Chapter 3), this, too, is a **collaborative life narrative** (Introduction II, d). Occasionally, Hills includes her own prompting questions. However, most of the time, Hills managed to keep herself outside of the flow of Neel's words. Therefore, this text presents a lively, energetic impression of Neel's actual conversation.

In the first excerpt, Neel recalls her early sense of vocation and her artistic training. In Philadelphia, Neel had choices unavailable to artists of previous generations. She could work at either the co-educational Pennsylvania Academy of Fine Arts or the all-women's Philadelphia School of Design. She must have believed that she would be taught oil painting techniques in a similar manner in both institutions. This text provides insights into Neel's independence and self-assurance, at least as she recalled it from the hindsight of about sixty years. She did not seem comfortable at the Philadelphia School of Design, recalling that she was "too rough" for that institution. What this means, exactly, is unclear, but her sense of not belonging and wanting to break out of the rules of art comes through quite clearly

I always wanted to be an artist. I don't know where it came from. When I was eight years old the most important thing for me was the painting book and the watercolors. I'm not like Picasso. He loved the Katzenjammer Kids. Even though I was given a book of the Katzenjammer Kids when I was ten years old, I hated them. I liked romantic couples, and pears and flowers, and that kind of stuff. And I'd get watercolors for Christmas. I didn't take art in high school, but I used to draw heads on the edges of my paper. I was so unsure of myself that the back of the head always went off the paper...

I never told anybody about my art. But even then, at night after work, I went to art school, to the School of Industrial Art, and then to another one in downtown Philadelphia. The teacher there was an old German, very dogmatic. In one picture I was putting the hair on the head like it grows, and he said: 'You don't have to do that. You can just put a tone in.' So he showed me how to fill in the side of a head with up and down strokes. I said: 'Well, that isn't the way the hair goes. I don't want to put in a tone.' So he looked at me in fury and said: 'Before you can conquer art, you have to conquer yourself. Even if you paint for forty years you may not get anywhere.' And I said: 'That's not for you to say because you are only my *beginning* teacher.' He didn't bother me though. I just kept going.

In the three years after high school I worked in various Civil Service jobs besides the Air Corps job. At the end I was making about $35 a week, which was a lot of money for then. Then I quit and answered an ad for a job in Swarthmore. I was offered a job for $30 a week. I remember walking home from the interview through the fall leaves and thinking how discontented I was just to go to work every day. Art was at the back of my mind, always. So I wrote the interviewer that I didn't want the job.

I then enrolled in the Philadelphia School of Design for Women, now called Moore College of Art. I didn't want to go to the Pennsylvania Academy of the Fine Arts because I didn't want to be taught Impressionism, or learn yellow lights and blue shadows. I didn't see life as a *Picnic on the Grass*.[5] I wasn't happy like Renoir.[6]

The Philadelphia School of Design was only a women's school. I liked that better, because I was young and good-looking, and the boys were always chasing me. And here at the Philadelphia School of Design I wouldn't even be able to notice a boy. Because I liked boys. It's all right at sixty or more to say that men are unimportant, but at twenty-one they can be the most important thing in your life. I went to a school that was just a girls' school so I could concentrate on art.

At that point I could always handle men easily. I much preferred men to women. Women terrified me. I thought they were stupid because all they did was keep children and dogs in order. Even though they were 'the conscience of the world,' I didn't think they had all the brains they should have, nor all the answers. I thought the most they ever did was back some man they thought was important.

Miss Emily Sartain was the dean of the school, a very conventional lady. And of course I got in all right. I paid the first year's tuition. It was only $100, I think, and I had saved a little money. They taught fashion there, too. I enrolled first as an illustrator, but that was a mistake, so I changed to fine arts before the end of that year. After that they gave me the Delaware County Scholarship because I was very good.

I was too rough for the Philadelphia School of Design. I didn't want to pour tea. I thought that was idiot's work. And I once painted a sailor type with a lighted cigarette. And, you know, when you paint a picture, there is a certain range. So having this lighted cigarette made the range different—from bright fire to the shadow—and it was very hard to paint. But none of them realized that. This shocked them. They liked pictures of girls in fluffy dresses with flowers better, so they didn't give me a European scholarship. I stayed until I was twenty-five and got a diploma, equivalent today to an M.F.A.

In the next excerpt, she discusses her attitudes toward art and politics during the 1930s. The text begins with her comments on a painting from that era, a rare still life, *Symbols*. She then segues to the trauma of her relationship with Kenneth Doolittle and her involvement with the Communist Party. Unlike Bonheur (Chapter 3) and most of the artists included in Parts 1 and 2, Neel had strong liberal political beliefs which she freely expressed to Hills. In response to Hills' question about the political effectiveness of art, she responds vehemently in the affirmative.

I painted *Symbols* in 1932. A short time before, Roger Fry [7] had written a book where he gave Cézanne's apples the same importance in art as the religious madonnas. The doll is a symbol of woman. The doctor's glove suggests childbirth. The white table looks like an operating table. And there's religion in this, with the cross and palms. In my opinion all of this is humanity, really. This wretched little stuffed doll with the apple, and you see we're still a stuffed doll. Look what's happening to us? Do you think we want to die of a nuclear thing? Do you want your son to go to war? We are powerless. I can't bear that. I hate to be powerless, so I live by myself and do all these pictures, and I get an illusion of power, which I know is only an illusion, but still I can have it, because I'm not confronted with this grim reality. You see all of the artists of yesterday, none of them have two cents of importance beside the great structure. The Pentagon is here. It's not the art world, it's the Pentagon. But you see, one thing they're learning here, maybe, is the importance of art, because the socialist countries always gave importance to art. They saw it as a great propaganda weapon. Here, they're finally learning that art has some importance. They never knew that before. They were too dumb....

In the winter of 1934, Kenneth Doolittle cut up and burned about sixty paintings and two hundred drawings and watercolors in our apartment at 33 Cornelia Street. Also, he burned my clothing. He had no right to do that. I don't think he would have done it if he hadn't been a dope addict. He had a coffee can full of opium that looked like tar off the street. And it was a frightful act of male chauvinism: that he could control me completely. I had to run out of the apartment or I would have had my throat cut.

This was a traumatic experience as he had destroyed a lot of my best work, things I had done before I ever knew he existed. It took me years to get over it. The level of the watercolors in this book show the level of the watercolors he destroyed. They were also personal history.

Since all this had been a major disaster for me, I was in a very rational mood when I painted Max White. Because of the irrationality of Doolittle's actions, I began to think that rationality was the most important thing. Anyway, I've always had a rational streak....

The first time I joined the Communist Party was about 1935, around the time I painted *Pat Whalen*. But I was never a good Communist. I hate bureaucracy. Even the meetings used to drive me crazy. I didn't participate in the meetings because I was too timid. I didn't dare to speak out. But it affected my work quite a bit.

I got an important critic on the WPA by lending him two pictures. The reason I loaned them to him—it was obviously dishonest—was because of left-wing influences. I had reached the conclusion that to eat was the most important thing in the world, and also I thought he knew so much about art that even though he couldn't paint he had a right to be on the project. Once he got in there he became a supervisor and a big theoretician and a great dictator. When he brought Elaine de Kooning[8] up to my house in the early fifties, I got drunk, and I accidentally told this story. And of course, he could have killed me.

I went to the demonstrations of the Artists' Union. We cooperated with the picketing workers of Macy's Department Store. We picketed, and an Irish policeman arrested a big batch of people. He walked up to me and said: 'No, I won't arrest you. You're too Irish.' And he didn't arrest me. But many people were in jail overnight. I hate to tell you that I was glad not to be in jail, because I had claustrophobia.

I was a Communist when I painted *Nazis Murder Jews*, about a Communist torchlight parade in about 1936. The people in the front are Sid Gottcliffe and others who were on the WPA project. I showed the painting at the ACA Gallery. A critic wrote: 'An interesting picture, but the sign is too obvious.' But if they had noticed that sign, thousands of Jews might have been saved.

QUESTION: Do you think that painting can be in the service of the revolution?

Look at Goya[9], look at the Mexicans! If it is real enough, it can be. Do you know how many lectures I went on this question? At least fifty. In the 1930s, this was the big question. The Communists said then—the big Communists—when there is socialism, there would be no need for art. I thought they were just stupid. They meant that everything would be so good you wouldn't have to correct it. Now I always hated being dictated to, although I myself painted these things.

In the following excerpt, Neel discusses her attitudes about being a woman and an artist.

Despite the progress of women artists, "painting like a woman" was still a very negative criticism, as it was in the time of Vigée-Lebrun (Chapter 1). Neel recognizes the need for a supportive network of women in her statement: "I always needed Women's Lib."

I didn't let being a woman hold me back. There was a man on the Project: 'Oh, Alice Neel!

The woman who paints like a man!' And I went to all the trouble of telling him that I did not paint like a man but like a woman—but not like a woman was supposed to paint, painting china. I felt it was a free-for-all. And I never thought it was a man's world. I thought women were always there, even though they may not have participated fully.

Art doesn't care if you're a man or a woman. One thing you have to have is talent, and you have to work like mad.

I was in the exhibition *The New York Group* in 1938 at the ACA Gallery—seven men and I. They were so embarrassed because I was a woman, but I didn't feel any different from them. They didn't understand.

I always needed Women's Lib. I had it inside of me, but outside, these people ran over me even though I was a much better painter.

Like many women artists, Neel's career suffered under the dominance of Abstract Expressionism, supported by the critical discourse of Modernism (Introduction to Part 3). In the following excerpt, she discussed her attitude towards this movement. While allowing artists a sense of personal freedom, she does resent the way that Modernist ideology devalued what Neel felt was more significant, the iconography of people: "What I can't stand is that the abstractionists pushed all the push-carts off the street."

Abstract Expressionism was becoming very attractive then. I'm not against abstraction. Do you know what I'm against? Saying that man himself has no importance. I'm grateful to trees and things that still put out their leaves. And skies that still operate for us. The Van Allen Belt has not collapsed yet. I think those things are very tolerant with human beings. What I can't stand is that the abstractionists pushed all the other pushcarts off the street. But I think when Bill de Kooning[10] did those women it was great. You know why? I think he had something the matter with him sexually and he was scared of women. He probably saw teeth in vaginas.

Ortega y Gasset was prophetic. He predicted in *The Dehumanization of Art* a whole era of art. I think he states there that Juan Gris[11] said Cézanne's[12] arm goes into a cylinder; whereas I paint a cylinder that perhaps becomes an arm.

There is room for different kinds of art. You know what the Bible says: 'In my father's house, there are many mansions.' And of course Robert Rauschenberg[13] is good today because he shows that the world is falling to pieces, and he shows the bombardment of the brain with all those things.

In the next statement, Neel discusses some of the techniques she used to create her portraits. Like Modersohn-Becker (Chapter 7), Neel also admired Cézanne's portraits. She talks about the process of developing a portrait. She clarifies the way the poses of her subjects are fixed and her desire to penetrate the psychology of her sitter.

I went to see a big show of Cézanne's, at least twenty-five or thirty years ago at the Metropolitan. He had a lot of portraits there, and I was amazed at his psychological depth. I didn't think he had it. And guess what he said: "I love to paint people who have grown old naturally in the country.' But you know what I can say? 'I love to paint people torn by all the things that they are torn by today in the rat race in New York.' And maybe one reason I love that so much is because as a child I had to sit on the steps in that dreary small town. But I also think I have an awful lot of psychological acumen. I think that if I had not been artist, I could have been a psychiatrist. Only I wouldn't have known what to tell them to do, but they don't know either.

I do not pose my sitters. I never put things anywhere. I do not deliberate and then concoct. I usually have people get into something that's comfortable for them. Before painting, when I talk to the person, they unconsciously assume their most characteristic pose, which in a way involves all their character and social standing—what the world has done to them and their retaliation. And then I compose something around that. It's much better that way. I hate art that's like a measuring wire from one thing to the next, where the artist goes from bone to muscle to bone, and often leaves the head out. I won't mention who does that.

When I paint, it's not just that it's intuitive, it's that I deliberately cross out everything I've read and just react, because I want that spontaneity and concentration on that person to come across. I hate pictures that make you think of all the work that was done to create them.

Like other women artists, Neel has paid attention to maternity. In a way similar to Kollwitz (Chapter 8), she has respected the specificity of the sitter rather that the abstract concept of "motherhood." But, Neel is unique in her depiction of pregnant nude women. While Modersohn-Becker (Chapter 7) created archetypal images of a "Great Mother," Neel painted specific portraits. In this statement, she mentions her portrait of her daughter-in-law, Nancy, and the reason why she felt it was important to paint these images of pregnant women.

It isn't what appeals to me, it's just a fact of life. It's a very important part of life and it was neglected. I feel as a subject it's perfectly legitimate, and people out of false modesty, or being sissies, never showed it, but it's a basic fact of life. Also, plastically, it is very exciting. Look at the painting of Nancy pregnant: it's almost tragic the way the top part of her body is pulling the ribs.

Neel sums up her focus on portraiture and the role of painting in this last excerpt. She describes her painting as a way to capture the "Zeitgeist" or "spirit of the age." It is a frequently quoted statement in which Neel is both defining and defending her life long painting project.

Art is a form of history. That's only part of its function. But when I paint people, guess what I try for? Two things. One is the complete person. I used to blame myself for that, do you know why? Because Picasso[14] had so many generalities. And mine were all—mostly a specific person. I think it was Shelley who said: 'A poem is a moment's monument.' Now, a painting is that, plus the fact that it is also the *Zeitgeist,* the spirit of the age. You see, I think one of the things I should be given credit for is that at the age of eight-two I think I will produce definitive pictures with the feel of the era. Like the one of Richard,[15] you know, caught in a block of ice—*Richard in the Era of the Corporation.* And these other eras are different eras. Like the '60s was the student revolution era. Up until now, I've managed to be able to reflect the *Zeitgeist* of all these different eras.

I see artists drop in every decade. They drop and they never get beyond there. That was one of the things wrong with the WPA show at Parsons in November, 1977. Hilton Kramer's[16] attitude toward that show was absurd. You can't dismiss the Great Depression as having very little importance. He flattered me. He said at least I didn't join the crowd and do just the same thing they were all doing. He was right, in a way. Those people dropped, back in the '30s, and they never got over it. Many artists developed an attitude and a technique, and they never changed. Even though the world changed drastically, they kept right on doing the same thing.

Alice Neel only achieved any serious recognition for her inventive psychologically penetrating portraits late in life, when the artist was in her 70's. The major primary source for Neel is a monograph of edited conversations that functions as a retrospective autobiography, from which these excerpts were taken. Neel's text is one of the first volumes which benefits directly from the increase in attention and recognition of Neel's work in the context of the Feminist Art movement of the 1970s. Interviewer/editor Patricia Hills created as reliable an autobiographical account as that of Vigee-Lebrun, also written from the perspective of the last years of her life.

Neel was not a writer and there are as yet no published sources for letters, diary, or other types of text; she was a talker. By capturing the rhythm of her conversation and her totally candid, ironic and at times humorous memories of her life we can find a source that connects us to the substantial body of portraits that are well known and documented. Neel went through a series of relationships and raised two sons, but her agency was her unwavering focus on capturing the appearance, and psychology of living people. No other artist active in these years so resolutely rejected the defining ideology of Modernism and its corollary, abstraction, to fix on the project of the artist who paints people. From the perspective of the twenty first century, this interest in individual biography makes her an important influence on the subsequent history of postmodernism (Introduction to Part 3). Neel anticipates and maintains loyalty to issues of identity, individuality, and the human form which is crucial to contemporary art as practiced by all artists, male and female.

Notes

[1] See the discussion of the founding of this school, in the Introduction to Part 1.

[2] Emily Sartain (1841-1927)

[3] See Introduction to Part 2, on the role of women in these government sponsored art programs.

[4] Patricia Hills, *Alice Neel* (New York: Abrams, 1983).

[5] Manet's *Dejeuner sur l'herbe* (1863).

[6] Pierre Auguste Renoir (1841-1919) was a French painter and leading artist in the Impressionist movement.

[7] Roger Fry (1866-1934) was an influential British art critic and defender of the Post-Impressionists. He wrote an influential study *Vision and Design* (1920) and a monograph on *Cezanne* (1927).

8   Elaine de Kooning (1918-1898) was an American painter and wife of Willem de Kooning.

9   Francisco Goya (1746-1828) was a Spanish artist who painted many images based on the atrocities of the Napoleonic wars.

10   Willem de Kooning (1904-1997) was one of the leading painters in the Abstract Expressionist movement.

11   Juan Gris (1887-1927) was a Spanish artist in the circle of Picasso and Braque who developed a personal Cubist style.

12   Paul Cezanne (1839-1906).

13   Robert Rauschenberg (1925-2008) was a major artist in Pop Art.

14   Pablo Picasso (1881-1973).

15   Richard, her son.

16   Hilton Kramer (b. 1928) was an influential art critic for the New York Times from 1965 to 1982. He was a supporter of Greenberg's Modernism.

Chapter 12. Judy Chicago (born 1939): *Through the Flower* and *Beyond the Flower*

Judy Chicago is widely acknowledged as one of the leaders of the Feminist Art movement of the 1970s. On the west coast, in the early 1970s, in collaboration with Miriam Schapiro,[1] Chicago spearheaded the Feminist Art movement, in her role as educator and in the creation of *Womanhouse*. Above all, it is her major installation *The Dinner Party*, which established her reputation, and for which she is best known today.

Chicago was born "Judy Cohen," into a Jewish liberal family, with no special predisposition towards the visual arts. However, like Kollwitz, her background did include a history of political and social activism. Her father, who died when she was only 13, was a union organizer. Chicago's first art training took place at the Art Institute of Chicago. She took classes while she attended public elementary and high school. Between 1960 and 1964, she studied at the University of California-Los Angeles (UCLA), earning her MFA. From this professional training, she emerged as a minimalist sculptor, with no gendered identity as a woman artist. In 1970, at her one-person exhibition at Cal State-Fullerton, she presented the visitor with the following manifesto, written on the gallery wall: "Judy Gerowitz[2] hereby divests herself of all names imposed upon her through male social dominance and freely chooses her own name, Judy Chicago." The significance of this name change is self-evident from a feminist perspective. However, Lisa E. Bloom has analyzed her self-naming from the perspective of "ethnic," i.e. specifically Jewish identity. Bloom believes this transition:

> "from the ethnically marked Gerowitz to the more American-sounding Chicago is seemingly central to her scripting of herself in public as an autonomous feminist subject and artist....
> ...the erasure of her ethnic name in favor of a national identity was not seen at the time as a public rejection of her ethnic group so much as turning away from patriarchy in general."[3]

By 1970, Chicago was developing a strong feminist awareness, although her art, such as the *Pasadena Lifesavers*, was still quite abstract and not fully comprehensible to the public as a feminist statement. That summer, Chicago moved to northern California and organized the first feminist studio art course in the United States, at Fresno State College. In 1971, she teamed up with Miriam Schapiro and together they developed a feminist art program at the California Institute of the Arts, in Valencia. The following year, they organized *Womanhouse*, which was composed of a group of installations in an abandoned building in Los

Angeles. *Womanhouse* is recognized as a major monument of the Feminist Art movement of the 1970s. But, Chicago's fame rests on *The Dinner Party*, her monumental and best known work, which was conceived in 1974-75 and completed in 1978. This large installation traveled across the country. After this tour it went into storage and was seen infrequently for the next 20 years. It continued to provoke controversy into the 1990s, when Chicago attempted to donate it to the University of the District of Colombia in Washington D.C. Under political pressure, the work was not accepted. Today it has finally found a permanent home at the Brooklyn Museum's Elizabeth A. Sackler Center for Feminist Art (Introduction to Part 3).

Chicago has continued to work on ambitious mixed media installations, most notably *The Birth Project* (1980-1985) and *The Holocaust Project* (1993). Both deal with themes of overwhelming human significance.

Chicago has written an extensive life narrative, spanning two volumes. These books are cogent narratives of both personal and professional events. *Through the Flower* (1975) deals with her life up to the creation of *The Dinner Party*, and *Beyond the Flower* (1996) describes her responses to the public reception of this work and the other issues in her life after 1980. *Through the Flower* is an important autobiography, since it is written by a woman artist, in full awareness of gender discrimination both in the art world and in the broader culture of American society in the 1950s and in the 1960s. Like many male autobiographies dating back to the Victorian era, Chicago's narrative is a focused, chronological account of her professional development. *Beyond the Flower* continued this sense of artistic mission in a clear, direct, and confessional style. Chicago is not troubled by postmodern issues of identity. Her self-writing conforms to the traditional type of autobiography, as defined by Candace Lang:

> "The 'sincere', 'authentic' autobiography, [is] by definition, an *oeuvre*: a referential, coherent, unified narrative, spoken by a single voice. The autobiographical work is the totalizing retrospective and introspective (i.e. self-reflective) account of a consistent subject..." [4]

Chicago accepts the male tradition of autobiographical narrative fairly uncritically. However, the subtitle of *Through the Flower* is "My Struggle as a Woman Artist." This theme of struggle and triumph connects Chicago's first volume with a long historical tradition of women autobiographers, stretching back at least to the Victorian era, contemporary with the world of Vigée-Lebrun or Bonheur, who could have easily accepted this subtitle for their life narratives (Introduction II,a).

The subtitle of Chicago's second volume, *Beyond the Flower*, is *"The Autobiography of a Feminist Artist"*, which foregrounds the importance of political feminism for her artistic identity. As is quite clear from the final entry which summarizes her aims for her books, Chicago sees herself as a role model, an example to other women artists. Therefore, I believe that Chicago's life narrative should be considered a **relational autobiography** which projects "the model of selfhood …as interdependent and identified with a community."[5] It can also be seen as a **Bildungsroman** of the feminist artist because of the sense of development and growth implicit in the "story" of the text (Introduction to Part 3).

Mara R. Witzling has made the case that Chicago's autobiography follows the male defined model of triumphs over obstacles, and ultimate success, in achieving her goal. Witzling states:

"The structure of *Through the Flower* follows a conventional pattern that defines the artist as a heroic outsider who creates because he is driven by inner necessity, and who struggles against the world whose misunderstanding only serves to make him more adamant in the pursuit of his unique vision." [6]

Witzling employs the male pronoun deliberately, since "the image that Chicago internalized and used as a model is the cultural stereotype of the dynamic, obsessed male artist."[7] However, the sense of being a "heroic outsider" is quite appropriate to the tradition of women's autobiographical writings, going back to Vigée–Lebrun (Chapter 1). Many Victorian women wrote life narratives which recorded their struggles against obstacles and their ultimate successes (Introduction II,a).

The first excerpt addresses Chicago's early sense of vocation and the key factors she perceived, in her family's background, which were instrumental for her desire to become an artist. She recalls her experiences at the Art Institute of Chicago. This is the same school where O'Keeffe had studied a half-century earlier (Chapter 9), but unlike O'Keeffe, Chicago shows no embarrassment or timidity in pursuing her goals.

Almost from childhood, my artistic life felt more real to me than any other aspect of my existence. Every Saturday, I would take the Number 53 bus from our home on the North Side, near the lakefront, which dropped me off right near the stone lions that flanked the steps to the museum. I always felt as if I were entering another world, one in which I could totally lose myself in the creative process. I would emerge from the cramped classes in the basement with a sense of satisfaction that I came to crave. I would walk up the wide stairway leading to the light-filled galleries, often spending the rest of the day there.

I loved wandering among the paintings and sculptures to study the millions of colored dots that together form Seurat's *Déjeuner sur la Grande Jatte* [8] or to marvel at the luminosity of Monet's[9] paintings of haystacks in the changing light. Standing in front of the ribald images by Toulouse-Lautrec[10], I traced his use of reds and noticed how the viewer's eye is made to move around the entire canvas. As observant as I was, however, the one thing that I totally failed to notice was that nearly all of the art at the museum was by men. But even if I had noticed, I doubt that I would have been at all deterred from my own aspirations.

I cannot remember when I first decided that I would be an artist when I grew up. I know that I spent countless hours by myself drawing, and I became the official school artist almost as soon as I entered grammar school. I illustrated yearbooks and decorated the gym for dances, activities that continued in high school, though by my teens my life circumstances were quite different. The one constant throughout these years was my ambition, which was to become a famous artist, to be part of the glorious art history I saw represented at the museum.

I have always, from my earliest days, had a strong sense of myself, which was encouraged by my parents. Years later, my mother told me that she had always known that I was different— "special," I think she said. For in addition to being artistically talented, I was also extremely bright. In the environment in which I was raised, these twin traits somehow afforded me such special treat- ment—from family, friends, and at school—that I never once encountered the notion that, given my gender, my aspirations were either peculiar or unobtainable.

My parents were Jewish liberals, with a passion for the intellectual life and seemingly endless energy for political activism. Some of my earliest memories include going to the union hall with my father, where I'd eat hot dogs while listening to him deliver some rousing political speech. He was a Marxist and a labor organizer, and I derived from him a lifelong passion for social justice, the belief that the world could be changed and, equally profoundly, that I could trust and be unconditionally loved by a man. I also learned that the purpose of life was to make a difference, a goal that has shaped my existence.[11]

In the following excerpt, Chicago presents an appraisal of her work around 1966. She very clearly articulates the pressures of being a woman in a male dominated art world. As her work became "neutralized," she grew more and more dissatisfied. This excerpt records the difficult and conflicted position of a talented, ambitious woman artist in the mid-1960s with great clarity.

The two people who helped me most were my dealer and Lloyd:[12] they supported me and stood up for me. My earlier naïveté about my situation as a woman artist was giving way to a clear understanding that my career was going to be a long, hard struggle. Fortunately, I knew that I was okay—that the problem was in the culture and not in me, but it still hurt. And I still felt that I had to hide my womanliness and be tough in both my personality and my work. My imagery was becoming increasingly more 'neutralized.' I began to work with formal rather than symbolic issues. But I was never interested in 'formal issues' as such. Rather, they were something that my content had to be hidden behind in order for my work to be taken seriously. Because of this duplicity, there always appeared to be something 'not quite right' about my pieces according to the prevailing aesthetic. It was not that my work was false. It was rather that I was caught in a bind. In order to be myself, I had to express those things that were most real to me, and those included the struggles I was having as a woman, both personally and professionally. At the same time, if I wanted to be taken seriously as an artist, I had to suppress anything in my work that would mark it as having been made by a woman. I was trying to find a way to be myself, still function within the framework of the art community, and be recognized as an artist. This required focusing upon issues that were essentially derived from what men had designated as being important, while still trying to make my own way. However, I certainly do not wish to repudiate the work that I made in this period, because much of it was good work within the confines of what was permissible.

By 1966, I had had a one-woman show, had been in several group and museum shows, and had made a lot of work that could be classified as 'minimal,' although hidden behind that façade were a whole series of concerns that I did not know how to deal with openly without 'blowing my cover,' as it were, and revealing that I was, in fact, a woman with a different point of view from my male contemporaries. At that time, I firmly believed that if my difference from men were exposed, I would be rejected, just as I had been in school. It was only by being different from women and like men that I seemed to stand succeeding as an artist. There was beginning to be a lot of rhetoric in the art world then to the effect that sex had little to do with art, and if you were good, you could make it.

Lloyd had moved into another studio on the same street, leaving me with a five thousand-square-foot studio to myself. He and I had been having a lot of trouble working together, and we decided it would be better if we each had our own place. This need was particularly strong in me because I felt that if people came to my loft and I was alone, they would be less apt to see me in relation to Lloyd. I felt convinced that the only way to make any progress in the art world was to stay unmarried, without children, live in a large loft, and present myself in such a way that I would *have* to be taken seriously.

The next text describes Chicago's motivations for developing the feminist art program at Cal State Fresno, in 1970.

I didn't know for sure if my struggle was relevant to other women, and I needed to find that out before I could use it as the basis for such a community. I felt a strong need to be with other women (something I had never done) and to find out if my own needs as an artist, my desire to build a new context, and the needs of other women interested in art could merge to become the basis for a viable female art community. I also felt a need to be in a place where male values were not as pervasive, and that meant a place where the art scene had less power. I wanted to feel safer, to open myself, to try to reverse the toughening process I had undergone in order to have a place in the male world. Also, I felt that if I worked with female students and helped them work directly out of their feelings as women, I could, through them, go back to that moment in my development where I began to move away from my own subject matter. I had decided to make another series of paintings. After having dealt with issues about the nature of my own identity as a woman, I wanted to move out, to go beyond my female identity into an identity that embraced my humanness. I wanted to make paintings that were vulnerable, delicate, feminine, but that also reflected the skills I had developed in the male-dominated world. I needed the support of a female environment to expose myself more than I had been able to at that point, and I hoped, by establishing a class for women, that I could provide a context for my students and for me that could serve us all.

At that time in California, schools around the state were hiring Los Angeles artists who 'had a reputation,' and although my reputation was not consistent with my development, I had made somewhat of a name for myself as an artist. Because of that, I found it fairly easy to get a job. I simply put out the word that I was looking and sent a few notes to places that, I had been informed, were hiring. I received a telephone call from Fresno State College, which I had never heard of. They were very eager to have me come there—so eager, in fact, that they were willing to accommodate me in any way, especially after they had received a recommendation from my former sculpture teacher that 'the best way to work with me was to let me do what I wanted.'

Given the importance of *The Dinner Party* for contemporary American art, this segment is Chicago's own record of the process which led up to her conception of the installation. The sense of a didactic mission is very clearly defined.

More and more, I was considering the idea of trying to teach women's history through art. First I conceived of a series of plates that would be entitled 'Twenty-five Women Who Were Eaten Alive,' a reference to the seemingly deliberate obscuring of women's achievements. Then I started thinking about doing one hundred abstract portraits of women, also on plates. Most of all, I was contemplating how to teach a society unversed in women's history something of the reality of our rich heritage. I began to cast about for a model by which I might reach a wide audience, at one point looking back to medieval art, which I had always admired. I found it instructive that the Church had taught Christian doctrine to an illiterate population through understandable visual symbols, and I thought to make my own iconography even clearer in order to accomplish a comparable goal.

I absolutely do not remember when I visited the china-painter who had spent three years executing complete place settings for sixteen. But my enduring memory is of exquisitely painted plates (including dinner, salad, and dessert); matching bowls (both soup and serving); similarly treated coffee cups and saucers; as well as a companion creamer and sugar bowl set. These were all arranged upon her dining-room table, where she kept them as a sort of permanent exhibition. While admiring the fine quality of the painting, I experienced an epiphany of sorts, realizing that plates are meant to be presented on a table.

This was probably the moment when *The Dinner Party* was born, because once I decided to present my abstract portraits of women within the context of a table setting, I immediately began to think about historical antecedents for such a tableau, notably the Last Supper. It seemed as though the female counterpart of this religious meal would have to be a dinner party, a title that seemed entirely appropriate to my desire to point out the way in which women's achievements—like the endless meals they had prepared throughout history—had been 'consumed.' In fact, when I thought about paintings of the Last Supper, I became amused by the notion of doing a sort of reinterpretation of that all-male event from the point of view of those who had traditionally been expected to prepare the food, then silently disappear from the picture or, in this case, the picture plane.

Before very long, I became very focused upon creating a series of plates that could constitute a visual narrative of Western civilization as seen through women's accomplishments. Like most folks educated in Western history, I had been taught to view this record in a linear progression, which is how I approached my chronicle of women's history. Whether this is, in fact, an appropriate or accurate way to present history is definitely debatable. But at the time I was engaged in conceptualizing *The Dinner Party*, I chose to work within this traditional framework.

However, instead of representing various historical epochs in this chronology through the accomplishments or exploits of, say, Plato, Aristotle, Alexander the Great, or Richard the Lionhearted, my intention was that the female heroines would stand for these same periods; Eleanor of Aquitaine, for example, would take the place of Richard as a symbol for the High Middle Ages. This substitution in the context of a 'dinner party' was intended to commemorate the sundry unacknowledged contributions of women to Western civilization while simultaneously alluding to and protesting their oppression through the metaphor of plates set upon and thus "contained" by the table.

In the second volume of her autobiography, *Beyond the Flower*, Chicago picks up her narrative where she ended in *Through the Flower*. In the following statement, she discusses her feelings about the criticisms directed towards *The Dinner Party*.

About this same time, I ran into Paula Harper, who had returned to Stanford after her tenure as art historian for the Feminist Art Program at Cal-Arts. She reported that she had been hearing many negative comments about *The Dinner Party* from her colleagues. But my own experience at this point was so affirming that I found it almost impossible to believe that there was such an undercurrent of negativity in the art community. I can still hear her saying sympathetically, 'Well, Judy, my dear, the prejudice [against women] in the art world is obviously much deeper than we had ever imagined.'

Given the passionate reaction of the general audience, one might ask why I cared so much about the art community. The answer is that it is within this community that art is ultimately validated. I had contrived something of an alternative support structure in order to accomplish *The Dinner Party*, but I believed that it was essential to earn acceptance and recognition within the art world. With hindsight, I can see that I must have been unrealistic in my expectations. I firmly believed that the size and ardor of the audience—along with the financial benefit from admissions and sales—would convince museums to show the piece, thinking that the planned museum tour would soon include more than the two other venues that Henry had secured.

However, even though I believed the overwhelming viewer response to be an indication of the power and allure of the work, I certainly did not assume that its financial success could be considered any indicator of its aesthetic achievement. I fully understood that the determining factor in the evaluation of art has traditionally been its importance *as art*; one can earn six figures and not be thought of as a serious artist, or be impoverished but considered significant. Art is, at best, about ideas and values, and art objects both reveal and help to shape our concept of what is important—more significant—what constitutes the universal.

In part, *The Dinner Party* was intended to test whether a woman artist, working in monumental scale and with a level of ambition usually reserved for men, could count on the art system to accept art with female content. The response of visitors to the studio, the support of Henry Hopkins and the San Francisco Museum of Modern Art, and the unbelievable audience reaction suggested that I had every reason to be hopeful, despite some negative press and a few disgruntled art historians. After all, one could hardly hope for unanimous accord.

However, a very pressing reason to have been more concerned about some of the hostile art world attitudes was that they would greatly affect the exhibition tour. First and inexplicably, the two other institutions scheduled to exhibit the piece canceled. On June 17 *The Dinner Party* closed, was dismantled, packed in crates, and placed in storage. I was in a state of shock, and the staff in Santa Monica was not much better. As Julie Myers put it, 'I can't even bear to think about it.'

Chicago embarked on her next major work, *The Birth Project*, in the early 1980s. Eventually this extensive series of tapestries, focused on the act of birth, would number over 100 images and be exhibited in many places across the country, to an estimated audience of 250,000. In this excerpt, Chicago describes her initial motivations for beginning this vast project.

In July, shortly after I returned from the Boston opening, my old friend Janice Johnson came to visit me. Since she had had four children, I thought I would ask her about her birth experiences, having realized with some chagrin that this was something we had never talked about. Somewhat sadly, we admitted to each other that it had never occurred to either of us for me to be invited to the births, even though they had all occurred while I was still living in L.A. Although Janice could recall many details of her birth experiences, she told me that they would recede in her memory until next time, when, in the throes of labor, she would angrily ask herself, 'How could I have done this to myself again?'

Listening to her made me wonder whether the absence of images depicting the birth experience might actually reinforce such lapses of memory. If women saw numerous images presenting the actuality of birth and were thus reminded of both the pain and the responsibility for another life ushered in by this process, would they still give in so often to what Janice and many others have described as an overpowering urge for a child?

Perhaps if I had felt the powerful desire for a child that I heard described by so many women, I might have felt similarly compelled. But I never did. Moreover, I have never regretted my decision not to have a child, because I always knew that motherhood would interfere with my creative life. I wanted my days to myself so that I could work in my studio. Moreover, while I was in my thirties, when many women reportedly feel their biological clocks ticking, I was steeped in research into women's history. Discovering that most successful women artists had been childless, I consciously chose to pattern my life upon theirs.

These insights helped shape my determination to make myself into a conduit for the unexpressed realities of the birth process, a goal that evolved out of my ideas, born in Fresno, of redefining the role of the artist so that my images might give voice to some of the unarticulated emotions of a larger community, thereby making an aesthetic contribution, while also helping to reconnect art to the fabric of human life. I also wanted to do something about the fact that, while men publicly celebrated almost everything they did, women seemed to deal with what were some of their most important experiences only in the privacy of the home. 'If men had babies,' I used to joke at the time, 'there would be thousands of images of the crowning.'

In this last excerpt, from *Beyond the Flower*, Chicago summarizes her experiences and her "struggle as a woman artist" the subtitle of *Through the Flower*.

Chicago positions herself, clearly, as a role model for other women artists. Chicago encourages her readers to help build a new feminist world and use her experiences, recorded in her autobiographies, as inspiration for their own life choices.

Even as the story of *The Dinner Party* shows us how hard it is to change the institutions, it challenges use to change ourselves. Most of us are prevented from making such a commitment, not by laws—these have all been altered, at least in the West, thanks to our foremothers who made *our* rights *their* priority—but by something equally binding: fear, guilt, and, most of all, a deep-seated belief in our own lack of worth. My own story exemplifies some of this. I have explained how I came to view my power as frightening and, as a result, how long it took me not to be bullied into feeling that there was something wrong with me and/or my art. In terms of guilt, I was lucky: I was raised differently from other women in that I was not made to feel guilty about pursuing my own needs, though I consistently (and confusedly) collided with everyone else's expectation that this was what I should do. Certainly, I had to deal with feelings of shame about my body and my sexuality and could not become fully empowered until I had overcome these feelings, primarily because self-worth emanates from self-acceptance, and one's self occupies a physical body with essential needs.

From my perspective, however, the tale that I have been relating about my own struggle has little meaning unless it helps provide the basis of growth for others. Similarly, all of the efforts that went into creating and exhibiting *The Dinner Party* will be rendered hollow unless it is permanently housed. One important lesson I derived from my study of the history of women's achievements was that if other people could do it, so could I. In discussing how I slowly overcame my fear of my own power, I was by implication urging my readers to do the same. In explaining how I was able to stand up to all the demands upon me and carve out time for my own needs without feeling guilty, I was trying to provide a path for others.

But foremost in my tale, in my estimation, is the importance, the price, and the rewards for taking risks. One might say that I have probably taken too many and, consequently, paid too high a price in terms of having provoked so much hostility (an entirely unanticipated result) and having altogether sacrificed financial security (a difficulty for me, especially now that I am older). At the same time, I have been rewarded in many other ways. Yet as much as I enjoy standing ovations and fan letters, I would like to express my impatience with those many people who seem to stand on the sidelines and cheer me on or admire me from afar. I would rather that their appreciation be expressed by active participation in achieving those goals of mine that are shared by them.

Judy's Chicago's two book length autobiographies are extremely detailed sources written by the artist at times in her life when she was closer to the narrated events than Vigée- Lebrun, Bonheur or Neel. These books are written completely by Chicago, without intermediaries such as Anna Klumpke or Patricia Hills. Chicago writes with a fluidity and confidence that is different from most of the women in the preceding chapters. She sees writing as part of her didactic mission as an artist. It would not be surprising to find that she will write a third volume documenting her life since 1996.

Chicago's sense of identity was forged in the trenches of the 1970s and so she tells her life story with the clarity of focus brought by the Feminist Art movement. Her work especially *The Dinner Party* has been subjected to such scathing criticism that we can interpret the second volume, especially, as a defense of this work and her subsequent artistic projects. The first volume was written and published before the outrage of criticism unreleased by *The Dinner Party*'s public exhibition.

Chicago is well aware of her historical significance and part of her identity is as a role model for younger women artists. Her books should be taken in that spirit as an honest, but also self-conscious narrative of a woman well aware of her controversial status in the history of contemporary art. Chicago did not have children, and while never assuming a traditional role of a "wife," she readily acknowledges the support of a male life partner, providing yet another way in which her life choices can serve as a model for younger women. As the comprehensive life narrative of a major figure in the Feminist Art movement of the 1970s, Chicago's autobiography is a valuable and unique primary source.

Notes

[1]   Miriam Shapiro (b. 1923).

[2]   She was married, briefly, to Jerry Gerowitz, a writer who was killed in a car accident.

[3]   Lisa E. Bloom, *Jewish Identities in American Feminist Art: Ghosts of Ethnicity* (New York and London: Routledge, 2006), 34.

[4]   Candace D. Lang, *Irony/Humor: Critical Paradigms* (Baltimore and London: The Johns Hopkins University Press, 1988), 183.

[5]   Sidonie Smith and Julia Watson, *Reading Autobiography: A Guide for Interpreting Life Narratives* (Minneapolis and London: University of Minnesota Press, 2001), 201.

[6]   Ibid.

[7]   Ibid, 209 note 6.

[8]   Georges Seurat (1859-1891) was the leader of the French movement of Neo-Impressionism or Pointillism and his masterpiece, *Sunday Afternoon on the Island of la Grande Jatte* (1884-1886) is in the collection of the Art Institute of Chicago.

[9]   Claude Monet (1840-1926).

10 Henri de Toulouse-Lautrec (1864-1901).
11 All quotes are taken from Judy Chicago, *Through the Flower: My Struggle as a Woman Artist* (New York: Doubleday, 1975) and *Beyond the Flower: the Autobiography of a Feminist Artist* (New York, Viking, Penguin Group, 1969). Reprinted by permission of Judy Chicago.
12 Lloyd Hamrol (b. 1937).

Chapter 13. Faith Ringgold (born 1930): *We Flew over the Bridge: The Memoirs of Faith Ringgold*

Faith Ringgold is widely recognized as one of the outstanding visual artists of her generation. She has created a well documented body of works which focus insistently on her identity as an African American woman. Ringgold is one of a handful of artists who were active in both the Civil Rights movement of the 1960s and in the black feminist movement of the 1970s. One prominent art historian, Freida High W. Tesfagiorgis, has identified Ringgold, along with Elizabeth Catlett,[1] as the two women artists who best exemplify the concept of "Afrofemcentrism."

> "Conceptually, Afrofemcentrism gives primacy to black-female consciousness-assertiveness by centralizing and enlarging intrinsic values, and as a result liberates 'black feminism' from the blackenized periphery of feminism."[2]

Ringgold occupies a nearly unique position in the history of contemporary art, both for her political activism and her creations in the visual arts, especially since the 1970s, which employ mixed media, oil painting, fabrics, and narrative texts in highly innovative ways.

Born in Harlem, during the Depression, Ringgold was educated in the public school system of Manhattan. She graduated from high school in 1948 and enrolled in the City College of New York. She has been an educator for most of her active professional career, teaching for eighteen years in the New York City public school system and, also, in a number of colleges and universities, including the University of California-San Diego (UCSD). In the late 1960s, Ringgold created paintings, including *Die*, which are quite famous as protests against racist oppression. By the 1970s, she became very active in the women's movement. As Lisa E. Farrington, author of a history of African-American women artists, has noted: "Already an experienced activist, Ringgold was an ideal candidate to help spearhead the gender crusade. She participated in the Ad hoc Women Artists Committee and co-founded several support groups for black women artists." [3] In this decade, she began making soft sculptures and using fabrics for masks and costumes for her performances. In 1984, at her first retrospective exhibition, in New York, she exhibited her first story quilt, *Who's Afraid of Aunt Jemima?* She is best known for her story quilts, including *Tar Beach* (1988). In the early 1990s, a major retrospective exhibition of her works toured the country.

Ringgold's paintings use both imagery and words to tell stories. She understood that her art was a form of communication and, therefore, was never interested in abstraction. In this sense, she is aligned with Alice Neel (Chapter 11) and equally excluded from Modernism (Introduction to Part 3). While her insistence on imagery and narrative marginalized her work in the 1960s, she was positioned on the cutting edge of the post-modernist changes in art in the 1970s and in the 1980s. Her stories relate directly to her personal experiences as an African American woman. In a statement published in 1990, she said: "After I decided to be an artist, the first thing that I had to believe was that I, a black woman, could penetrate the art scene and that I could do so without sacrificing one iota of my blackness or my femaleness or my humanity."[4]

Stylistically, one of her major contributions has been the inventive use of sewing and quilting techniques, which combine painting and fabric. Inspired by her fashion-designer mother, Ringgold incorporated the unconventional medium of textiles into soft sculpture and, later, as quilted borders, so that her works moved beyond the medium of oil paint on canvas. With her invention of the "story quilts," in which she actually wrote the story on the surface of the image, she found an exciting method to communicate with her audience.

Since Ringgold is a highly articulate public figure, who has enjoyed a good deal of recognition, there are several published interviews, which are valuable primary sources. However, in 1995, she published her autobiography, *We Flew over the Bridge: The Memoirs of Faith Ringgold* (edited by Moira Roth).[5] The following texts have been excerpted from this volume. Organized in a chronological manner, this life narrative speaks directly to Ringgold's sense of purpose as an artist, as well as her commitments to her family as daughter, wife, and mother to her two daughters. By using the term "memoir" in her title, one can relate her autobiography to the sense of historical documentation characteristic of the genre **memoir** (Introduction, II,d).

Sidonie Smith's characterization of the motivation to write a life narrative is especially appropriate for *We Flew over the Bridge*. Smith believes that many autobiographers write from:

> "the desire of autobiographical subjects to splinter monolithic categories through which they are culturally identified, such as the monolithic category of 'woman,' and to reassemble various pieces of identity, experience, and knowledge into another kind of subjectivity... For autobiography has continued to provide occasions for the entry into language and self-narrative of culturally marginalized peoples."[6]

Like Chicago, Ringgold's book should also be seen as a form of **relational autobiography** since she has a keen sense of herself as both African American and as a feminist, and thus "interdependent and identified with a community."[7] In addition to her feminist and racial identity, Ringgold's autobiography also recounts her life in the genre of a **Bildungsroman**. Her pride in overcoming social obstacles and pressures further connects her autobiography with Chicago's two volumes (Chapter 12).

However, in a manner that is unique among the artist/authors included in this book, Ringgold's text also foregrounds issues of race. Ringgold has an acute awareness of her position as a "culturally marginalized" individual, and her most insightful statements in her memoirs, address this issue very directly. Elizabeth Fox-Genovese is one of the most important theoreticians on African American women's autobiography. Her overview of the field is very helpful in providing a context for *We Flew over the Bridge:*

> "Autobiographics of black women, each of which is necessarily personal and unique, constitute a running commentary on the collective experience of black women in the United States…Their common denominator, which establishes their integrity as a subgenre, derives not from the general categories of race or sex, but from the historical experience of being black and female in a specific society at a specific moment and over succeeding generations." [8]

Margo Culley also comments on the importance of race to African–American women when she notes that "white women autobiographers *re*inscribe their gender in the title of their texts despite the redundancy of that act …but in the case of African-American women the sign of race seems to override the sign of gender in the titles of black women's autobiographies."[9] Although Ringgold does not use her race in the title of her autobiography, she is very aware of the significance of race for her identity.

Ringgold's life narrative relates to other autobiographies written by women activists from the Civil Rights movement of the 1960s. Arlyn Diamond has analyzed a group of women's autobiographies, including Angela Davis's *An Autobiography*, Anne Moody's *Coming of Age in Mississippi*, and Virginia Foster Durr's *Outside the Magic Circle*. The common factor among them is a "passionate engagement in the struggle for a radical transformation of American society" from the 1960s. [10]

"These autobiographical narratives…inhabit the uneasy realm where the personal and social merge into and confront each other…the comfortable division between 'public' and 'private' which American culture everywhere reinforces no longer work for them, as what they do and who they are become entangled." [11]

Ringgold's memories of her childhood in New York's Harlem are detailed and vivid. She recounts many aspects of her life, during these early years. The following two excerpts, however, are her recollections of her early and strong attraction to art. These early memories are also coupled with her insightful recognition of the racist biases of her teachers. As Farrington notes "Ringgold's tenacity and resolve, as much as her talent, are the bases for her phenomenal rise to prominence; these pivotal traits manifested themselves early."[12] Tenacity and resolve are very apparent in this excerpt.

Art was the one thing I had always loved to do. Yet, because I had never heard of a black artist, male or female, when I was a child, I did not think of art as a possible profession. In retrospect, I think I must have taken art for granted at this time-as something to do rather than be. I knew that I wanted to communicate ideas thereby make a contribution to society; and to do that would require a college education. This had been drilled into my head by my mother and Uncle Cardoza from the day I was born. Although I craved an education, I never really liked going to school. I loved the learning, but I did not like the teachers. Most of them were excellent but very racist. I am sorry to say I have lived my whole life in Harlem and went to school there, but I never had a black teacher in grade school, high school, or even in college…

At P.S. 186 I became the class artist. As soon as my teachers found out that I could draw, they had me drawing on the blackboard, or creating one of those huge murals on heavy oak tag; with big brushes and tempera paint. In the second grade I was asked to copy a scene in which George Washington's soldiers fed watermelons to some raggedy black boys. Each boy's head was centered in the middle of a slice of watermelon. All you could see of the boys were their eyes shining out of their black faces and their topsy-braided hair style. I told my mother about the subject of my proposed mural and the next day Mother was in school telling the teacher that black people had fought in the American Revolution and all other American wars-and that everybody likes watermelon. After all, there were some little white boys in the same picture. Why weren't they eating watermelon? Mother negotiated a change in composition so that I painted both white and black little boys eating watermelon.

Prejudice was all-pervasive a permanent limitation on the lives of black people in the thirties. There seemed to be nothing that could really be done about the fact that we were in no way considered equal to white people. The issue of our inequality had yet to be raised and, to make matters worse, prejudice was blindly accepted as beyond anyone's control. From time to time some kid would blurt out, 'You ain't no better than me,' but that was hard to prove in the thirties. All our teachers were white except for one or two black teachers, who were loved and admired by all the children. My teachers were men and women who "took no stuff." They thought nothing of our feelings and stereotyped all blacks as shiftless, lazy, and happy-go-lucky. We were taught the most degrading things about our history: slavery was presented as if it were our fault-a kind of deserved penalty for being born black. Some teachers taught us that black people enjoyed slavery so much that, after the Civil War ended, they wanted to remain with their former masters rather than go free.

I thought my teachers had more than a natural curiosity about the private lives of their black students-as if their own lives needed confirmation that they could only get by comparison with ours. Yet racists as they were, they did teach us. Nothing was watered down or made easier to compensate for our so-called racial disadvantages; in fact, just the opposite was true. Knowing this, our parents raised us to understand that we had to be twice as good to go half as far.

Despite this oppressive start, Ringgold did receive an adequate education in the New York public school system and at City College. For her first one-person exhibition, in 1967, Ringgold painting a series of large scaled works, including *Die* and *The Flag is Bleeding*, which are frequently reproduced and quite famous today. While she did experience a degree of professional recognition, Ringgold summarized her situation in the following statement:

By the end of 1967 I had had my first one-person show, had received positive reviews of my work in mainstream art publications, and had sold two paintings-*Bride of Martha's Vineyard* to Porter and *Hide Little Children* to Carol Bobkoff, a young art collector. The American People Series was complete, and I was excited about the new experiments in what I called 'black light.' But I was also apprehensive about painting more pictures when I had nowhere to show the ones I had already made. After all, despite the recognition I had received, I was still unconnected to the art world, black or white. I saw my lack of opportunity as an indication that being a black woman was a major drawback in my career and, therefore, needed to be addressed openly.

A few years later, in 1970, Ringggold became involved with the women's liberation movement. She describes the resistance she encountered within the black community to her political and outspoken feminism in the following statement:

It was not until 1970, however, that I got involved in the women's movement. In this year I became a feminist because I wanted to help my daughters, other women, and myself aspire to something more than a place behind a good man. The "Liberated" Biennale, the Whitney demonstrations, and the Flag Show were my first out-from-behind-the-men actions. In the 1960s I had rationalized that we were all fighting for the same issues and why shouldn't the men be in charge? I would be just the brains and the big mouth.

In the 1970s, being black and a feminist was equivalent to being a traitor to the cause of black people. 'You seek to divide us,' I was told. 'Women's Lib is for white women. The black woman is too strong now-she's already liberated.' I was constantly challenged: 'You want to be liberated-from whom?' But the brothers' rap that was the most double-dealing was the cry that 'black women's place is behind her man,' when frequently white women occupied that position.

The continued problems Ringgold encountered, as an artist, are further described in her recollections from the 1970s. During this period, she traveled, extensively, and presented public lectures documenting her career. During the course of these travels, she continued to experience many negative reactions from people attached to the New York art establishment and from southern black men.

In New York I found it difficult to exhibit my work because of my figurative style, the political content, the lack of social connections in the art world, and, also, because being black and a women was not as fashionable as the Civil Rights Movement and the Women's Liberation Movement might suggest.

When I first thought of being an artist, I thought I had too normal and simple a life. How could I be a suffering artist when my life of bringing up my children and teaching art was so steady and secure? Except for Earl and Andrew, I had never really experienced emotional pain. That was how I felt in my twenties and early thirties before I had actually begun to be an artist. Now I was about to find out what it really meant to survive as an artist: that feeling of creation for which I would have suffered almost anything.

In the 1970s I searched for and found an audience. To be successful you must find a market as well, but in those days making money from art was not nearly as important to me as making art. As long as I could produce, it didn't matter where the money came from. I had started touring colleges and universities in 1972, and the following year I quit my teaching job at Brandeis High School.

I accompanied traveling shows of my work and lectured on black and feminist art. The black men on campus avoided me because they believed I had come to preach. Some black women did, too: they had been warned that I was one of those feminists from New York who had come to separate them from black men. In the North I talked mostly to small white audiences. In the South, however, my audience had a large percentage of blacks, especially black women. Blacks in the South seemed to appreciate me for my cultural achievements. They knew how hard things were for us-they would tolerate my feminism. Yet, at Fort Valley State College in Georgia, I was warned: "You're in the South now. Our women don't want to hear nothing about Women's Lib-we men are king down here."

The urge for autobiographical expression has been strong and consistent for Ringgold. Her acute understanding of her art, as a form of communication, is underscored in this excerpt, in which she narrates the progression from painting to performance art.

In 1980 my career as an artist was in limbo and I was so preoccupied at the time that I hardly noticed I had turned fifty. I desperately needed a major New York exhibition to show the work I had made over the past twenty years. Although I had quite a large national audience from my many exhibitions in college museums and galleries around the country, I hadn't had an exhibition in New York in ten years. I was eager to document my experience of being a black woman artist-that seemed as important to me then as breathing. I had also just written my autobiography but could find no one interested in publishing it. Since I couldn't "tell" my story in either of these traditional ways, I looked for an alternative.

It occurred to me that performance art was a good way to have an oral publication of my autobiography. I had a lively schedule ahead of me of lecture dates at colleges and universities in all parts of the country and I was already familiar with the performance genre. After all, my first performance piece, *The Wake and Resurrection of the Bicentennial Negro,* was still enjoying a good audience on college campuses where students were eager to experience performance art. Why not now create an autobiographical performance? So in 1980 I designed *Being My Own Woman: An Autobiographical Masked Performance Piece.*

During the 1980s, Ringgold conceived of a highly innovative form of visual art, which she termed the "story quilts". She combined her own texts, painted imagery, and quilted fabrics to make works of art of great visual intensity and powerful expressive impact. The creation of *Who's Afraid of Aunt Jemima?*, which was her first story quilt, is retold in this statement.

The Story of Jemima Blakey, the name I gave to my radical revision of the character story of Aunt Jemima, flowed from me like blood running from a deeply cut wound. I didn't want to write it-I had to. I was tired of hearing black people speak negatively about the image of Aunt Jemima. I knew they were referring to a big black women and I took it personally. White people had Betty Crocker but I had never heard any of them say hateful things about her. I couldn't really understand the black artists of the 1960s, who portrayed Aunt Jemima as a gun-toting revolutionary, or the white people's stereotyped portraits of her as a despicable human being.

If you asked me, I'd say the Aunt Jemimas are the world's "supermoms." I've admired women like Aunt Jemima for their tireless devotion to nurturing. Personally, I was a reluctant supermom; I've always feared that a supermom could spend a lot of time in the kitchen feeding others, but never really feel fed herself.

Perhaps her most famous story quilt is *Tar Beach* (1988), since it migrated from the realm of the art world into her first children's book. In the following excerpt she proudly summarizes the transformation of her story quilt into a children's book, which expanded her audience and earned her a new level of recognition as a visual artist.

I had observed that many people read the stories on the quilts standing up in the gallery. Indeed, some people come back to an exhibition over and over again in order to read all the stories or to reread the same ones. Clearly, a story has to evolve quickly with as few words as possible. For that reason, the story quilts are actually written in the same way that I was to write my children's stories. However, children's stories can be much more imaginative than stories written for an adult audience.

Since 1987 I had tried to get my story quilts published but was constantly told, 'Oh, but they are art books and there is no market for them.' However, Andrew Cascardi, then the editor of children's books at Crown Books (a subsidiary of Random Hose), saw a poster of my 1988 story quilt *Tar Beach* (owned by the Guggenheim Museum), and recognized immediately that the story would make a good children's book. I must say I had not realized that I could write children's stories; rather, I was simply trying to recall my childhood experience of going up to "Tar Beach" and writing in a child's voice. (Michele had told me that a good writer has to develop a unique voice, just as an artist has a unique vision.) At any rate, *Tar Beach* launched my new career as a published writer and illustrator of children's books and it has won more than twenty awards including a Caldecott Honor, the Coretta Scott King Award, and the New York Times Award for the best illustrated children's book for 1991.

Tar Beach is a story of an eight-year-old girl named Cassie whose family takes her up to the roof ("Tar Beach") on hot summer nights. Cassie dreams of a steady good job for her father, who is a construction worker but was denied a union card because of racism. Cassie also dreams that her mother could sleep late (just like Mrs. Honey, their next door neighbor) and not cry all day when her husband goes looking for work and then doesn't come home.

Being on the roof with the stars all around her and the beautiful George Washington Bridge in the distance makes Cassie fantasize that she can fly over buildings and claim them as her own. Accordingly, she flies over the Union Building and gives it to her father. She also flies over the ice cream factory so that she and BeBe, her brother, can have ice cream every night for dessert. At the end of the tale, Cassie tells BeBe: 'Anyone can fly, all you have to do is have somewhere to go that you can't get to any other way and the next thing you know you're flying among the stars.'

The conclusion to her autobiography is a moving summation of the challenges, struggles, and innovative solutions she has brought to her career as a politically aware, African-American woman artist. The feelings expressed here convey a sense of pride in overcoming obstacles in a manner which is consistent with the attitudes of Vigée-Lebrun and other artists included in this book (Introduction II,a).

The issue of racism and sexism in the art world is a continuing problem that most people know very little about. Citizens don't demand equal rights for artists of color and women in museums and public funding agencies. Most people think if you're good enough, you'll make it to the top and so they don't urge their appointed officials to canvass the museums and other cultural institutions to see if they are spending public money to represent the best art done by artists regardless of race and sex.

Ninety-nine and nine-tenths percent of the significant art production of men and women of color is ignored by the major art institutions in this country and only token representation is given to the rest. I'd like to see that end-and it will. But right now the art world continues to have a field day and for the most part the only team players are white men.

Despite all of these obstacles, it has never occurred to me to stop, give up, and go away-even though I know that is what oppression is designed to make me do. I continue to look for alternative routes to get where I want to be. That is why I have worked the performances and story quilts in the 1980s; and so far in the 1990s the writing and illustration of children's books, the rewriting of history in *The French Collection*, and this autobiography. These things have given me a constantly expanding audience and the flexibility I need to continue working in the face of adversity.

Ringgold's pivotal role in the Civil Rights and Feminist Art movements makes her autobiography a unique resource. Ringgold's ability to draw strength from these movements and internalize this as personal power allowed her to create a highly innovative body of multi-media works, widely acknowledged as historically significant.

Ringgold's memoir when the artist was in her mid-sixties and narrates events from a clear retrospective position, since her most historically important works were created in the 1970s and 1980s. However, she is not as far removed from the actual narrated events as other texts written at the very end of the author's life. It is not a bid for immortality, like Vigée-Lebrun's or Bonheur's autobiographies, but it is a solid effort to tell her own story in her own works. Texts are an important part of Ringgold's art and so it is not surprising that she chose to write her own story in a more or less traditional format using a clear retrospective chronology to organize her chapters. However, her story is anything but traditional. Combining multiple roles of wife, mother and avant-garde African American feminist writer, Ringgold life is also inspirational, like Chicago's, and can also serve as an uplifting role model for younger women artists of all races.

Notes

[1] Elizabeth Catlett (b. 1915) is an American sculptor, painter and printmaker.

[2] Freida High W. Tesfagiorgis, "Afrofemcentrism and its Fruition in the Art of Elizabeth Catlett and Faith Ringgold" in Norma Broude and Mary D. Garrard, (eds), *The Expanding Discourse: Feminism and Art History* (New York: HarperCollins, 1992), 476.

[3] Lisa E. Farrington, *Creating Their Own Image: The History of African-American Women Artists* (New York: Oxford University Press, 2005), 151.

4   Eleanor Flomenhaft, *Faith Ringgold: A 25 Year Survey* (Hempstead, NY: The Fine Arts Museum of Long Island, 1990), 23.

5   Published by Little Brown and Co., Boston, 1995. All quotes are from this book and are reprinted by permission of Faith Ringgold.

6   Sidonie Smith, *Subjectivity, Identity and the Body, Women's Autobiographical Practices in the Twentieth Century* (Bloomington, IN: Indiana University Press, 1993), 61.

7   Sidonie Smith and Julia Watson, *Reading Autobiography: A Guide for Interpreting Life Narratives* (Minneapolis and London: University of Minnesota Press. 2001), 201.

8   Elizabeth Fox-Genovese, "My Statue, My Self: Autobiographical Writings of Afro-American Women" in Shari Benstock, (ed) *The Private Self: Theory and Practice of Women's Autobiographical Writings* (Chapel Hill and London: The University of North Carolina Press, 1988), 65.

9   Margo Culley (ed) "Introduction", in *American Women's Autobiography: Fea(s)ts of Memory* (Madison and London: The University of Wisconsin Press, 1992), 7-8.

10 Arlyn Diamond, "Choosing Sides, Choosing Lives: Women's Autobiographies of the Civil Rights Movement", in Culley, Ibid., 218.

11 Ibid, 221.

12 Lisa E. Farrington, *Faith Ringgold* (San Francisco: Pomegranate, 2004), 4.

Chapter 14. Louise Bourgeois (1911-2010): *Louise Bourgeois: Destruction of the Father/Reconstruction of the Father*

Over the course of a long career, Louise Bourgeois has created a varied group of works, using a wide range of sculptural media from the most traditional, bronze and marble, to the more radical, ephemeral materials of plaster and latex. Her sculpture is difficult to categorize, stylistically, but in terms of iconography, her works focus insistently on autobiographically driven, psychological situations, from the viewpoints of both the child and the adult woman artist. Her sculpture is among the most original, technically diverse, and thoroughly analyzed bodies of work created by a contemporary woman artist.

Bourgeois, herself, has repeatedly narrated the circumstances of her childhood. She was born in France, into a family of craftspeople who restored tapestries. Her artistic talents were employed, early on, in the family business, when she made drawings to guide the weavers. Her father brought a mistress into the household and for many years this created strong interfamilial tensions. Bourgeois attended the Sorbonne and studied philosophy and art history at the École du Louvre in the 1930s. She then studied art at the École des Beaux-Arts from 1936 to 1938, completing her formal academic training. She was aware of Surrealism, as well as the art of modernists, such as Brancusi[1] and Giacometti,[2] and actually studied for a period with Leger.[3] In 1938, she married noted art historian Robert Goldwater and moved to New York where she has lived since.

While raising three sons, Bourgeois began to create innovative wooden sculptures in the late 1940s and 1950s. These works were not well known and were only rarely exhibited through the 1960s. However, beginning in the 1970s, Bourgeois's reputation, like that of Alice Neel (Chapter 11), began to grow. Both women benefited from the renewed interest in women artists of an older generation, who managed to create art which reflected the female body, gender conflicts, and autobiographical insights. When Lucy Lippard published a drawing by Bourgeois, from the *Woman/House (Femme/Maison)* series, on the cover of her widely read collection of essays, *From the Center: Feminist Essays on Women's Art* [4] (1976), many more people became aware of her work. Lippard reprinted her *Artforum* essay, "Louise Bourgeois: From the Inside Out" in this book, and opened with this amazing statement: "It is difficult to find a framework vivid enough to incorporate Louise Bourgeois' sculpture".[5] In this feminist context, Bourgeois' installation and performance work *Destruction of the Father* (1974) became widely known and appreciated.

In 1982, when Bourgeois was over seventy years old, her sculpture was shown in a major retrospective exhibition at New York's Museum of Modern Art. This marked the first time that a large audience could view her work. This show traveled to Houston and Akron, as well. From this time forward, Bourgeois's art has been widely known and appreciated. Exhibitions have occurred on a regular basis, and a major traveling retrospective toured Europe between 1988 and 1991. In 1993, she had the significant honor of being the only American artist whose works were shown at the Venice Biennale. The subsequent exhibition, at the Brooklyn Museum, expanded the collection of works shown in Venice and was published with a catalogue, *The Locus of Memory.*[6] This exhibition included some of her architecturally scaled installations, known as *Cells*. She continued to create *Cells* through the 1990s, and one of her most famous assemblages, *Spider* (1997), was exhibited internationally. This work has been the subject of a detailed analysis by art historian Mieke Bal. In her essay *"Autotopography: Louise Bourgeois as Builder,"* Bal argues convincingly for an engagement with Bourgeois' art that goes beyond the autobiographical limits defined by Bourgeois herself. [7] Bal's essay confronts complex issues of interpretation. She grapples with the extent to which the artist's own intentions and autobiography can or should control the viewer's interpretation of the work. One can expand this argument to include the written primary sources.

In 1999, a freestanding *Spider* was commissioned for the new Guggenheim Museum, designed by Frank Gehry in Bilbao Spain, a rare mark of respect for a woman sculptor. A major retrospective exhibition of Bourgeois' work was organized by the Tate Modern, in London in 2007, and this show traveled to Paris, New York, Los Angeles, and Washington D.C. The accompanying catalogue added to the Bourgeois literature by including a "Glossary" of words, terms, and themes important for an understanding of her *oeuvre*.[8] Bourgeois' art has the power to inspire some of the most intelligent, contemporary art historians and theoreticians to engage with her work, thus the scholarly literature addressing her sculpture is extensive and highly sophisticated.

In a manner which supported Bourgeois' growing stature in the art world, a collection of primary sources was published by MIT Press in 1998: *Louise Bourgeois: Destruction of the Father/Reconstruction of the Father.* All the following excerpts were reprinted in that text, which conforms to more traditional autobiographies only in its chronological organization. This is a **literary self-portrait**, which is a post-modern genre of autobiography. In the accumulation of its fragments, *Louise Bourgeois: Destruction of the Father/Reconstruction of the Father* conforms to the concept of the "Barthesian subject," as first seen in *Roland Barthes by Roland Barthes* (Introduction I,c). Candace Lang describes the core of *Roland Barthes* as based on "the adoption of fragmentary writing...The use of fragments has the obvious advantage of precluding narrative continuity." [9]

The "Louise Bourgeois" who appears in *Louise Bourgeois: Destruction of the Father/ Reconstruction of the Father,* would seem to conform to the Barthesian subject since she emerges as:

> "a discontinuous, fragmented self, which the author explicitly opposes to the Baudelairean divided self. The fundamental problem of the postmodern autobiographer, Barthes demonstrates, is how to *avoid* irony: how to escape the illusion that the ego is a fixed, autonomous stable self-image..." [10]

The form of *Louise Bourgeois: Destruction of the Father/ Reconstruction of the Father* is unique among the primary sources used for *In Her Own Words*. Bourgeois' volume presents a complex, discontinuous sense of identity. Marie–Laure Bernadac, the editor, described this volume in the following manner:

> "This book attempts to take account of the multiplicity of her written and spoken statements, and of their diversity of levels: a diversity which matches that of her artistic work, reflecting the fundamental dichotomy between professional control and spontaneity..." [11]

Therefore, the following excerpts are a more diverse group than in other chapters. I have selected these texts because they seem to communicate with directness similar to the life narratives in other chapters of this book.

In 1982, upon the invitation of Ingrid Sischy, editor of *Artforum*, Bourgeois created the following text, accompanied by photographs, which she titled *Child Abuse*.[12] In this pithy text, Bourgeois sums up her own childhood mythology, which has been used frequently to interpret her work.

Some of us are so obsessed with the past that we die of it. It is the attitude of the poet who never finds the lost heaven and it is really the situation of artists who work for a reason that nobody can quite grasp. They might want to reconstruct something of the past to exorcise it. It is that the past for certain people has such a hold and such a beauty...

Everything I do was inspired by my early life.

On the left, the woman in white is The Mistress. She was introduced into the family as a teacher but she slept with my father and she stayed for ten years.

Now you will ask me, how is it that in a middle-class family a mistress was a standard piece of furniture? Well, the reason is that my mother tolerated it and that is the mystery. Why did she?

So what role do I play in this game? I am a pawn. Sadie is supposed to be there as my teacher and actually you, mother, are using me to keep track of your husband. This is child abuse.

Because Sadie, if you don't mind, was mine. She was engaged to teach me English.

I thought she was going to like me. Instead of which she betrayed me. I was betrayed not only by my father, damn it, but by her too. It was a double betrayal. There are rules of the game. You cannot have people breaking them right and left. In a family a minimum of conformity is expected.

I am sorry to get so excited but I still react to it. Concerning Sadie, for too many years I had been frustrated in my terrific desire to twist the neck of this person. Everyday you have to abandon your past or accept it and then if you cannot accept it you become a sculptor.

The following succinct statement reinforces the importance of her childhood memories in the formation of Bourgeois's sense of vocation, as an artist.

When and Why Did You Decide to Become an Artist?

Previously unpublished answer to a question posed by *Art News*, late 1980s.

The decision was made for me by the situation of my family. My parents made their living in the arts—they repaired tapestries—so I was born into it. In a very practical way I had to make myself useful around their atelier. But there is a more basic motivation. I was the third daughter of a man who wanted a son. So to survive I had to create ways of making myself likable. It was the only way of escaping the depression which came from feeling superfluous—from feeling abandoned. Having been privileged with a native energy switched from a passive role to an active one, which is an art I have practiced all my life—the art of fighting depression (emotional dependence).

Louise Bourgeois: Designing for Free Fall,[13] published in 1992, included a number of useful primary sources. The following text, edited from the original 79 succinct statements, titled "Self-Expression is Sacred and Fatal," will provide all students of Bourgeois' art enough material to discuss for the coming decades.

1

My early work is the fear of falling. Later on it became the art of falling. How to fall without hurting yourself. Later on it is the art of hanging in there.

4

When I was growing up, all the women in my house were using needles. I've always had a fascination with the needle, the magic power of the needle. The needle is used to repair the damage. It's a claim to forgiveness. It is never aggressive, it's not a pin.

5

My knives are like a tongue—I love you, I hate you. If you don't love me, I am ready to attack. They're very double-edged.

8

Color is stronger than language. It's subliminal communication. Blue represents peace, meditation, and escape. Red is an affirmation at any cost—regardless of the dangers in fighting—of contradiction, of aggression. It's symbolic of the intensity of the emotions involved. Black is mourning, regrets, guilt, retreat. White means go back to square one. It's a renewal, the possibility of starting again, completely fresh. Pink is feminine. It represents a liking and acceptance of the self.

11

Several years ago I called a sculpture *One and Others* (1955). This might be the title of many since then: the relation of one person to his surroundings is a continuing preoccupation. It can be casual or close, simple or involved, subtle or blunt. It can be painful or pleasant. Most of all it can be real or imaginary. This is the soil from which all my work grows. The problems of realization—technical, and even formal and esthetic—are secondary; they come afterwards and they can be solved.

20

The phallus is a subject of my tenderness. It's about vulnerability and protection. After all, I lived with four men, with my husband and three sons. I was the protector. I was also the protector of my brother; he knew it, acknowledged it, and used it.

Though I feel protective of the phallus, it does not mean I am not afraid of it. 'Let sleeping dogs lie.' You negate the fear like a lion tamer. There is danger and the absence of fear. There is no danger and yet no thrill with women.

25

Confrontation (1978) represents a long table surrounded by an oval of wooden boxes, which are really caskets. The table is a stretcher for transporting someone wounded or dead. So, there is one personage on one side, and one on the other. One creature is old, and as you can see by the shape, they are crinkled, they are definitely wrinkled and old. The other is absolutely fresh representing youth. Now, we are used to having stories and romanticism about the obsession of age with youth. That is to say, the falling in love of an old person with a young person. And when this happens, since love is never fulfilled, it always ends in death. Usually, we have the state of affairs where someone dies of passion for someone younger than himself, passion that is never achieved, never consummated. However, I assume and want to prove that the opposite is equally true, that a lot of young people are obsessed with the past, or with age, or with an older person, and they die of it. It's the young who just lose themselves. So there is an element of madness. It is the young who ask to be stricken by madness because they refuse to leave the past.

Each of these boxes represents one of us. We have to stop running and take our places in the circle and face ourselves in front of each other. That is to say, to face how limited and uninteresting we are. Every one of us has to do this in front of everybody else. At that point, we have grown up. Nothing can let us escape this confrontation.

We have to come to terms with ourselves, with how bad we are, how limited we are, how short our life is.

29

I need my memories. They are my documents. I keep watch over them. They are my privacy and I am intensely jealous of them. Cezanne[14] said, 'I am jealous of my little sensations.' To reminisce and woolgather is negative. You have to differentiate between memories. Are you going to them or are they coming to you. If you are going to them, you are wasting time. Nostalgia is not productive. If they come to you, they are the seeds for sculpture.

45

I am an addictive type of person and the only way to stop the addiction is to become addicted to something else, something less harmful.

...The sculptures reveal a whole life based on eroticism; the sexual or the absence of sex is everything. The desire to succeed and to know how to succeed is everything.

One must differentiate between sex, which is a function, and eroticism, which encompasses so much more. First, eroticism can be real or imagined, reciprocated or not. There is the desire, the flirtation, the fear of failure, vulnerability, jealousy, and violence. I'm interested in all these elements.

49

If a person is an artist, it is a guarantee of sanity. He is able to take his torment.

52

I'm afraid of power. It makes me nervous. In real life, I identify with the victim, that is why I went into art. In my art, I am the murderer. I feel for the order of the murderer, the man who has to live with his conscience.

The process is to go from passive to active. As an artist I am a powerful person. In real life, I feel like the mouse behind the radiator. It is mind over matter. You transcend real life in your art.

54

Self-expression is sacred and fatal. It's a necessity. Sublimation is a gift, a stroke of luck. One has nothing to do with the other.

I am saying in my sculpture today what I could not make out in the past. It was fear that kept me from understanding. Fear is the pits. It paralyzes you.

My sculpture allows me to re-experience the fear, to give it physicality so I am able to hack away at it. Fear becomes a manageable reality. Sculpture allows me to re-experience the past, to see the past in its objective, realistic proportion.

Fear is a passive state. The goal is to be active and take control. The move is from the passive to the active. If the past is not negated in the present, you do not live. You go through the emotions like a zombie, and life passes you by.

Since the fears of the past were connected with the functions of the body, they reappear through the body. For me, sculpture is the body. My body is my sculpture.

75

Breton[15] and Duchamp[16] made me violent. They were too close to me and I objected to them violently—their pontification. Since I was a runaway, father figures on these shores rubbed me the wrong way. *The Blind Leading the Blind* (1947-9) refers to the old men who drive you over the precipice.

79

The Existentialists disappeared when the Structuralists came in. Lacan[17] came in. The

Structuralists were interested in language, grammar, and words. Whereas Sartre[18] and the Existentialists were interested in experience. Obviously, I am on the side of the Existentialists. With words, you can say anything. You can lie as long as the day, but you cannot lie in the re-creation of an experience.

As La Rochefoucauld[19] said, 'Why do you talk so much? What is it that you have to hide?' The purpose of words is often to hide things. I want to have total recall and total control of the past. Now what would be the sense in lying?

Bourgeois has maintained a journal for much of her life. The selection of primary sources in *Louise Bourgeois: Destruction of the Father/Reconstruction of the Father* includes diary excerpts beginning in 1939, and continuing into the 1990s. However, the following text, "Tender Compulsions," first published in February 1995,[20] is a very cogent statement of the importance of both written and drawing diaries for her creative process.

I have kept diaries all my life, ever since I was a child, ever since I could look someone in the face—and catch visual emotions and remember my own. The diaries are for my private reflections. If they contain names, they are names of people I love (and perhaps would like to love me—although making someone love you is impossible). There are no glamorous names. I put down stories of the day, and what goes through my mind. Sometimes, without my knowing it, they are funny. When you try to be funny, you never are.

Now I am not talking about diaries that record the trivial aspects of life: whether you had dinner and with whom, or the art openings you went to and the famous people who were there. I was recently asked to review a book of diaries by a certain writer who also composes music. It seemed to me that his 'diaries' were kept for the sole purpose of boasting about the celebrities he met, the grand houses he visited, and all the titled people—real or imagined—that he seduced. I *abhor* this kind of 'diary.' It is a record of the non-essentials, a handbook of artificiality: what to wear, where to go, when to leave, all mixed with the suggestion of scandal. These publicized 'memoirs' make me think of wilted orchids worn by a silly goose.

My written diaries are never destroyed but they are not looked at either. If I had enough courage, I might look at them. But I don't want to. I'd be horrified by the things I said. For example, when I meet a person, perhaps I'm not sure the person likes me. There is a desire to please. In French, the phrase 'desire to please' has a special flavor, suggesting civility and gentility. My 'desire to please'—my analysis of the other person—goes into the diary along with an analysis of myself at that moment. Now you understand why I don't want to look at what I've written. It becomes a closed book.

I keep three kinds of diaries: the written, the spoken (into a tape recorder), and my drawing diary, which is the most important. Having these various diaries means that I like to keep my house in order. They must be up-to-date so that I'm sure life does not pass me by. Most people visit me, and I like to record our conversations or our dialogs.

But the only diary that counts is the drawing diary. I do the drawing during the night when I'm propped up in bed with pillows. There may be a little music, or else I simply listen to the hum of the traffic on the street. I preserve my drawing 'diaries' most preciously. They relax me and they help me fall asleep.

I make the drawings on notebook-sized paper that is comfortable to manage in bed. Sometimes the drawings are on plain lined paper, or else I use the gridded paper of a French notebook [see illustrations]. The grid is very peaceful. I enjoy the different qualities of paper. Quietly, I prepare my images. The images are personal: the tree, its branches, a sort of landscape rising and falling and whirling and spinning into spirals. Especially, I recollect the life I led near the water, in both France and New York. I have always lived near the river. The murmur of the water, the memory of that musical murmur, is calming.

Each day is new, so each drawing—with words written on the back—lets me know how I'm doing. I now have 110 drawing-diary pages, but I'll probably destroy some. I refer to these diaries as 'tender compulsions.'

Often, my diaries reflect an obsession of mine about being useful. Way, way back—I mean a long time ago—when a baby girl arrived, she was not considered useful, in some circumstances. And I would silently ask: 'Do you like me? Do you approve of me even though I am a girl?' For years, these concerns bothered me. Keeping a diary, finally, helped me resolve some of these questions.

This selection of texts would not be complete without including some of the most recent, previously unpublished diary entries from 1991 to 1997. Written from the vantage point of a famous artist, in her 80s, Bourgeois's insights are compelling.[21]

18 November 1991

The precipitation of an anxiety attack—if not jotted down on the spot it would be impossible to trace back—only a "poet" could get the notations.

8 January 1992

The sculpture speaks for itself and needs no explanation. My intentions are not the subject.

The object is the subject. Not a word out of me is needed.

27 March 1992

Sexuality is sublimated in the intensity of effort necessary to learn, to understand, to connect, to associate in creation, in triage, symbolize, or join, to orient to achieve, to make yourself understood, to convince, to defend yourself.

13 June 1992

The value of this sculpture does not stem from what it means to me. I have nothing to prove to other people. Self-expression is the motivation. Acting out is it. To be allowed to act out is a privilege.

5 January 1993

A catastrophic view of the world before it is conscious. Today, here and now, I was totally unconscious—explains in retrospect the sleepless (totally) night of yesterdays.

When I was born my father and mother were fighting like cats and dogs. And the country was preparing for war, and my father who wanted a son got me, and my sister had just died. Please let me breathe.

27 April 1993

Realization is a pursuit going faster and faster towards an accurate goal. The goal is the exact transfer of a need to express a thought more than an emotion.

20 August 1993

Art comes from a need to express—an idea or a concept—cutting, mutilating, self-mutilation. Pruning, control. How to prove to yourself. How to achieve sainthood, health, star status, self-knowledge, the curative aspect of Art, usefulness, how to prove to yourself that you are lovable. Make people love you through your art.

2 December 1996

The Runaway Girl who never grew up.
I need no support nor comfort.
I need no safety net, no breakfast.
No lunch or tea, no visitors no telephone calls
    nor little messages.
No little concerts, no hype, nor encourage-
    ment for big projects.
No ambitions, no spying on my neighbors.
I need nothing...I can wait, I am not afraid, I
    am an adult.
Nothing is lacking

13 October 1997

I am held accountable for my gift. My food is a gift, my jam and tea is a gift, my health, my disposition (smiling today), the sun coming into the room is a gift, my friend's phone call is a gift, the satisfaction of having done one's duty;

its accomplishment, is a gift. My sky blue shirt is clean and is a gift, very especially the weather, outside, and furnace is gift, the state of my stomach, gift from above, the presence of my loved ones.

Be ready to pay for your gifts in art.
Be ready to pay for your debts in art.
You are sacrificing your freedom for art.

12 December 1997

The power of integration, connect together, is enormous, overpowering—but evanescent. One responds to a need—are you together? Yes I am. I am a puzzle with all my forty-four pieces. *Tabula rasa* is needed. A map is an object of study, take your time. I am a map. You are a different map.

The form in which Bourgeois' primary sources have been codified is unique among the artists included in this book. The edited, fragmented postmodern subject whose identity can never cohere into a unified subject seems especially suitable to Bourgeois given the equally diverse forms of her art. It is hard to cite another artist who has employed more diverse materials and invented more unusual ways of creating art. Unlike Chicago and Ringgold the volume from which these texts are excerpted retains only the chronological organization of traditional biography. What makes this format important is the priority of biography in the Bourgeois myth, the primacy of the angry daughter and the strife of the nuclear family, worthy of Greek tragedy. Although Bourgeois was a wife and mother of three sons, it is in her role as daughter that her creative persona erupts.

The most important conduit for Bourgeois' creativity is the journal. But unlike Bashkirtseff's journal writing in which her sense of herself seems to accumulate in a strong picture of a young woman struggling again patriarchal oppression, Bourgeois' identity never builds to a unified form but constant breaks down in fragments, like the pieces of a mosaic that cannot be assembled into a coherent picture. This complex identity is what makes her statements tantalizing and ultimately frustrating. As readers we have to accept that there is not a "Louise Bourgeois" that we can grasp. We read her usually brief statements for their explosive power to provide those brief flashes of insight into the creative mind of an extremely gifted artist.

Notes

[1] Constantin Brancusi (1876-1957) Romanian-born sculptor, was active in Paris from before the First World War.

[2] Alberto Giacometti (1901-1966) was an Italian sculptor associated with Surrealism, whose mature period began in the 1930s.

[3] Fernand Leger (1881-1955) was a French artist who emerged from a cubist-derived style to produce a highly individual body of work.

4   Lucy Lippard, *From the Center: Feminist Essays on Women's Art* (New York: E. P. Dutton, 1976).

5   This essay was originally published in March, 1975. Lippard, *From the Center*, 238.

6   Charlotta Kotik, Terrie Sultan and Christian Leigh, *Louise Bourgeois: The Locus of Memory: Works 1982-1993* (New York: The Brooklyn Museum in Association with Harry N. Abrams, Inc., 1994).

7   Reprinted in Sidonie Smith & Julia Watson, (eds) *Interfaces: Women/Autobiography/Image/Performance* (Ann Arbor, MI: The University of Michigan Press, 2002), 163ff. See also Mieke Bal, *Louise Bourgeois's Spider: The Architecture of Art-Writing* (Chicago: the University of Chicago Press, 2001).

8   Frances Morris (ed) *Louise Bourgeois* (London: Tate Modern, 2007).

9   Candace D. Lang, *Irony/Humor: Critical Paradigms* (Baltimore and London: The Johns Hopkins University Press, 1988), 189.

10   Ibid., 13.

11   Marie-Laure Bernadac and Hans-Ulrich Obrist (eds) *Louise Bourgeois: Destruction of the Father/Reconstruction of the Father: Writings and Interviews 1923-1997* (Cambridge MA: The MIT Press, 1998), 19. All quotes are from this volume and are reprinted by permission of the MIT Press © 1998 Massachusetts Institute of Technology.

12   *Artforum*, vol. 20, no. 4, pp. 40-7.

13   Christiane Meyer-Thoss, *Louise Bourgeois: Konstruktionen fur den frien Fall=designing for free fall* (Zurich: Amman Verlag, 1992).

[14] Paul Cézanne (1839-1906).

[15] André Breton (1896-1966).

[16] Marcel Duchamp (1887-1968).

[17] Jacques Lacan (1901-1981) was an influential French psychoanalyst.

[18] Jean-Paul Sartre (1905-1980).

[19] François de la Rochefoucauld (1613-1680) was a French author, noted for his maxims.

[20] This was printed in *World Art*, no. 2.

[21] Certain passages translated from the French by Caroline Beamish and David Britt.

Chapter 15. Niki de Saint Phalle (1930-2002): *Niki by Niki* and Letters

Niki de Saint Phalle is an innovative artist best known for her large scaled, brightly painted sculptures of female figures, known as the *Nanas*. These joyous works are innovative, stylistically and in terms of iconography. Saint Phalle is the only woman associated with the 1960s movement of Nouveau Réalisme, which included Arman,[1] Yves Klein,[2] and Jean Tinguely.[3] Saint Phalle soon distanced herself from the all male group and began creating sculpture, which would remain outside of any easily defined categories. She used a variety of media and, like Neel and Bourgeois, she became more famous during the Feminist Art movement of the 1970s.

Although she was born in Paris, Saint Phalle was raised in New York. When she returned to France in 1952, her life as an artist began. She met Jean Tinguely and first achieved public recognition with her *Shooting Paintings* [*Tirs*] series (1960-61), in which viewers were invited to shoot at paint filled balloons to create the work of art. In this early performance oriented project, she poked fun at the "action painting" of Abstract

Expressionist artists, such as Jackson Pollock.[4] In the letter, reprinted below, addressed to Pontus Hulten,[5] she recounts the history concerning this rather notorious project. Through these works, she became associated with the group of French artists known as Les Nouveaux Réalistes (New Realists) and exhibited with them in 1961. In the early 1960s, Saint Phalle began to make fascinating assemblage sculptures, such as *The Bride* (1963) and *Pink Birth* (1963-64). These works used dolls and other small scaled toys in innovative ways. Painted a uniform color they were among the first in which the myths of the female body were exploded, anticipating the interest in body imagery of Feminist Art of the 1970s. From this assemblage period, she began making the *Nanas*. These sculptures were over life-sized in scale, painted in bold colors, and positioned in playful poses. In 1966, she was invited by Pontus Hulten, director of the Moderna Museet, in Stockholm, to create a massive installation, *Hon*, for this museum. This famous work was architecturally scaled. Viewers could enter into the "body" through a door in the vagina. A milk bar was installed in one breast, and a film was projected on the inside. In the final letter, reprinted below, Saint Phalle recalls its creation in some detail.

The *Hon* is historically significant because it anticipates the fascination with goddess imagery and with the female body, which would become key themes in the Feminist Art movement of the 1970s. Following this experience, she focused on monumental sculpture and sculptural installations. One of her most accessible works is the *Stravinsky Fountain* (1982-83), which was created in collaboration with Tinguely, which is now installed outside the Pompidou Center in Paris. Another large installation, *The Tarot Garden*, begun in 1979, took its inspiration from Gaudi [6] and the iconography of the Tarot deck. In 1994, she moved to San Diego, where she died in 2002.

Saint Phalle's works are well known and well documented. Her early supporter, Pontus Hulten, who had invited her to create *Hon*, was now the first director of the newly opened Pompidou Center. In 1980, she was given a retrospective exhibition with a published catalogue at this museum. Another large retrospective, in 1992 was organized by the Kunsthalle of Bonn. This show traveled to Glasgow and Paris, exposing her works to a broad European audience. The catalogue to this exhibition reprinted the letters in this chapter. Throughout the 1990s, her works continued to be exhibited around the world. A retrospective exhibition of her work traveled through South America between 1994 and 1999. A catalogue raisonné of her complete works to 2000 appeared in 2001 and then, in the year after her death, a monograph, *Niki de Saint Phalle: My Art, My Dreams* was published. [7] The first excerpt, *Niki by Niki*, was published in this book.

St. Phalle has written an insightful autobiographical statement which is a compressed professional history of the major phases of her career. *Niki by Niki* is a unique example, in this book, of an **Autobiography in the third person.** By shifting her mode of address from the customary first person "I", Saint Phalle finds a less self-important voice, which seems consistent with the playful qualities of her sculpture.

Niki by Niki

Niki is a special case, an outsider: Most of Niki's sculptures have a timeless quality, are reminiscences of ancient civilizations and dreams. Her work and life is like a fairy-tale full of quests, evil dragons, hidden treasure, devouring mothers and witches, birds of paradise, good mothers, glimpses of paradise and descents into hell.

The same themes occur again and again in different forms, colours and materials.

Periodically throughout history and in all cultures myths and symbols have been reinvented and recreated. Niki shows us in her very modern way that these myths and symbols are still alive.

Take the *Nanas*. They are very much sculptures of today, yet we can't help thinking of the *Venus of Willendorf* when we look at some of them.

Tell me, is Niki a reincarnation from some ancient time? I am convinced she has had several lives and that in one of those lives she was burnt as a witch. In another life she was certainly involved in sacred rites in Mexico.

And why was it her destiny to make the *Tarot Garden*? Was she involved with the cards in the fourteenth century or was she linked to the cabbala? Is it no accident that she is creating this garden in Italy? There is a reason. Her hand is guided. She follows a path that has been chosen for her.

Niki's work is intelligible to the general public because there is something familiar, something haunting about it that arrests people. It is their own past or their unconscious dreams that they see in Niki's work. Sometimes it is the lost vision of a forgotten paradise or of hell. Some dream remembered from another time and made real in the present.

I see Niki as a devouring mother who has devoured all sorts of influences, from Giotto,[8] early Siennese painting to *le douanier* Rousseau,[9] from Mexican and Indian temples to Bosch[10] and Picasso.[11] They have been eaten and digested, and the child that is born from the feast is invariably a Niki.

One of the reasons why very little has been written about Niki's work is that she is difficult to categorize. Is she a twentieth-century artist or an archaic sculptor? Which is the critical period in Niki's work? Is it the early oil paintings which disclose all her future avenues of approach? Is it the shooting, New Realist period with its altars and assemblages? Or is it the Romantic, tormented period of the white hearts, the brides, the women giving birth? This particular period has usually been most overlooked, but for me it is the most important.

Or are the *Nanas* perhaps more important? The *Nanas* which have made Niki famous and put everyone in a good mood and are the opposite side of the coin to the white reliefs? Some of the *Nanas'* forms come from ancient antiquity. In others we can see the influence of Picasso or Léger and be reminded of Matisse by the colours. Yet they too remain *Nanas*.

Then comes the devouring mothers series, which is extremely ironic with its violent, social commentary. These works are unpopular as they remind us of our nightmares of being devoured by the evil witch. They are among my favourite sculptures though they sometimes scare me, too.

Many artists have been inspired by their love affairs. It seems that Niki has been inspired by the roles women have had to play in life. What is behind roles? Myths? The bride, the whore, the woman giving birth, the devouring mother, etc.

One very important factor in Niki's work is the passion with which she experiments with different materials: oils, plaster, guns, chicken wire, cloth, wool, *objets trouvés*, toys, clay, polyester, and finally—her new big loves—glass, mirrors and ceramics.

It seems as though Niki is always on the move, always on some new search. Sometimes she moves too quickly, not developing certain periods thoroughly enough. For instance, the almost abstract skinnies, which look like plants, the lamps, which are like drawings in the air. I feel she could have—and would have—gone much further with them. But there is no time, because she is working on the biggest project of her life: the *Tarot Garden*.

There is urgency in everything she does—as though she is always pressed for time, afraid it is running out, afraid she will not finish what she was meant to do. What is this obsession she has with the monumental? Does it come from her life-long admiration of Egyptian art, or is it her urgent necessity, her destiny, to show that a woman can work on a monumental scale?

Why is it that very few museums have exam-ples of Niki's work? Is it because she is an outsider, a 'special case' who is difficult to categorize? It's not Pop Art, it's not Op Art, it's not concep-tual art. What is it? Or is it the fact that she is a woman? And what about her architecture? What kind of crazy architecture is that? Her *Tarot Garden* is in the classic tradition of fantastic gar-dens and certainly the most ambitious one since Gaudi's *Parc Guell*.[12]

So let's leave her now. I'm getting tired of writ-ing about her. It's exhausting thinking of all that work. I would like to give her a piece of advice. Take it easy. Relax more. Take those walks you want to take every day with your dogs. Read a bit more. But she can't do that. WORK, WORK, WORK.

P.S. I forgot about her graphic work. All her ideas come from her drawings, lousy little scrib-bles on generally bad paper for essential ideas.

Drawing—as soon as she has a pen in hand, her anxiety goes.

P.P.S. Do you know something interesting? She cannot draw in three dimensions. Is it a formation or malformation of the brain? She has been shown the tricks of perspective but cannot assimilate them. Tell me frankly, do you think she is mad?

P.P.S. All of this is just Niki trying to do art criticism. The essential is not here: the mystery remains.

The next excerpts are "letters" written as "autobiographical texts". These letters were never actually sent to their intended correspondents. Uta Gorsenick has defined them as "stories in which the artist takes friends into her confidence and tells them a chapter of her life story, a story in which they themselves have played a part." [13] All of the following letters were published in an exhibition catalogue accompanying her retrospective in 1992.[14] Because these letters were written specifically for publication, they are similar to the epistolary format of Vigée-Lebrun's *Souvenirs* (Chapter 1). The "letter" functions as an "enabling" device, permitting the author to write an autobiographical text.

One of the key figures in Saint Phalle's life was Jean Tinguely. In the following letter, addressed to Tinguely, written in 1990 one year before he died, she recounts her memories of their first meeting and the beginning of their relationship. They were both married to other people when they first met in 1955. Eventually, they were married in 1971. This letter is important, because it traces the key groups of artists and artistic ideals which inspired Saint Phalle. She notes the separation from her husband and three children, and Tinguely's split from his wife.

Dear Jean,

I remember very well meeting you and Eva for the first time in 1955. I was 25 years old. I immediately fell in love with your work. Your studio looked like a huge pile of iron garbage hiding wonderful treasures.

A long, black and white moving relief was hanging on the back wall of your studio. It had a little hammer hitting a bottle and numerous little wheels with wires which were trembling and turning. I had never seen anything like it and I was crazy about it.

Harry and I didn't have much money but we decided to buy it. You were very pleased: you and Eva had just enough to eat and work. You used to steal the coal to heat your studio in winter from the piles behind the hospital adjacent to l'Impasse Ronsin where you lived.

Your dealer at the time, used to buy your entire production. For this she gave you less than $100 a month, starvation wages...

I talked to you about Gaudi and about the Facteur Cheval[15] whom I had just discovered and who were my heroes and the beauty of man alone in his folly without intermediaries, without museums, without galleries. You were against this idea; you thought art ought to be in society, not outside of it. Then I provoked you by saying that the Facteur Cheval was a much greater sculptor than you.

'I never heard of that idiot.' you said. 'Let's go and see him right away.' you persisted. ..

I started to talk to Harry about separating and living alone for a year or two, to go to the end of my potential as an artist. I felt I needed solitude.

Harry wasn't happy, but he never did anything to hold me back. He had many weapons he could have used, like the children. Perhaps he had too much respect for me and my art to use them.

I had a brief love affair with a well known artist at the time that was running after me. He was married or at any rate he was living with someone and his specialty was to break up couples and seduce the wives of friends. I wasn't in love with him but he held me in a certain way. I didn't like this dependence so I bought a gun to kill him symbolically. There were no bullets in the gun. The revolver was in my handbag and it made me feel better.

One day I had the idea to do his portrait. I bought a target in a toy shop, a target to throw darts at, and I asked him if he would give me one of his shirts. Then I put a tie on it. All of this was glued on wood. I called it 'Portrait of my

Lover.' I started to have fun by throwing darts at his head. It was successful therapy because I began to detach myself from him.

You came to my studio one day with Daniel Spoerri[16]. They saw this relief and both of them were crazy about it and decided immediately to use it in a new exhibition where the New Realists were shown. I was delighted.

There was a lot of aggression in me that was starting to come out at this time; one night at "La Coupole," which was still only a café-brasserie where artists used to hang out in Paris, I was with Jean Paul Riopelle[17] and Joan Mitchell[18]. Giacometti[19] was at the table; later Saul Steinberg[20] arrived. It was quite late at night. He started coming on too obviously. I didn't like it and I felt humiliated by his exaggerated attention. But I liked his great mustache.

He was carefully and extravagantly dressed. He had on a beautiful grey cape. A great uncontrolled violence suddenly surged up in me. So I took a glass of beer that was on the table and threw it at his head. Giacometti was so thrilled by my doing this that he kissed me on the mouth and spent four or five hours talking to me.

Giacometti talked about art and about his hatred for Picasso. I've always been a great admirer of Picasso and was amazed by the hatred he aroused in many important artists. Picasso was very important to me. I liked his immense freedom with materials and his continual research. His changing of styles stimulated me. For everyone else, at the time, it was Duchamp[21] YES, Picasso NO. I always liked both, and Matisse[22] too.

I started putting my violence into my work. I made reliefs of death and desolation. One of them had the revolver which I had bought to symbolically kill my lover. The moon in these reliefs was always black, with images of violence. Yes, I was starting to descend into HELL.

I started living alone. Harry generously bought my paintings which permitted me to live very modestly. I was able to work on my art all day long without getting a job. It seemed logical for the children to stay with Harry as I didn't have enough money to look after them. I came to see the three of them often.

Daniel Spoerri started to court me. I wasn't indifferent to his charm. He looked like Louis Jouvet, whom I found attractive. You were Daniel's best friend and I noticed that you didn't like this very much.

You and Eva had separated. ...

Jean, I used to see you often at this time. You would come by and I would accompany you to the iron yard and choose pieces that excited you. We continued our interminable discussions on art. You talked to me a lot about the Dadaists. You and Yves Klein saw the abstract expressionists as the enemy to be defeated. You wanted your vision of the universe to replace theirs.

The day of my 30th birthday, October 29th, 1960, Harry bought me a gorgeous white curly lamb wool jacket. I looked very spectacular and Jean and Daniel were enthusiastic. I was very proud of my new jacket. Daniel invited me to have dinner with him. I accepted with pleasure and I asked myself: would he be my next lover? When Daniel turned his back, Jean, you came to me and said, 'I forbid you to go out with him.'

I was very surprised and replied, 'Why?'

'I want you to have dinner with me,' you said.

I didn't want to break the friendship between you and Daniel nor mine with you. I responded,

'OK, but what do I tell him?'

'Just lie, invent anything.'

I saw in your eyes that something had changed. You looked at me differently. I asked you,

'What is it? What's going on?'

You continued, 'I can't bear the idea of his going out with you in that beautiful coat. I like it even less than the idea of his touching you.'

Two days later I didn't resist your eyes anymore. You were looking at me in this new way I found very disturbing. We didn't leave each other anymore. (It's sometimes dangerous to buy too beautiful clothes for your wife.)

I wanted to be independent, FREE. I had no intentions of becoming a couple. I saw myself rather as a Mata Hari of art having plenty of adventures and eventually returning to Harry a year or two later.

Life, however, is never the way one imagines it. It surprises you, it amazes you and it makes you laugh or cry when you don't expect it.

Pontus Hulten supported Saint Phalle's career and brought her work to a broad public over the course of several decades. In the 1992 catalogue there are several "letters" addressed to Hulten. In the following undated letter, she narrates her memory of the origins and exhibition of the *Shooting Paintings*, also known as *Tirs* which were the first works which brought Saint Phalle a notorious type of fame and established her originality, in the art world. They are so historically important that photos of her "shoots" are used in the front and back cover flaps of the catalogue for *elles@centrepompidou* (Introduction to Part 3). In the essay printed in the catalogue for the show, "Fire at Will", Quentin Bajac refers to the *Tirs* as "the founding actions of a certain type of woman artist, one that is engaged and militant...the gesture itself...has become a symbol for an entire subsequent generation of women artists."[23] This is a powerful assessment of Saint Phalle's historical position.

Dear Pontus,

You asked me about the Shooting Paintings.

One spring day in 1961 I was visiting the Salon de Comparisons exhibition in Paris. A relief of mine was hanging in the show. It was called "Portrait of my Lover."

There were darts on the table for spectators to throw at the man's head. I was thrilled to see people throw the darts and become part of my sculpture. Near my work, there hung a completely white plaster relief by an artist named Bram Bogart. Looking at it—FLASH! I imagined the painting bleeding—wounded; the way people can be wounded. For me, the painting became a person with feelings and sensations.

What if there was paint behind the plaster? I told Jean Tinguely about my vision and my desire to make a painting bleed by shooting at it. Jean was crazy about the idea; he suggested I start right away.

There was some plaster at l'Impasse Ronsin. We found an old board then bought some paint at the nearest store. We hammered nails into the wood to give the plaster something to hold onto, then I went wild and not only put in paint but anything else that was lying around, including spaghetti and eggs.

When 5 or 6 reliefs had been finished, Jean thought it was time to find a gun. We didn't have enough money to buy one so we went to a fairground in the Boulevard Pasteur and convinced the man at the shooting stand to rent us his gun. It was a .22 long rifle with real bullets which would pierce the plaster, hit the paint in little plastic bags embedded inside the relief, causing the paint to trickle down through the hole made by the bullet, and color the outside surface. The man from the shooting stand insisted on coming along. Maybe he was afraid we wouldn't return his gun.

We had to wait a couple of days before he came which, of course, added to the excitement and gave us time to invite a few friends including Shunk and Kender, photographer friends who documented the first shoot-out. Jean also invited Pierre Restany[24] who then and there decided, while watching red, blue, green, rice, spaghetti, and eggs (where was the yellow?) to include me among the New Realists. I was getting a great kick out of provoking society through ART. No victims.

We took turns shooting. It was an amazing feeling shooting at a painting and watching it transform itself into a new being. It was not only EXCITING and SEXY, but TRAGIC—as though one were witnessing a birth and a death at the same moment. It was a MYSTERIOUS event that completely captivated anyone who shot.

We nailed the reliefs to a back wall of l'Impasse Ronsin. There was a long, grassy field in front of the wall which gave us plenty of room to shoot.....

For the next six months I experimented by mixing rubbish and objects with colors. I forgot about the spaghetti and rice and started concentrating on making the shooting paintings more spectacular. I started to use cans of spray paint, which, when hit by a bullet made extraordinary effects. These were very much like the Abstract Expressionist paintings that were being done at that time. I discovered that when paint fell on objects, the result could be dramatic. I used tear gas for the grand finale of my shooting performances. Performance art did not yet exist but this was a performance.

The smoke gave the impression of war. The painting was the victim. WHO was the painting? Daddy? All men? Small men? Tall men? Big men? Fat men? Men? My brother JOHN? Or was the painting ME? Did I shoot at myself during a RITUAL which enabled me to die by my own hand and be reborn? I was immortal!

The new bloodbath of red, yellow, and blue splattered over the pure white relief metamorphosized the painting into a tabernacle for DEATH and RESURRECTION. I was shooting at MYSELF, society with its INJUSTICES. I was shooting at my own violence and the VIOLENCE of the times. By shooting at my own violence, I no longer had to carry it inside of me like a burden. During the two years I spent shooting I was not sick one day. It was great therapy for me.

The ritual of painting a relief over and over again in immaculate virginal white was very important to me. The theatricality of the whole performance appealed to me immensely.

It was late Spring 1961 that I met Jasper Johns[25] and Robert Rauschenberg.[26] They had already met Jean Tinguely at the time of his *Homage to New York* at the MOMA.[27] We soon became friends. I found both of them gorgeous and was fascinated by their being a couple. They had a grace that comes with beauty allied with exceptional talent and intelligence. It was electrifying being with them.

I made homage to Jasper. It was a relief with a target and a light bulb painted in his colors. I asked him to finish it by shooting. He took hours deciding where to shoot the few shots he finally fired at the target. Bob Rauschenberg, however, shot his piece in a few minutes and screamed, 'Red! Red! I want more red!' ...

I think it was around February or March of 1960 that I met you, Pontus. Jean had told me a great deal about you and I also knew that you were the director of the Moderna Museet in Stockholm so I was in awe of meeting you. You quickly put me at ease. Whenever there was something to twiddle or play with, like a piece of string lying on the table, it was irresistible to you and you would pick it up and play with it for hours. I understood you were one of us. Your enthusiasm for the shooting paintings was a great support for me. At the time I was being attacked by the newspapers constantly.

The first time you visited my studio... you spent hours looking at my old paintings. I had disowned them thinking they were no longer interesting. We argued about this but I was secretly very pleased that you liked them. A few years later you would buy one for the museum.

It was June 1961 that I had my first one-man show in Paris at the Galerie J. I was finishing 'The Shooting Stand' on the day of the show. Visitors would be allowed to shoot at a painting. Three reliefs would be prepared and shot at during the show. Jean had put a big sheet of rusty iron behind the reliefs to protect the wall and a contraption to catch the paint that ran down from the painting so that it wouldn't drip to the floor. Jeannine de Goldschmidt, the gallery owner and Pierre Restany's wife, stayed marvelously calm during the proceedings and it seemed not to bother her at all that there would be shooting every day in her gallery with a .22 long rifle (by that time we had found the money to buy a gun).

An hour before the show opened a man with a degenerate face came in and asked, 'When can I shoot?' I explained he would have to wait a bit until we had finished hanging the show.

'Why don't you come back in a little while?'

'No, I'm not going to leave. I'm going to stay right here until I can shoot.'

Every ten minutes he would ask, 'Can I shoot now?' I finally got annoyed and went over quietly to Jeannine and implored, 'Can't you find some nice way of getting rid of that guy. He's a nuisance.'

Jeannine declared, 'Are you kidding? That is Fautrier!'[28] I was a fan of Fautrier's work even though his preoccupation with paint and space were very far from mine. I came back to him and said, 'O.K. you can start shooting.' Later, when the crowd started arriving, he had difficulty giving up the gun. He kept shooting at the center and was trying to make one of his own paintings out of the shooting. When someone else was taking a shot, he would scream, 'The center, the center! Shoot at the center!'

My other fellow artists were also fascinated by the fact that by shooting at a painting they could finish a work of art. They, too, were caught up in the spellbinding dynamics of the Shooting Paintings, a feeling as indescribable as making love. Bob Rauschenberg thrilled me by buying a sculpture of mine at the opening night show.

Autumn 1961, Larry Rivers[29] moved into one of the studios at L'Impasse. He was there with his new bride, Clarice. I would go and chat with them often. Jean was suspicious of these people he didn't know and refused to meet them. When Jean felt I had been chatting with them too long, he would take my gun and start shooting in the air. I knew it was time to come home. One day he could no longer resist the smell of Clarice's homemade soup which won him over; after that we had lunch with them everyday. We almost lost their friendship, however, by forgetting to warn them that we were going to use the front of their house to shoot at my new relief with a small cannon Jean had just built. By mistake, Jean mixed in a little too much gunpowder with the paint in the cannon. When the cannon hit the relief, the entire house shook. Larry came out screaming, "What are you trying to do, kill us?" After much apologizing, our friendship was saved and we continued to enjoy our great lunches together.

Why did I give up the shooting after only two years? I felt like a drug addict. After a shootout I felt completely stoned. I became hooked on this macabre yet joyous ritual. It got to the point where I lost control, my heart was pounding during the shootouts. I started trembling before and during the performance. I was in an ecstatic state.

I don't like losing control. It scares me and I hate the idea of being addicted to something—so I gave it up. I was tempted to return to shooting when I suffered extreme depression and also while I had rheumatoid arthritis and could hardly walk.

I wanted to shoot my way out of the disease. I decided against it because I wasn't able to think of a new way to make the Shooting Paintings and I didn't want to do the same thing I had already done. IT HAD TO BE NEW OR NOT BE, so I gave up the idea.

It was also hard to give up all the attention in newspapers and newsreels I was getting from the shooting. Here I was an attractive girl (if I had been ugly, they would have said I had a complex and not paid any attention) screaming against men in my interviews and shooting with a gun. This was before the women's liberation movement and was very scandalous.

It was not surprising that hardly anyone bought these works and they mainly belong to me today. Bill Seitz[30] from the MOMA made a statement that my attitude was harmful to art and that I had set back modern art by 30 years!

From provocation, I moved into a more interior, feminine world. I started making brides, hearts, women giving birth, the whore—various roles women have in society.

A new adventure had started.

The next letter, dated autumn 1966, is addressed to Larry Rivers' wife, her friend "Clarice."[31] Here Saint Phalle describes the creation of her famous work *Hon*.

Dearest Clarice,

You asked me what it was like working and making the HON, the BIGGEST NANA I ever made. She was 90 feet long, 18 feet high, 27 feet wide. Pontus Hulten, director of the Moderna Museet in Stockholm asked me to go there in the Spring of 1966 with Tinguely, Martial Raysse and Oldenburg[32] to build a monumental sculpture in the big hall of the museum. Martial Raysse declined the invitation. Oldenburg couldn't come at the last moment and Jean had just started some new work in Soisy and wasn't in the mood. It looked as though the whole project would fall through, but a secret voice kept telling me that I must go, that it was important. I listened.

The first few days we met in Stockholm were unsatisfactory. My enthusiasm convinced Jean to come also and many ideas were tossed about by Jean, Pontus, myself and the Swedish artist who joined us, Per Olof Ultvedt. Pontus suggested we all go to Moscow for a few days (Jean and I had never been there) and either the city or the vodka would inspire us. We were about to buy our tickets when Pontus had a brainstorm. EUREKA! He suggested we build a huge, penetrable Nana that would be so large she would take up the entire hall of the museum. We suddenly became very excited. We knew we were entering the sacred land of myth. We were about to build a goddess. A great PAGAN goddess.

As you, Clarice, were the original Nana, consider yourself the model for the GREAT GODDESS.

Jean assumed the technical direction of a team of volunteers that Pontus found for us. One of them was Rico Weber, a young Swiss artist, who was to remain afterwards as assistant collaborator for Jean and me for many years. Rico was working as cook at the snack bar of the museum. We had six weeks to produce our huge giantess and must have worked 16 hours a day.

We named our Goddess HON which means SHE in Swedish. I made the original small model that gave birth to the goddess. Jean, by measuring with eyes only, was able to enlarge the model in an iron frame and have it look exactly like the original. After the chassis had been welded, chicken wire was attached to the immense surface of the Goddess. I cooked, in huge pots, a mass of stinking rabbit skin glue on small electric heaters. Yards of sheet material were mixed with the glue and then placed on the metal skeleton. Several layers were necessary to hide the frame. I often felt like a medieval witch brewing this glue. When the sheets dried and were stuck to the metal, we painted the body of the Goddess white. I then made my design using the original model with some modifications. Later, with the help of Rico Weber, I painted the sculpture. Pontus worked night and day sawing and hammering and participating in every way he could with us. Meanwhile, Jean and Ultvedt were occupied with filling the inside of the body of the Goddess with all kinds of entertainment. Jean made a planetarium in her left breast and a milk bar in the right breast. In one arm was shown the first short movie starring Greta Garbo, and in a leg was a gallery of fake paintings (a fake Paul Klee,[33] Jackson Pollock, etc.)

The reclining Nana was pregnant and by a series of stairs and steps you could get up to the terrace from her tummy where you could have a panoramic view of the approaching visitors and her gaily painted legs. There was nothing pornographic about the HON even though she was entered by her sex.

Pontus knew he had embarked on a perilous venture with this great lady and decided to keep the entire project secret. Otherwise, the authorities might hear distorted rumors and shut the show before it opened. We constructed a giant screen, behind which we worked; no one was allowed to see what we were doing.

I remember laughing with Pontus many times about enjoying his last moments at a museum before he was asked to leave by an outraged Cultural Minister. He was willing to take the risk as he always does when he believes in something. Pontus Hulten had already brought many innovative artists to Stockholm. He was the first to show Jasper Johns, he bought Rauschenberg's 'Goat.' He arranged for Jackson Pollock to be seen in Sweden and for John Cage[34] to give his first concert which everyone left horrified.

During this time I was painting the HON like an easter egg with the very bright, pure color I have always used and loved. She was like a grand fertility goddess receiving comfortably in her immensity and generosity. She received, absorbed and devoured thousands of visitors. It was an incredible experience creating her. This joyous, huge creature represented for many visitors and me the dream of the return to the Great

Mother. Whole families flocked together with their babies to see her.

The HON had a short but full life. She existed for three months and then was destroyed. The HON took up all the space of the big hall of the museum and was never meant to stay. Wicked tongues said she was the biggest whore in the world because she had 100,000 visitors in three months.

A Stockholm psychiatrist wrote in the newspaper that the HON would change people's dreams for years to come. The birth rate in Stockholm went up that year. This was attributed to her.

The HON had something magical about her. She couldn't help but make you feel good. Everyone who saw her broke into a smile.

The two types of texts included in this chapter show a resistance to the form of traditional autobiography such as the book length memoirs of Chicago and Ringgold. The first text, is a brief, rather playful summary of some of the highlights of Saint Phalle's career, but written in the third person, as if the ability to write in the first person was too powerful to encompass her life. The other texts are "letters" in the same sense that Vigée-Lebrun's *Souvenirs* employ an epistolary format to disguise the power of writing about one's life. Yet the inherent modesty of these forms of life narratives is not consistent with the historical significance of Saint Phalle's work. As noted above, her first original "works" the *Tirs* may be viewed as the founding symbol of Feminist Art. Following this the *Hon* clearly anticipates many of the key concepts of the movement. Subsequently, St. Phalle was fortunate in that she had opportunities to create sculpture on an environmental scale which was extremely rare for a woman artist of her generation. Therefore, her texts are important because they are the form of life narrative in which this highly gifted and historically important artist chose to recall the key moments in her career. As both a writer and a visual artist Saint Phalle uses humor, playfulness, and even a form of self-deprecation to enclose important ideas.

Notes

[1] Arman (1928-2005) was an innovative sculptor noted for his "accumulation" works.

[2] Yves Klein (1928-1962) was a French artist who was best known for his monochrome paintings.

[3] Jean Tinguely (1925-1991) was a Swiss sculptor and one of the founding artists of the movement, Nouveau Realisme. He became Saint Phalle's husband in 1971.

[4] Jackson Pollock (1912-1956) was the leading artist of Abstract Expressionism and known for his "drip" technique.

[5] Pontus Hulten (1924-2006) was a distinguished Swedish museum curator, who was a powerful presence in the contemporary art world, from the 1960s to the 1990s. He was the director of the Museum of Modern Art in Stockholm in the

1960s-1970s, and founding director of the Centre Georges Pompidou in Paris from 1974-1981.

[6] Antoni Gaudi (1852-1926) was a Catalan architect.

[7] Edited by Carla Schulz-Hoffmann (Munich, Berlin, London, New York: Prestel, 2003). All quotes are reprinted by permission of the NCAF, the Niki Charitable Art Foundation.

[8] Giotto (1267-75-1337) was a major Italian fresco painter, active in the fourteenth century.

[9] Le Douanier Rousseau (Henri) (1844-1910) was the archetype of an untutored artist and one of the first masters of "naïve art".

[10] Hieronymus Bosch (c. 1450-1516) was a Netherlandish painter of fantastic imagery.

[11] Pablo Picasso (1881-1973).

[12] Gaudi designed the large environment, the *Parc Güell* (1900-1914) incorporating public space, fountains, a market hall, and colorful mosaic decoration.

[13] Uta Gorsenick, in Pontus Hulten, *Niki de Saint Phalle* (Verlag Gerd Hatje, 1992), 144.

[14] Ibid.

[15] Le Facteur Cheval (Ferdinand) (1836-1924) was an artist associated with Jean Dubuffet (1901-1985) and the movement of "Art Brut".

[16] Daniel Spoerri (b. 1930) was a Swiss sculptor, and one of the founding members of Nouveau Réalisme.

[17] Jean Paul Riopelle (1923-2002) was a Canadian painter and sculptor.

[18] Joan Mitchell (1926-1992) was an American painter and expatriate who lived in Paris and painted in a style associated with Abstract Expressionism.

[19] Alberto Giacometti (1901-1966) was an Italian sculptor living in Paris, and associated with Surrealism.

[20] Saul Steinberg (1914-1999) was an American illustrator, draftsman and cartoonist.

[21] Marcel Duchamp (1887-1968).

[22] Henri Matisse (1869-1954).

[23] Quentin Bajac, "Fire At Will" in Camille Morineau, et al., *elles@centrepompidou: Women Artists in the Collection of the Musée National d'Art Moderne, Centre de Création Industrielle* (Paris: Editions du Centre Pompidou, 2009), p. 48.

[24] Pierre Restany (b. 1930) was a French critic who drafted the manifesto of Nouveau Réalisme, in 1960.

[25] Jasper Johns (b. 1930) was an American painter and one of the founding figures in Pop Art.

[26] Robert Rauschenberg (1925-2008) was an American artist, known for his assemblages, partner of Johns, and one of Pop Art's founding figures.

[27] Museum of Modern Art, New York.

[28] Jean Fautrier (1898-1964) was a French painter and printmaker who won the International Grand Prize at the Venice Biennale, in 1960.

[29] Larry Rivers (1923-2002) was an American painter associated with the Pop Art movement.

[30] William Seitz (1914-1974) was curator of painting and sculpture at the Museum of Modern Art in New York, from 1960 to 1970.

[31] Clarice Rivers was the wife of Larry Rivers. (See note 28) identified in Grosenick, in Pontus Hulten, *Niki de Saint Phalle,* 145.

[32] Claes Oldenburg (b. 1929) was a sculptor known for his soft sculptures and associated with Pop Art. Oldenburg was Swedish by birth, but was raised in the United States.

[33] Paul Klee (1879-1940) was a Swiss born painter associated with the Blue Rider and Bauhaus groups.

[34] John Cage (1912-1992) was an influential experimental composer associated with the Pop Art movement, in the post World War II period.

10772650R0

Made in the USA
Lexington, KY
18 August 2011